Project Domain

S.L. Luck

This is a work of fiction. Names, characters, places, and incidents are either the product of the author's imagination or are used fictitiously. Any resemblance to actual persons, living or dead, events, or locales is entirely coincidental.

Copyright © 2022 S.L. LUCK

All rights reserved. No part of this book may be reproduced or used in any manner without written permission of the author except for the use of quotations in a book review. For more information: info@authorsluck.com

FIRST EDITION

www.authorsluck.com

ISBN 978-1-7780083-0-6

Hardcover ISBN 978-1-7780083-2-0

E-Book ISBN 978-1-17780083-1-3

Cover design by 100covers.com

Edited by C.B. Moore

Other Novels by S.L. Luck

Redeemer

Interference

Lords of Oblivion

Foreword

Straight up, I've made mistakes. I'm not a doctor or a scientist. I've never been a police officer, nor have I served for the military. But I love mashing bits of these professions together, giving them a good swirl of fantasy, and seeing what happens. Errors of conduct, science, and rank are all mine. But I hope you can forgive me. I did what I had to do. Just like M2.

S.L. LUCK, July 2022

1. Everyone Loves a Potluck

Everyone loves a potluck, Cora thought. She pressed a button on her transceiver and spoke low in case Hollis was still around. "Tower, this is Mighty Duck. What's the twenty on Hangman?"

There was silence, then static when Mitch answered. "Mighty Duck, Hangman has been cut loose. Taillights are fading on the Dover. All clear, my dear. Light 'er up."

Cora dove under the desk and retrieved her shoulder bag, in which a pot of rice pudding had been sitting since she'd made it this morning. Unless the sky fell, Hollis wouldn't be back until 7:00 a.m. He hadn't subjected them to one of his surprise inspections for quite some time, but Cora—who knew everything— knew that today was his wife's birthday. Horrible Hollis might be many things, but he was apparently a decent enough husband because he was still married, against incredible odds. She settled into the reassurance that a surprise inspection would be unlikely today and opened her bag.

Mitch's voice cracked through the radio. "Mighty Duck, save me some pudding."

Despite her hurry, Cora smiled. Mitch Iverson had been her son's friend before James suffered a fatal seizure exactly a week after his wedding eight years ago. Mitch had served as a groomsman and pallbearer within the course of a month. They had leaned on each other that terrible day and every minute since. James and Mitch had had the same bright eyes and the same over-the-top—often grotesque—sense of humor, and Cora had come to think of Mitch Iverson as a son, almost as a stand-in for James. Her son couldn't be replaced, of course, but Mitch's presence helped ease the pain that would never go away. She tucked the pot under her arm and said into the receiver, "I made one specially for you."

Even in their bleak environment, those listening to the communication couldn't help but grin. Hollis would have blown a fuse and burnt his ugly toupee right off his chemically tanned head had he heard any of it, but the hothead wasn't there, so fuck him. For a few short hours they would talk the way they wanted to, piss on Hollis' chair if they felt like it, and amidst decades of constraint no one would tell Cora or Iverson to remember the protocols for taking small freedoms.

Cora left her office with the pudding. As always, darkness struck her blind. For reasons foreign to her, the Under Facility Office—UFO to the science geeks aroused by mystery—was underlit and underheated. Two thousand meters underground at the base of a five-kilometer decline, the office felt like a leaky freezer under the ocean. Dim. Cold to the point of making her hands hurt if she left the comfort of the small heater near her feet for more than a few minutes. Damp as though a million little rivers had surrounded them and were leaking their way inside. By the time the lift collected her at the end of the day, she often looked like she'd been swimming with her clothes on.

But that didn't bother her much. It was the isolation that got them. Sometimes it was so isolating they forgot that they had coworkers or that forty-seven long-term guests required constant attention. *Guests* was one of Hollis' terms. Something he conjured to make the employees feel less like guards and the guests less like prisoners. As she was in administration, though, this didn't affect Cora much.

Once the lift took her underground, it was only ten feet to her office, a journey with no aluminum oxynitride glass with which to observe the creatures on the other side. She waited until her eyes adjusted and proceeded two dozen steps to the lunchroom. Over the years she'd made a point of ingratiating herself with Lieutenant Deborah Mills, who oversaw the Under Atmosphere, among other things. Mills, Hollis' right hand, had been intractable until Cora discovered her profile on a salacious dating website called DirtyMatch.com.

It was the anniversary of James' death, and Mitch was drunker than a skunk in a barrel full of whisky when he called her in the middle of the night. Her husband Gary, God bless him, put on his shoes and drove her to Mitch's apartment without so much as a yawn. When she arrived, she and Mitch relieved their pain by seeking a woman for Mitch. Short or long-term, it didn't matter, only that she was willing. This led them to the website where Lieutenant Mill's cat-eyed face puckered seductively beneath a wild blond wig. One mention of *Gina Titswither* when Cora passed the lieutenant the next day and Cora was granted a five-degree temperature adjustment in her office as well as the installation of two ceiling-mounted heaters and floor-mounted running lights that led from her door to the lunchroom. It wasn't bright and balmy, but it was better.

Inside the lunchroom, Iris was stirring something that smelled like beef and tomatoes. Steam rose from the slow cooker as she turned around. "I'm not here," she said when she saw Cora.

Cora put the pot of rice pudding on the table. "I'm going to pretend you didn't cook for your own retirement party." She narrowed an eye at the smaller woman, made smaller in recent months by her husband's stage-four liver cancer diagnosis.

"Bernie was hungry last night," she said. "But I made too much. It's just leftovers. I didn't want it to go to waste." Behind her glasses, there were tears on her eyelashes.

Cora hugged her. She didn't ask how Bernie was. The shadows under Iris' eyes explained everything. She leaned over and smelled Iris' stew. "No one's going to want my rice pudding after this," she said.

Iris nudged her arm. "Not a chance."

Together they tidied the table. Cora set plates and cutlery where the serving line would begin. Iris unfurled white paper cloths and smoothed them on the rectangular tables. Little touches of battery-operated candles and plastic flowers (a bit on the gaudy side as Cora was wont to do) made the typically bleak room not quite delightful yet satisfactory. For once, it didn't make Cora want to hang herself.

"Holy hotties!" Clint Maclean growled behind them. He was twenty-something with the tact of a pubescent boy raised by barn animals, but Iris and Cora loved him. "If you two keep bending over like that, I'm going to need a few minutes in Hollister's office. I'll spread it like confetti." He jerked a fist near his crotch. The women tittered.

"I thought you weren't in until tonight," said Iris.

"And miss my girl's last day? Not a chance." He squeezed her rear and kissed her on the cheek. Iris' grief-greyed skin pinkened.

Cora could have also used a rear-squeeze, but she said nothing. Iris was leaving and there would be plenty of time to have Clint fondle her lady parts. She knew he meant nothing sexual by it, her being old and round and him being young and . . . well . . . everything she wasn't. Still, a firm tickle from strong hands every now and then boosted a lady's ego. As lovely as Gary was as a husband, he had been stricken with carpal tunnel for years and couldn't squeeze a bubble, let alone Cora's rear. Sometimes she and Gary liked to talk about

Clint's hands when it was dark and the lights were out, but she'd never tell Clint that.

Break time in the Under Facility Office usually consisted of cold food and sideways insults at Hollis' expense. Microwaves weren't allowed because they agitated the Venusians and put the Uranians to sleep for days. But an armada of slow cookers and heating plates defied their challenges and now everyone was filing in, licking their lips and rubbing their bellies, awaking as if from comas as long as their tenures.

Cora raised a wooden spoon. "We don't have long, so let's get everyone sitting."

Cheryl Pickett's big teeth glowed white as she beamed at the gathering. Jennifer Tibbs, Don Sendall, Bo Wilco, Victor Petrarch, and Luis Helzer dropped into their seats. Beside them at the adjacent table, Russ Tenor and his quick-tempered cronies—three brothers with the shared brain capacity of a turkey—grunted that they were hungry.

"Now," Cora said, relishing the attention of the almost two dozen attendees. She reached under the buffet table and withdrew a small silver bag stuffed with tissue paper. When she stood again, her eyes were wet. "I honestly hoped this day would never come. In our own little way, we're family here and . . ."

Tenor cleared his throat loudly enough to get a nasty look from Tibbs. "Asshole," she said. Wilco and Helzer, both bigger men than Russ Tenor, squeezed him in the vices of their eyes. Tenor surrendered and sat back, quiet.

"A little something to remember us by," Cora said quickly, and thrust the bag at Iris.

Iris' small fingers disappeared in the paper and pulled out a small velvet box. She gasped at the pendant inside. The others in the room respectfully watched the exchange, but then the shuffling of feet and the repositioning of hands and legs overwhelmingly pushed the moment to an end.

"Thank you," Iris breathed tearfully.

Cora clasped her hands together and once again commanded the room. "I'd like everyone to line up and fill a plate, but I'd ask that you remember our one and only rule."

"Don't tell Hollis," they chanted in unison.

2. Bad Pudding

In all, Iris' retirement party lasted only forty-five minutes, but it was enough. After they ate, they queued up to give Iris last hugs and departed the way they'd come: Tibbs, Wilco, and Helzer to their patrol of Sector East, Sendall, Petrarch, and a quiet mumbler named Jones to Sector West. Tenor stomped with the others to Sector Center, where the most agreeable guests were housed. Cheryl Pickett followed Maclean back to the surveillance room in Sector Zero, where Mitch Iverson held post.

Built in 1946 by a team of Canadian military engineers, the Under Facility Office—deemed *Project Domain* by the then Minister of National Defence (Air), Major-General Andrew Hutton, the UFO had never suffered an escape. Hutton's repository for the extraterrestrial onslaught following WWII was an airtight, soundproof, transmission-proof, two-by-three-kilometer underground detention centre designed to withstand nuclear and alien attack. Hutton used the sharpest minds in the county, employing the same team of Canadian military engineers responsible for the country's northernmost airfield in Resolute Bay, the Bailey Bridging system that sped the movement of Allied Forces in Europe, and the tunnels of Gibraltar, a critical defensive outpost in the Mediterranean. Project Domain featured 32-inch concrete walls, a mess hall, library, twenty-five isolation cells, a surveillance room, conference room, living quarters, industrial kitchen, infirmary, three administrative offices, a laboratory, bathing facilities, and control center, situated just over two kilometers directly beneath Garrett, Ontario's one and only waste management facility.

Over time, with the capture of twenty-eight wayward Martians, three Saturnians, five Venusians, three Plutonians, six Uranians, and two Kepler Mimicas—or Mimics— from Kepler-186f, the Under Facility Office eventually jettisoned its library and mess hall to gain space for twenty-five more cells. Hutton's design had also since been fortified with additional airlock chambers, including those fronting the Venusian, Uranian, and Mimic enclosures, through which meals, magazines, and medication were passed. Through good behavior and an absolute unwillingness to do anything but laze around and get fat, the Martians had been the only guests granted the subjective freedom of iron bars instead of oxynitride glass, of which they liked to remind the testy Saturnians at every opportunity.

Iverson grinned as Pickett passed him a plate; beneath it was his own tub of Cora's cinnamon rice pudding. He pointed at monitor three, at the top right of the display. "Mendawall is at it again. Cheeky little bastard."

On the screen, a small silver-skinned Martian was stretching his hands between the bars, beckoning with the middle of three fingers for a Saturnian in the adjacent cell to come closer. A Saturnian they called Templeton spilled its fluid body toward the Martian enclosure, curious. A small Martian shoe struck the glass in front of Templeton. Had it been a Plutonian, they would have had to scrub an explosion of red goo off the walls. But Saturnians didn't explode like Plutonians. Saturnians retaliated in other ways. Templeton drew up his body, shuddered once, and gave Mendawall a terrible headache. Then he oozed back to the bunks where the other Saturnians played at dripping from the ceiling.

Mendawall grabbed his head. In the surveillance room, Iverson and Maclean laughed.

"That'll serve him right," Maclean said.

"Until he does it again," said Iverson; and just like that, Mendawall tossed another shoe.

On the screen, Russ Tenor shook a finger at Mendawall, but the Martian just yawned and patted his belly. Tony Groper, Tenor's right hand, seconded the scolding with a shaking of his own. Mendawall's beard elongated and twisted into the shape of flowers, which he then pushed through the bars at the guards. Tenor and Groper smacked Mendawall's offering aside.

"One day I hope he makes a knife and shoves it right up that bully's ass," Cheryl Pickett said. She burped and spit into the wastebasket.

Iverson shook his head. "A knife's too good for him. Let's hope it's an anvil."

"Ouch," Maclean pulled a face.

Maclean and Pickett relieved Iverson to eat. They assumed their positions at the monitoring station while Iverson went to the lunchroom. Over the next few hours, a change began to settle on the otherwise immutable facility. Sourness coated stomachs. Bowels liquefied. Nausea infiltrated bodies. Shivers and chills took hold of Cora, Helzer, Sendall, and Petrarch. Then Wilco. Maclean. Iverson. Eleven others. Everyone who ate the rice pudding that had been sitting under Cora's desk beside her heater went from white, black, or brown to a sickly shade of green.

Tenor, who had been with Groper and a guard named Evan Anderson in Sector Center since the potluck, was leery about the Martians and so never risked leaning against the bars. Now he did so without care.

"You don't look so well, Mr. Tenor," said Mendawall formally. The Martian reached his hand through the bars and with a slim finger touched the nape of Russ Tenor's neck. "And you don't feel so well. You're as hot as Y2." The reference to the Venusian the Martians had encountered during The Gathering of 1952 drew no response from Tenor. Instead, Tenor leaned into Mendawall's cool fingers. Then he clutched his stomach and vomited.

Anderson jumped back from the splash. The Martians turned up their noses and fell away from the bars.

"He's sick. Oh dear moon pies, he's sick!" cried Pintree, the youngest of the Martians. Unlike her male counterparts, Pintree didn't have a beard with which to express herself. But her eyelashes fluttered like the wingbeats of honeybees and her silver skin danced like minnows under water.

Anderson bent to help Tenor to his feet, but then Anderson himself felt a stirring in his stomach. He gagged his lunch onto the other man.

In Sector West, meanwhile, Don Sendall had just passed the Venusians and Plutonians their nutrient cakes through the airlock chambers when a cramp pierced his side. He stretched his back and cursed himself for not drinking enough water. "Eat up, fuckers," he hissed, and slid three meatloaf and potato dinners over to the Uranians, who could tolerate such food. The blue creatures, tall and bipedal, moved to their trays. The hard tentacles on the bottom of their feet scraped onward like the opening of too-tall doors against concrete. Sendall wrinkled his nose. "Do you have to do that?"

"There is no have. Only *do*." The Uranians chanted in an English-like language, for they always spoke as one. They took their plates. "Would Officer Sendall join us? You can sit and soothe your cramp," they said, intuiting his pain.

Sendall frowned. "Not a chance. And keep the fuck out of my head. We warned you about that."

PROJECT DOMAIN

Four eyes on each of the Uranians' narrow heads blinked their vertical lids. "Thank you for the food, Officer Sendall. We hope it is better than yours," they said, and scraped to their small dining table near the encyclopedia library Lieutenant Mills had supplied not long after they deduced her Gina Titswither pseudonym.

Don Sendall smacked their airlock chamber. "What's that supposed to mean? *We hope it's better than yours.* Huh?" A current of agony blazed through his intestines, doubled him over, and thrust him toward the bathroom with both hands on his rear. The Uranians watched him go, knowing, while the Plutonians and Venusians basked unaffected in their super-heated rooms.

"I think it's something we ate," complained Petrarch.

"Uh-huh," mumbled Jones.

They, too, clutched their stomach, clenched their rears, held their erupting mouths.

Petrarch clawed at his radio. "Tower, this is Petrarch in Sector West. We need you to cover—" he swallowed the bile creeping up his throat. "We need you to cover for us. I think we ate something bad." He released the receiver and farted a little too solidly.

"Sector West, this is Tower," Iverson reported from the surveillance room, not yet feeling the effects of the rice pudding. "I got you covered. Do what you need to do."

Petrarch and Jones sped away. Iverson scanned Sector West's console, saw the Plutonians, Venusians, and Uranians quietly eating their dinners, and sat back in his chair. All was calm.

A few minutes later, Iverson patrolled the monitors once again and saw something strange. His human counterparts had all become almost incapacitated. None of Sector West's guards had yet reported back from their washroom breaks, and over in Sector Center, Tenor, Groper and Anderson seemed to be alternately cleaning each other off then getting sick. Every creature in Sector Center had retreated away from the mess as far as possible, even the Saturnians, who were protected by Level-10 glass. Iverson's stomach gurgled sourly at the sight, but he continued at his post.

"You see this?" he asked Pickett, who had been scanning the waste facility above them for potential voyeurs of the operation.

Pickett wheeled her chair around. Her face was pale and sweaty. She looked at Iverson's monitors. "Looks like Gina Titswither's photo's been leaked." She laughed weakly.

On any other day, Iverson would have rolled with Pickett's joke, but two things bothered him. One: he knew the illness taking over the facility wasn't a coincidence. Because of the timing, it had to be something they'd eaten at the potluck, and *that* could cause some serious trouble for all of them. Hollis would lose his fucking mind and was known to transfer offenders of even the most minor infractions to their sister facility in the north, where sunshine and warmth were only faraway memories. Second, whatever was taking hold of his colleagues had begun to teeter inside Iverson like a sinking ship. He felt a sickening whirl within his guts. A tidal force of bile and nausea surged up his esophagus. Typhonic pressure gusted into his colon, and as he looked at Tibbs and she at him, they both knew they were doomed.

Pickett yanked open her desk drawer and snatched the bottle of antacids. She fumbled the cap open, pushed a handful of colorful tablets at Iverson and downed a handful of her own. The crunch of the tablets was loud in her head, and she closed her eyes against the sound.

"Fuck." Saliva-softened antacid dribbled down Iverson's chin, but it didn't concern him. It was the monitoring console for Sector East, where the Mimics were housed.

Sector East was the facility's most secure arm. If one were to visit Sector East, he or she would first deposit all personal belongings in an appointed locker in the twenty-meter corridor designed for traffic to and from the eastern wing. Here the concrete walls were 40-inches thick, but visitors would be as aware of this as they might be of the growth of their hair from one hour to the next. They would be too preoccupied removing their personal identities to be concerned with anything else. Earrings, necklaces, wedding bands, and watches must go. So too must elastic bands, hair clips, hair extensions, wigs, bandages, sutures, plaster casts, nipple, navel, and genital piercings. Fake nails. False eyelashes. Clothing. Only visitors with perfect eyesight and no tattoos or discernable birthmarks were allowed to enter. Hair must be natural. Nails must be short and neatly groomed. Polish was forbidden. Pregnancy, illness, or allergies of any kind would be rejected. Dental appliances were a definite no.

Having shed their individualities, visitors would then proceed, naked and barefoot, to the decontamination showers for a good dousing. They would be dried and given antiseptic-smelling clothing, new shoes, and a radio. But since the Mimics' arrival in 1963, there had been only a handful of visitors. Besides Hollis Brubaker, his two predecessors, and Lieutenant Mills, all of them had been highly trained special-forces officers, three of which were now rolling across Iverson's screen.

Wilco had his back to the camera, but by the look of his hung head he appeared to be vomiting. Helzer had been ill on his uniform, and though he was pawing at his radio, Iverson and Pickett saw Helzer's fingers slip in his own sick, unable to operate it.

Tibbs was on her knees, her forearm to her mouth. "Tower, we need help." She looked into the camera, speaking to her radio. The camera magnified on her chin what had moments before been in her stomach. She helped Wilco and Helzer back into their chairs then limped to her own.

Iverson pressed a button on the control panel. "Overlook, this is Tower. We need three bodies to Sector East, stat." The antacids mixed with the poison in his stomach and made him retch.

Above ground, in an uninteresting, squat grey building six hundred meters opposite the waste-management facility, the occupants of Adequate Accounting mobilized.

3. ALL WAS CALM

As with any good prison, all communication was monitored. Iverson's request, though unusual, didn't immediately alarm Theo Carver as it should have. No alarm signal had been sent, and when he pulled the UFO's surveillance footage to his own screen, he saw three guards in Sector East sitting in their respective chairs. The Mimics, two tiny beings the shape and size of ice cubes but with the weight of semi-trucks, were gathered in the center of their cell. No reason to panic. Still, the request was curious. Theo summoned his three best officers, professional soldiers relegated to impersonating lumpish accountants.

Jeffrey Acres, Dalton Byrd, and Foster Cupps—the ABC team—skidded into his office. Theo ordered them to Sector East through the northeast tunnel. The men consented in unison and were gone.

Theo looked at Sector East's monitors again. No change. As always when he saw those two insignificant cubes, he had a hard time believing they were dangerous. During his thirty years in the military, he'd known danger. He'd seen landmines obliterate children. He'd seen terrorists pull triggers and detonate bombs and slash necks and heads and hearts. The two little cubes in the center of the floor looked nothing like the assassins he'd known. They didn't strap explosives to their bodies. They didn't shout demands or spew hatred. They didn't say anything at all. Unlike the Martians and the Uranians who spoke English, and the Plutonians, Saturnians, and Venusians who communicated using their minds, the Mimics had never uttered sounds besides their screams during experiments. Lia Geller, a physician-scientist and the UFO's director of Bioprocess Technology, postulated it was because of their strict diet. They were basically two pebbles in a holding cell.

But when Theo took the assignment, he had been heavily warned. The Mimics weren't just dangerous, the reports stated, but *lethal*. Their capture in 1963 had claimed the lives of seventeen civilians and twenty-six soldiers in the bloodiest operation the overseeing commander had ever witnessed. *They seek only the brain*, Commander Barca wrote. *M1 and M2 allure victims by replicating friends, family, co-workers, anyone known to them. Then they use their brute strength to tear out the sides of victims' brains.* The proceeding pages accounted, in detail, the depth and location of the victims' injuries. As was mandatory, Theo studied every grotesque image. An older woman with two blood-stained craters on the side of her head. A much beloved local librarian with his skull cracked open and two divots of tissue missing from his brain. Five limp soldiers in a grisly heap. All had been discarded like tissue. Dutifully, Theo had read on.

Later reports identified the scavenged areas of the brain as the temporoparietal junctions, the right and left locations in the brain where the temporal and parietal lobes meet. Most interestingly to the scientists that collaborated on a recent review of the report, it was the part of the brain believed responsible for mimicry—a person's ability to copy something they've seen or heard. This revelation led Lia Geller to add, in a footnote: *Cannot discount the possibility that*

M1's & M2's ingestion of the temporoparietal lobes intensify their ability to replicate. Further study required. This had made Theo laugh. He could see Geller's enrollment sheet: *Brains to spare? We are conducting a scientific experiment and we need you! Sign up today!*

Still, it was hard for Theo to reconcile the reports he'd read with the little cubes. One of the first things he'd learned in the military was to never underestimate an enemy, so he would be cautious, of course. But be afraid of creatures smaller than his toes? No. Theo couldn't bring himself to do that.

Once again he checked the monitor. All was calm in Sector East.

4. Rope In The Wind

By now, Helzer, Tibbs, and Wilco could only patrol the sector with their eyes. Their stomachs ached and there was acid in their bowels, but they held their ground. Thankfully M1 and M2 hadn't moved from their spot in the center of the cell, so none of the guards were yet concerned.

Helzer's watch beeped. He lifted his wrist as one would a sack of wet sand. "It's their dinner time," he said.

"Ugggh," Jennifer Tibbs groaned. Her body hurt; God, did her body hurt.

"Got to be done," Helzer insisted.

Wilco's eyes swept over the dice, who were still and silent. "You think they care? Overlook'll take care of it when they get here. Let them do it."

"The schedule . . ." Helzer moaned insistently.

"You do it," Wilco said to Helzer.

Helzer, who over the summer had been severely reprimanded for a three-minute delay to the schedule, couldn't afford another mark on his file. Lizzy would leave him if Hollis sent him north. He wobbled to his feet and dragged himself to the pneumatic tube. A hiccup brought his curdled lunch to the back of his mouth, but he swallowed it back down. Across the room, Tibbs and Wilco swayed in their seats. Helzer entered his identification number and selected from the menu a dinner nutrient cake, which their pharmaceutical chef loaded with tryptophan in the evenings to help the Mimics sleep.

The Under Facility Office employed four chefs. Upon receiving a nutrient request, the duty chef ordinarily verified the request against the identified creature's standing authorization. Each time a request was approved, the duty chef input the desired meal into the BioChef instrument panel, which measured, blended, infused, heated, pressed, turned, cooled, and presented the requested meal in a sealed capsule. Capsules were then carried by the duty chef to the corresponding creature's pneumatic tube and off the meal went. The entire operation was completed without any outside exposure. This was especially critical for the Mimics. Should a foreign creature such as a fly or mosquito find their way into a capsule and the capsule continue to the Mimic enclosure, the Under Facility Office would officially be breached and a lockdown ensue.

Outsiders might scoff at the protocol, but there were reasons for it. First, during the capture massacre of 1963, Kepler Mimicas were observed to not just imitate their prey, but transform some targets into replicas of *themselves*. Before one soldier was killed, he had taken the appearance of a five-legged, nine-mouthed towering beast, as M1 and M2 sometimes appeared during transport, then that of a cube. The unfortunate soldier, twenty-three-year-old Jeremy Ribach, was subsequently obliterated by his comrades. In all, mistaken identity had accounted for over a third of the victims.

The second reason for the precaution was that the Under Facility Office had made no advancement in identification technology. Early experiments with mice and hamsters demonstrated M1's and M2's exacting ability, yet none of the UFO's employees or machines had been able to correctly identify which rodents were the Mimicas. When asked, a member of the biohazardous cleaning crew had accurately pointed out M1, but later admitted it was only a guess. And while larger animals couldn't possibly escape the enclosure, insects were another matter. Their microscopic scale did not inspire confidence of containment, no matter how well the cell had been sealed.

Simon Puskel, the shift's duty chef, was the UFO's most conscientious employee. He had never been late. He had never made an error. He had never let so much as a tiny mite escape his notice. So steady was he that Hollis himself had cited Puskel for a national award. But today Puskel had made the mistake of eating not one but *three* portions of Cora's famous rice pudding. Steady as he might seem, Puskel was as lonesome at work as he was at home. He had needed the potluck as much as they all did, so he had savored the rare treat of company and multiple trips to the buffet table. Trips that filled him with more staphylococcal aureus than anyone else.

A familiar double beep signaled Sector East's request for two nutrition pucks. The tingle Simon Puskel had felt in his esophagus and dismissed as mild indigestion had spread to his stomach. It had become not just uncomfortable but painful. Simon Puskel had the sensation of being repeatedly stabbed with a serrated knife. He gasped each time the blade went in and blubbered on his lab coat each time the blade went out. He felt his insides being masticated like grass under a mower. It was a ripping pain. A tearing pain. A pain that gripped all his attention. The rest of his body worked automatically. And for the most part, Simon Puskel succeeded in creating M1's and M2's nutrition pucks. The BioChef beeped and whirred and dispensed the two capsules, exactly as ordered.

Simon lurched to the dispensary tube and pressed the release button. The airlock depressurized and hissed the capsules out. Here was where Simon would normally retrieve a capsule, verify the contents of the label against the approved requisition, put the capsule into a pre-navigation sterilization chamber, then enter the section and cell information—and off the capsule would shoot in the pneumatic tube to its destination. Puskel would perform this operation for each capsule. For seventeen years, he had done this flawlessly.

But Simon Puskel thought he was dying. Absolutely sure of it. His bloated stomach pressed painfully against his belt buckle. His torso prickled like a million needles were inside and trying to get out. The muscles in his arms, his legs, were as sturdy as wilted flowers. The moment the BioChef depressurized, his brain began leaking its sense. He forgot what the capsules were for, then remembered. He scooped them up in one arm and swayed on his toes as he groggily spied the labels. Something, not his brain but maybe instinct in that moment, remembered an emergency signal. A button or lever. A string? Something he maybe he should think about. Or maybe someone he should talk to. No. Maybe he shouldn't. Maybe he should lie down and . . .

Simon fell on the capsules.

The crash tumbled his sensitive stomach. The nausea jarred him. He stood, capsules in hand, and remembered his duty.

He entered M1's location into the transportation chamber and watched the capsule fly away. M2's capsule, meanwhile, had suffered a crack when it broke the chef's fall. On a good day, Puskel would have seen the crack and disposed of the capsule. But his vision had blurred. He could type from memory but he could no more see the keys on the computer or the crack in M2's capsule than he could see Kepler-186f with binoculars. Nor did he see the fruit fly that had followed his malty scent from the washroom to the kitchen lab where Puskel, dizzy as a top, had forgotten his decontamination.

"Urp." Puskel retched and out came the pudding on his shoes. He wiped a smear off the capsule with his sleeve.

The smell of Puskel's vomit aroused the fruit fly. It hovered near Puskel's shoes then fled the movement of Puskel's long and quivering legs. It went to the capsule Puskel had put in the open sterilization chamber and slipped inside while Puskel fumbled through M2's details on the computer.

M2's capsule whizzed away. Then Simon Puskel fainted.

Over in Sector East, Helzer, Wilco, and Tibs awaited relief. Overlook wouldn't arrive for several more minutes, which felt like hours, *days*, to the guards. The three soldiers sagged with nausea. Tibbs and Wilco blinked dizzily at the Mimics, who hadn't moved.

Helzer's legs trembled as he waited for the second capsule to drop. He leaned heavily on the counter.

"You all right there, Luis?" Wilco asked from the comfort of his seat. "You're swaying like a rope in the wind."

Helzer flapped a hand to indicate he was okay. He was okay because even though he was clenching his rear and swallowing back down his rotten old lunch, M1 and M2 would be fed on time and he wouldn't be banished to the north. Lizzie wouldn't leave him. It would be okay.

M2's capsule arrived with a plop. Helzer released the airlock on the pneumatic tube and retrieved the capsule. By now, Tibbs and Wilco hadn't even the strength to oversee the feeding, as was protocol. Their heavy eyelids felt like bricks swaying in their sockets.

"Let's get this over with," Helzer said, and brought the uninspected capsules to the feeding chamber. He opened the drawer and put them inside. Then Helzer stumbled back to his chair. All done.

5. Fruit Flies and Fatties

Millions, if not billions, of years of impulse fixed the fruit fly to a droplet of Simon Puskel's chunder that fell through the crack and onto M2's nutrition puck. There it flitted and sucked, oblivious to what it was about to become. On the other side of the glass, the three humans were as energetic as cows in a heat wave, and about as useful as them too. Neither Helzer, Tibbs, or Wilco knew it, but something was occurring in the Mimic enclosure. The little cubes had had so little interaction since their capture that they were attuned to new movement. They were aware of microscopic wing beats and of the diminutive pulses of Puskel's pudding being sucked through pseudotrachea, and of hundreds of eggs being laid on the nutrition puck. M1's and M2's gentle movement toward the feeding chamber gave the impression of two blocks of sugar on a sleepy conveyor belt. Helzer, Wilco, and Tibbs had seen this routine many times.

M1 glided forward and unfolded her layers. She grew to the size of a boot, to the height of a broom, to the width of a grizzly bear. Nothing unusual to the guards. M1 nudged M2's capsule. The dark shadows of her many hands grasped the capsule while, down below, M2 looked on.

"That ain't yours, shit for brains," Wilco burped to the slightly whiter cube that had become a monster.

It didn't really matter, however, because the nutrition pucks were always the same, every day, for both creatures. But Bo Wilco was the sort of person who grew important with control, presiding in superiority like a toddler over its toys. As long as everyone did what they were told, Bo Wilco was happy. He had lorded over the M1 and M2 for thirteen years, and they had behaved as ordered. "Just . . . just eat . . ." Wilco wanted to say more, but he was so close to unconsciousness that the words would have depleted the rest of his energy.

M2, still in his innocent form, rose and took his capsule from M1. The creatures, now dark and fluid as the sea, looked at the guards and at their rations and knew their time had finally come. They waited until Wilco lost interest, then M2 opened his capsule.

Alien lifeform swelled inside the body of the fruit fly as fast as the lifeform of the fruit fly swelled to the shape and size of an ice cube in the space where M2 had taken his meal. M1 shrank back down and assumed her gentler surface beside the fly that was now a cube. M2 wasted no time. He zoomed to the feeding chamber. It was sealed tight. He raced to the ventilation shaft and leaned his small body into the down blast. Up and up and up M2 pushed but then felt the tingle of an electromagnetic current that threatened to fry him if he came any closer. He inspected the floor-wall joints and wall junctions and the overhead light that was always on. He darted to the waste receptacle. The floor bolts. The experiment chamber on the western corner of the cell that rendered them powerless, and where he and M1 had surrendered themselves for pokings and proddings, cuttings, scrapings, twistings, compressings, expandings, zappings and every other savagery the humans could think of. No escape.

Below, the fruit fly was rigid in its new body. M1 was anxious but still, so still.

Tibb's radio crackled. "Sector East, this is Overlook. We're two minutes away."

Jeffrey Acre's voice should have been reassuring, but it was as comforting as acid on a hemorrhoid. The *A* in Theo Carver's elite ABC team, Jennifer had learned after a boozy one-night stand, stood for *grade-A asshole*. The Under Facility Office had a strict no-dating policy, but it didn't stop employees from *encountering* each other from time to time. Jennifer Tibb's encounter with Jeff Acre had started along the Callingwood River, where their jogging routes had intersected one cloudy evening not long ago. In the austere confines of their working world, she hadn't had the chance to get to know him before she agreed to go for a post-workout coffee, but she reasoned that a colleague, of all people, would be nice company. The coffee had led to wine, and the wine had led to tequila shots, and the tequila shots had led to a painful fingering against a garbage can and Jeff's come on her favorite pants. Then he'd grabbed the inside of her thigh and told her to keep running if she wanted the real thing next time because Jeffrey Acres didn't fuck fatties. Jennifer wasn't skinny, by any means, but neither was she fat, and she would be dammed if she would let a guy like Jeff Acres make her believe otherwise. She hadn't wished food poisoning on anyone, but now she willed it on him with all her might. She wanted him to feel like his intestines were going to rocket out of his own ass. She wanted him to vomit and shake and sway and then *she* would grab hold of his balls and tell him that no amount of exercise was going to make his *real thing* bigger than his pinky, so she'd pass on the offer, thank you very much.

"Copy that," she said now, and hoped she could sidle away behind Helzer or Wilco without the asshole seeing her when he came in.

The Mimics heard everything. They had minutes, possibly only seconds, before the replacements arrived. M1 imparted to M2 the need to hurry. M2 flew to the door, dove to the brackets where their beds hung on the back wall, scuttled to the observation window on the eastern wall.

"M1, M2, return to your squares," said Wilco over the intercom.

M1 began her slow slide to their shift-change positions. The fly, looking much like a resistant M2, did not move. M1 went to it now and nudged the fly cube to M2's square.

"What's going on, M2?" Wilco asked, painfully now, for his cramps had intensified.

"Maybe they're sick too," Helzer said.

"He's probably just curious about us," Tibbs said. "They've never seen us like this before." Wilco thought she was probably right.

The intercom, meanwhile, had given M2 an idea. He rushed to the circle in the upper corner where Wilco's sick voice had come out. M2 raced through one of the many holes in the metal dust cap and scoured the cone. There was a space, infinitesimally small, but then so was M2. He folded his wings behind him and squeezed through. He went through coils and plates and baskets and much weaker electromagnetic fields. He lost a wing. Then a leg. But just as the replacements were released from the sterilization chamber, M2 was free.

6. Irma

Scotty Waymore stared into the field, smoking a cigarette. He could see little in the darkening light, only the faraway floodlights of the landfill where he worked and the darting silhouettes of scavenging birds over the pit. Frank would be pissed at their mess, and Scotty would pretend it pained him to send Frank to clean it up. A chuff of laughter escaped him and echoed in the night. The porch post groaned as he leaned against it, but Scotty thought that maybe it was laughing with him, like some of the voices he'd heard.

He put the cigarette out with the toe of his boot and left the cool air to itself. Inside, his small house was warm, with just enough heat left in the wood stove to boil a can of soup. The loaf of bread Meredith had baked for him was on the verge of mould, but the soup would mask the bad parts. He broke off a chunk, set it on a plate, and waited for the soup to boil.

The few minutes before dinner were the best time to think. His dog-eared notebook and pencil lay beside his thinking chair, and these he took up as he sat down.

PROJECT DOMAIN

The scrawl on the opposite page did not assure him of his sanity. It never did. But still he recounted his day and things that were strange to him and the moments when he had heard the Voice. Scotty pushed his sleeve up and looked at the notes he had written. There were twenty-seven rows of smeared blue ink on his pale fish-belly arm.

6:14 a.m. Nest
6:52 a.m. Truck
7:01 a.m. Gravel
7:29 a.m. Here
8:11 a.m. Here
8:33 a.m. Here

He recorded his memories in his notebook. That morning, he'd discovered a robin's nest in the rain gutter above the kitchen window, where there hadn't been one before. And his truck had taken seven seconds to start, when usually it idled within *two* seconds. Also, the gravel had sounded weird, almost hollow, at the landfill when he walked to his office. Whatever state of mind Scotty was in, he knew gravel shouldn't sound like that. And there had been the extended toilet flush and the flicker of the porch light. At least he thought it'd flickered. Most likely it had.

Lastly . . .

. . . lastly, the Voice had come early today.

Scotty wrote until bubbles of boiling soup began to hiss on the stove. He ladled himself a bowl of Campbell's tomato and sat at the table, feeling older than he was.

Before the Voice came, Scotty had been a regular guy. He'd been a husband and a father and as sociable as a celebrity. He and Meredith had been volunteers at the Good Boy Animal Shelter and regulars on one of Southern Ontario's premier bowling leagues. Scotty himself had been second only to the Pocket Rocket, a sweaty Pole named Przemo Wójcik, who weighted his ball and had the manager grease his lane for a cut of the payout. And besides running Garrett's only waste facility, Scotty regularly tendered his janitorial services to St. Jude's middle school, where their daughter, Claire, was a teacher. His efforts helped save an after-school art program from being cut and gave him the opportunity to spend more time with his only child.

It hadn't been an easy life, but it had been a good one. One that made him happier than any man had a right to be. And one that was now so far gone it felt like it had never been his at all.

He sipped his soup and stared at his spoon. He looked like a turtle. His upside-down face, the only version of himself he could stand, belied the true horror of what he'd become. The spoon blurred his skin so it didn't look as much like a disked field. It smoothed the coin-slot ruts the Voice's serrated timbre had carved into him. It made his eyes look less lunatic. His mouth less like a flappy hound dog's. The image was so small, you could almost believe his ears were the same length. Like he hadn't sliced off one to stop the sounds the spoon couldn't hear.

Here.

Here.

Here.

Over the years he'd grown accustomed to the sound in his head, as well as to the solitude that came with it. Everyone thought he was crazy, Scotty knew that. The doctors. Meredith. Claire. The police. Douglas Radway, the fat kid who called him *Skitzo* (as in Schizophrenic) *Scotty* and bombed his front door with steaming bags of dog shit every Saturday afternoon. All the jackasses around the city that slapped alien stickers on his truck whenever he went on a grocery run. *Screw them all*, Scotty thought, thinking it would be okay with him if everyone but Meri and Claire were collected and compacted with the rest of the trash. That would be fine. Just fine.

He was washing his bowl and spoon when a sound jarred him. Scotty set down the dishcloth and strode to his desk beside the bathroom, where not one but all his sound amplifiers were active. The seven parabolic microphones, eleven UHF audio receivers, two GSM listening devices, six vintage transistors, and four bionic ears—scavenged over time and as vital to Scotty as his own heartbeat—transmitted something Scotty hadn't heard before. Their scattered reports melded into one. His fifty-six-year-old heart constricted.

The Voice was different.

Come; it crepitated like wind through a door jam. It was an echo in a lonely room. It was the reverberation of misery from a broken heart. It brought the hair on Scotty's arm to attention.

Scotty twisted knobs, rolled dials, pushed buttons, and adjusted levers. He was in it now. In his space, listening to the One that only he could hear. He slipped on his headset.

"Talk to me," Scotty said. "I know you're out there, buddy. Talk to me, okay? Don't let me think I'm crazy. Do that for me, and I'll give you anything you want. Just talk to me."

The cabin was silent. Scotty tuned his radios, listening with the ears of a soldier. Crackling erupted from the Zenith.

"Nnnnn," the Voice said.

Scotty ran a hand over his balding scalp. He hadn't heard that before. Every day for eight years, he'd heard *here* and what sounded like desperate cries of pain. More rarely, he'd thought he heard laughter. But it had been muffled, as if a hand had been clamped over the Voice's mouth.

"Nnnn? What the hell does that mean?"

He slid the pad of his thumb over the tuner, slowly, so slowly. The Zenith buzzed with static. It whistled and hissed and trumpeted enough key minors to make Scotty's skin crawl. He drew up his shoulders and ticked the knob. He came upon a radio program from Toronto plugging the airways with a seedy commercial for a used car dealership that promised the best prices in the city. Then a wavery evangelist threatening the fire of God to those who didn't take the Saviour into their hearts immediately but reminded listeners that for

$19.99 an iron-on patch could be sent to their homes as a reminder of the Urgent Commitment. The dial moved a hair's breadth. The Leafs were losing to the Habs again. Another nudge. Scotty overheard a taxi being dispatched to an address down Yonge Street. Another nudge. Garrett's classic rock station warned, "Hang on to your tighty whities, people. We've got a special weather statement from Environment Canada. Looks like we're in for 80–90-kilometer-per-hour winds, gusting up to 110. They're warning that power outages could occur and that you'll want to stay off the roads for this one. Another nudge. "Who's Daddy's princess? Yes. You are. You urrrrrp—" A father gagged as the tell-tale tear of a baby's diaper being opened sounded through the Zenith.

"Where are you?" Scotty sighed. "Come back."

The Zenith went silent. Scotty ran through the gamut again. Nothing. He leaned back in his chair, cradling the back of his neck. He huffed his frustration at the ceiling.

Outside, wind had begun to scratch at the windows. Small sticks and pebbles dusted up and hit the glass. Scotty looked at the entrance window beside the front door and saw nothing but himself. The darkness spat his reflection back at him as if to say, "Get a good look, old boy. It's only going to get worse."

He pinched the skin between his eyes like the psychologist had taught him. Years in that chair and nothing had stuck with him but that. The pressure eased his anxiety. Scotty was taking long breaths when the Zenith woke once again, crackling like a punctured lung.

"Nnnn," whispered the Voice, so quietly Scotty turned up the volume and put his good ear to the speaker. "Nnnn," sighed the Zenith.

Scotty spoke to his instruments as carefully as a parent would a soon-to-be-sleeping child for fear of provoking it before closing its eyes. Gently. Reassuredly. Encouraging it toward peace. "I'm here, buddy. I'm not going anywhere. Stay with me."

"Nnnn," said the Voice. Then, more insistently, "Nnnn. Nnnn. Nnnn. Nnnn."

"Help me understand," Scotty said softly.

"Nnnn. Nnnn. Nnnn." The Voice responded, faster now. Faster. "Nnnn. Nnnn. Nnnn." It pulsed like dripping water. The ripples of its urgency spread to one of the bionic ears. Then the Motorolas. The Sennheiser. The rest. "Nnnn. Nnnn. Nnnn." They cantillated into Scotty's space. All instruments. One voice. "Nnnn. Nnnn. Nnnn. Nnnn. Nnnn." On and on the Voice seemed to *plead*, imploring with the pledge of its own life. But for what? What could the nameless, faceless entity want? And what could Scotty possibly do to help it? While Scotty pondered, the Voice began to slowly ebb away . . . away . . . away.

Scotty could barely hear it now. "Tell me," he whispered. He put his worry-rutted head to the Zenith and tapped it with his finger, listening.

"Eeeeeeeee!" A pestilent screech pierced his bad ear. From the Zenith, the Motorolas, the Sennheiser, an atom-splitting percussion blasted free. His water glass shattered. The ashtray on the coffee table exploded. The jar of Old Maria pasta sauce he kept above the fridge burst open. A spray of red splashed everywhere in the kitchen.

Scotty covered his ears. The bulb in the table lamp imploded. His binoculars popped. All around the house, his few possessions were exploding like targets in a shooting gallery. His eyes swept to the bottle of CC on the kitchen table just in time for him to think, *not that, not my whiskey*, when it shattered.

Then it was quiet. The equipment silenced. Not a buzz or murmur or whisper came forth. The only sounds were of Scotty's house taking stock of its injuries. Whiskey trickled off the table. Splatters of Old Maria slid toward the floor. The broken binoculars swayed on the hook. In the aftermath of the auditory assault, Scotty counted himself lucky the windows didn't break; small miracles and all that. He lifted himself from his chair and began cleaning.

Twenty minutes later, most of the glass was in a double-lined trash bag. He pushed a mop around to collect the shards he couldn't see, then dabbed the floor with paper towel. Scotty finished with his broken house and then lit a cigarette outside. The cold April wind seemed to flee the field toward him. It patted his legs, ruffled his clothes, stung his cheeks. He worked his cigarette to the filter, thinking about the Voice. He was sure something was wrong with it, maybe that it had been harmed. Probably it was. Maybe he'd never hear from it again. Meredith would like that. Claire, too. But it would crush Scotty. Because then there would be no proof that it was real.

Just over two acres of land separated his rented widower's cabin from the southern edge of the wasteyard. What Scotty loved the most about the quiet space was that even on the hottest day, there was no smell. Most people—the Douglas Radways and alien sticker slappers of the world—sniffed that anyone would live so close to a dump. But they didn't know what Scotty knew. The dump, perhaps it is the case with all dumps in Canada, was one of the most peaceful places on earth. There were no noisy or nosy neighbours. And nighttime traffic near the outlying waste-management facility was uncommon. Scotty could nap on Fletcher Road if he wanted to. He observed the field with an ironic gratitude that calmed what the Voice had stirred up.

Wind-pushed grass shuddered toward the porch. Stronger gusts rattled the loose floorboards. The house groaned, but she had been built well and would stand her ground longer than Scotty ever could. He patted the railing and turned to go inside.

From the field came a whisper.

Scotty frowned. He squinted at the moon-slicked field. Winter mould dotted the land like constellations in a midnight sky. But for the wind, the dusty carcasses of old growth that spread as far as the dump were quiet. Farther still, the coyotes scavenging more lucrative spaces were gathered near the compactor. The heads of the animals spooked up. Then one, two, three—they bolted away.

Scotty's eyes swept over the field. "Hello?" he said.

There was movement to his right. The grass crackled—it was the same sound he'd heard from the Zenith. Scotty scrambled into his house and locked the door. His heart thundered. *The Radway kid is right*, he thought. *I'm insane.* Still, he was afraid to look outside. He slid his back against the wood and spied the field through the side window. The feeble porch light exposed little past the front step, just the worked-up dust and moths flapping against the glass. He sighed. "I need a dog," he said aloud, feeling a little silly. His heart slowed, slowed, but then steps bounded toward the house. Through the grass. Over the gravel. Up the stairs. As heavy as sandbags dropped from an airplane.

The door shuddered. A blast hit it full force, rattling the hinges. *Oh God*, Scotty thought. *Oh God, it's real and it's coming to get me. No. No. No!* He pressed hard against the door. But then the shaking subsided. Scotty chanced another glance at the side window.

It was filled with an old woman's face.

Irma Madinger, the night clerk at Garrett Grocery, was standing on his porch. Her jacket was undone and her apron flapping around her waist. Worse, her mouth was open, gaping like a fish's. She captured Scotty with her unblinking eyes.

He wheeled back. "Irma?" he said, too quietly for her to hear. Then, more loudly. "Irma? Are you okay, Irma?"

Irma's tiny hands scratched the window. Her mouth opened and closed as if to feed.

Scotty protectively twisted his arms over his torso. "Can I help you with something, Irma? If you can hear me, shake your head." He shook his own to show her what to do.

Irma mimicked him, but her eyes never blinked and her mouth never stopped working. The old woman should have been trembling against the wind, but she neither trembled nor was afraid of the shadows around her. She stepped closer to the window and fogged it with her breath.

"Irma, I'm not going to open the door until you tell me what you want. You're not yourself and I don't want any trouble. Sorry, but that's the way it is. Tell me what you want and maybe I can help you." He had drawn back from the window, but he could see the woman scrawl with a thin finger on her breath fog. As quickly as she scribbled, the wind carried her words away.

"I don't know what you're trying to say." Scotty was shouting now.

The woman's mouth never stopped working, but her hands went to the sides of her wind-messed head and returned wet and red. Her fingers spidered back to the glass and wrote *coming* in blood. At once, the instruments on his desk awoke. *Coming*, they crackled and hissed and gurgled. *Coming. Coming. Coming. Coming.*

. . . HEEEEEREE.

Scotty shrieked. "I'm calling the police," he yelled to his bloody window. But before he could, oncoming red and blue lights flashed near the landfill.

The cashier sped away on her hands and feet.

7. Sound The Alarm

Long after Jennifer Tibbs, Bo Wilco, and Luis Helzer were relieved by Theo Carver's elite ABC team, all but one of the employees who'd been at the potluck was still at the facility. Most had suffered through hours of nausea to complete their shifts, and all but the guards in Sector East reported nothing unusual in their end-of-shift logbooks. Their unspoken pact was an act of preservation for all since they knew that if even one of them divulged the secret of the potluck, every last one would either get fired or sent so far north they'd need blow dryers just to keep their eyelids from freezing shut. And Tibbs', Wilco's, and Helzer's reports indicated a mild nausea from what each suspected was a stomach bug caught in the community. Nothing they could help.

When the call came in, Jeffrey Acres had been happy to abandon his pallid pretense of a dorky accountant. Prior to what they told him was an *elite* assignment, he'd been active in Iraq, Syria, and Sudan. It had been risky work, but he thrived on it. Artillery strikes. Suicide bombings by Western resistors. Uncoordinated stabbings that kept him thrumming. He liked to thrum. He liked the zing it gave him. It was like a cattle prod to his psyche. Fucking energizing. Almost better than sex. It was frowned on to enjoy it as much as he had, so he quietly lamented his duty to those who asked. A necessary evil.

But fuck, was it fun.

Not fun to Jeffrey Acres, however, were four years of useless paperwork in a stuffy office. He supposed they'd sent him here as a punishment, a pre-emptive strike against a too-eager war boy. Something to cool his jets. Like an occupational vasectomy. No more release from confrontation or combat. Before, he got to put his hand up the skirt of violence and grope her rough and wet spots. Now he had to settle for the nudie-mag equivalent. The New York Times. CNN. Global News. They satisfied him as much as an over-the-jeans pat-down, so when Iverson's call came for him to replace the guards in Sector East, Jeffrey Acres prepared to run the bases.

Tubby Tibbs had almost ruined it for him. She had smelled as rotten as a truck stop washroom. The other two, Wilco and Helzer, had contributed their fair share, of course, but Tibbs had the added odor of revulsion. She despised Jeffrey so much that she wouldn't face him. This led to a prolonged view of her sweaty backside, where a smear of sick could be seen on her calf. In his zealous state, it had almost made *Jeffrey* chuck and given him a one-way ticket back to his stodgy desk at *Adequate Accounting*. He would have fucking killed her if that had happened. Not really, but he would have imagined it, like the war boy he was.

Truthfully, he'd expected more of Sector East. Alien rebellion. Hot-tempered cursing to keep them in line. But so far he'd found none of that. The two cubes just sat there like sticks on a sidewalk. Where was the fun in that?

"Are they going to just sit there all night?" he asked no one in particular.

"They don't move much, do they?" Dalton Byrd said, picking his teeth. The men watched the immobile cubes for a time, then Dalton added, "Beats the office, though."

Foster Cupps, the biggest yet gentlest member of the ABC team, folded his arms. The effect was of two twined-up sleeping bags trying to copulate. "This is fine by me. They might look like they can't hurt you but remember the file. They're killers. They'll rip our heads off if we're not careful. No need to rile them up. I prefer it quiet and peaceful." He stretched his long legs and crossed them at the ankles. Helzer's vacated chair creaked beneath him. The silence in the room was heavy on all of them. Their quiet exhalations boomed like leaking faucets. Foster studied M1 and M2 and frowned. "If I was locked up as long as they've been, I'd be messed up, man. It's not good to be isolated like that. It makes a guy go crazy." To the little cubes he said, "Sorry, guys. I know it sucks. I hear you. I hear you. And I'd help you if I could. You like music? I could sing for you. Would you like that?"

M1 and M2 said nothing.

"Weak-ass fuckhead." Jeffrey rolled his eyes.

Dalton leaned his ear toward the Namibian, for he'd heard Foster's voice many times. It gave the impression he was sheltering an orchestra of angels within the folds of his throat.

He didn't disappoint. The slow swell of Duke Ellington's "In My Solitude" floated from Foster's chair, brushed Jeffrey and Dalton's ears, and sounded through the speakers into the Mimic enclosure.

"You want to depress them?" Acres scowled. "At least sing something happy, for goddsake."

"All right, all right. Chill, man. I got this. Let's see." Foster drummed his fingers on his shiny scalp, thinking. His eyes widened. "Ah! Let's see how the little ones like this." He stood and went to M1 and M2's cell and brought with him a little Freddie Mercury. His rendition of "Don't Stop Me Now," so good he could've been on stage, had even Jeffrey tapping his feet.

"What'd you think?" he said to the unresponsive Mimics when he finished. "Want another?" The fly cube that was not M2 jostled forward the space of a pencil eraser. It was not much, but far enough for the men who'd never seen a mimic move in person. Foster dropped to his knees to get a better look at M2. "Hey! You see that? Did you see it? I think they like it!"

Dalton pointed a hairy arm at the enclosure. "It's your lucky day, little dudes. Enjoy it while it lasts. Sing 'em another, Fos'."

From his knees, Foster sang "I Want to Break Free." His delivery was lullaby-soft so as not to overexcite the lethal cubes too much. The chuff of Acres' laughter grated on him, but he sang the words to his little audience. Then he sat back on his heels and smiled to M2, who was now jittering quite a bit.

"My pleasure, little dude. You be good for me, I'll be good for you."

M2 sputtered and shook against the floor. As Foster Cupps smiled down at him, M2 sprang like popped corn. Up. Up a little higher. Each time skidding back down like a plane trying to but not quite managing to take off.

Dalton rose and eyed M2. "Is he supposed to be doing that?"

"Beats me," Acres said, but he didn't think so.

Sector East's daily logs read like all the Canadian social studies textbooks pushed at him in school. So mind-numbing he rarely made it past a sentence or two. Like queuing up to read the dictionary. Even his teachers fell asleep. The Mimics never did anything, and Acres counted on them to continue to do nothing whether or not he properly reviewed the logbooks.

"He's doing the jitterbug." Foster chuckled. "Look at him go." The big man jived to show the Mimics how Namibians did it. He shook his hips, dipped his shoulders, opened his chest. Subtly, of course, because Sector East wasn't a nightclub.

"Hollis is going to tear a strip off you," Acres warned. He went to the enclosure and bent to inspect the little cubes. One was so still it

38

might have been dead, but the other was twitching enough for both. "You fucked him up, Fos. Look at him."

"He's just happy," Foster told Acres.

"I don't know, man." Dalton squinted at the squirming cube. Something about it made him uneasy, so he strode to the desk and retrieved the close-focus binoculars Sector East used to track the Mimics within their cell. For a second, he thought . . . no . . . it couldn't be . . . it couldn't . . . it would be disastrous if it . . .

He adjusted the binoculars.

Wobbling beneath the cube were three pairs of legs, thin as eyelashes. They were bug's legs, Dalton knew. No doubt about it. His breath caught.

"Report, Byrd," Acres ordered, for he was the most senior officer. "What do you see?"

A wing sprouted from the jumping cube. Then another. Dalton blew the front of the binoculars to rid them of dust. The wings and legs were still there. "The fuck?!" Dalton Byrd reported, as etiquette had not the words to describe how screwed they were.

"What? What is it?" Foster pulled the face of a child getting a needle.

Away from the Mimics, Dalton swept the binoculars east to west, back to front, up and down, looking for another cube. Perhaps M1 and M2 were playing. Dalton, Jeffrey, and Foster weren't the usual guards, after all. Maybe this was normal.

But they knew it wasn't normal.

"I said, 'Report, Byrd'," Acres growled, stomping his foot.

The lenses of the binoculars once again captured the bug cube. It had eyes now. Eyes and legs and wings and a little square body. Then the unmistakable frame of a fruit fly. The binoculars trembled. "Sound the alarm," Dalton Byrd said. "Sound the goddamn alarm!"

8. Anthrax and Kitchen Naps

Hollis Brubaker sat up in bed. He'd been dreaming of a change-of-command ceremony where outgoing Commander Meyer Stanton's responsibilities as the Chief of Defence Staff were transferred to him. The Governor General had extolled Hollis' accomplishments and was about to relinquish the podium to the Prime Minister when someone in the reverential crowd clashed together a pair cymbals. It was if someone had hooked him and yanked him from where he most wanted to be. He tried settling back into his dream to get his promotion, but then his phone rang again.

Only, it wasn't ringing. It was trilling the sinking-submarine alarm he'd heard years ago when one of the Plutonians escaped to the kitchen to beg for a better meal. He slapped on the phone and put it to his ear. "Tell me," he said.

Theo Carver's usually steady voice bore an accent of fear that woke Hollis more than a kick to his balls. "It's M2, sir. He's out. We don't know how it happened, but we've got everyone on it. Facility's on lockdown."

Bloody images of the Mimics' kills flashed in Hollis' head. The soldiers. The civilians. The babies. "How sure are we that we've got him contained?"

There was a pause, then Theo said, "We're not, sir."

"Ops?

"Cobra and Tracer are on their way."

That Carver had engaged the special operations teams before calling him was a good decision. Hollis had command, but control ultimately depended on his officers' acumen. The UFO's continued secrecy and security depended not on kissing his ass but on doing what had to be done *when* it had to be done. Carver's quick thinking might save all their necks, but Hollis wouldn't celebrate that. M2 shouldn't have gotten out in the first place. He would celebrate when whoever was responsible was strung up and skinned. He put on his glasses and spied the time on his alarm clock. Not even three in the morning. Beside him, Karen was stirring. Compared to the shit pile he was heading into, her loveliness was almost a sin.

"Roll call in twenty," Hollis said to Carver. "I'm on my way." He hung up the phone.

Theo returned the private receiver to its holder. When the alarm had sounded, he was the first to arrive at Adequate Accounting. His apartment above the bar next door, The Sleepy Sloth, afforded him the luxury of being able to dash from his bed to his office in the time it took most people to brush their teeth. He bulleted from under his blankets, jumped into one of his issued, saggy suits, and made for Adequate Accounting.

Any other night, Waste Way (aptly named for its proximity to the dump and the lesser-known, soul-sucking narrative of Adequate Accounting's sequestered soldiers), would be barren. There would be no cars—for those were always hidden—no office lights, and no people bustling around. To outsiders, it was a lifeless office near a dump. Not worth the footsteps or the gas to visit, especially for the exorbitant rates posted on the company's website. But when Theo burst out of the apartment, Adequate Accounting was lit up like a Canada Day night sky. Behind closed blinds, windows glowed. The cricket-chirp silence he sometimes enjoyed during evening walks was pregnant with unease. The Sleepy Sloth, too, had quickened her pace. While M2 cavorted to God knows where, the bar became a tigress in long grass, honed to movement.

Five minutes later, after Theo had been apprised of the situation by Overlook, Adequate Accounting's all-seeing-eye that routinely consisted of five tech nerds stationed at dozens of surveillance screens, he called Hollis. Now he took the elevator down to a floor that didn't exist on the designation panel, where a knee-quivering soldier waited for him.

"Major Carver, sir!" said the man, saluting with a shaky hand.

"Master Corporal Rollins, is it?" said Theo.

"Yes, sir!" said Rollins a little too loudly. His words echoed off the cavern walls and bounded back to them. *Yes, sir, sir, sir . . .*

Theo sighted a G Wagon parked near the tunnel entrance and walked past Rollins. "Rollins, I need you to get me to Sector East as fast as you can, and if something happens along the way I need you to be prepared to back me up or continue shooting if I'm dead. Can you do that?"

The soldier scurried to the vehicle as though a bag of spiders had been dropped down the collar of his shirt. He flinched. He cowered. He quaked. "Yes, sir. I'm sorry, sir. I'm not normally like this but M2 is . . . is . . ."

"Is what?" Theo asked as the engine fired up.

"Worse than war."

Theo hadn't heard it put that way before, but it was perhaps the most accurate way to describe the Mimics. With the right words and the right promises by the right people, war could be averted. Most countries perpetually campaigned against war and so had become experts at avoiding it. And in the rare cases where war became inevitable, rules of what could and could not be done were clear, else face consequences. But there was no negotiating with M1 or M2. Because they would rip your head off before you could utter a single word.

"I won't tell you they're not killers, Rollins. In fact, I think that's exactly what they were built to do. But we've had them contained for almost sixty years. *Sixty*. They might be nasty, but we've got the upper hand. How far did you read into the folder, Rollins?"

"I'm not sure," Rollins said as the G3 sped down the winding shaft while cones of light carouselled past them. The rough road made the men bounce in their seats. "What I mean is, I don't have access to the restricted file. There's more, sir. I just don't know how much." The apple in Rollins' skinny throat rolled up and down as he swallowed.

"Ah," said Theo. "Well then, this may or may not be news to you. Do you know they're interdependent?"

Rollins squished up his face. "Come again, sir?"

"They *need* each other. They can't be farther than a few kilometers from each other or they lose their ability to replicate. And if they can't do that, they're stuck as little cubes. Then they're harmless. We've got the benefit of *boundaries*. M2 can't go far."

This was no consolation to Master Corporal Rollins. He was driving Theo toward Sector East, which meant his head, and Theo's head, were vulnerable. He lifted the collar of his jacket as if that would protect him and depressed the gas pedal as much as the bumpy roads would allow. He would do his job, but as fast as he could.

When Rollins was able to speak past the lump of fear clotting his throat, he said. "May I ask why M1 and M2 are together, sir? I mean, if they're not dangerous when they're apart, doesn't it seem the sensible thing to do? Then we wouldn't have to go through all this."

The look Theo gave him was that of a frustrated educator to a dullard. Rollins could feel the other man's cold blue eyes sizing him up.

"Ever been to Winnipeg, Rollins?"

"Once, when I was little," Rollins admitted. "We visited my grandma and she took us to the zoo."

"All right, then. Did you know that while you and your grandma were ogling polar bears and smearing your cotton-candy hands on the penguin habitat you were only twenty minutes away from some of the deadliest diseases on earth? Diseases so terrible they make anthrax look like hay fever?"

Rollins shook his head.

"I didn't think so. It's public knowledge, but most people don't know about it, either because they choose not to know about it or they're too busy insulting the home team to look past the rink and read the goddamn paper. We—as in our government, our syrupy-sweet, wholesome Canadian government—has in its back pocket enough hemorrhagic, respiratory destressing, bowl-bursting diseases to murder the entire planet. Right in Winnipeg. Almost smack dab in the center of our country. Why? Because we can. Because if you want to defeat your enemy you have to *live* with it, understand it, get to know all its wicked parts so you can create weapons to destroy it on its own turf. We *need* M1 and M2 together, Rollins. It's the only way to study them and the only way to prepare for an invasion. You want those bastards knocking on your grandma's door, Rollins?"

"O-of course not, sir," the young soldier stuttered.

"Then we got to put up with what we got. And what we got is whatever our beloved government throws at us." Theo unrolled the window and spat. Rollins gripped the steering wheel and wondered if it was too late to change careers.

The G3 careened down the slope, lower, lower, until they were two kilometers below Scotty Waymore's dump. Rollins jerked the car to a stop and was about to peel back to the subterrane when Theo instructed him to wait. "Standby, Rollins. I may need you."

Immediately after Theo disappeared past the twenty-ton blast door, Rollins wished he'd gotten into a safer career like accounting and unholstered his gun.

There were three thresholds between the blast door and the official entrance to Sector East, each with a biomechanical airlock chamber and biometric access control, and entry was further delayed by a decontamination chamber between the second and third thresholds. Rollins might have sped Theo to Sector East in record time, but nothing, not even M2's escape, could hasten Theo's approach inside the building. One escape was catastrophic. Two could very well be the end of the world.

When he cleared the last negative pressure zone, the door hissed and opened onto Sector East. Theo wasted no time. "Acres, report," he demanded.

Jeffrey Acres, rigidly center of Byrd and Cupps, explained what they knew. They had relieved Wilco, Tibbs, and Helzer, who had been suffering from a stomach flu. M1 and M2 were present and accounted for when they arrived. But exactly six hours and twenty-three minutes later, M2—the slightly darker cube—began to behave strangely. Theo ran his finger down the logbook Acres pushed at him. From the time when M2 first moved to the time when Byrd spotted the fly legs sixteen minutes had passed. He tapped the entry and glared at Acres. "Sixteen minutes? You let that go on for sixteen goddamn minutes and didn't sound the alarm?"

"I've never seen M2 move in person, sir," Acres replied. "Only on the videos. It didn't seem abnormal until the end if I may say so, sir."

"You may not *say so*," Theo growled. He turned and glared into the Mimic enclosure where M1 innocently idled. The nutrition capsules should have been cleared away once the creatures fed, but they had been left on the floor. "Engage the divisor. I want to see those capsules," he said.

The *divisor* was the Under Facility Office's most advanced piece of equipment. An ultrasonic, 10,000-volt electric, demagnetizing dome that, when deployed near M1 and M2, effectively blocked their symbiosis, hence their deadliness. It was UFO's lifeline in the care and containment of the Mimics, as well as their compliance to ongoing scientific discovery. M1 and M2 hated the divisor, but they had learned that if they wanted to eat, they had to put up with it.

Acres went to the control desk and engaged the divisor. An alarm warned the divisor was about to come down. A red light flashed, and then M1 glided to her designated ready station. The fly, long since zapped by an overhead laser when its presence was discovered, did not. Another button and then penetrating radar scanned the cell. M2 was still unaccounted for. Acres completed the operation and the divisor inched shut.

Theo proceeded to the cell's east antechamber where M1 and the nutrition capsules were. He had the mind to kick M1 as a warning to M2, but he restrained himself. Instead, he entered the cell and closed the door behind him. Even as a little cube, he could feel M1 watching him, wanting to tear his head off. Imagining the pulp of his brain inside her many mouths. He pointed at the bank of lasers in the ceiling.

"Don't get any ideas. The power of ten atomic bombs is pointed at you if you so much as *sweat* in my direction." He bent by the capsules. There was nothing unordinary about M1's capsule, but he spotted a small fracture in M2's. Theo rubbed his fingers over the fissure. "Byrd, I want to know who was in the kitchen last night. Get me the names of the chefs from zero-five-hundred to now. And I want them present, understand?" His voice carried through the speakers to the men on the other side.

Dalton Byrd nodded. "Yes, sir!" He rushed to the monitoring desk.

"Cupps!" Theo shouted to stimulate the men. Inches from the glass, Foster Cupps stood ready for Theo's order. "Get Lia Geller here ASAP. Not tomorrow, not five minutes from now. NOW."

Foster Cupps hurried away. Theo glared at M1 one last time. *I know you can hear my thoughts, you little bitch. You better hope we bring him back alive, because if I'm the one who catches him, I'll rip him to fucking pieces.* Then he said, "Be a good girlfriend and stay put."

He had just exited the antechamber when Byrd called out from the monitoring desk. "Major, sir!"

"Report," Theo said.

"From zero-five-hundred to now three chefs were on duty. Jimmy LaVar, Leela Ware, and Simon Puskel. LaVar and Ware are on their way, but Puskel isn't answering. We're checking his home, sir."

"And the kitchen?" Theo asked.

"Kitchen closes at nine, sir. No one is there."

"Are you *sure* no one is there, soldier?"

Byrd swallowed. "I will check it myself."

About fucking time, Theo thought, and dismissed Byrd. He checked his watch. Hollis would arrive any minute, then the *real* hell would break loose. "Acres," he said. "Have we found anything yet?"

"Nothing, sir. Overlook is quiet. Radar hasn't found anything, but I'm not sure it's accurate. Depending what form M2 has taken, it might not pick him up."

"Keep looking."

"Will do, sir."

A vaccumous suction of air from the negative pressure zone indicated company. Lia Geller, director of Bioprocess Technology, and the person M1 and M2 most despised, gusted in. As per protocol, she'd donned the sterilized uniform, but her usually made-up face was bare and pale. Her hair had been hastily tied in a high ponytail and a pattern of pillow marks on her left cheek slightly resembled a tic-tac-toe grid. A small mole was in the center square. Unlike UFO's security contingent, the defense scientist did not kowtow to Theo. Officially, they were equivalents, though Theo had an edge in terms of subordinates. She had only a few, but they were Einstein-smart and competent when independent. The rest of the defense personnel could barely tie their shoes without affirmation.

"How did it happen?" she said without preamble.

"I was hoping you could tell us," Theo said. "One minute they're there and the next, we've got a cube with bug legs. Byrd was the first to see it, so he can tell you more. Got anything to add, Captain Acres?"

Jeffrey peered at the scientist. She was *fi-ine*, if a little dark under the eyes. A natural beauty, some would say, though from what he'd heard went on in her lab, only on the outside. Her insides were as rotten as a toilet on chili day. Her eyes bore into him as he described the events of the evening, omitting Foster's singing and dancing. At least until they reviewed the tapes, Foster would owe him, and Jeffrey Acres liked to be owed.

Finally, he said, "I can't explain it."

Theo raised M2's broken capsule. "Can you explain this?"

Jeffrey Acres blinked. *The capsule*, he thought. *It was the fucking capsule.*

Lia trapped Acres with her guillotine brows, so ready to come down on him that Jeffrey Acres took a step backward. "You didn't see the capsule?" she said crisply. "Was it broken before or after it arrived in the enclosure?"

"I'm not sure," Acres said reluctantly.

Her guillotines came down. "You had one job, Captain Acres. It's not that difficult, even for a guy like you. Either there was a crack when the capsule arrived or there wasn't. Further, you failed to promptly retrieve the capsules after they fed. You do realize that your lapse in judgement could cost lives? Not only have you jeopardized our operation, but if we haven't contained M2, everything we've ever done here could be exposed. To the citizens in this small city, to all Ontarians, to every human being on this planet. There is no room for uncertainty here, so I'll ask to think hard. When was the capsule broken?"

Theo watched the captain squirm. Acres had been exiled to the Under Facility Office in an effort to extinguish his aggression, but now it colored his cheeks a deep, boiling purple. He wasn't averse to chastising the captain, but it was *his* job to do so, not the scientist's.

"It's curious, yes," Theo said. "But for all we know, M2's escape might not have anything to do with the capsule. And you weren't the one to feed M1 and M2, were you, Captain?"

"No, sir." Acres drew himself up. "Helzer fed them."

"Then *he* would have been responsible for retrieving the capsules?"

"Yes, sir."

Lia glared at the men, both as deep as dinner plates. She was not about to let Theo cover up the most colossal screw up the UFO ever experienced. With an exasperated sigh, she addressed Acres as though he were an incontinent mutt. "How soon after they were fed did you relieve Lieutenant Helzer, Captain Acres?"

Jeffrey looked at Theo, who offered no answers, then back at the witch. "We arrived just after, ma'am."

"A minute after? A second? Be specific, Captain Acres."

"I—"

"We'll review the tapes just to be sure," she said. "In the meantime—"

Lia was interrupted by Dalton Byrd, who'd rushed past the negative pressure zone, panting. "I tried calling," he breathed. "But no one picked up."

Theo shot a look to Cupps, who was on the phone directing a contingent to Simon Puskel's apartment. "What did you find?"

"The chef, he . . . he . . . he's unconscious, sir."

9. Head Games

Dan Fogel gasped. The night was black but for a sliver of moonlight, and even with that he couldn't miss the wreckage of Irma Madinger's poor head. She'd been returning home from her shift at the grocery when she'd hit something near the dump and a passerby called in the accident. The damage to her car suggested something as big as a moose, but there was no hair or animal blood on the crumpled hood and no tracks leading to or from the accident. He agreed with his constable's assessment that Irma Madinger seemed to have hit an invisible brick wall but advised her to refrain from including that in her report.

"And unless you have proof she's been speared through her temples, don't include that either."

Constable Oaklyn Cox flashed her brown eyes at him. "I never said she was *speared*, Dan. That's so medieval. I said she was possibly stabbed or smashed. I've seen plenty of car wrecks in my time, no thanks to traffic duty—"

"Everyone has to do it."

"Anyway, I've seen my share of bumps and bashes, but I've never seen a steering wheel or windshield do what's been done to that woman's head. I mean . . . *look* at it. Her brain's been *scooped*. I don't care what she hit, whatever happened to her head wasn't an accident." She wrinkled her nose at Irma's corpse.

The police chief sighed. It hadn't been two years since the city suffered a series of unexplained murders, beginning with a bus full of casino-loving tourists and ending with two children and his friend, Ed Norman, dead. That is, unexplained to the *public*. He couldn't record the unearthly circumstances surrounding the deaths as he himself would have been locked up in a sanitorium in London faster than the ink could dry on the paper. It had taken a lot of maneuvering to record the events as if he hadn't gone completely mad. There was a lot of conjecture, heaps of simplification, loads of artistic diversion, scads of evasion, and volumes of partial truths, big stretches, and outright fabrications. Somehow, perhaps because everyone wanted to push that grim period aside as quickly as possible, he had never been questioned about his findings. Now, looking at Irma Madinger's busted head, he wondered if the demon had ever really gone away.

"There's got to be an explanation," Dan said to Oaklyn, who was searching Irma's ancient Toyota Corolla for answers.

"You know what this looks like, Dan? If I were a crazy person, and I'm not, I would say that the animal she hit was mighty hungry. Big guy gets smacked in the road, but he's so big that he outweighs the car. Not a scratch on him. And then he gets testy—because who wouldn't be, right? Irma, God bless her . . . well, if she's conscious, she unrolls her window. She's a little woman and she's alone, see? She unrolls from the safety of her car to see what she hit, and the animal takes a bite out of her."

Dan's hands went to his hips. "She's got chunks out of both sides of her head. What? Did she turn and offer him the other side? With part of her brain already missing?"

She pointed to the driver's side window. "Maybe he came in through here."

"And yet we've found no fur and there is no blood but that on the victim."

"Yet. We haven't found fur or blood *yet*," Oaklyn countered.

"She probably hit a moose," Dan said. "And as for her head, my guess is that the impact was so severe her brain got jostled around a little too much. The impact could have fractured her skull." *Like a stone in a jar*, he thought. *Shake it hard enough and it will crack and the contents fall out.*

Oaklyn made no attempt to hide her doubt. It was one of the reasons she had become one of his favorite constables so quickly. He never had to guess what she was thinking because, whether he wanted to hear it or not, she always let him know.

"Forensics?" he asked after a cursory glimpse of Irma's trunk.

"On their way," Oaklyn said.

"The witness?"

She pointed at the cruiser near the speed limit sign, near where her partner, Constable Mark Stringer, had erected the north perimeter. "Family of three called it in. When dad went out to see if Irma was okay, he saw her head then called 911 and sent his wife and son home so they wouldn't have to see it. We have dad in the car."

"He stayed with the body?" Dan asked.

"Uh-huh. Says he stood near her door. In the middle of nowhere, with a dead woman on a road with no lights. Either he's got balls the size of frisbees or he's slow. Can't figure out which."

"I'll talk to him," Dan said, and strode over to the cruiser.

The man leaning against Oaklyn's cruiser had one hand hooked on a belt loop and with the other he was tapping a cigarette, vacantly staring at the dirt road beneath his boots. He was bent so low he had to look up when Dan approached. Peter Brace, Dan learned after introductions, had picked up his son from a late-night gaming session at a friend's house then the family came upon Irma's car.

"When it's this late, Adam usually stays at Ravi's house, or vice versa, but we have a thing in the morning," Peter said, still looking at the dirt.

"Lucky your wife came for the ride and was able to drive your car home," Dan said, digging as his profession obliged. "So late and all."

Peter took another puff then flicked the cigarette on to the road. "Yeah. We're going through some things right now. Therapist tells us we need to do things together, so she came with me."

"Ah," Dan said. "Been there myself. Not easy, but worth it if you have kids."

"Did it work for you?"

"I never had kids." As the other man stayed silent, Dan pushed on. "What can you tell me about the accident, Peter?"

He shrugged. "Not much. We were coming down the road when we saw her lights kind of at a weird angle. I slowed down a bit because there are a lot of deer around here, sometimes moose, but it's gotta be years since I've seen one in the area."

Dan took notes as Peter spoke, writing in the elementary scribble that only he could decipher. "Was she still moving?"

"No. She was stopped by then. At least her car was. I know because the one headlight that was still working was pointed toward the dump." He raised an arm to show Dan what he was talking about. "Right there, see? The gates are lit up."

Past the flashing emergency lights and the stretch of rustling elephant grass that bordered the landfill along its ditches, Irma Madinger's one head light beamed at the chain-link fence and the attached hours of operation sign. *Open 8:00 a.m. – 6:00 p.m. Monday – Friday. 9:00 a.m. – 4:00 p.m. Saturdays. Closed Sunday.* On a post high above the control panel for the automatic gate was a camera that Dan intended to investigate.

"Can you describe what you saw when you first approached the vehicle?"

The nasty winds from a few hours earlier had somewhat abated, but its lingering fingers pulled at their collars and ruffled their hair. More than once, the police tape Constable Stringer erected had broken and other officers rushed to retie it. Peter pulled the hood of a sweatshirt from under his jacket and settled into it.

"To be honest, if my son and wife weren't with me, I would have just called 911 and drove on. It's probably not what you want to hear, but when you see someone's head torn up like that, it's not something you want to be around. Worse than any horror movie I've ever seen, and I've seen some good ones."

"You had no doubt that she was dead?"

Peter shook his head. "None. Not the way her head was. I knew Irma. I think everyone in Garrett knew her. She was just a nice lady, you know? After working on her feet all day, you'd think she'd close up early given the chance, but that wasn't her. How many times did she find us rushing to beat closing time, but she'd see us through the window and wave like she'd been hoping we'd come. She just made you feel good. There's not many people like that."

"She was an excellent cook, too," Dan said, recalling the lasagnas and the soups and casseroles Irma passed on over the years since his and Brandy's divorce, fearing for his bachelorhood as if she were his own mother.

"Best chicken pot pie I've ever eaten," Peter agreed. They looked at the car, thinking of their next grocery runs with gloom.

"One last thing. You didn't happen to see what she hit, did you? No animal limping away, or maybe a vehicle that got the better of the crash?" When Peter said he didn't, Dan thanked him and shook his hand. "Well, we appreciate you staying, Peter. We'll be in touch if we need to review your statement. If you give me a moment, I'll have one of my officers drive you home."

Dan stepped away, instructing a very resistant Oaklyn to drive Peter Brace home.

"I'm not a chauffeur, Dan." She eyed the man drooping against the cruiser. Her thick braids flapped against her shirt.

"You'd be a terrible chauffeur, Oakie. Most people want their drivers to be quiet."

She elbowed him. "Then why me, when Stringer or Nilbit can do it?"

"Because neither of them is as good as you are at talking. A woman's been killed. Whether it was an accident or otherwise, we have almost no evidence. Maybe daylight will help, but I'm not confident. See if there's anything else you can get from him. Casually, of course. Maybe the wife or kid noticed something. People tend to relax when someone's not writing down what they say."

"You're lucky to have me."

"Never said I wasn't. Go do your thing, and I'll see you in the morning. I'm heading to the station for a few hours."

"She got you on the couch again?"

Oaklyn eyed him. The entire department had seen Dan's divorce wither him like a dried flower. He had skinnied out then puffed up, looking so much like a bloated fish at one point that Oaklyn herself put a hook on his desk and told him to bite it. She knew it was crass, but she didn't pussyfoot around. You were honest with people you respected. And when his new girlfriend came in, the city's nosiest reporter, Jessica Chung, Oaklyn had told him that she hoped the woman at least rode some life back into him.

A year later, Dan was more alive than they'd ever seen him. His hair stopped greying and he'd lost the weight his rejected heart caused him to gain. The hound-dog look Brandy authored had, with Jessica Chung's spicy seduction, become assertive and, damn it all, if he were Oaklyn's type she would have even thought he was sexy now.

"Nah. She's *painting*," Dan said of Jessica. "Saw some article in one of those magazines and now my house isn't white enough for her. The walls were already white, for Pete's sake. The only room that doesn't make me choke from the fumes is the kitchen, and only because she's already done that."

"Small price to pay for happiness," she said as she dug the keys to the cruiser from her pocket.

"I'm not complaining," Dan said with a grin that belied the melancholy he felt for Irma Madinger.

They left the scene in Mark Stringer's capable hands. Officers deterred the curiosity of occasional traffic, slowed to gape through holes in the perimeter. Oaklyn escorted Peter Brace to a narrow two-story across from Timothy Lumley Junior High School in a semi-forested suburb barely ten minutes away. And while Dan was pulling into the station, his phone rang.

He backed the cruiser into his stall and hurried to the restroom to relieve his over-burdened bladder. There, his phone rang twice more. He washed his hands and wet his face and by the time he was back at his desk with a tumbler of three-a.m. coffee and feeling decently alert, his phone was trilling with a number he didn't recognize.

"Fogel," he said, because anyone who had his number and the latitude to call him in the middle of the night must be familiar to him.

"Chief Daniel Fogel? Goes by Dan?"

"The one and only," Dan said.

"Dan, I do apologize for calling at such an unearthly hour, but I do need to speak to you. Hollis Brubaker with the RCMP, Security and Intelligence."

Dan sat up. "I'd say I was dreaming but the station's coffee is burning a hole in my esophagus, as usual. Hollis, you said? What can I help you with?"

The lie from Hollis' lips flowed from mouth to ear like ice melt to river. "Among other things, my department is responsible for pursuing some of the most violent murderers in Canada. We've been tracking forty-eight of them from Nova Scotia to Vancouver, and we have it on good authority that one has made it to your city. You know the Zombie Killer?"

On the other end of the line, the corner of Hollis' mouth lifted in a sideways smile. When he assumed command of the Under Facility Office, he had been assured by the retiring authority that the institution was inescapable. But an attempted escape by Ebba, a Plutonian with a picky palate, to the kitchen some seven years ago necessitated a contingency plan, should any of the aliens ever escape beyond the facility. The Martian plan included a media release warning the public of an accidental deployment of robotic gnomes, intended for use in a Hollywood Christmas movie, with a $10,000 reward for the safe capture and surrender of each gnome to a fake company established by Lieutenant Deborah Mills. The final contingency plan—deemed *Project Assemble*—fashioned the Venusians as clusters of endangered coral reef, mobile with hordes of flesh-eating sea bugs, the Plutonians as rabid red porcupines, the Uranians as bipedal snakes escaped from a genetics laboratory, and the Saturnians as pulsating slime molds that, if touched, caused paralysis in seconds.

Those narratives had been relatively easy to conjure, but they had to be especially careful with the depiction of the Mimics because they were the only aliens capable of assuming human form. Serial killers were the most natural choice. A few Jane Does and some plug-and-play, and Hollis had created the most dangerous killer that never existed.

"Still got you?" Hollis said when Dan was silent.

"I'm here," Dan said.

Of all serial killers in Canada known to the department, the Zombie Killer turned the most stomachs. This was because both BOLO (Be On The Look Out) and Intelligence Reports noted that the Zombie Killer had an eerie propensity for snacking on the brain matter of dying victims. Identical saliva samples collected from victims' wounds confirmed a male human, though the killer's DNA hadn't matched any of the profiles in the National DNA Data Bank.

Most active in the early nineties, with a few decapitations in late 2010, the Zombie Killer was an especially evasive predator. One Dan definitely didn't want in Garrett.

"Hollis, please tell me there is another Chief Fogel that I'm unaware of. Someone in another city, very far away?" He pinched the bridge of his nose.

"I'm afraid not, Dan. I know it's not the best news I can give you, but the good news is we are prepared to hunt him down. I'm deploying a unit as we speak."

Dan's insides constricted. He'd done his fair share of cooperating with federal agencies. Some partnerships were a boon to good policework, but others, well, others were as useful as an amputation. He sipped his coffee, now wondering about the timing of Hollis' call. Irma's injuries suggested she'd encountered the Zombie Killer, but the fact that Hollis hadn't called him until *after* he claimed a victim didn't seem quite right. Why would the RCMP let someone die if they could prevent it? God only knew the scandals the agency experienced in the past, which should have made it much more diligent, but this conversation didn't give Dan much hope.

"Maybe the coffee hasn't hit me yet, so forgive me as I try to understand this, Hollis. I have a victim out near the dump on Waste Way that fits your killer's modus operandi. She was a good woman and she died in no ordinary car crash. She might have hit a brick wall in the middle of the road, for all we know. As you can expect, I've seen my share of accidents, but not one that's ever done what's been done to our city's favorite grocery clerk. Now, if what you're telling me is true, I have to wonder how long you've suspected the killer was in Garrett; and now that I'm really thinking about it, why do I get the feeling that what I've told you isn't news? There's no way you could have known we had a victim down a back country road, could you? Not so soon, unless you had a car out that way and didn't report it, but that wouldn't make any sense." A small snort of laughter came out of him. "I tend to ramble when I'm tired, so bear with me on this one."

"Dan, I give you my word we weren't confident about the killer being in Garrett until just before I called you. All signs were pointing to Mississauga. But you *do* have me on your victim. We picked up some ham radio chatter a few hours ago. Not sure if it was before or after you discovered your grocery clerk, but word was there was a woman in the area with what seems to be our killer's trademark on her skull. Before you ask, it was too quick to triangulate, but damn it, we tried."

"Your unit . . ." Dan said.

"Will take the lead on this one only if we confirm your clerk's wounds are our guy's, but I expect a reciprocal partnership regardless."

"Fair enough. The quicker we get this son of a bitch, the better," Dan said. "Though I do have a question for you before you go. Any chance you've figured out how the Zombie Killer reaches his victims? I recall the reports being vague on that, mostly victims had been found in fields or ditches, a small truck or car was mentioned, nothing recognizable, of course, but our clerk's car is smashed up like a summer piñata. Assuming our clerk met with your killer, I wonder how he did it. Is the guy driving a tank? No evidence of tracks that I've seen, but it's dark and we're just coming off one hell of a windstorm. The gravel was knocking about quite a bit without us walking on it."

Hollis groaned theatrically. He had planned for this. Lieutenant Mills insisted it had been overkill, but the Mimics packed more power in a single atom than a Bengal tiger, a detail that could literally *and* figuratively crush the project. In a situation like this, their might *had* to be explained. "I wish I could tell you no, Dan, but two of his Jane Does did meet rather fortunate ends in single-vehicle collisions just like yours. I say *fortunate* because they were dead *before* he'd gotten to their heads. At this moment in time, the military has a number of decommissioned tanks unaccounted for. Could it be one of those? My guess is most likely, but those things don't exactly come in like mice. Could be he's either knowledgeable enough to modify it or he has help, in which case we're looking for more than one perp." *And good luck finding them*, Hollis thought.

"I'll inform my team," Dan told him, and suggested they meet later in the morning.

Hollis wanted to meet with the chief as much as a proctologist. He'd managed to remain concealed for years, avoiding the wider city so adeptly that only his staff recognized him. His hope was that M2 would be captured before the day—hell, the *hour*—was over. He would call Dan and claim victory and recede like a footprint in the sand. "I'm tied up, but I'll send an inspector your way. Gina," Hollis tittered to himself, "Totswither. She knows everything I do and has full authority."

When he ended the call, Dan felt he had aged ten years. He'd known death couldn't be separated from his career. It was as much a part of his life as his own family. On its own, Irma Madinger's tragedy wouldn't make him lose sleep or worry for the city, but Hollis' call summoned a fear that shredded his nerves. Garretters were good people. They didn't deserve to have their brains eaten. He shuddered, logged into his computer, and attempted the gruesome task of familiarizing himself with the Zombie Killer. And Hollis Brubaker.

10. Little Spark and Big Bitch

Waste management wasn't the most alluring profession, but to Scotty Waymore it was a beautiful reprieve from an ugly world. He got to watch the sun wrap its amber arms over the surrounding fields and paint them gold, and in the evenings see the throat of the sky swallow it all down to its starry stomach. He got to see foxes, squirrels, chipmunks, raccoons, and swirls of birds, all hungry, and none who called him *Skitzo Scotty* or *Scotty van Gogh* or anything at all. Even after a night like last night, with Irma Madinger gone mad at his window and the Voice screaming through his transmitters, the peace he felt for his landfill soothed his confusion.

Last night's weather had pushed on toward Manitoba, so when he walked from his cabin through the field to the office, he had only needed a sweater. Warm though he was, he felt a chill creep through him as he remembered Irma bounding away like a cheetah in the middle of the night. If the grass ruffled, it was Irma coming to get him. When a faraway car bounced past, it was Irma thrusting herself at him with her gaping fish mouth.

Scotty hurried along. A few minutes later, he was at the back gate, unfastening the latch of his own private entrance. Most days, Scotty liked to arrive before his staff, but his restless sleep had been crippled from Irma and the Voice. The moment he closed his eyes, one would gape and the other would scream. So he kept them open until sleep finally took him not two hours ago. Waking wasn't so easy.

"Shit, Scotty. You look like hell," Chad Copper, one of his long timers, said. He was slurping an *Ener-Wake* energy drink, filled with enough caffeine to keep a platoon of new parents awake until their infants graduated. There was a smear of pizza sauce on the top of his bald head, compliments of the gas-station submarine sandwich balanced on his knee. "That skunk under the porch again?"

Scotty shook his head. Above their makeshift coffee station was the small mirror Vera hung when she started almost three decades ago. It was as rusty and cracked as her, so when Scotty glanced at it, the man staring back at him had rust-wrinkles across his already weathered skin.

He swiped the air in front of his face. "Wish it was," he said, draining the last of Vera's weak coffee from the canister into a paper cup. He turned and leaned against the trailer wall. "That skunk wouldn't have done to me what Irma did."

Vera Kingsley's office, if it could be called that, was an over-heated, over-stuffed afterthought slightly larger than a portable toilet, the handicap variety, suffused with layers of smoke so thick, the outdated pictures of her family could not be reorganized without her having to repaint the walls. She bumped her way between her desk and the filing cabinets and squinted at Scotty. "What'd you say about Irma now?"

"I said she gave me quite the scare last night," he told her. "Came tapping on my window in the middle of that storm. Scared the lights out of me. I said, 'Irma, is that you?' And her mouth just opened like a trout's. Holy mighty, I never seen anything like it. So I ask her if she needs help, you know, because she didn't look right, and she just took off like a . . . a dog or something."

The look Chad gave him suggested Scotty had grown horns. "You hearing that Voice again, big man?"

"It wasn't the Voice," Scotty said. "It was Irma, I tell you. Swear to God. She must've been sick or something." He dug a hand into his front pocket to quell his trembling fingers.

Vera's puckered pink lips were working like she tasted something sour. Her eyes darted to Chad then back to Scotty. "What time was this?"

Scotty rubbed the back of his neck. "I don't know. Midnight, maybe. Give or take. It was dark. Too dark for a woman to be running around like that."

"Irma's dead," she said matter-of-factly, studying Scotty's face for a reaction. She swiped Chad's cigarettes from the table and lit one. "You didn't hear the crash last night? It was near the front gate."

"Crash?"

It was Chad who nodded. "Look at the camera. There's still police tape in the east lane."

The gravel road in front of the dump didn't really have *lanes*, but Scotty knew what Chad meant. He strode to his office, slightly larger though much cleaner than Vera's, and turned on his computer. The old machine chugged and wheezed awake, then Scotty pulled up the live-feed security footage. There it was. Tape roped around the gate. Tape roped around the speed limit sign. Little orange flags staked in the grass.

"You didn't hear it?" Vera eyed him. "Whatever she hit stopped her like a brick wall. I have a friend in Beaver Ridge. She heard it all right. Said it shook the house."

Usually, Scotty couldn't avoid hearing the traffic on Waste Way but last night the Voice had been shrilling through the cabin like a steam whistle. Of course, he couldn't tell Vera and Chad that. He said, "What do you mean *whatever she hit*?"

"Some asshole hit her and took off. Heard it on the radio this morning. Police are asking people to look for a truck or larger vehicle with unexplained damage." Chad took another bite of his sandwich while Vera puffed her smoke at him.

Vera said, "They didn't say it was Irma, but everyone knows it was her. Some shitheads passed the accident and posted it on that site. Facegram or Instabook, I don't know where people are puking out their lives these days. Cops didn't visit last you last night, then?"

Scotty said they hadn't, but knew they would. They would want to talk to him. They would want to know if he'd heard the crash, and they would want to see the security tapes. The way Irma had been acting on his porch, it was obvious now that she'd been in an accident. She'd come to his door seeking his help and Scotty had been too goddamned afraid to help her. He sighed and dragged his hands over his head. "No one came. Just Irma. God, I wish I could've helped her. Are you sure it was her?"

"I mean, there's a *chance*..." Chad said unconvincingly, fingering the thick gold chain around his neck.

"And I'm the CEO of Tim Horton's." Vera tapped her cigarette into Chad's not-quite-empty energy drink can. "There's too many people saying it for it not to be true. Internet doesn't lie."

The merit of her logic often found them at ends with each other. She had come with the place like a diseased tree. There so long, one couldn't be separated from the other without killing the roots. She wasn't anyone's favorite, and she wasn't a particularly hard worker. More often than not, Vera's nose was in trashy romance novels as she sipped her four tablespoons of sugar coffee and dragged her dry lips over long-filter cigarettes. But ... and this was a *big* but, Vera Kingsley stored in that smoke-smelling head of hers more information than the all the filing cabinets and Scotty's computer combined, much of it incriminating. She knew a temporary driver had illegally dumped 9,000 litres of leachate in a wooded area a few hundred meters north of the facility. She knew that Fat Frank drove one of the bulldozers into the entrance shack when Scotty refused him overtime pay after discovering Frank had been leaving the site for hours-long *weed and feed* binges in the middle of his shifts. Vera knew that Scotty, Frank, Chad, and even Scotty's right-hand, bubbly Brian Dunn, sometimes scavenged from the site, something the company strictly forbid. And she knew Scotty heard voices, as they all did.

He looked at his watch and said, "Battery collection come yet?" Chad shook his head. "Go see that Frank hasn't messed them up like last time, then have him fix the cover. I said ten inches, it's ten inches. That layer's got more holes than a net. It's scattered all over. Tell him he can clean that up after he's done with the cover."

Chad groaned. He stood, hitched up his jeans, and left the trailer.

Scotty was about to turn toward his office when Vera lassoed him with her yellow eyes. "You sure it was Irma?" He nodded. Vera thought about this, twisting her crimpled mouth so much she might have been chewing her tongue. After a time, she said, "I didn't like her anyway," and slithered back to her office to read.

Her departure left a tolerable peace in the trailer. He went to his office, still close enough to hear her choke up pebbles of phlegm and spit them into tissues and stuff them into an empty coffee can that she kept on her desk. There was a small radio beside the printer, and he flipped this on to drown out the noise. Then he turned to his computer and retrieved the recording of last night's security footage.

From the time he left until the wind picked up at around eight, the footage played like a still. The evening was quiet and uneventful. The footage continued. For minutes, there was nothing. Then the screen showed a breeze beginning to pick over the road, dusting up pebbles and dirt. The gate banged in its latch. Loose litter cartwheeled one way, then another. Trees churned like an angry ocean. Branches sailed by. Whirlpools of leaves swirled across the gravel. Occasional traffic slowed, slowed, until for a long while there was none.

He was biting his pen cap, frustrated at the speed of the tape, when the Voice came into his head.

Coming.

Scotty looked around. He had been visited by the Voice at work a few times. It put a pallor on him that made his team think he was going to faint, though he actually did only twice. Chad, Frank, and Brian never gave Scotty any trouble about the episodes, but he knew Vera amassed them in her arsenal, so he worked hard to conceal the visits.

He slid out from behind his desk and quietly closed the door, careful to slowly release the latch so it didn't catch on the strike plate.

Coming, the Voice said again.

No. That wasn't quite right. It wasn't *coming*. The Voice had spread the word into two syllables. It was *com-e*, so that it sounded like *come-ee*.

Come here, more clearly now.

"Where?" Scotty whispered to the room. "Where do you want me to go?" he said more quietly.

There was a bang at his door.

Vera had never warmed to calling him Scotty. Instead, she barked his name as though he was a soap scum remover instead of a human being. "*Scud*! What the hell do you want in there? I can't hear you if the door's shut."

"Vera, I am on the phone—" he called from his desk. He could see the shadow of her feet beneath the bottom of the door. Something slid against the wood and Scotty knew that it was the woman's ear. "I'll let you know if I need anything," he said, informing by his tone that he knew she was spying on him. He began clacking on his keyboard again when the shadows finally receded.

The Voice did not come back, so Scotty returned to the security footage. It was as unremarkable as before. He was sighing into his chair, watching for so long his eyes grew dry, when a small flash

PROJECT DOMAIN

in the bottom of the screen caught his attention. It was the tiniest thing, really, like a cigarette being lit on the ground. He increased the magnification, but the system was too old and cheap to reveal the spark more clearly. He squinted, forwarded the feed, stopped, rewound the feed. He thought that someone most likely had tossed a lit cigarette out a car window. Wind like that could have easily carried a stub down the road, maybe for miles.

After watching the spark for some time, he concluded that it didn't move like a discarded cigarette. For one thing, the spark never went out, and for another, the spark's movement was too smooth to have been caused by the wind. Scotty watched some more while Vera played at being

productive by shoving things in her office. Soon the road brightened with the slow approach of headlights.

Then it happened.

As the dim intensity of the headlights grew almost white on the dark road, the little spark zipped in front of the car and promptly went out. A terrible darkness rose where the spark had been. Glistening black projections unfurled outward and upward as though an ink spot had developed on the camera and was being blown like straw painting across the screen. Scotty tapped the side of his laptop, thinking the darkness was a glitch. He rubbed the screen with his forefinger, but the inky blotch did not go away. "What the hell?" he muttered to himself, and was squinting around the webs of black at the light of the oncoming car when it slammed into the darkness.

Irma's car—it had to be Irma's—crumpled. The hood crushed inward. The windows shattered. The short head behind the wheel lurched forward, hit the dash, and snapped back. At least, this is what Scotty *thought* he saw. It was hard to tell what was really happening behind the black ink. But it was easy to tell that the crash had been lethal.

There was the rusty taste of blood in his mouth when he realized he'd bitten his pen cap to a jagged point. Scotty spat in the trash bin, unable to look at the screen any longer. Seeing a woman die wasn't on his list of priorities, but it superseded any anxiety he'd felt about the Voice.

Vera banged on the door again. "Scud, you have a visitor. Don't make the *officer* wait." As often as their personalities clashed, sometimes so forcefully they couldn't be within miles of each other, Scotty realized that Vera was warning him.

He closed the surveillance feed and opened the budget spreadsheet he'd been updating, then hurried to the door.

In their combination lunchroom and meeting area, Police Chief Dan Fogel was declining the pack of Vera's outstretched cigarettes. "No, thank you," he said politely, and held his ground under Vera's inquisitive glare.

If any officer had to visit, Scotty was glad for it to be Dan. The man was known as much for his compassion as his discretion. Dan himself had attended the personal safety call when Scotty took a blade to his ear to stop the Voice. Unlike many departments where police chiefs were reluctant to involve themselves, the Garrett Police Department ran as lean as a lemonade stand. It did not have the manpower for Dan to *not* get involved.

Scotty tipped his chin to the one person in the room he respected and shook his hand. "You here about the accident?"

"I am," Dan admitted. Then, when Vera's tight lips gave the impression that she was disinclined to give them privacy, he said to Scotty, "You have time for a walk?"

Smoke puffed from Vera's nose. They left her scowling and went outside.

As during Dan's previous visits, they walked the red clay loop that surrounded the facility. Dan absently watched a cacophony of swooping birds while he slowly strode alongside Scotty. "Besides enduring that employee of the year back there, how are you doing?" He jerked a thumb toward the trailer where Vera's moldering face appeared in the window.

Scotty chuckled. "She makes me want to cut off my other ear some days."

It was a crude joke, but Dan smiled and patted him on the back. "Remind me to give you a pair of ear plugs before I go. I have a pile of them in the console just for people like that. Best protection I can give you." They rounded the bend near the oil depository, where, on the other side of a nearby fence, the marshy toe of one of Garrett's three conservation areas flashed its cattails. After a time, Dan said, "You doing okay, Scotty?"

He could have lied, but Dan Fogel wasn't an easy man to lie to, nor did Scotty want to lie to him. "To tell you the truth, I'm not so sure," Scotty said, and looked at the sky. "It's not the Voice that's bothering me, Dan, it's . . . ahh . . . I hear Irma Madinger died in that accident." He nodded toward the road.

Dan sighed. "She did."

"She came to my porch last night," Scotty said without looking at him. He relayed the story in all its terrible confusion, skipping only the incidence of the Voice. Dan listened quietly, occasionally glancing sideways at Scotty to see his trembling cheeks, but they never stopped walking, Dan fearing Scotty would stop talking and Scotty fearing Dan would lock him up.

"You say she *bounded* away like a cat? On her hands?"

Scotty nodded. "That's what I saw, swear it with my life. She couldn't have been right in the head. I know I'm not the guy to say something like that, but she wasn't right, Dan." He thought of Irma's bloody hands and vacant face, and of the stain on the back of her pants when she bent and ambled away.

"Where did she run off to, do you think?"

"God knows. She took off. Back to the road, it looked like, but it was too dark to see anything once she went into the grass. But why go back like that?" When Dan didn't speak, Scotty said, "Was she close to the car when you found her?"

Dan shook his head. He was as attuned to lies as mothers were to infants, but he sensed no dishonesty in the waste manager. Still, Scotty wasn't exactly a model of mental health. His story had a lunatic kind of logic that brought more questions than answers. There was no doubt that Irma had died. Her stiff body on the autopsy table proved it. But while a crash like that could have instantly killed her, Dan couldn't discount the possibility that instead she'd become disoriented and gone to Scotty's for help.

In the state she'd been in, she wouldn't have considered that he was no more prepared to help her than she herself was. If this were the case, returning to her car would be a natural reaction. After an impact like that, however, he wasn't convinced that Irma could have crossed the field, banged on Scotty's door, galloped to her car, and buckled herself back in. So far, the evidence simply did not support that. And until it did, Dan had to pursue the theory of a hit and run by the Zombie Killer, or that Scotty Waymore could somehow be involved. Or both.

At last, he said, "She was buckled in."

The way Scotty's face gathered gave the impression of a dried out Shar-Pei. "Why would she do that?"

"You tell me," Dan said, though without conviction.

They came upon the compressor station, which, though relatively advanced for a city the size of Garrett, sounded not unlike a speeding train. Here Scotty stopped, put his hands in his pockets, and observed the building as a museum-goer would abstract art. "I know my word might not mean much, but I have no reason to spin a story like that. You think I want to sound crazier than everyone thinks I am? This had nothing to do with me. See the tape. You'll know what I'm talking about. She crashed into *something*, but God only knows what."

It wouldn't be the first time that Dan's department requested surveillance footage from the landfill. There was a period one spring, during a home renovation frenzy, when Scotty's crew arrived many mornings to find discarded carpets, toilets, drywall, and rotten lumber heaped in front of the gate. Scotty had asked Dan to find the culprits responsible, who refused to abide by the landfill's operating schedule. One of the city's most disreputable contractors was promptly fined enough to make the activity stop. Two murder investigations by departments in London and Toronto also found Scotty submitting the landfill's surveillance footage, though nothing had ever come of it.

"You watched the tape?" Dan asked now.

"'Course," Scotty told him. "When I heard, I had to see for myself what they were talking about." He explained about the spark that didn't move like a spark and how, when it went out, something big and black appeared in the road, and how Irma's car crumpled when she had struck it. "It was like she hit a brick wall," he said.

Or a tank, Dan thought, remembering his conversation with Hollis.

They completed the loop and rounded back toward the trailer where Dan's cruiser was parked. Vera was still in the window, but she had opened the screen to see if she could hear anything. To their right, Frank was cursing at Chad that the cover was damn well high enough, but then he spotted Scotty and stomped toward the bulldozer.

Scotty went inside to copy last night's surveillance footage to a flash drive while Dan grabbed a handful of ear plugs from his console. They traded and shook hands, each promising the other to connect soon.

Proceeding at a snail's pace, Dan pulled away from the trailer, down the gravel road toward the gate. Unaccustomed to police visits, all the staff—Vera, Chad, Frank, and now Brian Dunn, who was pulling into the site—nervously watched the chief examine their workplace as he drove. From behind her window, Vera thrust a middle finger at the car. The cruiser's brake lights came on, but Dan was only turning onto the side road, not returning to arrest the woman for having the demeanour of a face punch, as Scotty hoped.

He went to his office and turned off his computer to keep Vera's prying but computer-illiterate fingers from getting anything. Before she could speak, Scotty closed his door and said, "I'm going out."

"I saw Meredith at the bank the other day."

"Oh?"

The woman's bottom teeth tugged her upper lip. She looked so much like a yellowed yak, Scotty worked hard to keep a straight face. "She was with a fella. Not an ugly one, for once. Two ears, too." She worked that in like a knife and waited for his reaction.

"It's a good thing you didn't have children, Vera," he said, looking at her looking at him. "One devil is enough for this world." He saluted her then, feeling her indignation on him like a heatwave. Then he got in his truck and went to find Meredith.

11. Roundup

It had been fourteen hours since M2's escape, though just under twelve since the Under Facility Office became aware of it. The spring sun had risen and settled on the little city with its gentle warmth and birdsong, but two kilometers beneath Scotty Waymore's landfill, the chill of an apprehensive gloom took root in Cora Hughes. It might have been winter, for all the warmth down there. And no one could talk without fear of having their tongues caught because Hollis wasn't just frosty but *glacial*.

She'd been summoned to the office at the ungodly hour of four a.m. As with the others, she arrived promptly and was subjected to saliva swabs and corralled into the command center in Sector West by Lieutenant Deborah Mills. They were given no coffee, no chairs, and no chance to pre-emptively tender their resignations. Still suffering from sour stomachs, the pale hostages groaned uncomfortably while they waited their indictments.

Mitch stood beside her, letting her lean on him to soothe her arches. "Bet you Anderson forgot the head count again," he whispered to Cora.

"It's the potluck," she whispered back. "He knows. Oh, God, we're all going to get fired." Unlike Iris, who was now officially retired, Cora still had four years to work before she could collect her pension and put her feet up. If she were fired now, she would have to find another job, and who would hire her with a twenty-year gap in her resume? She couldn't exactly put that she worked underground with aliens, now, could she? She leaned on Mitch, biting her lip.

"Naw," he said cheerfully. "They wouldn't do that. Who would take care of the place? It's never as bad as you think."

But it was worse than any of them had thought.

They were kept in the room for two hours and no one was allowed to leave. Even Jennifer Tibbs, who—in addition to the food poisoning— was suffering from a painful urinary tract infection but was not given permission to use the washroom. Whenever she yipped in pain, it was Jeffrey Acres, guarding the door under Hollis' orders, who snapped at the woman to shut up. They were tired and burdened with their own mistakes, imagined or otherwise, sweating up the place like a high school locker room. When Hollis finally came in, Cheryl Picket and Don Sendall were asleep in the corner and Bo Wilco and Luis Helzer were one blink away from joining them.

Hollis strode to the front of the room where a platoon of six men from Overlook flanked him. His wiry orange hair was severely flattened over his anger-flushed scalp. He put his hands in his pockets, rocked on his toes, his heels, and snorted at them. Collectively, they took a step back.

"Never," Hollis said, the searchlights of his eyes swinging at them. "Never has such gross incompetence been gathered in one place. Look around. *Look*!" Veins erupted on the sides of his over-tanned face. His eyebrows arrowed, nocked and ready, then he shot his venom at them.

"Not one of you is worth the dirt I walk on. Not one. Dirt does what it's *supposed* to do. We have one rule. One goddamn rule more

PROJECT DOMAIN

important to the country—the *world*—than any one of your insignificant little lives. Any one care to tell me what that rule is?"

No one offered an answer.

The way Hollis pursed his lips suggested his jaw was broken. They came so far out you could almost hear his brittle skin tearing. "*Always. Be. Aware.* Not sometimes. Not when you feel like it. Not when you think I'm looking. *Always.* Every goddamn minute of every goddamn day. Because you know what happens when you close those pathetic eyes of yours? The baby gets out of the gate." He paused, gazed up at the ceiling, and back at them. "That was one of my predecessor's terms. *Baby.* Doesn't sound so bad, does it? You let a baby out, you get it back. Right? It might even come back to you on its own. But what you've done, you incompetent little shitheads, is let the devil out of the basement. M2 is missing."

They gasped. Hands went to mouths, eyes opened in terror, and the frightened drumbeats of knocking knees thundered around the room. Tony Groper, who had always been quick-tempered with the aliens, started hyperventilating. Don Sendall shook so violently the keys in his pocket jangled. Jennifer Tibbs released her bladder in a stinging pink stream down her pantleg. Leela Ware, one of the morning chefs, fainted.

"This is how you *should* feel. You should be terrified. But you're too busy having *potlucks* to remember that you are surrounded by creatures that want to kill you and every other thing on this planet."

Oh God, Cora thought, wondering if the Bargain Mart would hire her. They were always hiring ex-prisoners and homeless people. They had to hire her, didn't they?

Mitch glanced at Cora. Hollis wasn't exactly wrong, but neither was he entirely right. The Martians were as aggressive as dandelion puffs. And the Saturnians were constantly healing headaches. When Iris's husband had been diagnosed with cancer and she had been unable to sleep, it was Templeton who touched her wrist and cured her insomnia. The Plutonians might behave like menopausal women with straying husbands, but when they were done blowing their steam, all they really wanted was someone to talk to. And as for the Venusians and Uranians, not one had ever been violent. Two bad apples didn't spoil the whole bunch, in Mitch's opinion.

"You have something to say, Iverson?" Hollis speared him with his eyes.

There was a swish of footsteps as everyone around him backed away. Only Cora remained nearby, mentally fabricating her resume.

"No, sir," he said.

For a time, Hollis just looked at him, venting through his nose. Somehow Mitch knew that if he looked away, Hollis would make an example of him and ship him to the ice hell up north where the water froze your balls and you had to have sex with your clothes on if you wanted to survive it. As much as it nauseated his already tender stomach, Mitch held his ground.

"Iverson, I'm going to give you some advice. Would you like to hear it?"

The deadfall trap Hollis had him in hung heavy over his head. One wrong move and Hollis would yank the stick away and Mitch would be crushed.

"I'd suggest you and the rest of your idiot companions get your praying hands together," Hollis said. "You're going to want to squish 'em so tight they *bleed*. You see, early this morning we found our chef, Simon Puskel, unconscious in the kitchen. Down, just like that." He snapped his fingers. "*Food poisoning*. Greener than a leprechaun in a pot of kale. And by the look of it, some of you are not that far behind. At this very moment, Mr. Puskel is under the care of the doctors at Garrett General, but we need him to recover. Because every second he can't tell us what happened is another second M2 is loose. Could be he's in this very room. One of *you*, even." He pointed at them.

Suspicion swelled in the room. Former friends retreated from each other. Those who had been in the vicinity of the Mimics before

PROJECT DOMAIN

M2 escaped discovered people around them not slinking but *diving* away. From above, it appeared that Jeffrey Acres, Dalton Byrd, Foster Cupps, Luis Helzer, Bo Wilco, and Jennifer Tibbs had been caught peeing in the pool. Wherever they waded, paths were cleared.

"Could be any of them," Hollis agreed. "But don't underestimate M2's cunning. He could be you, and you, and you." He pointed at Adequate Accounting's actual accountant, then at a twenty-five-year janitorial veteran, then at the scientist Lia Geller, the only one who didn't shrink away. "M2 could have been every single one of you during the space of this conversation and we'd never know it. That's the shitstorm you've put us in. So we have only one solution. You will remain here until we find M2. Rooms have been readied in Sector South—"

Lindsey Tanzer, an IT technician and single mother of three young boys, shook her head. "I'm sorry, but I can't stay. I have kids."

"And if you don't want them to find M2 hiding in their closets, you'll report to Sector South," Hollis said.

The woman, now envisioning M2 springing from their closets and biting their tender little heads, hardened her conviction. Teddy, Mika, and Andy needed her, and she would be there to protect them at all costs. "Fire me if you want to, but I'm not staying." She made for the door, but two of Overlook's soldiers blocked it.

"All right, then," Hollis said. "You're fired. And . . . Osborne?" A soldier at the back of the room stepped forward. "Osborne, in interests of national security, we need you to detain Ms. Tanzer and bring her to the isolation quarter in Sector South."

Dozens of murmurs rumbled through the room.

"But—"

"Anyone else interested in joining Ms. Tanzer?"

A single, timid hand rose above their heads. Cora said, "I'll do whatever you need us to do, sir, but I've never heard of Sector South. Is that in Garrett or in another facility?"

"Of course you'll do what we need you to do, *Mrs. Potluck*. You, of all people, have no choice. But since you asked, Sector South is right under your traitorous toes. Sixty-four thousand square feet of contingency chambers equipped for every imaginable species, including lumps like you. Major Carver's team will see you to your rooms." He abruptly turned and exited the room.

No one had ever heard of Sector South, but their experiences in sectors East, West, and Center conjured memories of nutrition pucks, tasers, scientific experimentation, isolation, and the complete visibility of inmates whether they were sleeping, dressing, or using the toilet.

Negotiations quickly ensued.

Evan Anderson, an avid gambler, had been pulled from the casino on a rare night Lady Luck attended with him. He offered all (well, almost all) of the thirty-three hundred in his wallet to Foster Cupps, who was ordering the crowd into a line, to let him slip away.

"Ah, man, you know I can't do that," Cupps told him regretfully.

Anderson upped the ante with the full thirty-three hundred and a pair of VIP tickets to the Toronto Jazz Festival. He didn't have them, but let Cupps think he did.

Cupps walked the line. Anderson followed him.

Interaction between Overlook and the Under Facility Office had been historically sporadic. Employees who reported two kilometers underground every day felt that Overlook was out of touch. They didn't work directly with the aliens, so they didn't experience the Plutonians' rage or the Martians' sensitivity or the Venusians' superiority. They didn't guard two of the most dangerous creatures on the planet. They didn't share in the shame when an alien cried out from one of Lia Geller's experiments. And they weren't shoved into darkness for entire shifts, only to clock out when the sun was already down.

Overlook, on the other hand, generally regarded Under Facility employees as inferior *because* of those responsibilities. UFOs (*Under*

Facility Outcasts to Overlookians), were not smart enough or strong enough to be assigned to Overlook, nor were they called to duty when *real* trouble arose. They were basically glorified babysitters, alien ass wipers, degenerates of the incapable kind.

UFOs who were familiar with Foster Cupps knew him to be one of the nicer *Overlords*, but his tolerance only went so far. When Anderson's frantic attempts at bribing Cupps proved unsuccessful, he grabbed the elite soldier's formidable wrist and whispered in the larger man's ear, "Let me out or everyone will think you're M2 and you'll be just as fucked as me."

Foster Cupps might be friendly, but he was not a man to be grabbed nor a man to be threatened. He thrust one of his big punching-bag fists at Anderson's face. The crack of Anderson's nose breaking and the subsequent crumpling of his body to the floor drew a scream from one of the chefs and under-breath cursing that spread through the crowd like brush fire. Any rebellion in the line was immediately extinguished.

Lia Geller, one of the few UFO employees not reporting to Sector South, quietly left the detention debacle and returned to her office to find Hollis and Theo on her laptop. She didn't begrudge Hollis access to her files. He was the keeper of the entire operation, and so it was only natural to expect him to bulldoze his way into whatever he wanted, whenever he wanted. But Theo's pretentious fingers on her keyboard grated like road rash.

"If you tell me what you're looking for, maybe you'll find it," she said, dropping into one of the guest seats with an exaggerated sigh.

"The PT test," Hollis said. "You had some interesting results."

"We did," Lia agreed. Her department's epigenetic study—particularly of environmental effects on genes—consisted of twenty-four active and fifteen passive tests conducted on a daily, weekly, or monthly basis. The PT or *Pain Tolerance* test subjected the aliens to varying levels of physical and psychological trauma to deduce potential benefits of resilient alien genes for human use. It was the test that most haunted both the aliens and their human researchers.

Lia recited what she remembered. "When we began the program eight years ago, we set out with the hypothesis that—"

Hollis rolled his eyes. "The basics, Geller. We don't want your mumbo-jumbo shit. We want to know if anything happened to M2 during that test that could explain how he was able to escape."

Lia knew that if anything was going to help them, it *was* her *mumbo jumbo shit*, as Hollis so eloquently put it. She might not be a soldier like Theo or Hollis, but she knew that if you wanted the upper hand against an enemy, you had to know your enemy. She, of all people, knew M2. She knew the way his mouths shuddered when she inserted the electrical probe. She saw the gouges on the reinforced steel gurney from M2's nails when she sliced into his soft backside and when she dripped acid into incisions she herself had made, just to see if M2 could recover. And she knew that if M2 had been in that room when Hollis made his announcement, she would have been the first to have her brain gouged out.

She removed her glasses and set them on the desk, then looked at the adolescents as an exasperated teacher. "Similar to what happens in humans, the pain tolerance of all the aliens have plateaued over time, *except* for M1's and M2's. With the others, there's just so much they can take, but with the Mimics . . . it's almost a game to them. They hurt, yes, but it seems the more we throw at them, the more they bolster their defenses, if you understand. Not only do they learn, but their bodies are able to adapt to new trauma and recover even quicker than in previous tests. They're really a marvel." When they didn't speak, she said, "And, no, there's nothing I could think of that would explain M2's escape, except that with each test there had always been a greater potential for him to escape, as I've noted in every report since we discovered its cause and effect."

Hollis slammed her laptop shut and swept her papers and phone to the floor. He spoke through his teeth. "And once you discovered this cause and effect, why did you continue the tests on M1 and M2?"

"It was your order, sir," she said, knowing she might as well slap the man.

Theo's eyes darted from the scientist to Hollis, but there was no explosion. It was rumbling, all right, bubbling under Hollis' parchment skin like a geyser about to blow. But a detonation wouldn't help anything. It would only make the scientist resent the blowhard more than she already did, and when she was in one of her moods, she was as useful as a hangnail. He said, "See if there's anything that can help us, Lia—whether it's the PT test or something else; anything at all that can help us capture him would be helpful."

They left her retrieving the things Hollis had thrown on the floor with a plan to meet later in the afternoon, unless M2 was captured sooner. Taking the hallway to Sector East, Hollis asked, "What's the word on Cobra and Tracer?"

Theo strode fast to keep pace with the older man. "Nothing yet. Our best lead is the Madinger woman. The whole city knows she's dead. Cobra is working her family. She's got a husband and two grown kids. A couple of grandkids. To our knowledge, none of them have seen grandma's ghost yet. Tracer is working the grocery store, her church, and this knitting circle she was in. No sightings there either."

"He can't go far," Hollis said. "M1's the focus. We have a three-dimensional perimeter around, above and below M1. Deploy as many units as possible without drawing attention from the city. People start snooping and we'll be more compromised than we already are."

"Grizzly, Shadow, and Bloodhound were deployed an hour ago, sir."

"Missile?"

"Plainclothes tourists on a memorial tour. They're staying in the city for a week to honor their dear departed friend who loved fishing in Lake Huron. Three couples are checking into the Garrett Hotel as we speak," Theo said.

Hollis nodded. "Smart."

They reached the sterilization chamber and went quiet while the room hissed around them. When the hissing was over, they proceeded into Sector East and the Mimic enclosure where M1 sat immobile on her bed.

Since M2's escape, she hadn't released herself to her natural form, even for the breakfast and lunch nutrition pucks. Her capsules—thoroughly examined—had been retrieved, untouched, and returned through the pneumatic tube to the kitchen.

"I think she's sad," said Foster Cupps, who was relieved to be free of the detainment chaos in Sector South.

Hollis hammered the glass with his fist and glared at the little cube. "She's not *sad*. She's *planning*. Don't fool yourself. In that blockhead costume of hers, she's trying to figure a way out so she can shred your insides."

He watched M1 for a time, knowing she was thinking of M2 and his escape, maybe even communicating to him from below to his hiding place. He wanted to pry out her thoughts—with pliers if need be—when an idea struck him. The symbiosis between M1 and M2 was perhaps the only constant they could work with. Their bond was unlike any the Under Facility Office or the Arctic League in Extraterrestrial Naturalization (ALIEN) had experienced. So strong was it that any pain felt by one was pain felt by the other. Emotional responses studied by Lia Geller's team were equivalent whether M1 and M2 were together or separated or—most notably—even when only one of them was subjected to pain or pleasure. A current of understanding flowed through him now, so clear Hollis could picture it in his head. They could devote themselves to hunting M2, but that did not mean they would find him. No. They would have to *draw* him home, splash the facility with pheromones of suffering, lure him with M1's blood. M1's *life*, if necessary.

He drew his phone from his pocket to call their mad scientist-in-residence when the negative pressure door hissed and Lieutenant Deborah Mills entered, carrying a briefcase. Though she was wearing a loose-fitting suit, Hollis couldn't help but imagine the woman in a nipple-baring bra and cheap blonde wig. She had a body, he'd give her that, but that's where the attraction ended. She also had a brick-like chin and a nose that dripped like mortar. *Gina Titswither's* online picture did her justice only because she'd mastered the art of shading. Hollis enjoyed her personality as much as he had his vasectomy, but, like the later, he knew that a little pain would benefit him in the long run.

"You gave the chief a whole lot of nothing, I hope?" Hollis said.

She stood in front of the Mimic enclosure, glanced at Cupps, who was noticeably appraising her ass, and shrugged. "Couldn't have been easier. Compliment the local apple pie, tell them their pee wees play like midgets, and they'll believe anything you say. They suck, by the way."

"The pie or the hockey players?" Cupps asked from his place near the wall.

"Both," she said. "Actually, the pie's pretty good. Anyway, I gave him our file on the Zombie Killer. He went fifty shades of white, but he's sharp for a small-timer. He asked how long we we've been in town. I told him what we discussed. He *did* question why we think the killer is still in the city when most get the hell out of dodge when they know someone's onto them. I pointed him to the file and showed him that the Zombie Killer tends to stay in smaller cities for a while. Good thinking on that one, by the way."

"Anything else?"

She fingered her chin. It was such a long sweep it gave the impression of a traffic cone. "He looked you up online, as we knew he would, but he didn't press. He was more focused on the victim than anything else. Just our luck M2 killed the town's sweet old aunt. Had he got one of those junkies off Mitton, we wouldn't be having this conversation. But since we are, I'd like to have someone on Peter Brace. He was the good Samaritan that called it in."

"A witness?" Hollis asked instantly.

She shook her head. "The parents were returning from picking their son up at a sleepover or something. Mother and son stayed in the car while dad went to investigate. I have a copy of the guy's statement." She produced a folder from her briefcase and gave it to him. "He sent his family home and waited with the woman's body until the police arrived."

"Necrophilia?" Hollis said, drawing a gag from Cupps.

"Unlikely. Just a guy who didn't want his son to be around a woman with two holes in her head. A constable Oaklyn Cox drove him home. She told the chief he seemed a bit nervous in her car, but nothing more than that. It might help to determine if he saw anything he didn't include in the report. Few people would want to admit seeing a nine-headed monster."

"No one would survive seeing that nine-headed monster."

"Probably not," she agreed. "But a peek at the guy couldn't hurt."

Until now, Theo had been silently watching the exchange. His mentor, Colonel Hershel Eyre, had ingrained in him that noise interfered with clarity, so it had become his habit to observe and quietly evaluate. In the short time since they'd returned to Sector East, he'd processed the developments more clearly than Hollis because Hollis proceeded out of anger, whereas Theo proceeded out of logic. Theo couldn't feel anger toward the Mimics. They were foreign souls, cornered in Lia Geller's house of terror. Of course they wanted to escape. But Hollis' plan of drawing M2 to M1 by torturing her wasn't as simple as drawing a puppy to a chow dish. Push any dog the wrong way and he'll attack.

He said, "Dalton Byrd can help you with Peter Brace. He's a good investigator when he wants to be."

Deborah nodded, her dark hair swaying across her shoulders. "Perfect."

"As for M1," Theo gestured to the little cube, who had slid toward them as if to hear better. "I would hold off on doing anything to her. We don't know what M2 will do if he thinks we're hurting her. There are people out there—"

They watched M1 watching them. Theo, Hollis, Deborah Mills, Foster Cupps. "That's why we need to make him *want* to come back," Hollis said. "The longer M2's out there, the longer the city isn't safe. I have a meeting to prepare for. In the meantime, tell Lia M1's due for a PT test. Throw everything we have at her." He left the room.

12. Kitchen Knives and Port-a-Potties

Scotty had been waiting in his truck for an hour before Meredith came out. He had caught her at work, Garrett's own Axccor Construction, in the middle of a staffing dilemma she couldn't escape from.

"I'm sorry, Beverly," Meredith had explained to an irate woman; one of Axccor Construction's employees had parked in front of her driveway. "Our paving crews know better than that. We'll find him and get him to move his car."

The woman shouted loudly enough for Scotty to hear her through the phone. "You damn well better because if it's not gone in ten minutes, I'll back into the piece of shit."

Meredith had put down the receiver and looked at him with those doe-like eyes that never failed to soothe him. She was frazzled, to be sure, but the saint she was, she always had time for him, even after their divorce. She asked him to wait while she sorted the problem out, so he went to a drive-through for coffee and picked at a bagel until it had become a pile of cold crumbs in an oil-stained bag.

He had just finished his coffee when Meredith knocked on the window. A light breeze played with her hair and she was hugging a sweater to her slender body. He unlocked the door and cranked the heat. "Figure everything out?" he asked, glancing at the spray of freckles on her nose and so badly wanting to touch them and make everything normal again.

She shook her head. "Beverly McKinnon just hit Nick Penner's car, and she's sending *us* the bill for the damage. I swear, some days it's like babysitting. The crews, the customers, the people... uggh."

He laughed knowingly then they grew quiet, him looking out over the steering wheel and Meredith staring at her own fidgeting hands.

"How've you been, hun?"

He rubbed the back of his neck, as nervous as he'd been those years ago on their first date in the very same truck. "I've been hearing it, Mer."

She wasn't surprised. "Have you started taking the pills Dr. Huxley prescribed?"

"Mer—" he started.

She put a hand on his knee. Her voice was as soft as it ever was, with a timbre that suggested fragility, though she was perhaps the toughest person he'd ever met. She said, "I've never said I didn't believe you. Not once. If you say you're hearing voices, Scotty, then you are. But I don't think it's healthy to close yourself up the way you do. Pills might help that. It would be nice to see you out here a little more, you know?"

He didn't answer. She knew he didn't want the pills. It was part of the reason she'd divorced him. That and the self-mutilation and his almost manic paranoia.

"Vera called me."

Scotty groaned. "What did she tell you this time?"

"She said you thought you saw Irma last night. You know she—"

"I know she died," he said harshly.

Her eyes swept to the street, which was busy with lunch-hour traffic. "She didn't come out and say it, Scotty, but you know how she is. She's suggesting you might've had something to do with it."

He pinched the bridge of his nose and sighed so long and so hard a little patch of breath fog bloomed on the windshield. Vera had painted him as many things but never as a murderer. It shouldn't have surprised him.

"I know you didn't, hun, of course I know you didn't have anything to do with it. I'm telling you this because you're an easy target. I know you'd never hurt a living soul, but the last few years . . . with the voice and the equipment . . . your *ear* . . . it's hard for people to look past that. All I'm saying is that you need to be careful. I'm your sounding board. I will *always* be your sounding board. You can talk to me, but I'd be careful who you share those experiences with."

"How's Claire?" he asked, changing the subject.

"She misses you, but you know how it is."

Scotty hated how it was.

His relationship with his only child had deteriorated since he began hearing the voices. In the beginning, she received his madness compassionately, visiting him more often, calling from the middle school where she taught, listening to him talk about the Voice in his head, sympathetically observing while he set up newly purchased transmitters on the dining room table. This went on for some time. Then came the flat tires and the cross-street insults and the shit bombs on the front door.

Scotty was fine. He'd learned people could be shitheads. But the shitheads didn't stop at Scotty. They went for Meredith and Claire with the zeal of hungry dogs. It wasn't just *Skitzo Scotty* who was bullied like a trailer park dog, but *Meltdown Meredith* and *Creepy Claire*. Axccor Construction suffered hundreds of prank calls from guttural teenagers asking if Meltdown Meredith could fuck voices into their heads, too. And Claire, poor Claire, had been warned by the school principal that if vandals didn't stop breaking their windows and scrawling images of *Creepy Claire's Cunt* all over the schoolyard, they would have to consider "reassigning" her.

Meredith took her abuse with a stiff chin, but the slow unravelling of their daughter cut them deeper than any knife could have. Divorce on Meredith's part and estrangement on Claire's hadn't mended the wound, only kept it from splitting wider.

She touched the remains of his ear. "What's inside you, hun?"

He hung his head, letting her fingers remember him. "I think something's happening, Mer. It was different this time. It's like . . . it's like he's coming or wants me to come to him. That's what he's saying: *come here*. I heard it clear as day right before Irma came knocking the door."

"Take me back to that," she said. "Was Irma really there?"

He nodded and explained everything of the night, even the screeching of the Voice, which he hadn't shared with Dan Fogel.

She took his story in, worked it in her head, nodding, never once doubting, even if it hurt her. Her lips pressed together, then she said, "Whatever this is, you have to see it through. Men don't go cutting off their ears for nothing, Scotty." She paused, sagging the way she had when she'd given up on him and slid him the divorce papers that awful September night. "But I think that this has to be it. You can't go on like this forever and *I* can't go on like this forever. It's *hard, Scott*. It's not the life I've chosen, nor is it the life either of us want for Claire. It's not fair to her. She's so young. She's got the whole world ahead of her, but she can't live it because that thing inside you won't let her. Tell me you agree on that."

"It's not *me*, Mer—"

"It doesn't matter *who* it is. What matters is Claire, and it's high time you remember that. I'm here for you, don't think that I'm not. But now you have Vera accusing you of *murder*. What do you think would happen if *that* gets out?" She rolled her eyes. "They wouldn't just toss a shit bag and run, Scotty. Claire's already sleeping with a knife under her pillow."

His heart constricted. He hadn't known that. He was about to tell her he would stop, that he would get rid of all the equipment and stuff his ears with granite, if need be, when a woman appeared beside the truck.

It was Judy Stalder, Meredith's co-worker and long-time friend. She had her hand over her mouth, and it was apparent from the blotches of mascara running down her cheeks that she was crying. She used the hand with the tissue in it to tap the window.

Scotty unrolled it.

The woman's breathy little sobs shook her drooping shoulders. "Meredith—" she sputtered and burst out crying.

"What happened? Did someone call me? Is it Claire?" His ex-wife trembled, fumbling for the door handle. He understood then how badly he'd wrecked their lives.

Judy blubbered. "No. It's not Claire. Steve just called. They found Nick behind a port-a-potty out near the switchyard. He's been . . ." She hiccupped a cry. "He's been killed. His head's been bashed in."

Meredith gasped.

"They tried finding him to tell him to move his car, and when Nick didn't answer his calls, Steve drove around looking for him. He saw his foot in the grass. He thought Nick was sleeping." When Judy started hyperventilating, Meredith got out of the truck and put her arms around her.

Scotty had been leaning toward them but now he slumped back. Outside, both women were crying. He felt it would seem heartless if he didn't share their sorrow, so he wiped his dry eyes with the back of his hand, doing his best to appear adequately affected. Nick Penner wasn't a saint, by all means. He was a known philanderer and had kept his silence about one of the city's deadliest fires, which Nick alone had witnessed, until he was exposed by a local reporter. How soon Nick forgot his own public browbeating one night, when he joined the other shitheads and pushed Scotty to the ground outside Shooter's, calling him Skitzo Scotty and spitting on him. But did the man deserve to have his head bashed in? No. A black eye or solid gut punch would have been enough.

"You said his head was bashed in? Did he fall? Or maybe something fell on him in one of those construction sites?" Scotty asked.

"Steve said it looked like Nick was attacked. Like someone bit him on the head. He saw Nick's brain. His *brain*. Can you believe it?" Judy spoke over Meredith's shoulder, her pressure-strained neck venting the words in quick staccato sobs

"Now how could that happen?" Scotty wondered aloud. "No bears around here." He thought of Irma's bleeding head appearing at his door.

"The police are there." Judy sniffed. "But they're not telling Steve anything. Simon's on his way to talk to them."

Meredith, who had been at Axccor Construction since Claire was a toddler, said, "I'm closing the office. Let's go for lunch." She looked at Scotty. He nodded and left them to commiserate.

13. Old Soldier, Many Eyes

No school on earth was as bad as St. Jude's, and no class anywhere was as bad St. Jude's soul-sucking, ego-crushing, morale-murdering gym class. These were Adam Brace's thoughts as he flailed up the rope like a guppy on a fishing line.

From the mat, Penny watched his twiggy legs flap ineffectually around the rope. He closed his eyes, trying to forget that she was there. He was sure she could see his balls, squiggling against the rope like two mice up a greased pole.

"Come on, Adam, just to the second knot. You can do this." Julia Fowler, St. Jude's seventh grade gym and science teacher, clapped her hands and shook an encouraging fist.

There was no way Adam was going to make the second knot. He'd never made it to the *first* knot. He'd never made it *half-way* to the first. Even when Ravi boosted him.

"Bet he shits himself," Douglas Radway jeered.

"Won't be the first, won't be the last," Julia said brightly. "It's okay, Adam. Reach. Lift your knees. Clamp your feet. Just like I taught you."

"This is inhumane," Ravi said beside Penny, wincing at Adam's struggle. "Did you know that most schools did away with these barbaric drills years ago? What are we going to do? Board a ship?"

"It's good to see what your body can do," Julia told them.

"We see what his *balls* can do," Douglas said.

Penny elbowed him. "Be nice, Douggie. He can't help it if the uniform doesn't fit him."

Adam looked at Douggie, looked at Penny, and heaved himself upward. His muscles burned, his balls hurt, the skin on his fingers had broken open, but still Adam pulled and yanked his hundred-and-ten-pound frame up . . . up . . . and fell to the mat.

Julia patted his back. "Good job, Adam. Three more inches today. This time next week you'll be *scaling* that rope, I know it."

Adam lay limp on the mat, breathless.

Ravi patted his stomach. "In a few years this will all be a memory, and no one will care if you can climb a rope." He rubbed his hands together and sprang at the rope. Ten seconds later, Ravi was past the fourth knot and going for the metal beam.

Julia cringed. "Not that high, Ravi. We talked about this. You fall from that height and we're all dead. Please come down."

Douggie, who had only made it to the second knot, cupped his pudgy hands and called up to Ravi, "If you're going to fall, let me get one of the javelins first."

"If I fall, I'm aiming for your head, you fat fu—"

"*Mis-ter Das*!" From the entrance to the gymnasium, Principal Irving Hahn stood with his hands clasped behind his back. He walked slowly, silently into the gymnasium. The fifty-nine adolescents from grade 7A and 7B stopped everything. Lopsided cartwheels were halted mid spin. The badminton birdie cresting near the stage found no opponent and fell to the ground. The boys messing around on the springboard and vault stepped away. The girls practicing handstands on the tumbling mat returned to their original positions and clasped their hands in front of them, just as Irving Hahn had behind his own back.

Adam, happy the school wasn't leering at him for once, gestured with his eyes for Ravi to come down.

"What's he doing up there?" Penny whispered to Adam, as Ravi was frozen at the top of the rope.

"I don't know," he whispered back.

Principal Hahn made a perfect diagonal toward the ropes, one of which had been promptly vacated by a falling student once he appeared. He wore an old moss-colored suit and wine-colored tie, and his fashion and expression never changed. Graduations. Fire drills. First days. Chemistry explosions. Irving Hahn was as obdurate as gravity, as consistent as time. To the students, he was a serious and sedate ruler. To his teachers, Irving Hahn was a wise, avuncular figure, a professional counsellor whose intuition was almost never wrong. He signed their paystubs with a line of advice written at the bottom in his slow, careful script. *A faithful career is a loving companion. It's always a good time to learn something new. Perspective is in the pencil.*

Julia's eyes swung to Ravi, who was still at the top of the rope. She waved a hand at him. "Get down," she breathed from the side of her mouth.

"Please don't make us wait, Mr. Das," Irving said, now standing behind Adam.

Ravi climbed down. He bowed his head.

"Now. I want everyone to hear this. Please be sure you can hear me. I did not call Ravi down because he was hanging off our roof. That is a good thing. If our ropes went to Jupiter, I would tell young Ravi to climb away—provided we could safely catch him, of course. I called Ravi down because he was so close to the rope, he almost burned his *tongue*. The f-word in your mouth, Ravi. Was it *fire*? Were you going to say fire?"

PROJECT DOMAIN

Ravi's cheeks burned the color of beets. "Fire," he said. "Yes, sir. Sorry, sir."

"Ah. That's what I thought. Carry on, students."

The slow resumption of activity reverberated around the gymnasium.

Julia, who felt toward Irving Hahn greater affection than that toward her own father, pointed to the rope and winked at him. "Race you to the top?" she challenged.

Little wrinkles fanned from the corner of his eyes. "Wouldn't want to show you up in front of the kids," he said.

"He's too old," Douggie shared quietly to Penny. "*Adam* could climb farther than him."

By all accounts, Irving *was* old. Presently, he was sixty-three. His hair had abandoned him so long ago he'd forgotten the feeling of a full head against a cold pillow. He had more age spots on his face than the sky had stars, and less muscle on his bones than deserts had water. But Irving Hahn's *hearing* was ever so sharp. He glanced at the ceiling, then to Julia. Then he removed his jacket.

"Will you?" he asked Penny, who accepted his jacket as though it were fine china. "Shall we go to Jupiter, Ms. Fowler?" He rolled up his sleeves.

"Tell us when to blast off," Julia told Adam.

A crowd was gathering now. Irving grabbed hold of his rope. Julia grasped the other.

"One. Two. Three. Blast off!" Adam shouted, and their principal and their teacher left the ground.

Julia moved like a caterpillar, working her way upward, curving her rear not the way she taught her students, but the way she felt would give the principal a fighting chance. Kowtowing to the boss was unnecessary, however, for Irving bounded up the rope faster than Ravi, faster than any seventh grader at St. Jude's ever had. He was up and down before Julia made it to the second knot and even had time to roll down his sleeves and retrieve his jacket from Penny before Julia's feet returned to the mat.

All the students cheered, except Douggie, who was gaping at the principal as though fish had dropped from his pants.

"Now," Irving said, breathing only a little more heavily. "Besides showing you what an old man can do"—he looked at Douggie— "I came for a purpose. I need to steal Adam from you. Adam?"

Adam rose and followed him out of the gymnasium, to his office in the opposite end of the school.

"That was incredible," Adam confided when he sat and no one was around to hear.

"Incredible even for *me*," Irving admitted. "I'll be feeling that one until you graduate. But there's a lesson there for you, Adam. Never let anyone, including yourself, tell you that you can't do something. Believe it and mark my words, you'll give Ravi a run for his money by the end of the year."

When he closed the door, Adam swallowed. "Am I in trouble?"

Irving gave a little chuckle. "I have to work on my people skills, it seems. Of course you're not in trouble. I had a call from your parents. Nothing to worry about, everyone is fine, but your father is going to be picking you up for the day. We need you to pack your things and we'll see you bright and early tomorrow."

A hesitation lingered on the principal's face, as though he wanted to talk about something. The situation rang strange to Adam because whenever he was picked up by one of his parents, he'd never been summoned to the principal's office. He was always told by his teacher, Ms. Fowler. And Adam had been around his parents enough to know when someone was hiding something.

"Do you know why they're picking me up?" he asked.

Principal Hahn leaned forward good naturedly. "I believe that is for them to tell you, but your father mentioned something about a family interview."

Shit, Adam thought. He was sick of family interviews. It was his parent's bubble-gum term for their counselling sessions. They were always at night and on weekends, but now they were taking him out of school to talk about their fuckups. Or, rather, his mother's inability to stop sleeping with her boss and her boss' boss. Maybe even the guy higher than that.

"I get the feeling you're not looking forward to the appointment."

"No," Adam admitted.

"You know what I do when I have to do something I don't want to?" Irving asked.

"What?"

"I do it as quickly as I can to get it over with. And I do it *first*, so it doesn't hang over my head like a bowling ball. And," he added, "when it's an appointment such as you have and you can't speed it up, I pretend it's the most important thing I'll ever do, even if it's not. Because if I don't do it right—*engage*, as in your case—it just prolongs the suffering. Does that make sense to you, Adam?"

Adam's thin shoulders went up.

Irving stared at the boy for a moment. "I'd like to tell you something, Adam. Call it small-city telephone—you know how news spreads around here—but I understand you might have witnessed the accident everyone is talking about."

A groan escaped Adam's lips. "*Ravi.*"

"No, no. Don't worry. I don't want to talk to you about it. I just want to be clear that if you ever want to talk to *me* about it, well, you'll always have a safe place here. I say this because you're not the first kid around here to see something unpleasant. Remember Bus 587?"

Adam nodded. It was a casino tour bus that went over a guard rail and into the Callingwood River last year. Of the forty-odd people on the bus, only one had survived. It had been Garrett's worst accident, and students were still talking about it, as both Adam and Irving knew.

"A few of our students were there that day. It was tough on them, but they're getting through it. Just like you will, Adam. My office is always open."

"Thanks."

Irving checked his watch. "Your father will be out front in a few minutes. Let's not keep him waiting." He watched the boy exit the school and waved politely as they departed, then he went back to his desk to think.

Along with fifty-eight other grade-seven students, Adam had started at St. Jude's Middle School this past September, and the Brace family had suffered for as long as Irving had known them. Gossip was as endemic in Garrett as kangaroos were to Australia, but news of Gia Brace's infidelity hadn't come to Irving through the city's grapevine, as most information did. It had come from Peter himself. The man, perhaps folding from heartache, had confided to Irving one evening after a parent council meeting. Then after a parent-teacher interview. Then at a junior boys' basketball practice when Peter thought Adam wasn't looking. Sometimes Peter left Irving phone messages loosely related to Adam, but when they were unpacked, they always came back to Peter's marriage.

Irving learned that Peter and Gia Brace had been married for seventeen years and that one morning Peter found Gia, naked, in his boss' office. Irving's experience in education taught him not only lessons about children, but about the complexities of their families and the necessity for him to be a confidante and counsellor to those who sought his advice. He believed it served the children well, though how well this extended to their parents, he wasn't sure. Irving felt that at least in the Brace family's case, he had managed to make them comfortable because Peter's call today was about a family interview with the *police*, not their therapist.

Peter confided that they came upon Irma Madinger's car and that he himself was the one to call the police. "Gia and Adam stayed in the car, so I don't know why they want to talk to them," he had told

Irving on the phone. "They didn't see anything. It was dark as hell out there."

For reasons unbeknownst to Irving, the police had urgently requested a meeting with the entire family. It couldn't wait until the afternoon blocks were over and the children were dismissed. The urgency was unusual, especially for a traffic accident. But Irving, ever so perceptive with his satellite ears and his x-ray eyes, had heard that maybe it *wasn't* a traffic accident. That maybe Irma Madinger had hit something and was attacked. Word spreading around Garrett was that an animal had taken a healthy bite out of the poor woman's head, but Irving didn't believe it. He didn't know of a species that would do that without leaving a trail, which led him to something much more sinister: a person.

Irving was a pacifist, which he felt made him more sympathetic to the needs of those around him, but it hadn't always been that way. Before he became a teacher and succeeded to principal, he had been an infantry soldier, all testosterone and ambition. He was drawn to danger and the idea that *he*—a lanky, knock-kneed boy from Southern Ontario—could fight his way up and one day lead a battalion, if it ever came to it.

But the puff went out of him after two quick trips during which his unit was stationed to support the transportation of refugees in Vietnam and electoral observers in Zimbabwe. Irving was struck by the ongoing needs of postwar countries and realized that he could be better utilized not by firing a gun but by helping postwar countries elevate their populace. Education was critical. So for four decades, from September to June, Irving had taught and mentored Canadian children. And for four decades, from July to August, Irving had used his salary to fly to Zambia, where he volunteered at a secondary school in Chipata. *Those* kids had never stopped needing him, and Irving worked hard to champion their causes, no matter the distance. And he adopted the same stance toward his Canadian students, whatever their concerns.

He pulled a peppermint from a tin on his desk and stuck it on his tongue, whirling it about his mouth as he thought. Currents of training came back to him when he considered Irma Madinger and Adam and Peter Brace. Something about the situation summoned his instincts. Made him try to understand the urgency. Maybe the boy had seen something, maybe he hadn't. But a hasty police interview sat uneasy in Irving's mind. He opened his planner, thinking of an excuse to call Peter Brace tonight.

After Peter divulged the reason for the mid-day pickup, mentioned more as an afterthought than a serious discussion, Adam suffered yet another one of his father's attempts to alienate his mother.

". . . I mean, if she's going to be with him, she should just be with him," Peter was saying while Adam looked out the window. "None of this back and forth, you know. It's not fair to you. It's not fair to me. The *indecision* . . . it's unhealthy. I don't know. Maybe she's sick. They say you shouldn't ignore the signs. Grandpa had Alzheimer's. You think that's it? Oh, what am I saying? Sorry, Adam."

Adam pulled the hood of his sweatshirt over his head. His mother didn't have Alzheimer's. She just didn't like ambitionless men. His father floated between jobs and Adam often came home from school to find him lounging on the couch, playing video games. There wasn't a year when his father didn't have some existential epiphany and put them all through months of financial insecurity and pretentious blather about self-worth and warped capitalism. He loved his father, but Adam couldn't really blame his mother, though he would never say so.

There was an unmarked car in the driveway when they pulled up to the house. Inside, Gia was pouring coffee. The man at their kitchen table had a pizza-shaped face, extra wide at the temples and tapering off to a neat little point at his chin. He had a long, fine nose, and thin lips that disappeared when he smiled.

He offered his hand first to Peter, then to Adam.

"Don Bower," Dalton Byrd said. Once everyone was seated around the table, he got right to it. "I'm hoping this won't take too much of your time, but it's important we understand what happened last night. The report you filed with—" He opened a leather folder and flipped through the papers, none actually containing Peter Brace's report.

"Oaklyn Cox," Peter offered helpfully, pulling her card from his back pocket. She had written her name and badge number on the back of a standard card with the station's contact information. Peter slid it across the table to Dalton.

Dalton tapped the paper as though the name had come to both at the same time, "Yes. Constable Cox. We appreciate the information, Peter. Not a lot of folks are willing to stick around and help, so thank you for that." He pretended to review words that weren't written, then he sat back with his pen poised over his folder, while the woman, Gia, looked nervously toward her son. Dalton wondered if the boy had seen something and told his parents, or if the mother simply didn't want her son reliving the tragedy.

She raised a small hand. "Adam doesn't know what happened last night. He and I were in the Impala while Peter stayed. I'd prefer it if you don't discuss the details in front of him."

Adam had been as lively as an old dog, but now he rolled his eyes toward the ceiling. "Everyone knows, Mom."

Dalton seized on this. "Knows what, Adam?"

The boy, slumped so low in his chair Dalton was sure his ass was going to fall, turned his can of Coke around and around. "That lady died."

"Did you see this, Adam?" Dalton asked.

"No."

"While you were in the car and your father was out of the vehicle, did you see any other traffic? Or any people around?"

Adam shook his head. It had been late and dark, and his parents had been fighting again. His father had been questioning his mother about the scent of cologne on her when they saw Irma Madinger's car stopped across the road. When his father went to investigate, his mother had quickly sent messages to someone who was not his father. Repulsed by the cologne, Adam, meanwhile, had opened the back window to air out the car. He had been breathing the cool, middle-of-the-night air when movement outside caught his eye. There was a grunting, quiet—but with his parents at odds, Adam was used to listening for quiet sounds. He rolled up his window slightly and squinted at the darkness. The grunting stopped but just outside the cone of the Impala's lights, off to the right toward the dump, something had bounded into the ditch.

"You said something, Adam?" his mother had asked disinterestedly when he drew in his breath.

Suddenly, the door had opened and his father appeared. His face had that ashen look it got whenever he found unfamiliar tokens in his mother's purse. She understood immediately, raising her eyebrows to his father as though Adam didn't know what they were talking about.

His father had inclined his head ever so slightly. "Go on and take Adam home," he instructed. "I'll wait here until the police arrive."

It was the one time his mother hadn't argued. Adam considered pressing to stay, but he knew that after the argument in the car, his father probably needed space and that a dead person might be better company for him than Adam's mother.

They were pulling away, with Adam's mother driving and Adam with his arms crossed and looking out over the back seat, when he'd seen it. There, low in the muddy slough of the ditch, a black figure with many heads. Dozens of eyeballs glinting in the moonlight made him shudder. It had been too dark and his mother had been driving too fast for him to get a good look at the creature, but in that moment it looked like a giant overturned spider.

"Stop!" he'd cried to his mother, for his father was alone outside. But then the spider came slightly onto the road and into the cloudy residue of Irma Madinger's one remaining headlight.

"He'll be fine," his mother called back, peeking only for a moment in the rearview mirror.

Adam had been about to *make* his mother stop if he had to when the spider thing disentangled its heads and became an old woman wearing a Garrett's Grocery apron. Then the woman had bounded into the field and was gone.

"Adam?" Mr. Bower said, and Adam realized they were all looking at him.

"No one was there," he said, and turned the Coke can.

Dalton nodded appreciatively and wrote in his folder, *eyes on origin*, meaning Adam. He clicked his pen several times. "Thanks for your help, Adam. I don't have anything else for you, but I'd like to speak to your parents now." He offered his hand to the boy, but Adam had already bumped his way from behind the table and left the kitchen.

"Kids," Gia said with an apologetic shrug.

"Tell me about it," Dalton lied and pointed toward the basement door where Adam went. "Got two of my own not much older than him. I would've had to tie them down to talk to me." He laughed. Then Dalton got serious. "Listen, Gia, Peter." He caught and held their stares, breathing slowly and forcefully out of his nose so they understood that easy time was over. "The reason this couldn't wait is that we don't believe it was an ordinary traffic accident. We've been tracking a violent predator across the country and we think he may have found his way to Garrett. As you can tell by the victim's injuries, he's ... cannibalistic."

Gia gasped and pulled back. Tendrils of her long, wavy hair fell into her coffee. Peter pulled them out. "You think that was ... that he could've been there when we stopped? That's why you asked Adam if he saw anyone?" Peter's hand went to his forehead.

"We're not one hundred percent sure; there's a possibility it was an animal, or that Mrs. Madinger had her head in such a way that would cause the damage it did when she was struck, but our preliminary findings are pointing to the Zombie Killer."

Dalton let that sink in. It had been Hollis' idea to tell the Braces about the Zombie Killer because the likelihood of Dan Fogel informing the city it had a serial killer on the loose was slim to none. Only UFO and Overlook knew how lethal the situation really was, and as much as Hollis might be an occupational tyrant, he didn't want M2 to slaughter innocent civilians. If the Braces knew, the city would know, and that was the best Hollis could do while still maintaining anonymity.

"The Zombie Killer?" Peter's mouth fell open.

Gia took his hand, which was the first real sign of requited affection between the two Dalton had seen.

"Will he . . . come after us?" Gia's lips quivered.

Gotcha, Dalton thought. "No. Serial killers don't tend to go after the people who find their victims, but they are like bees in that they tend to stay close to the honeycomb. There's a buffer zone between their homebase and the honeycomb—the neighbourhoods—they forage. It's no consolation, but you're not in any more danger than anyone else. I would suggest being careful, lock your doors and all that, but you're going to be okay and we're going to do everything we can to catch this guy. Trust me." Reassurance slid off his tongue. This was where Dalton Byrd *excelled*. He wasn't as imposing as Foster Cupps, with his oil-barrel arms, nor as Jeffrey Acres with his arrogant everything. Dalton was a digger and a smoother, a relationship archeologist if there ever was one.

He closed his folder and stood, pretending not to notice that the hood of Adam's sweatshirt was peeking from behind the basement wall.

"We'll be in touch, but if you think of anything that might help us, give me a call." He handed his fake-as-flowers business card to Peter and left.

14. Rats, Bagged and Shaken

The Garrett switchyard, through which seventy percent of cross-country trains travelled, was busy even on slow days—but today traffic was paused, and sixteen freight trains lay waiting in the corridor along the Callingwood River for Nick Penner's murder investigation to conclude. So, too, were commuters stopped, bumper to bumper, along the east section of Novadale Road, where police cars clustered to shield them from the grisly sight of Nick Penner's body being lifted from behind one of the switchyard's portable toilets.

"Sweet Jesus," Oaklyn Cox had said when her eyes fell on the remains of Nick Penner's head. Like Irma's, his temples had been gouged, as if with a spoon. She wrinkled her nose. Unlike Irma, the man had not been well-loved in the community. He had been a known philanderer and all-around seedy guy. Few people would miss him, but they would talk, oh, they would talk. "Not saying he deserved it," Oaklyn said to Dan, "but—"

"Don't say it," Dan warned.

She raised her palms to him. "Not saying anything. Let's just say I think he's found his peace."

"Amen," Mark Stringer had said, shaking his head between them.

Dan had sent them to corral several onlookers who'd breached the perimeter and was now in his cruiser, waiting for Gina Totswither to arrive. Cloudless spring sun glossed the awakening trees and slumbering rail lines so brightly that Dan put on his sunglasses. *Where are you?* he wondered, looking out at yet another murder scene.

A moment later, he spotted Gina walking toward him, holding two cups.

He exited his cruiser. "Are we celebrating that you found the bastard or is this an apology for letting him loose in my city in the first place?" Dan said, for he felt his earlier meeting with the detective had been too vague and that she had not told him all she knew.

She passed him a cup. "Go easy on me. I don't like this as much as you do."

He didn't apologize. They drank, each one surveying the yard as though the answers they sought were right in front of them. "I know I sound bitter, but I don't think you or Hollis have been completely honest with me, Gina. This call"—he motioned with his cup to where Nick Penner's body was being loaded into the medical examiner's van— "didn't seem surprising to you. Why is that?"

"Nothing surprises me with serial killers," she said. "Do we want it to happen? No. Are we surprised when another body shows up? No. You know how it is, Dan."

Besides the BOLO and Intelligence Reports, Dan had zero experience with serial killers. Not the years-long, cross-country, brain-eating type anyway. "It's always a surprise to me," he said.

"Stay that way, okay?" She put her cup on the cruiser's hood and pulled out her phone, scrolling on it to review her notes. "Any news since we last spoke?"

He thought of fragile Scotty Waymore. "We have a possible sighting of Irma Madinger last night. Unsure what to make of it."

"Oh?"

"There's a local fella here. The dump manager, Scotty Waymore. Quiet guy. He was just like you or me, but then a few years ago he started hearing voices. Docs say he's not schizophrenic, but he's paranoid. Even van Gogh'd his own ear a while back." He nodded when she turned her head and gaped at him. "Honestly, he's never been any trouble. It's the bullies that keep us busy. They're nasty to him. Anyway, the dump has a security camera at the front gate. I went to collect it this morning and he said that Irma showed up on his porch last night; he lives in a cabin south of the dump."

Deborah gritted her teeth, trying not to react, but the muscle in her jaw contracted like a beating heart. *The fucking camera.* Theo was supposed to get the video before the dump opened this morning. "Did you get the tape?" she asked.

"The camera's not aimed at his porch," Dan said.

"I assume not, but maybe it corroborates his story?"

"I haven't looked at it yet." He gestured to the medical examiner van pulling out of the yard onto Novadale. "As you can see, your killer is keeping me busy."

"Why don't you let me review the video, Dan?" she said as though she were really trying to assist.

He shook his head. "I'd like to see if it matches up with what he told me. He knew we were going to ask for the security footage, but he was so worked up after he heard she died that he reviewed it before I got there." He drained his cup, put it in his cruiser, and started walking. "Apparently something was on the road, but it wasn't a car. Scotty said it was a spark, like the tip of a cigarette, then . . . I don't know . . . *shadows*, I guess. There's a video analyst we work with in Toronto sometimes. I might have her—"

"We'll take care of that," Deborah said.

A tired sigh came from him. They had crossed several sets of tracks and were now trudging the flat gravel beside a cluster of yellow retarders clamped outside the last line. "I believe Hollis said this would be a reciprocal partnership, but I get the feeling that my department's not good enough for you."

"You know how it is when you're too close to a case. Nothing's good enough," she said.

"I'll drop the flash drive off when I'm done with it. Final offer."

The conversation was getting worse and worse for Deborah. It would make Dan suspicious if she pressed, and the last thing they needed was a bored cop seeing M2. The crazy guy had cut off his own ear, so even if *he* saw M2, no one would believe him. As long as there was no video to prove it.

Either Hollis would have to throw his weight at Dan and make it clear that Hollis' team was in charge, or Theo would have to do his fucking job and *Mission Impossible* the flash drive from Dan's office.

She shrugged. "Can't blame a girl for trying. Tell me, what time did he say Irma went to his house? If he really did see her and she went to his house for help, she would've been in a world of pain. Did he speak to her at all?" A thought congealed in her head. Was M2 walking around as *Irma Madinger*? Even though the Mimics could replicate, they couldn't speak human. Instead, their vocalizations sounded like the squeal of rats, bagged and shaken. Only their *screams* were understood, for whenever they were with Lia Geller, they screamed a lot. Pain being the universal language.

"Few hours after dinner," Dan said. "He says she just showed up out of nowhere, opening her mouth like a fish. He was too scared to open his door. Imagine the brain damage she would've sustained, to show up at someone's house who wasn't all there to begin with? Would've scared the lights out of him. There are so many other ways that could have gone. Why did it have to be him?"

M2 was mimicking the car crash victim, Deborah was sure of it. She would have to distribute the woman's picture to the Ops teams ASAP. They would either have to catch her or, if need be, they would have to kill *Irma Madinger* a second time. "I'd like to talk to him."

"I don't think that's a good idea. I've built a level of trust with Scotty and I don't want to go spoiling it now. I'd prefer to handle that on our end."

"But what if . . ." She paused, kicking gravel onto the flattened grass. "What if he had something to do with the accident? Are you able to be subjective?"

Dan stopped walking. He turned to face her. "Insinuate anything like that again and you can consider this *reciprocal* relationship over." He air-quoted what he thought of their relationship.

With the affinity between them warm as snow, Deborah pulled from her bag of tricks the heartbreaker she had prepared for emergencies like this. "I'm sorry, Dan. I don't want you to feel in any way that you're not a good cop. I've read about you. The shit you've been through the last few years . . . I don't know anyone who could've managed it. I know you're the real deal; don't think I don't know that." She willed tears into her eyes. "Look. I didn't want to tell you this, but this one's personal for me. About five years ago"—she wiped a counterfeit tear from her eye— "the Zombie Killer got my cousin. Remember the nursing student?"

Images and information rolled through Dan's head. "Western U. On her way home from a play?"

"We grew up together. She wasn't even twenty." Deborah worked a quiver into her lips, a tremble into her chin, and a flush into her cheeks for the cousin that had never been born. "Forgive me if it seems like I don't think you're doing enough, but I promised my aunt I would catch the bastard, and that's exactly what I'm going to do."

A handful of locals watching the exchange saw Deborah crying and started taking pictures with their phones. As long as he'd been in the service, Dan hadn't been able to escape the attention. "Why don't we watch the tape together?" he suggested. "And I'll see about meeting Scotty afterward. He doesn't like to be surprised, so I'll call him and set something up."

She sniffed and they began their return over the tracks. "I just need a few minutes. Shall I bring dinner?"

"The vending machine at the station serves a pretty mean bag of chips," he offered.

"Ritzy," she said. "Ours hasn't worked since I got there. There's a bag of ketchup chips that's put in more time than I have."

They laughed. Dan excused himself to talk to Oaklyn and Mark, and Deborah hurried across the railyard to her car to call Theo and Hollis.

15. Seventh Neck, Right Hand

Strapped to a gurney in lab three, M1 awaited pain. After the divisor came down, she knew she was in trouble. She was powerless in the divisor's span of control and could do nothing but let them unfold her and tie her down. Rough hands squeezed and pried. Someone's boots had come down on her back. And when she yielded her necks like raised, surrendering hands, they whipped her until she bled. By the time they strapped her down, luminescent smears were all over the floor.

They must have assumed M2's escape made her stronger because they used more straps than usual today. Three around each of her necks, arms, and legs, and five around her body; the not-to-be-fucked-with military-strength straps that choked her and made it impossible to move. There was no doubt they were going to punish her for M2's escape. The red-faced crab in charge had made it clear. She reached for M2 with her mind, got static back. He was there. She could feel him. Somewhere around, but too far to help.

PROJECT DOMAIN

The negative pressure zone outside the lab inhaled a great breath and Lia Geller entered the room with three assistants, head-to-toe in hazmat suits. White suits were reserved for tests that didn't expel M1's or M2's fluids, but today the four were wearing the beige ones that hid the true severity of the torture. It was what the scientists needed to sustain efforts of cutting, scraping, burning, pulling, squeezing, battering, choking, poisoning, and whatever else their creative minds could conjure without the filaments of sympathy slowing their progress.

"We are ready, I see?"

Lia Geller's mask-covered face leaned close. Her circular voice amplifier brushed one of M1's necks, where her ear canals were located. The membrane covering her canals constricted to shut out the sound, but the scientist inserted a gloved finger deep into a canal and tugged it open.

"Today we are going to do something different. Let's call it PT *squared*. If you cooperate, it will be easier on you."

The scientist was lying, for after hundreds of tests M1 had learned that cooperation only made it easier for the *scientists*. How was a being, any being, to be still when stabbed or injected with Ebola or cancer or sulfuric acid? Worse, how could any being remain still when *told* it was going to be stabbed or injected? Not all creatures understand the words of the torture they endure, but their sixth sense makes them acutely aware and acutely afraid. M1 and M2 not only understood the human words but also their interminable language of torture. It made the Mimics all the more determined to escape.

M1's twenty-eight eyes narrowed on the Mad Scientist.

"Be a good girl and call him back," Geller whispered in her ear. "Call him back and we don't have to do the test."

The top strap on M1's seventh neck hadn't been secured as well as the others, so when the scientist thrust another finger into M1's ear canal to make sure she was listening, M1 struck out. She gnashed at the scientist with layers of needle-sharp teeth. Then she forced her ear canals closed, trapping two of Lia Geller's fingers inside her neck.

"Get her off me!" Geller screamed, pulling her arm now with one hand, now with two, now with the help of the nearest assistant.

Another assistant—Arlo Sims, by the look of his stomach—rushed to tighten the strap on M1's neck and was effectively amputated at the wrist by M1's second, third, and fourth rows of teeth. Contrary to belief, neither M1 nor M2 enjoyed being carnivores, but now M1 chewed Arlo Sim's hand with the pleasure of a castaway at a buffet. *Cooperate with **me**,* M1 thought smugly, *and I'll save you some meat.*

The negative pressure zone belched and in came five hazmat-suited soldiers with rifles. They hurled themselves at the gurney. Arlo, who hadn't stopped screaming, swiveled about the lab, spraying his blood on the equipment. Assistant Katy Morris hurried a tourniquet over Sims' arm but the other assistant, Ernest Rask, had fainted and was now being trampled on by the soldiers trying to subdue M1's thrashing mouth.

"Tranq her!" Geller ordered, still trying to yank her fingers out. "Tranq her, goddamn it!"

Darts flew at M1's body like buzzing insects. M1 swallowed Arlo's hand. Then she was out.

When she woke, M1 found they had doubled the straps on her body. The eyes that hadn't been beaten by the soldiers blinked and looked around the room. She had been moved to lab five, the Under Facility's most soundproof room.

"I've been a scientist for two decades."

Lia Geller's amplified voice came from the corner, where she stood in the center of a line of soldiers and assistant scientists. Arlo Sims had been replaced by Thomas Carson, two years senior, and Ernest Rask, also on route to the infirmary, had been replaced by Juliette Hooke, three years Carson's senior. Lia stepped toward the gurney and glared down.

"*Two decades,*" Lia continued. "And it has been the most rewarding experience of my life. Science is the bridge to truth; did you know that? All those little answers just waiting to be discovered. Limited only by your imagination. I know I'm part of something good. And I know the work we do here matters, that's why I appreciate the hard work our subjects do for us. You might not feel that way, but I want you to know that until that little stunt you pulled, I admired you." She gave a little laugh. "I even thought of finding a way to get you back home to show you how much we appreciated your service. We could have done that. Shipped you in a rocket. Set you free with all those cretins over there."

On the counter, something was bubbling over a Bunsen burner.

"But when we make those decisions, we have to ask ourselves why we have done what we've done. Do we enjoy your discomfort?" Her hazmat suit creaked like wrung rubber as she shook her head. "Of course not. We've done what we've done in the name of truth, but not just any truth. We keep you and the others here to discover your potentialities; how your uniqueness might help ease suffering, speed healing, calm nerves, make us all more resilient. We've spent billons on this, yet we were no closer to answers than you are to your own planet. But *you*"—she walked now to the Bunsen burner and retrieved the steaming flask— "you've given us more since these experiments began than all my work combined. In fact, I've found that the more we work with you, the faster we progress. Five years ago, it took us months of trial and analysis to discover a single advantage your DNA could bring to our population. Now we're discovering them weekly." She went to the gurney and put two pinched fingers in front of M1's eyes. "We're this close to adapting your genes. *This* close. And we will never get sick. And we will be strong as tigers. *Disguise* ourselves at the snap of a finger. So it might be painful, but pain is progress, yes?"

M1 stiffened.

"You understand," Lia Geller said. "Good." She gestured to her assistants. They flanked the gurney. Hooke and Carson plunged speculums into M1's reproductive canals.

Help me, M1 thought. She didn't send her cry to M2 because no matter how much they tortured her, she didn't want him to return. They would just torture him. Instead, she centered her terror inside herself like a great ticking bomb.

"Call him back," Lia Geller said.

Before this is done, I will take your head and feed it to the Red Crab. M1 thought, and then the Mad Scientist nodded to her assistants. The speculums were cranked open.

"Last chance." Lia waited, letting the steaming flask hover near the specula.

M1 closed her eyes and willed her body to reject the coming pain.

"Remember that this was your choice," Lia said, and tipped the flask.

16. Mushroom Hunter

In the darkened basement of an abandoned warehouse, the former body of Irma Madinger padded barefoot over broken glass. The woman's mouth had hung open, but now it crunched the thin bones of a squealing mouse. Habit, it was, for all creatures to eat. The congealed blood glopping from the woman's lacerated feet drew the mice and the insects, so it was easy picking. But it was the only thing that was easy.

The newness of freedom clamped down on M2 like a glacier to plains, grinding him with foreignness. He felt flat without M1. Two dimensional. Below, their bond had been almost covalent. There was not one part of M1 that was not M2, and no part of M2 was not M1. If M1 ate the slop disk, M2 felt full. If the Mad Scientist burned M2, M1 felt the heat on her skin. Their joys were shared, as were their fears. It had been this way for millennia, since before the Red Crab's ancestors had scuttled out of the ocean and learned to make fire.

M2's escape had been crucial. It was the only way out for both of them, but separation was like living with a dyssynchronous heart. He felt weak. Nips from the woman's brain helped to syncopate him with M1 again, though the bond didn't last long. The construction worker's effect lasted only slightly longer. He thought that brain matter for him and M1 might be like what drugs were for humans. Temporary power. And using it only made you want it even more. M2 hadn't had a taste of real food in so long, the woman's brain had almost made him collapse, such was his delirium. He'd done better with the man he'd left behind human-waste capsule. But the feeling had passed, and now M2 trudged the warehouse floor in his not really human skin, wondering what to do. He couldn't imitate the woman much longer, but neither could he expose himself. The Red Crab's people would know the dead woman walking was him. They would capture him and let the Mad Scientist teach him a lesson. He walked and thought, walked and thought.

From somewhere in the dark, a bottle rolled across the floor. M2 had been so focused on how to help M1, he hadn't noticed that he was not alone. He sniffed the air with the woman's old nostrils. It was a person. A woman. He stiffened.

"That you Eddie? Shine a light for me so I can see you." Papers rustled on the floor. A woman stumbled about blindly. Her foot thudded against the wall. Several mice scurried away.

M2 could smell the woman's sick. It was the same smell the guard Bo Wilco had after some weekends. *Crack*, M2 thought it was called, from when he had breached the man's psyche. Crack brains smelled like rotten mushrooms, so M2 closed his nasal passages and backed away from the woman.

"Don't fuck around, Eddie," the woman said, stumbling toward him. "Don't . . ." She burped and mumbled.

Just then a rumbling came down the stairs. The dim light of the upper room spilled into the basement like deep-sea gloom, but it was enough for the woman to recognize her partner. She shuffled toward him in the dark.

"Charity, where you been? I told you to wait—who's that?" The man—*Eddie*, M2 realized—was pointing at him. "You're in the wrong place, Grandma. This ain't no place for you."

"I thought that was *you*," Charity said. "What's your grandma doing here?"

"She's not my grandma," Eddie said.

"Then whose grandma is she?"

They started toward M2.

"Granny, Granny. Here, Granny, Granny," Eddie said.

I don't like mushrooms, M2 thought. *Mushrooms make me sick, but I will eat mushrooms if I have to.*

"We won't hurt you," Charity said with a slur that sounded like, *"Wewo were you."*

"Maybe she can't talk," Eddie said. "You know how they escape from those homes sometimes? Maybe she's lost."

"Awww. Are you lost?" Charity said, leaning toward M2.

The stick figures crept closer and closer, unaware that M2 could kill them more quickly than the crack could reach their mushroom patches. M2 backed Irma Madinger's likeness into a corner, then felt the itchy filaments of M1's fear wrap around him.

"She's scared," Charity said with her blistered lips and her weedy teeth.

What's happening? M2 reached urgently to M1. Her screams detonated in his head. His lobes convulsed with her pain.

Eddie pointed at Irma Madinger's feet. "Hey. Hey, you all right, ma'am? You should have shoes on. It's not good to be walking around like that. Let's get you out of here." He reached for her.

Throbbing with rage, M2 released Irma's likeness and unfurled his arms, his legs, his necks. He *roared*. Glass that hadn't been broken now sprayed from the warehouse windows. Underfoot debris trembled against the ground. And the two sour-brained stick people cowering below him clutched one another, yelping like dogs.

From Lia Geller's lab, M1 cried out.

M2's fifth mouth clamped around the woman's leg and his fourth arm wrung the man's neck. He didn't like mushrooms, but weeding the garden was necessary. He lifted the screaming pair and bashed them against the wall. Then again. Then again. Charity's broken leg flapped around itself. Eddie' head dangled from his disconnected neck. Then M2 *shredded* the pair. Blood and bones and organs splattered on needles and broken bottles and excrement left to rot.

A shriek rang through his lobes. He tore at the walls and flashed up the stairs. Then M2 went mushroom hunting.

17. Regin of Arachnicobra

Friday night, and only the fragrant scents of Binita Das' curry could mask the sour odors of three teenage boys sweating in her basement. She carried their plates of chana masala, lamb koftas, and rice downstairs, smelling Ravi's bowl when Douggie's clammy armpit opened to reach from the platter she carried.

"Uh, uh, uh." She shook a finger at Douggie, who was already stuffing his mouth with food. "You boys wash your hands first, and maybe some of your body spray, Ravi, huh?"

"*Mom.*" Ravi rolled his eyes.

"Go," she said.

Douggie pushed past Ravi and Adam toward the bathroom, spearing them with his elbows.

"Did you have to invite *him*?" Adam asked when Mrs. Das returned to the kitchen.

"Wasn't my idea," Ravi said, for in his whole young life there had never been a time when he had invited Douggie over. Douggie's presence was the work of Ravi's mother, a sweet woman with an approachable temperament who loved to cook and mouths to cook for. This week, Douggie had been over more than usual because he had set his kitchen on fire and his parents had taken extra shifts at the hospital to help pay for the damage their insurance wouldn't cover. Only two weeks ago, Douggie had forgone the dinner instructions his mother left on the kitchen table. After gas had been seeping into the oven for twenty minutes and the house did not fill with smells of cooked cheese and pepperoni, Douggie finally read his mother's instructions, opened the oven door, and twisted the ignition. The resulting blast singed the nascent hairs on his face, but hadn't blown his attitude away, much to Adam's disappointment.

A few minutes later, Douggie came out of the bathroom, doing up his zipper. "Warmed it up for you," he jeered at Adam.

For a moment, Adam envisioned smearing Mrs. Das' spicy chana masala on Douggie's eyes. He quietly went upstairs, washed his hands, and returned to the basement, where one of Douggie's fat fists were reaching for his plate. Adam whipped it away and glowered at him.

"There's more upstairs, asswipe," Ravi said to Douggie.

"The exercise will be good for you," Adam added.

"Whatever, fuck twads," Douggie said. He took up the controller and resumed *Reign of Crucor*, the newest multi-player medieval warfare game played by everyone in the school. His character, a three-headed giant brandishing a spiked club, swung indiscriminately at the other players. Realistic blood oozed from his victims until they flickered away and were reborn at the starting point. Ravi and Adam watched the carnage intently, alternately spooning curry into their mouths and shouting at Douggie to *watch out*, *run*, or *get him*! Douggie's three-headed giant smashed a passing giantess with his club and her brain splattered the screen. "Just like that old lady," Douggie said, and smashed the giantess again.

"It wasn't like that," Adam said.

"You said she had holes in her head," Ravi said.

When the accident happened a few days ago and the school was delirious with gossip, Adam did what any moderately unpopular kid would do: he used the seeds of first-hand knowledge to cultivate social currency. It was unlikely that the *Garrett Gazette* would publish the gruesome details of Irma Madinger's death, so Adam became St. Jude's sole source of information. He *might* have said Irma Madinger had holes in her head, and a few more kids *might* have gathered around Adam and Ravi during lunch, but he'd relayed the story so many times, he wasn't sure what he told whom and how much he embellished the truth.

"She did," Adam said. "I just don't know how many. My dad won't tell me. My mom said there were two, but she didn't see it. Only my dad did."

"Maybe someone shot her," Douggie wondered aloud. He was sitting cross-legged in front of the TV, furiously pressing buttons. His tongue peeked from the corner of his mouth, now the other corner, in deep, teenage concentration.

But Adam didn't think that Irma Madinger had been shot. He wanted to talk to Ravi alone about it, but that would just cause another fight with Douggie, with whom there was only social *debt*. He ate the last of his lamb and put his plate on the coffee table, thinking again of that overturned spider in the darkened ditch.

He said, "If I tell you something, swear you won't tell anyone?" The naïve belief that neither Ravi nor Douggie would tell, and that whoever *they* told wouldn't tell, and that whoever *they* told wouldn't tell settled like heavy snow on a steep slope in the periphery of Adam's mind.

Douggie paused his game.

Ravi's eyes went from Adam to Douggie and back again. "Now, man?" he mumbled to Adam so that Douggie couldn't hear.

Adam shrugged.

"Were her brains all over the car?" Douggie asked rapturously.

"Nothing like that. Well, maybe a little, I think. I told you I didn't see her, but when my mom and I were driving away, I saw... well, there was ... something in the ditch." He paused, aware that if he told them, he could never take it back, and that they could think he was just as crazy as *Skitzo Scotty*, the one-eared dump manager.

Ravi and Douggie leaned in.

"What was it?" Ravi asked.

"Not human," Adam said at last.

"What's that supposed to mean?" Douggie cuffed Adam's arm. "Was it a dog? A gorilla? What?"

"What was it?" Ravi seconded.

Adam glanced at the stairs. Then he quietly went and shut the basement door. "Remember when we were at Pissly's last summer?"

Ravi and Douggie nodded. They, along with Penny Ma's brother, Zhen (nicknamed Zen-Zen by his friends), and Cory Oliver, had spent a sweltering summer night in Cory's tree house. The father-son project, complete with rope bridge, compostable toilet, bunks and electricity, seemed like a classy contradiction to the younger Oliver's propensity for pissing off the roof whenever his friends were crossing the bridge. It was the summer before they started junior high, the summer they discovered that running women in horror movies often didn't wear bras. None of the movies had been approved by their parents—some deemed too graphic even for adult audiences—but the boys devoured them with adolescent glee.

"Remember *Arachnicobra*?" Adam asked. It was one of the cheesier movies about an amateur who bred a King Cobra snake with a Goliath Birdeater tarantula.

Ravi and Douggie nodded.

"Well, when my dad went back to the lady's car, I saw this *thing* in the ditch. It was like the thing in the movie, but way bigger. And it had like all these things coming out of its body with eyes—don't look at me like that. I'm telling you what I saw."

"In your fucking dreams." Douggie laughed.

"Cut it, Douggie," Ravi warned. He unpaused Douggie's game. Several giants immediately surrounded and were beating Douggie's character.

"C'mon!" Douggie scrambled back to the controller. "I *died*! Now I have to go back to the beginning." He tossed the controller aside and threw his hands up.

Ravi, who was slightly more popular than Adam because he never took any of Douggie's shit, said, "I'll do it again if you can't shut your mouth. He's telling us something. Either you listen quietly or go back to what's left of your kitchen. Go on, Adam."

"It's nothing," Adam started feebly.

"I'm listening," Douggie said. "Spider snake in the ditch. Did it cocoon the old woman's head and suck her brains out?"

Ravi pointed to the door.

"Okay, okay," Douggie said. "Spider snake. What happened next?"

Adam continued. "Well, it was just looking at me. It had all these eyes—" He wiggled his fingers near his face. "And then it turned into that lady and ran away."

Ravi frowned. "You need to stay off the internet. Like the whole thing. Forever."

"I knew you wouldn't believe me," Adam said.

"Wait a second," Douggie lifted a finger. "I heard about this. Shape shifters, right? Like when girls put makeup on . . ." He spit laughter.

"Whatever. Don't believe me. But if that thing comes for you, it's not my fault." Adam stood, picked up his plate, and carried it upstairs to Mrs. Das. Ravi followed. Doggie went back to *Reign of Crucor*.

In the kitchen, Mrs. Das had been spooning cinnamon kheer into bowls for the boys when her phone rang. She had it to her ear, sprinkling slivered almonds on top, when her hand dropped to her side and the almonds fell to the floor.

Adam and Ravi looked at each other, then Ravi touched her shoulder. "Mom?"

She shushed him with a finger and sat down. "*No*," she gasped to whoever was speaking. "The whole station? Everyone? What . . . how . . .?" The boys listened quietly, but her ear was pressed so tightly to the phone they couldn't make anything out. She dabbed at her eyes with the corner of her apron, sniffling. "They can stay here. We'll make room. Okay. Okay. Poor Sanvi. I know. See you soon." When she pulled the phone from her ear, the screen was wet. "Kabir's sisters will be staying here tonight. There's been an accident and . . ." She hiccupped a little sob, "Vishi . . . didn't make it. Oh, those poor kids. Poor Sanvi."

The Chawlas had immigrated to Ontario only fourteen months earlier when the father, Vishi Chawla, accepted a role as a software engineer manager for a blockchain development company out of Toronto. His flexible schedule allowed him to work remotely from Garrett most days, where he could spend more time with his wife, Sanvi, and their children, four daughters and a son. Garrett's growing East Indian community was close-knit and received diaspora like mothers received babies, nurturing them with care until they could walk on their own. Though Ravi had known them from the Bharatiya Culture Association most East Indians in the city belonged to, none of the Chawlas were in junior high. The girls were all still in elementary school while Kabir was already in high school and working as a lifeguard at the YMCA. Vishi's death meant that Sanvi would be a single mother with five children to support.

Ravi wrapped his arms around his mother. He rested his chin on the top of her head and she began weeping into his chest, trying but unable to compose herself.

"What happened?" he asked.

She extricated herself and accepted a tissue from the box Adam offered. "Jeeva said he was picking Kabir up from the pool and a truck hit them. It . . . it drove through the bus station Kabir sometimes waits at, then, then it *hit* them. Kabir is in the hospital, but Vishi tried to stop the driver—" She didn't finish.

"Hey Mrs. D, got any more of those lamb things?" Douggie said as he entered the kitchen. She pointed without looking to the platter of koftas on the stove. Douggie glanced at the three, shrugged, and carried the platter downstairs.

"I'm sorry, Mrs. Das," Adam said. Then to Ravi, he said, "I should go."

Ravi nodded.

A short time later, Adam's mother's SUV pulled up in front of the house.

"Have a good time?" Gia asked, ruffling his hair as he fastened his seatbelt.

"Douggie was there."

"Ah. You should've called earlier," She smiled and turned on the radio because her attempts at small talk since the counseling sessions began always ended with Adam crossing his arms and turning away from her.

They were turning out of Ravi's suburb when the blue and red lights of multiple police cars signalled that the southbound road was closed ahead. An officer was directing traffic to an eastern detour down Dundas, and they followed the few cars in front of them as those red and blue lights appeared again.

"What is going on with this city?" Gia said, looking at the sky where the faint outline of a crescent moon was appearing high above the April dusk. She turned the car down Littlewood Road.

Shape shifters, Adam thought gloomily, watching shadows emerge behind hedges, under windows, beside doors. He was sad for Mrs. Das' friends, he really was, but the overturned spider wouldn't leave his mind. His mother had told their therapist that Adam was imagining things when he said that passing in the school bus one day, he'd seen her and his father's boss entering the Dartree Motel. She was so adamant it hadn't been her that the therapist explained the mind was a powerful conjurer and sometimes made people see what they wanted to see. He didn't believe his mother, nor had he believed the therapist, not about the hotel. But now he wondered if his parent's issues weren't playing tricks with his mind, taking him back to last summer when his mother wasn't a cheater and women in horror movies didn't wear bras and *Arachnicobra* was just a movie they laughed at.

Gia hit the steering wheel. "Bloody hell. Adam, call your father and tell him we're going to be a while. There's another accident." She had turned north toward the switchyard when an ambulance blocked the road. The blast of an arriving police car made Gia yelp. She stopped, put the car in park and waited for the officer to direct the line of traffic.

Adam used his mother's phone to call his father. He was waiting for his father to answer—*probably playing video games*, he thought—when he spotted on the right side of the road a bus station with shattered glass. He thought of Mrs. Das' friends and the accident near the YMCA. Two bus station accidents seemed unlikely, unless some disgruntled maniac was wreaking havoc on commuters, but it made Adam think. There was a bus stop close to where the police cars had stopped by Ravi's house. Adam had taken the bus there many times when his parents couldn't drive him. And was there another stop by the second accident? He couldn't be sure, but something told him that there probably was.

"Hello?" Peter answered. "Gia? Are you okay? Is Adam with you?"

"It's me, Dad," Adam said. "We might take a while. There's a lot of police cars and accidents everywhere—"

"Adam, Adam, listen. You two get home safe, you hear? Uncle Arty just called me and said there's something going on out there. You know that guy in the chicken costume at the Chicken Kitchen?"

Adam said he did.

"Uncle Arty say's he was in the drive-through and these dark clouds came down on him. I don't know, he said it was something like a tornado on the guy. One minute the guy was waving that sign and the next . . . he didn't have the top part on. The tornado ripped it off him. His head . . ." Peter started but decided not to tell Adam. "It's happening all over the city. Just get home, Adam. Keep the windows rolled up and get home, okay? Put your mom on for me."

"I'm driving, Peter," Gia groaned when Adam pushed the phone at her.

"Tell her to get on the goddam phone, Adam," Peter shouted loudly enough for Gia to hear.

She took the phone and subsequently hung up. "It's illegal to talk and drive unless you have hands-free, Adam, and since your father chooses to sit on the couch and not commit to a proper job, we can't afford it. He can talk to me when we get home."

"But—"

"I'm trying to concentrate on the road."

He slouched further in the front seat and turned away from her. He leaned his head against the window. A procession of emergency vehicles passed on his mother's side—and on his, officers were webbed out from the road to the auto repair and metal fabrication shops across the street. The evening was almost dark now and flashlights swung this way and that, illuminating garbage cans, windows, fences, roofs.

Traffic started moving again. An officer tipped her chin and directed them to make a U-turn, then right onto Rogan, where a detour was being marked. His mother spun the Impala around and followed the line of cars inching out of the area.

Adam stared at the rows of trains parked at the tracks. Police tape flapped from the entrance and on a number of trees and signs. With the flashlights receding behind them and the streetlights in front of the switchyard in desperate need of replacement, it was almost impossible to see past the train closest to their car.

A pedestrian ahead slowed the pace and once again the Impala stopped. Adam fogged the window with his breath and drew a circle. He traced several lines upward from the circle and wrote *Arachnicobra* underneath, then he squinted through the circle at the switchyard.

There, a man sat atop a train car.

Adam pressed his face to the glass. He pulled back and wiped the window with his sleeve, then pressed his face to the window again. The man was still there.

"There's a guy there," Adam said, pointing to the train car where the man cradled something against his chest in faint silhouette. "He's on the train. Look!"

Gia swiped the air in front of her face. "Druggie. They hang out here all the time. You've seen them, Adam. Don't stare or they'll think we have money." She double-checked to make sure the doors were locked and all the windows were rolled up. "C'mon already," she muttered at the car ahead of her.

But Adam didn't think the man was a druggie. For one thing, he wasn't slumped over like the people he saw outside the liquor stores or under the bridge near the river. And for another, he couldn't see a druggie making it all the way up to the roof of the train car. He unrolled his window just enough to see without the glass fogging up or reflecting back at him.

"Honestly, Adam," Gia huffed. "If he starts coming this way, you better roll that thing up."

"I will," he said, and squinted through the darkening dusk at the man on the train. There was no way for Adam to tell what the guy was holding or even what the guy looked like, only that it was a man.

But then the amber lights of an approaching tow truck illuminated the man only for a second. It was enough. In that thin slice of time, the man's silhouette brightened, and Adam saw the face of a guy who'd made the paper because he didn't report a deadly fire a long time ago. Adam couldn't remember his name. But he wasn't mistaken about what was dripping from the man's chin onto his shirt.

Blood.

18. Ick

An auditory layer of sirens buried the city so that by the time he swung his truck into St. Jude's parking lot, Scotty had a terrible headache. He opened the glovebox for the Tylenol and swallowed three pills dry. Sometimes this blocked the Voice, but Scotty didn't care. He couldn't clean the school while his head was under bricks and didn't want to try.

He'd come earlier than usual, afraid that the accidents simmering all over the city would keep him from seeing Claire. Not that she wanted to see *him*, of course. Softball practices in the back fields were just finishing, so Scotty skirted the grounds and sat, alone, on an empty bench in the only unoccupied field. Spectators paid him no notice, but parents arriving to pick up their children avoided the space he occupied as though he might reach out and attack them. Scotty pretended not to notice, just went on loving his only daughter from afar.

Before long, the erect figure of Principal Irving Hahn waved to the students and came over to him.

"Beautiful evening," Irving said. He had his hands tucked into his pockets and now he lifted his neck to look at the stars just beginning to reveal themselves. "You had no trouble getting here, I hope?"

"I had to detour down Habitstrom," Scotty said of the tertiary sideroad he'd used. "Can't figure it out. You know anything?"

The principal had sat on his right side, looking with Scotty toward the students finishing their practice. It made Scotty self-conscious whenever anyone but Meredith was on that side of him, and he automatically tilted his bad ear away.

"About the fuss out there?" Irving gestured to the streets. "Not yet. I made a call to the police and they said to tell everyone to drive carefully and avoid the main roads. They might as well have told me to send my students into oncoming traffic, for all the help that was. I tell you, I don't know about the world sometimes. I tell myself it would be easier to pack it all in and move to a cabin in Yellowknife, read and ice fish for the rest of my life, but I'd probably get eaten by a bear."

Scotty laughed.

"Look out!" someone yelled, and before Scotty had a chance to react, Irving was on his toes and whipping the ball back to the outstretched mitt of a pale, gum-chewing boy.

"Sorry!" his pubescent voice wobbled.

"I'm lucky you came," Scotty said when his heart stopped racing. Had Irving not been there, Scotty would have believed the toss had been intentionally aimed at him, and a flicker of indignation fluttered through him.

"Luck seems to be spreading," Irving told Scotty, sitting back down. He pointed to Julia Fowler, who was gathering bats and balls alongside Claire while students were collected by their anxious, traffic-frightened parents. "Our Julia must have kissed a leprechaun because she just won a contest. A tour around the world. She's leaving us for six months. Now I have to figure out how to fill the hole she'll be leaving. You interested in teaching?"

They both knew he was joking, but Scotty appreciated his humour. It warmed him to know that Hahn didn't buy into any of the *Skitzo Scotty* rhetoric. "They couldn't handle me," Scotty said honestly, then added, "and I couldn't handle them."

Irving patted his arm. "Some days I can't either, but we're one of the fortunate schools with teachers who are especially adept at herding cats. God bless them. But now we'll be down one hell of a cat herder." He spread his hands. "For some reason, everyone in our regular supply pool has been deployed to London, so they're sending us someone from Toronto. If we can scrub the city out of him, I might let him stay." He winked, then nodded toward Claire and Julia, who were tugging the equipment back into the school. "They like keeping us on our toes, don't they? We change their diapers, spoon-feed them, do everything we can to protect them and yet they grow up and forget who taught them how to walk."

"Sydney still with the . . . tattooist, is it?" Scotty asked.

"She is," Irving said. "And God forbid I suggest he takes that ring out of his chin when we guilt her into dinner." He stood. "On that note, I have a beef stew calling my name. If it gets any colder, Norma will put a ring in *my* chin. Have a good night, Scotty, and thank you again."

Scotty hurried into the school, hoping to catch Claire before she snuck away. He walked down the hallway and found her in her classroom talking to the other grade seven teacher, Julia Fowler.

"Hi Mr. Waymore," Julia said. She grinned so brightly that the fluorescent light was glinting off her teeth, and Scotty couldn't help but be happy for her. In all the years he had cleaned the school, she had never warmed to calling him by his first name. Her habit of addressing her students' parents by their last names carried over into her personal life, she had told him, and she was equally taken aback when addressed by her own first name. Her eyes darted to Claire, whose freckled face began to blush.

"I came to congratulate the contest winner," Scotty said, leaning against the door frame.

"Eeee! Isn't it crazy? I don't even remember entering a contest, but I must've because they sent me flowers and money, too." There was a box on Claire's desk and Julia picked it up. "My mom's coming with me. We're leaving tomorrow."

"Already?" Scotty asked.

Julia nodded. "They've been trying to contact me for two months, but I didn't get their messages until yesterday when they showed up at my door. It was like one of those *Publishers Clearinghouse Sweepstakes*. You know those commercials where they show up on someone's door with a big cheque and balloons? It was like that. I have to vlog—that's *video log*, like a video diary—of the trip and send it out to all my followers. I don't even have many followers, but I guess I will now. All of my students just followed me." She giggled then threw an arm around Claire and hugged her. "I'll miss you, girl."

"Don't accept drinks from strangers," Claire said, hugging Julia tightly.

"I won't, *Mom*," Julia said, and released her.

Scotty stepped aside to let her leave but then Julia hugged him too. Scotty's stiff arms stayed by his side, but he chuckled, wishing almost to the point his heart hurt that it was Claire hugging him now.

"Have fun, kid," he said to Julia, and then she was gone and he was alone with Claire. He risked her aversion by stepping into the room. "A trip around the world, huh? I could use one of those," he said a little awkwardly.

"Would that've changed anything?" Claire asked flatly. Her hair was long and as red as her mother's but now she tucked it behind her ears as she put a small stack of binders and books in her bag without looking at him.

"Claire—" he said.

"I'm just curious, Dad. Would it?"

His hand went to the back of his neck, and he pressed his lips together and shrugged. "I don't know. It probably would have helped *you*, at least." They were both quiet, him desperate for Claire to show a little love, Claire desperate for him to not be *him*. "How's Ty?"

"He's good," she said. "Better now."

Inside, Scotty cringed. His grandson was *better now* that he hadn't seen his grandfather in almost a year. Better now because he stopped being bullied for having *Skitzo Scotty* as a grandfather. Better now because *Creepy Claire's Cunt* wasn't drawn on his locker or scribbled on his desk. Better now because he didn't step in Douggie Radway's bags of shit every morning when he left the house. As a single mother, Claire had put up with a lot, but she was unwilling to accept the burden of having her son bombarded because of her father. The sharp severing of their relationship when Scotty refused to take Dr. Huxley's pills had been hard on everyone, but especially Ty, who adored his grandfather despite his eccentricities.

"That's good," Scotty said. "Good."

"He'll be even better if I can get him to eat his vegetables," Claire admitted. "I have to practically tie him down to eat anything green."

This little tidbit warmed him, and he was about say so when his ears rang and he realized that he and Claire were not alone.

Here, said the Voice. *Help. Here. Come.*

Not now, Scotty thought. *Not now. Not when she's finally talking to me. Please, no. Please.*

She tilted her head and stared at him. "I got to go. Ty's waiting on me. It was nice seeing you, Dad." She passed him with a tight smile.

"I'd like to see him," Scotty said softly.

She stopped. "I'd like that too. You tell me when you start taking those pills and maybe we can make that happen. I love you, Dad. I miss you, and Ty misses you too, but it's not good for us if you refuse to take care of yourself."

"I told you, Claire—"

Here. Come. Help. Help. Help.

"I know. You think it's real. But the sad part is that you care more about those voices in your head than you do me or Ty. It's your choice, not mine. Have a good night, Dad, but please don't come early next time. If you do anything for me, do that, okay?" She turned and walked down the silent school corridor without a backward glance.

Scotty wasn't an emotional man, but now he cried. He went to the janitorial closet, weeping. He swept and mopped the floors wishing he could close the valve in his head that let the Voice inside. Today the Voice was unusually frantic, *frenetic*, even.

Help! The Voice cried. *Help! Home! Help!*

He could feel it inside his head, pulling at him. Usually, he cleaned the school with the lights on but the way the sirens hurt his head, he'd only left the hallways lit. It was enough for him to scoot into classrooms and do what he needed to do, but the Voice seemed to animate the shadows. The walls crawled with movement. The floors reached for him. And even the innocent sketches of Mr. Dawson's class appeared to creep off their pages and surround him.

There was a noise behind him. "Hello?" he said. Scotty whipped around and realized, embarrassed, that it was the end of the broom hitting the wall. He dragged a hand over his face and craned his neck toward the ceiling. "Can't a guy get a break?"

Break. Break. Break, said the Voice. He froze. It was the first time the Voice had ever repeated him, and Scotty wasn't sure if it meant that the Voice had been himself all along or that it had learned to speak to him. "Let me help you," Scotty said, and listened. "At least tell me your name. Are you . . . are you *me*?"

Had anyone been in the hallway, he knew what it would have looked like, but he didn't care. Not when he was so close to his long-time companion. For several minutes, he waited for a response. When it didn't come, he hurried about cleaning the rest of the rooms, locked the janitorial closet, and left the school.

Outside the sirens had abated, but there was the unmistakable shimmer of emergency vehicles beyond the hill. The truck was parked near the pair of dumpsters between one of the portables and the gymnasium, and Scotty had to skirt the south end of the building with the yellowed exterior lights dully smoldering above him.

He was a good twenty feet from the truck when gravel dusted up against someone's feet.

"Hello?" Scotty called out.

Gravel skittered across the parking lot.

"Anyone there?" His keys jangled in his trembling hands. He instinctively tucked several of them outward between his fingers and clenched his hand into a fist. The best defense was awareness, but if he was attacked, he would fight like hell. Like a man crazy enough to take his own ear.

Shuffling up the slanted pavement, a man appeared. He was in the dark space between the weak parking lot lights so Scotty couldn't get a good look at him but saw that the man was slumped over like an old scarecrow loose from its stake. His feet dragged under him. They *slid* toward Scotty. Pebbles tumbled slowly, then began to crack like marbles being thrown against a wall. He was gaining speed, churning like an old engine starting up, and a sound grunted up his throat. *Aghh. Aghh. Aghh.* Faster now. *Aghhhhh. Aghhhh.*

The Voice burst into Scotty's head. *Break. Break. Help. Come. Home. Break. Help. Coming. Coming. Coming.* Scotty tried to push the Voice away, but it wouldn't go.

"Stop right there," Scotty said. His keys were so tight in his fingers that the little peaked triangles of the sun-shaped key cover Ty had once owned cut into his palm. He tensed. "Identify yourself. Identify yourself or I'll call the police."

But the man came closer. His foot appeared beneath the farthest light. Only, it didn't look right. There was something *wrong* with it. Scotty narrowed his eyes, trying to focus on the man's foot when he slid his other foot into the light.

"I said stop!" Scotty shouted. He reached into his back pocket and pulled out the pencil he carried. It wasn't much, but it was something, he figured, and he clenched it beside his hip. That and the keys should protect him, he hoped while staring at the man's feet. He realized why they looked so strange. They looked strange because the man wasn't walking on his feet. He was walking on his *ankles*, lugging his feet like *chains*.

Scotty gasped. He glanced at the truck, still twenty feet away. Then he ran for it.

So, too, did the feet-lugging man.

The spraying gravel beneath the man's ankles grew closer as the man gained on him faster than any of Douggie Radway's shit bags and faster than Vera's attitude whenever he entered the office. *Aghh. Aghh. Aghh*, came the grunts behind him, so close that even his phantom ear tingled. Scotty glanced backward. He'd gone half the distance he needed to cover, but the man had almost caught up to him and his fingers were reaching toward Scotty—no—*snaking* toward him like vines. Scotty did a double-take. The face was familiar.

"Nick?" Scotty asked, knowing that it couldn't be Nick Penner because Nick Penner was dead. Judy had told Meredith that not two days ago through the window of Scotty's truck.

Nick, said the Voice in Scotty's head but as Scotty heard it, he also saw Nick's jaw move.

Scotty was two feet from the truck now. Nick Penner grunted his dead man's grunt and Scotty realized in that terrible moment that *getting* to the truck was one thing. *Opening* it was another. He wheeled around and put out the hand with the keys. Closer to the school where the light was only slightly better, the keys in Scotty's hand looked like tiny claws. The outdated picture of Claire and Meredith at a breakfast table in Disneyworld dangled against his trembling wrist.

"Stop Nick! Stop this right now!" he shouted.

Of all things Scotty thought would happen, Nick stopping was not one of them. Yet Nick had skidded still as though he'd struck glass. Scotty had cowered with his hand out, expecting Nick to strike him, but Nick had stopped mid-dash and was now only inches from Scotty, working little grunts from his mouth. The way Nick's tongue poked out reminded Scotty of when Claire was a baby and learning to talk. "Hel—" Nick said in a strained voice, as though someone were sitting on his chest.

Help, Scotty thought. *He's going to say help. Home. Come. Break. He's going to say it and then he's going to kill me.* His lips trembled. "P-please d-don't."

Nick cleared his throat. He tried speaking again but when the words didn't come out, he reached up with his hands, clamped onto his head, and twisted his neck. The crack made Scotty's blood run cold. He squeezed his eyes shut and whispered a *Hail Mary*.

"Hell-o," Nick said in Scotty's head.

From his crouching position, Scotty could see Nick's bones jutting over the tops of his shoes. Splashes of dried blood stained his socks and the places where his broken ankles skidded against the road were a crusted black-brown mess.

"Hell-o," Nick repeated, and stretched out his hand, palm down, as though he were a priest and going to pray over Scotty's head.

"Nick?"

"Ick," Nick said without audible words. He swayed a little, like a man after a few too many drinks or a man without feet, and it gave Scotty the creeps.

Scotty stood and faced him. Nick staggered and took a step back, then seemed to get his balance. In the state Nick was in, he should not be walking, let alone running across a parking lot in the dark. Either Judy was wrong about Nick being dead and he had somehow wandered from the hospital with enough morphine in him to stun a heard of elephants, or . . . or this wasn't Nick Penner.

"Tell me your name," Scotty said.

Nick's mouth stretched and narrowed. His tongue clicked several times.

"I don't know what you're saying."

The whites of Nick's eyes overtook first his irises then his pupils and then he was reaching to Scotty, lowering his bloody hand to Scotty's temple. *Run*, Scotty thought. *If I don't run, I'll die. Run, goddamnit, run!* But like all the times he heard the Voice, Scotty couldn't turn his back. He had to *know*. He leaned into Nick's hand.

Then M2 introduced himself.

19. FATHER ROSS AND THE RELUCTANT TEACHER

Deep underground, a guttural scream shook the facility. The aliens had learned to repel the sounds of torture for the sake of their own sanity, but now the Martians pressed their ears to the walls, the Venusians extracted the commotion from the air, the Saturnians sponged soundwaves into themselves, the Plutonians burrowed into the speakers as far as their jellied bodies could go, and the Uranians intuited everything with rapt attention. The sound hurt M1's valves and she tried to shut them, but the Mad Scientist made it so she couldn't. She lay on M2's bed, thinking of him, hoping Hollis was shouting because the ceiling had caved in on him.

In Sector Center, meanwhile, Jeffrey Acres had already dodged a stapler, a full cup of coffee, and the telephone, which Hollis had also threatened to wrap around his neck.

"You tell those son of a bitching bootlickers that if they don't eat, we'll *make* them eat. There's room for every last fucking one of them in the lab. And if they won't open their mouths, you sure as hell know we'll open their fucking *bodies* and shove it in." He took a picture from the wall. It was the one of him and the Prime Minister in a charity rugby match. He whipped it at Acres.

Geller's PT test on M1 had been the most severe test ever conducted in the facility. Part of what made Geller's team so good is that none of them seemed to have hearts. They didn't imbibe social or moral integrity like most people but were from that infinitesimally small subset of the human species unaffected by feelings. Geller and her assistants could be slabs of slate, for all they cared. M1's cries did not hurt their hearts, for there were no hearts to hurt, but their *ears* were another story. They strapped big leather belts around her mouths to quiet the noise but after Geller emptied the flask, M1's terror shook the gurney and cracked a window graded to withstand jet propulsion. Hollis had told Geller to do what had to be done to get M1 to bring M2 back, but he hadn't thought it would lead to a goddamned hunger strike.

"Who's responsible?" Hollis asked Acres now, jabbing his finger on his desk. "It's that Mendawall, isn't?"

Acres nodded. "He filed a petition on behalf—"

"Filed a *petition*? Who does he think he is? That's it. We've been too soft on them. Revoke their privileges. Martian wants to act like he's in charge, well, we'll show him who's boss."

"It's not just him, sir," Acres said. "Templeton is refusing his medication and the Uranians have stopped using the toilet. Their room is filling up with . . . you know . . . and Crygee is making everyone in Sector Center itchy like they've fallen in poison ivy. They're *mad*, Sir. They say we've gone too far."

"What on earth do they have to be mad about? The roof over their heads? Nutritious food? Heat? And what do we ask for in return? A little experimentation. *Humans* across the world volunteer for experiments and do they complain or go on hunger strikes? Of course not, because the ones that do *die*. Do me a favor and pass *that* on to them."

"Yes, sir." Acres stomped his foot, spun on his heels, and left to deliver the news.

No sooner did Acres depart, Foster Cupps rapped on the doorframe.

"What is it now?" Hollis groaned. He'd tasked the soldier with the containment and transfer of employees from the command center to their cells in Sector South, where they would be held until M2 was captured. From the look on Cupps' face, Hollis wasn't going to like the reason for the visit.

Cupps stepped inside Hollis' office and was going to sit, but then saw that Hollis hadn't completely depleted the ammunition on his desk. A small clock tossed hard enough could hurt even a big man like Foster Cupps, so he stopped just inside the door. He spread his hands. "Sector South is secure, sir, but they're not happy."

Hollis pointed to the scratches on Cupps' arms. "Give me the names and I'll ship them up north."

Cupps swallowed. "I appreciate the gesture, sir, but they can't be transferred if they quit, can they?"

"What do you mean?"

The room was too hot for Cupps and he began to sweat. "May I speak frankly, sir?"

Hollis flapped his hand irritably. "*Now*, soldier."

"They're not taking too well to the plan, sir. The women have been getting weepy and it's working up the men. Anderson—"

"You broke his nose?" Hollis interrupted, having seen the incident report.

"Had to be done, sir," Cupps said.

"And his cheek?"

"Same punch, sir. I only hit him once."

Hollis pursed his lips together appreciatively. "Evan Anderson had one of the finest surgeons in the world fix his face and has some of the best nurses in the world tending to him down there. He's not trying to bully his way out again, is he?"

"That's just it, sir. He's started a riot. They're wrecking their rooms. They say they're all going to quit if we don't let them out."

"Cupps, what do we say about replaceability?"

"Everyone but *you* can be replaced." It was the adage they'd learned on day one.

"That's right. Tell them if they don't cut it out, none of them will have jobs when this is over—and I'll make it so the only action they see is the squirt gun games at that hick festival in the summer. I don't know a single carny who gets a pension, do you?"

Cupps said he didn't.

"And if they still won't behave, let's see if we forget to feed them for a while. They can thank Mendawall for that idea." His angry face tightened into an eerie grin.

From the floor where he had thrown it, Hollis' cell phone rang. Cupps picked it up and passed it to him, then excused himself to deliver Hollis' warning.

"What?" Hollis growled into the receiver.

"I was thinking the same thing," Dan Fogel said.

Hollis rolled his eyes. The cop had been calling him all day and until now, he had successfully managed to avoid him. "Dan," he said. "I've been meaning to return your calls."

"My old boss, Tom Widlow, always told me that intention is about as useful as a vest on a hanger. You can intend all you want but if you're not wearing it when shit goes down, it can't save you. We've been at this cat-and-mouse long enough for me to understand that you're playing with me, Hollis. I might not be part of your big-budget tactical hoopla or whatever you've got going on over there, but I know that cooperation doesn't happen in a vacuum."

"Now, wait a minute—" Hollis started, but Dan interrupted.

"You wanted full disclosure on my end, but I won't be party to a bona fide cannibal picking off my people. Thirteen dead, Hollis. *Thirteen* with chunks out of their brains. Students. Fathers. Sisters. Children. I don't know how your Zombie Killer gets to thirteen people across seventeen kilometers, but I've effectively closed every bus stop in the city. Now, I have to ask myself how does a single man immediately go from fifth street to Dundas? The answer is, he *can't*—unless he has help. Tell me, Hollis. How many Zombie Killers are you hiding from me? My guess is more than two because of the sheer distance the murders covered. And—excuse me for thinking out loud—I suspect there's this... *thing* they're doing with the bodies."

"I'm listening," Hollis said, which was especially hard for man used to talking.

"We had a sighting on Irma Madinger, the first victim, by our waste facility manager. It seems she visited him *after* the crash, then took off into the field and buckled herself back into her car. The dump has a security camera pointed at the very spot, but I went to verify the footage the manager gave me and got nothing but static. Scotty says she was acting strange. And we've received reports from concerned citizens that Nick Penner was stumbling around those bus stops. Either victim number two resurrected himself from the morgue or your Zombie Killer has a thing for playing doll. Which one is it?"

Hollis sighed. "It's best if we talk about this in person."

There was a pause on Dan's end, then he said, "The press is breathing down my back and I've already got dozens of families camped out in front of the station looking for answers. I have a news conference scheduled in an hour. If you're not here in twenty minutes, I won't keep your Zombie Killer a secret. I don't care what that does to your investigation."

"Let's not be—"

"Twenty minutes. Or should I come to you? I'll leave right now."

There were only thirteen RCMP detachments across Ontario, with the nearest being an hour away in London. As far as Dan knew, Hollis' team had temporarily commandeered space in the sleepy Adequate Accounting office, where they could be closer to the action until the Zombie Killer was caught or moved on to another city. Civilians errantly venturing into the building for cheap accounting services took in the shabby interior and lethargic employees and almost always walked right back out. Deal-seekers who insisted on quotes consistently received astronomical estimates many times higher than even the most exclusive firm in Toronto, so in all the years Adequate Accounting had languished on Waste Way, it hadn't secured a single customer or genuine interest. But Dan Fogel was sharp, and Hollis couldn't risk him blowing the project's cover. He said, "I'm on my way."

"Don't be late," Dan snapped and hung up the phone.

No one snapped at Hollis. He brooded over having to eat Dan's attitude. Once M2 was captured and this was over, he'd pull every string in his arsenal to have Dan reassigned. Maybe security detail at Garrett's shitty little strip mall or night shift at the hospital. Let him deal with the midnight junkies and the shit-flinging nuts from a narrow little booth.

He palmed the clock on his desk and chucked it at the wall. Then he stomped out of his office, into the cool damp hall dividing the Martian and Saturnian enclosures.

Mendawall glared at him. "Stab the Red Crab, stab the Red Crab," he chanted through the bars, though without much conviction. It wasn't in Martians' nature to be mean, and the effort of insulting Hollis took the shine out of Mendawall's silver skin.

Pintree's eyelashes elongated then thatched into a rippling image of Lia Geller with horns and a trident. Hollis snatched it and yanked the little Martian into the bars. She yelped in pain. "No more out of you," he growled. "No more out of any of you, you hear me?" He glared at the television in their room, where a fluffy-haired artist was painting happy little clouds above a mountainscape. "And if you don't end that hunger strike of yours, you can say goodbye to Bob Ross."

Twenty-eight miniature shrieks rang out. Since the Martians' incarceration, television had been the only thing to calm their night terrors, and Bob Ross had become the only human to soothe their souls after Lia Geller's PT tests, since he was most like themselves. *Father Ross*, they called him, and the Martians simply could not do without him. They could not, would not, do without him.

"Hunger strike is over," Mendawall called out glumly, and his twenty-seven compatriots put down their offensive facades, picked up their cold dinner trays, and began to eat.

One of the guards who had been watching the exchange said, "Bob Ross, who knew?"

Hollis did. It was his job to know everything about everybody involved in Project Domain. The new guard also should have known that. "Report to ALIEN tomorrow, soldier. You've been reassigned," he said.

"Up *north*?" the soldier, Tim Gyles, asked dazedly.

"Let me give you some advice," Hollis glared at the man's embroidered name tag, "*Gyles*. The aliens up there make these ones look like itty-bitty tinker toys. Stuffed teddy bears. Happy little bouncing balls. Know your enemy, Gyles, or they will hunt you and rip you apart like sharks."

The other two guards waited until Hollis disappeared through the vacuum chamber then consoled Gyles, who had started to tremble.

A minute later, Hollis arrived at the blast door where Deborah Mills was waiting beside Theo Carver, whose eyes were currently being photographed by the biometric access control scanner.

"You took care of Mr. Waymore's flash drive, I see?" Hollis said to Lieutenant Mills.

She moved a thumb toward Theo. "He took care of it."

"Cyber Ops did, actually," Theo said, pulling back from the scanner and blinking moisture back into his eyes. "I had them access Dan's phone, laptop, and personal computer. They scrubbed the recording as he was playing it." He said this casually, as though it had taken no effort and Cyber hadn't been sweating until the entire recording was deleted.

Hollis didn't tell Theo he'd done a good job, nor did Theo expect to hear it. The blast door hissed open. "Ride with me," he said. They followed the quick thud of his steps into the tunnel where Master Corporal Rollins waited inside the idling G3.

The soldier was steadier today than when M2 first escaped, but he'd since developed the nervous habit of biting his lower lip whenever he wasn't talking. Several small scabs were in various stages of healing on his lip, but he'd broken the biggest one on the left just moments ago when ordered down the decline to collect Hollis. He sucked the small bead of blood into his mouth so they wouldn't notice, nodding respectfully when they got in.

"I visited Irma Madinger's husband—" Deborah started as she sat, but Hollis cut her off.

"M2's already moved on," Hollis said. "The switchyard victim—Penner—has been *resurrected*. We need all eyes looking for him."

Rollins, who hadn't yet learned to keep quiet unless spoken to, kept his eyes on the road. "Only him, sir? I mean, M2 could be *anyone*."

"Mind the road, Rollins," Hollis snapped.

Theo leaned toward Rollins from the back seat. "That's actually a fair question." He glanced at the front passenger seat, from which Hollis flapped an annoyed approval.

"You told me your grandmother took you to the zoo when you were little. How's she doing now?" Theo said.

Unsure where Theo was going with the question, Rollins said, "Dead, sir. She died when I was in high school."

"What happened?" Theo asked.

"Cancer," Rollins told him, squirming at the suppressive authority of the three listening superiors.

"Okay, cancer," Theo said. "I had an aunt who had cancer. But it wasn't the cancer that got her. It was a stroke. I didn't know that people with cancer are more likely to have a stroke than people without cancer. Do you?"

Rollins looked in the rearview mirror. Theo looked right back at him. "No, sir."

"The reason I say this is because I remember visiting her. She had forgotten how to walk, and never took another step, but the woman *beside* her did. She said that her mind remembered how to walk, but her *body* had to be taught again. It's exactly like M2. He knows how to replicate, Rollins. His mind hasn't forgotten that, but his *body* is out of practice. He has to go for easy targets until he learns to run again. And we need to catch him before he does."

Rollins thought about this for a moment, then breathed the easiest breath he'd taken all week. He deposited them at the subterrane lift that would take them up to Adequate Accounting and returned to his post near the tunnel.

"Clever," Deborah said as they entered the elevator and Rollins was out of earshot. "Your *aunt* would be proud."

"A little embellishment never hurt anyone. I figured he was going to chew off his damn lips if we didn't settle his nerves."

Hollis had been quiet throughout the story but now he clapped Theo on the back. "A master storyteller, good, good. Perfect for your next assignment."

Theo raised an eyebrow. He'd never shied away from an assignment, which is partly what made him indispensable to Hollis, but the sudden show of affection boded poorly. It meant that Hollis was buttering him up. Probably for an assignment that would kill him.

"Dalton's interview with the Brace family—he didn't get much but he *did* think there was something with the kid. Adam's his name. We've been at this too long not to have answers. I need someone on him in case he knows anything. Someone that no one in this shitty city has seen yet. Someone good. Capable of spinning a story. Getting close to him."

Theo's blue eyes swept to the floor designation panel; the green light was scrolling as they rose. "You want me at his school."

"You start tomorrow," Hollis said. "The teacher you're replacing won a contest and will be away for six months." He grinned. His tan-damaged skin crinkled like tissue paper. "The only time the government pays for a vacation and it's not prison. She better damn well enjoy it."

Of all the work Hollis could have assigned, Theo figured this one might actually kill him. He hated kids. That's why, at forty-five, he still had none of his own. At least none that he knew of, but he was as careful as an adulterous executive, so he anticipated no surprises. He wished Adam were in elementary or high school. *Those* kids could be reasonably bribed to behave. But junior high? A bunch of militant adolescents with zero self-control and the emotional stability of manic depressives? Well, Theo would rather go a few rounds with M1. He'd still have his self-respect and the Mimic would expect him to strike, but he couldn't strike a kid.

"I look forward to it," he said.

20. Bulls on a Rink

It was the first nice day of spring, weather so warm it could almost be considered summer, and though winter had finally relinquished its hold on the city, not a single citizen celebrated. Mourning like the lowing of cattle flung through windows and drenched kitchen tables. The keening cries of grieving parents, wives, husbands, and children were met with an armada of casseroles such as the city had never seen. In the homes not personally touched by death, embraces were tighter and words were kinder than they had ever been.

In the midst of the melancholy, however, Adam, Ravi, and Douggie maneuvered away from their parents with promises to call, to stick together, and to be home before dark.

Adam wanted to be around Douggie as much as his father wanted to talk about his mother's lovers to their therapist, but he had invited Douggie to come along because Mrs. Das feared their low numbers would make them easy targets for deranged drivers. He had assured Mrs. Das that Penny and her brother Zhen were also going to meet them, and that he would sacrifice himself to save Ravi's life, if need be. Well, not actually that last part, but he suspected she was wishing

PROJECT DOMAIN

it when Vishi Chawlas' widow, Sanvi, phoned and asked Mrs. Das if she wouldn't mind helping her with Vishi's funeral arrangements.

Instantly, her worry had whipped from Ravi to Sanvi and Ravi was free to go, with the stern warning that if he wasn't home before the sun went down, she'd ship him to Bangladesh for the summer. "You'll spend two months putting ointment on Nani's feet if you're one second late, Ravi," she had said as she shook her finger at him.

Now, after discussing the calluses on Ravi's Nani's feet for some time, they pedaled their bikes out of Ravi's subdivision, toward the dump. Douggie, as athletic as a bar of soap, panted furiously. "I thought w-we were meeting Zhen-Zhen at Mac's? I need a Slurpee."

"They're coming later," Adam said, glancing at Ravi, who knew that Adam hadn't called Zhen. Zhen didn't know about the snake spider because if they found nothing in the ditch, Adam didn't want another friend thinking he was crazy. And as for Penny, well, she just made Adam nervous.

Douggie heaved his bike over a curb and followed Adam and Ravi onto the gravel road, where pedalling was as easy as running in sand. Soon he was lagging so far behind the others, he couldn't tell the difference between Adam's red t-shirt and Ravi's orange zip-up. "Hold up! Slow down!" he called between breaths.

Adam pedalled faster.

Ravi stood on his pedals and glanced back at Douggie struggling in the dust. He shouted ahead. "He annoys me, too, but we need him, Adam. If a monster chases us, we're faster than *him*."

A quick shoulder check confirmed Ravi's assessment. Douggie had given up. He was off his bike and sitting on the edge of the road. Neither of them really wanted Arachnicobra to eat Douggie, but in that moment, they couldn't help but imagining it. Douggie would scream like a girl. But that wasn't the worst part, nor was the idea of a giant spider thing cocooning Douggie's head and sucking his *Reign of Crucor* blitzed brain out. The worst part was that if they left Douggie to be eaten by Adam's maybe-not-imaginary monster and he survived, Douggie would kill them.

Groaning, Adam swung his bike around. Ravi followed, occasionally wheeling away from center when a car or truck passed with loads the city wouldn't collect.

"It stinks out here," Douggie said when they returned.

"Spring runoff." Ravi pointed to the ditch behind them where a steady stream of murky water flowed toward a storm drain under a side road.

"Smells like your *face*," Douggie said stiffly for no reason other than his tender ego. His cheeks were a fierce red and his hair was sweat-stuck to his forehead. He tossed a handful of pebbles at their feet.

Adam straddled his bike but held on to the handlebars, ready to take off if Douggie went after him. "Go back if you want to."

"You never wanted me to come anyway."

"If you weren't such an ass twad, we would," Ravi said honestly. He stretched one of his long brown arms out and pointed up the road. "The dump's just over there. Maybe five minutes. Come check it out with us. Or be an ass twad and go home."

Douggie's puggy little eyes narrowed. A mouthful of steam puffed his cheeks, but his curiosity got the better of him and he let it out in a long, slow, noteless whistle. He picked up his bike and they flanked him, riding at Douggie's pace.

"If there's nothing, it doesn't mean it wasn't there," Adam told them, pedalling slowly for a boy who could cross the city in forty minutes if he wanted to, an hour without even trying.

"What if that guy's there?" Ravi asked with a touch of apprehension. "The creepy one you saw on top of the train."

Adam shuddered. He had told Ravi and Douggie about what he had seen while he and his mother were stuck in traffic. Twice Adam had explained that the man who had been in the paper had been sitting—shoeless, he remembered—atop a train car with blood all over his shirt. When he came home, he used his laptop to look up the name of the man who had been in the paper and found that it was Nick Penner and that Nick Penner, although not entirely a criminal, was a societal pariah if ever there was one. He'd seen a fire and didn't report it, and two people died. When the news came out just last year, Nick's face had been plastered on the Garrett Gazette and nearly every other media outlet across the province. Until now, Adam hadn't ever given him a thought. But presently the memory of Nick, spaced out and bleeding on top of that train, made Adam shiver.

"He's probably one of the people that died yesterday." Adam thought of the thirteen unnamed victims that had made the morning news. "Maybe it just wasn't, you know, *instant*."

"We can take that guy," Douggie said confidently. "There's three of us. Let the fucker try anything and I'll hammer him." He had brightened since they'd collected him, and his ego was beginning to swell the way it did whenever he recovered from an indignity. One of his meaty elbows came up and he swiped the air with it, wobbling only slightly on his creaky bicycle.

They let him have his moment because, in the fragile state Douggie was still in, any slight would send him paddling home, squawking to Mrs. Das that Ravi and Adam were alone out near the dump, looking for a monster.

The sun had grown hotter since they'd left, and by the time the boys reached the waste management facility they were all sweaty and wishing they had brought water. Just past the gate, Adam slowed and pulled his bike to the side of the road. The tire marks from Irma Madinger's Corolla had since disappeared, the gravel like an ebbing ocean refusing to give its secrets, but there were several little orange flags still staked in the grass and tattered yellow police tape still fluttering from the speed limit sign and several trees.

"This is where she . . . where that lady . . ." Ravi said, but was too mesmerized at the proximity to death to finish. He pulled his bike beside Adam's and stared at the emergency markings as though they were entrails freshly hung.

Douggie shrugged, unaffected by the markings of death, more interested in Skitzo Scotty's shitty little cabin slumped far in the field like a pile of old manure. He thought of the shit bombs he'd tossed at Skitzo Scotty's door and the delirious high that had overcome him each time the door wooshed open and Scotty came out running and shouting that he was going to "get you, you little bastard."

He gave his friends one of his impish grins and said, "Let's see if he's home."

Neither Adam nor Ravi were interested in disturbing the house and said so. Douggie huffed something neither of them could hear, and Adam pointed to where he'd seen the spider snake in the ditch.

Adam eyed the speed limit sign and the dump's main gate. "We were *here*." He dug into the gravel with his heel to mark the spot. "And her car was *here*." It looked different during the day with the sun beating down and making everything many shades brighter, but he thought he'd seen the spider snake just behind the speed limit sign, before it morphed into Irma Madinger and bolted into the field. "And the . . . thing . . . was right here. Then it took off that way." He pointed toward Skitzo Scotty's cabin.

They investigated like gold diggers, carefully, methodically, with the tools they had, which really was nothing at all. One way Adam studied the ground, another way Ravi inspected the trees, while Douggie ventured aimlessly around them, stirring up what they were trying to explore. But on the road, in the grass, on the trees, there were no distinctive marks of any kind.

"I swear it was here," Adam said when Douggie asked if he'd possibly started smoking the reefer Bud Ziegler had stolen from his parents.

Ravi and Douggie looked at each other, then Ravi said, "*Sarach* kind of looks like what you said your spider thing looked like. We were playing *Reign of Crucor* right before your parents picked you up. Maybe you thought you saw him because of the game."

He shrugged to let Adam know that it was okay to admit he might have been mistaken. Kids enduring parental strife could be forgiven almost anything, and Ravi's simple shrug said more to Adam than if Ravi had screamed it out loud. Douggie did not know what Adam had been going through, however, and Adam was glad that Ravi had kept that confidence.

"We came all the way out here for *Sarach*?" Douggie threw up his hands.

Sarach, one of the evil mutants in Reign of Crucor, *did* have the heads and body of the spider-thing, Adam admitted to himself. But Sarach was in a video game. He did not creep around the dump, turn into little old ladies, and bound away.

Adam grabbed his handlebars and began walking his bike through the ditch toward the field in front of Skitzo Scotty's house.

"Where are you going?" Ravi called after him. If any of his mother's friends saw him on the road, he could reason his way out of trouble. But he couldn't reason himself out of Skitzo Scotty's field. No way. His mother would send him to Bangladesh for the rest of his life if he did that. And there wouldn't be just Nani's calloused feet to slather, but many, many aunts with weak arms and endless chores.

"We're going to ask him if he's seen it," Adam said.

"No. No way, Adam. Are you out of your mind? He'll kill us. Especially with the shit-tosser here," Ravi said, thumbing toward Douggie.

Ravi was right. Douggie had been *terrible* to Skitzo Scotty. There was no way he was going to help them with Douggie around, Adam realized. If anything, they'd all end up compacted with the garbage and no one would ever find them. He stopped walking. "You better stay here."

Douggie, who hadn't really believed Adam's story about the spider-snake but knew it would come for his head the moment he was alone, deliberated for only a second. "Uh-uh. I'm coming with you. He won't see me, I promise. I'll hide, I swear." He hurried behind them, quietly for a while, then groaned. "I'm thirsty."

"Shhh," Ravi said. They were nearing the house now. Out in the open field with the spring grass still awakening near their ankles, they were as inconspicuous as bulls on a skating rink. "He's going to hear you, ass twad."

"He can see us, Rav. All he has to do is look out his window. I need water," Douggie complained.

"Shhh," Adam said to both of them. He held up a finger and stopped, then he popped out his kickstand and parked his bike. "You two stay here."

They didn't argue.

Most kids were afraid of Skitzo Scotty, but not Adam. In elementary school last year, he had been as nervous as any other kid around the man, and had admittedly engaged in schoolyard rumours, even making some of his own. (*Skitzo Scotty misses the potty. I heard he eats kids. Bet he buries people in his basement.*) But when he got to junior high and he encountered the volunteer janitor after basketball practices, Scotty had politely said hello and stepped aside. The time Adam dropped his jacket when he rushed through the hallway to meet his father outside, Scotty had hurried to their car to give it to him. He might've heard voices and he might've cut off his own ear, but Adam didn't believe he was as evil as everyone said he was.

He glanced back at Ravi and Douggie, now shoving each other around, and stepped from the field onto Scotty's front lawn.

"Ask him if he has water," Douggie called from under Ravi's armpit.

"I'll drown you with it," Adam said without looking back.

Swallowing the lump in his throat, he stared at the house. From the road, Scotty's cabin had seemed uninhabited. But up close, he found many signs of life. A stack of wood piled neatly next to the house. An impressive mansion-like bird feeder filled with seeds. A garden hose neatly coiled. A pair of boots on a thickly bristled mat. There was a small wicker table and two chairs and a pot of small white flowers that probably wouldn't survive the evening frost. Under the window, a long, rugged table held several tools tidily arranged by function. The wires from satellite dishes and antennae hung slightly over the roof of the porch, but besides that, nothing seemed untended. The curtains in the window were drawn, so Adam couldn't tell if Scotty was home, but he glanced at the box of Scotty's truck parked next to the house and knocked on the door.

Ravi and Douggie held their breath mid-tussle. Adam nearly fainted.

The movement inside was like the scattering of dogs. Nails scraped. Legs thudded. Low-throated moans swept like wind past the poorly sealed door. Adam had the brief thought of picking up the hammer on Scotty's table, then shook it off, realizing Douggie had gotten to him. He waited as calmly as a boy about to have his tooth pulled.

"It's Douggie," Ravi called through cupped hands. "He doesn't want to see him."

Waiting for Scotty to answer the door, Adam suddenly felt foolish. What had he been thinking, calling on him like this? What was he going to say? *Excuse me, sir, but did you happen to see a monster in the area? A spider-thing that transforms into a woman?* The same awkward nervousness that jittered up his spine during tests practically blasted him off the porch and he reached for the doorknob to steady himself.

"What are you *doing*?" Ravi shrieked.

There was no reason for him to turn the knob, but that's exactly what Adam did. He touched the cold metal just as it turned and flew open. Scotty Waymore's stern face appeared, but he wasn't looking at Adam. He was looking *past* him, to where Douggie crouched in the short, dead grass like a pig in a garden.

"You boys better turn around before I call the police," Scotty said over Adam's head.

Adam put his hands up. "We don't want any trouble, Mr. Waymore, honest. I . . . I just have a question for you. You don't have to answer it if you want . . ."

"Get off my property!" Scotty boomed, pointing at Douggie. "*Now,* or I'll take every blasted shit bag you've thrown at my house and bury you with it. Now go!"

Douggie didn't even bother to pick up his bike. He ran to the road through field as though it had suddenly become lava. Torn between waiting for Adam and following Douggie, Ravi picked up Douggie's bike and went still on the field.

"I didn't mean to bother you, s-sir," Adam started but then Scotty tipped his weathered chin at him.

"That boy's bad news," he said. "If you're trying to pull a prank on me, son, you can tell your friends you did. Now have a good night." Scotty's face receded as the door slowly began closing.

One of Adam's matchstick arms jerked into the doorway. From the field, Ravi gasped.

Scotty didn't think this boy was a troublemaker, but he didn't like his twiggy little fingers where they shouldn't be. He raised his eyebrows. "You taking lessons from your friend? I saw you in the hallway at school. Never took you for *his* sort." He made no movement to push the fingers out because even a brush of skin could turn him from Skitzo Scotty to the Paranoid Pervert before the fat kid even reached the road.

"I'm sorry Mr. Waymore. I promise I'm not here to cause trouble. Please. I was just wondering . . . my parents and I saw that accident on the road there." Adam pointed past Ravi to the spot where Douggie was hustling onto the gravel. "Well, we didn't see it, actually, but my dad was the one to call the police and ... and ... you know how they don't know what the lady hit ..."

"My dinner is getting cold," Scotty said. Inside the house there was a faint scratching sound. He glanced behind him and squeezed the door almost closed. Only his foot and Adam's fingers were between the door and the jam. One of Scotty's darting eyes fixed on Adam, then away, then on Adam again.

"Something was there that night, Mr. Waymore. I swear it. It was dark, but I saw it in the ditch and then it—*changed*, I guess—and ran into your field. I know I saw it."

"But your friends don't believe you," Scotty said, interested.

"No," Adam admitted.

How does it feel to be like me? Scotty thought but didn't say anything.

"What's he doing?" Douggie's voice carried from the road.

"Let's *go*, Adam," Ravi hollered.

The low-throated moan Adam had heard before Scotty opened the door now rumbled through the house. But it wasn't just one moan. It was several. Like when he and his parents were thinking of buying a dog and walked through a gloomy kennel and left without choosing one because they were all in tears and couldn't stomach the lonely, captured melancholy.

"You have dogs?" Adam asked, now rising on his tip toes, trying to peek over Scotty's shoulder.

"Sorry I can't help you," Scotty said abruptly and closed the door a little more. He had slid his foot back so that only Adam's fingers prevented the door from closing.

The old man was hiding something. Maybe something harmless like a woman. Adam's own mother had many lovers, so it wouldn't have been unusual for Scotty to have one, or some, stretched out inside. He wondered about the unhappy moans and if Scotty had someone or many someones on the bed, maybe even tied up. Could be true, he figured, but then why would Scotty answer the door? It would make more sense to pretend that he wasn't home and that he'd left his truck behind to go for a walk and pop into work at the dump across the field.

"Tell me if you saw it," Adam insisted, dropping back onto his heels. "That's all I want. Did you see it, Mr. Waymore?"

Something behind Scotty gulped.

Adam's eyes swung to narrow space of floor. A black mass undulated across the hardwood like a snake, thickening and thinning its body. It became a foot, became a leg, became a torso, became a head. And then the man that Adam had seen on top of the train with blood down his shirt was standing behind Scotty Waymore.

Then Adam was peeling off the porch, hollering to Ravi to run.

Chapter 21: Tyler Cagey

Theo was in hell. He had reported fifteen minutes early to Principal Irving Hahn's office wearing an itchy tweed jacket and second-hand corduroy pants that were so stiff they seemed to split his balls in half. He was so hot his impenetrable antiperspirant disintegrated. He smelled sour. The chair was uncomfortable. And the crispy-haired secretary—*Joan Tobbles*, by the nameplate on the reception desk—had been ogling him like his perspiration was coconut body oil and he had asked her to rub it all over him under a tropical beach umbrella. He had smiled politely and when she smiled back, bright pink smears of lipstick were on her teeth and he had to stifle the urge not to point it out.

"You're a new one," she purred when he gave her his name—*Tyler Cagey*. "Emma and Lauren are our usual supply teachers. Sometimes Morgan. You're going to be with us a while, huh?" Her eyes darted to his left hand where there was no wedding ring.

He avoided looking at her left hand; didn't want her to think he was interested. "Got lucky, I guess."

She took his brief answer for nerves. "First-day jitters?"

Theo nodded. "Is it that obvious?" He flashed his save-a-country smile, the one that got him into beds and out of trouble whenever he wanted. The more she liked him, the easier this would be. "I haven't taught in a while. My sabbatical that lasted much longer than I thought."

"I always thought of taking one myself," Joan said, rising from her chair and coming around the reception desk. "Travel somewhere warm, explore new cultures, maybe meet someone." She leaned against the desk. Her too-large suit consumed her cigarette-slender frame, as though she were a straw bunched inside a parachute. Even through his own sour sweat he could smell tobacco on her and when she opened her ashtray mouth to continue, Theo noted that the lipstick was gone and that her teeth were little brown-yellow capsules in need of a good bleaching. "Where did you go?" she asked.

"Cambodia," Theo said. "My wife and I planned to volunteer in this village."

Disappointment creased her face. "That would have been an amazing experience."

He nodded. "It would have been, but she passed away shortly after we arrived. There was a malfunction with her scuba gear." He cast his eyes downward, remembering his fake wife and her terrible, fake death.

Joan's hand went to her mouth. It was a major improvement. "Oh, oh dear I'm so sorry. That's terrible." She moved as if to reach out and hug him but then two pimply latecomers stumbled into the office. She gave him a sympathetic smile, scowled at the teens, and retreated to her desk to give them purple slips of paper.

He saw it in her eyes that she wanted to talk more, perhaps offer a shoulder of sympathy, but Irving Hahn walked into the office, shoes soaking wet. Behind him was a boy with his head hanging so low that he appeared almost headless. Only when he tripped over Theo's feet did he raise his eyes, and Theo saw that the kid was on the verge of tears.

"Mr. Cagey, I presume?" Irving said, motioning Theo to his office. Theo followed and sat across from Irving, beside the downcast boy. Hahn removed his shoes and tipped the water from his heels into the pot of a giant philodendron in the corner.

"Elijah must've known you were coming, but instead of welcoming you like the rest of us with applause at an assembly or in the student newspaper, he has gone all out with fireworks in the east wing toilets." He leaned over the desk and looked at Theo's shoes. "But I see you missed his welcoming party."

The subject of Hahn's diatribe shrank in his seat.

"Usually an escapade of this magnitude demands a call to the parents, but since you're the guest of honor, I'm wondering what you would suggest, Mr. Cagey."

"Military school," Theo said automatically, having read the intelligence report on Hahn. According to the file, Hahn was soft on his students but liked to scare the troublemakers with military school whenever a more serious misdemeanor necessitated it. Hahn himself had been a student of the Robert Land Academy in Wellandport, the hefty tuition being doled out by his father when Hahn was just twelve years old, after failing to abide by a strict curfew. Intelligence noted that Hahn hated the school and had authored several articles condemning all boarding schools for long-term psychological trauma on their wards.

Elijah yelped. "Please. I'm sorry Mr. Hahn. Don't tell my parents. Please. My dad will kill me."

"Ahh. The proverbial murdering father. The world seems to be full of them," Hahn said, leaning back in his seat.

Theo watched the contemplating principal and the squirming boy. It was taking too long. He needed to be in the classroom near Adam so he could find M2, not sitting here playing *what's the punishment*.

"How many toilets did you break?" Theo asked Elijah.

"I don't know."

"Three," Hahn said. "Three shattered bowls and one with just a small crack, thanks to the Red Devil that didn't ignite."

"Three," Theo repeated. "That's about four, conservatively three, *hundred* to replace. Each. Do you have twelve hundred dollars Elijah?"

Elijah said he didn't.

"May I?" Theo asked Hahn, who was watching the exchange with interest. Hahn nodded. Theo turned to Elijah. He steepled his fingertips together on his knees. "A long time ago, a group of students pulled something similar at one of the schools I worked at, but with paint. They thought it would be fun to redecorate the halls, if you know what I mean. They also had murdering fathers and about seven dollars between the four of them. The school was old, not as new as St. Jude's, and needed quite a few repairs. We agreed that if they spent their lunch hours repairing the school until their debt was paid off, we wouldn't send them to the wolves. The thing is, they enjoyed the work so much they offered their services free of charge long after they had to." He raised his eyes to Hahn. "What do you think?"

"I think the question is what Elijah thinks. What do you say? We do have quite a bit of graffiti that needs a good scrubbing. And the baseboards near the shop class need to be stripped of glue before we can reattach them."

"I can do that," Elijah said.

"You can and you will," Hahn agreed. "And you will help reinstall the toilets you broke so you can understand the work that goes into getting them there, and maybe next time you will think twice about destroying them." He asked Elijah if he wanted to discuss the arrangement with his parents, but the boy declined then hurried to class.

"That was a good story," Hahn said when they were alone. He wrung out his socks in the planter and drew a pair of running shoes from a cabinet under the printer. "I thought *I* was good but *you*, you are better. My contact at the board usually sends me files on our supply teachers but I have to admit, yours seemed rather thin. You haven't taught in a while, I see."

Though Hahn was occupied with his wet feet, Theo knew he was being sized up. The old man guarded his students with the grace of a swan but the ferocity of a sly crocodile. On the surface Hahn might seem gentle, but underneath his claws were flexed. Theo relayed the fable of his dead wife, willing just the right amount of grief into his face. He wasn't sure if Hahn believed him, but he accepted the man's condolences and followed him to Julia Fowler's noisy class.

They scanned the unattended room through the observation window. Paper planes and wet spit balls zoomed from hands and mouths to heads, walls, and Theo's new desk. Music thrummed from prohibited cell phones. In the back of the classroom the faces of two teens were mashed up against each other, while closer to the front several students were tapping furiously on their devices. Three students were sleeping, if that was even possible, and another was applying lipstick to a puckering blonde.

"Welcome back, Mr. Cagey," Hahn said, and opened the door.

A vacuum of silence swept through the room. It was the same kind of silence that overcame the Under Facility Office whenever Hollis appeared.

"Students," Hahn said simply. He leaned on the edge of the desk and stretched his long legs out. Twenty-seven sets of eyes were suddenly rapt with attention.

"Good morning, Principal Hahn," the students chimed.

"As some of you are aware, Ms. Fowler has swallowed a leprechaun and won a trip around the world." The students whooped with excitement. "Yes. Yes. If we all could be so lucky. Speaking of, we are fortunate to have Mr. Cagey assume the exceptional responsibility of shaping your minds while Ms. Fowler is away." He stretched an arm toward Theo. "Mr. Tyler Cagey, won't you please tell us a little about yourself?"

Theo stood in his stuffy clothes and told them about his imaginary life and his make-believe work experience. Overnight, Cyber Ops had made a point of inserting *Tyler Cagey* into the largest school system in Ontario—Toronto, to be exact—where there were 584 schools, nearly a quarter of a million students, over 40,000 full and part-time staff, and the inability to recognize change when it invaded their system. No doubt Hahn would investigate Theo's background, but no doubt Cyber Ops was prepared for the peek.

"Be easy on him," Hahn told the students before he departed.

Then Theo was alone with twenty-seven teenagers. He opened Julia's status report and quickly identified the appropriate block (English) and tasks in progress (read up to chapter seven in Gary Paulsen's *Hatchet* and write a few paragraphs on what their own reactions would be to awakening after a plane crash in the wilderness). He instructed the students to continue their work on the assignment while he familiarized himself with Julia's notes, but mostly he was watching Adam Brace.

The boy, as gangly as a wet calf, was tapping a pencil on his notepad. The kids that Intelligence had identified as his closest friends—Ravi Das and Douglas Radway—flanked Adam and were leaning over his desk, no doubt discussing anything *but* school.

Theo closed Julia's report and began to tour the rows, starting with Adam's. He came upon the distracted trio so quietly that they jerked and gave sudden yelps of surprise when he spoke. "Anything I can help you with?" he said. He spied Adam's notebook, on which the boy had not written words but drawn something that looked like a fat caterpillar. *A turd,* Theo thought. *The kid's drawing a fucking turd, and I'm the master turd instructor.* He wondered what Dalton Byrd had seen in the boy, and for a brief moment Theo Carver figured he might have been fooled. With Theo away from Overlook, Dalton might perhaps wiggle his way into Hollis' favor. Maybe even get a promotion. But he put on his practiced teacherly smile and said, "I believe art is at the end of the day . . . What are your names?"

The boys mumbled what Theo already knew.

"And is that part of the assignment?" He pointed to the fat caterpillar Adam was attempting to hide under his arm.

"No sir," Adam said, and Theo did not miss the look he exchanged with the other two.

"Let's put that away and work on the assignment, huh?"

The Das kid swung back to the desk in front of Adam's and the Radway kid slumped back into the seat behind. He didn't want to start the wrong way with them, especially since he needed them to talk, so he said, "I wasn't much of a reader when I was your age and, I tell you, it was *torture* to do my assignments. I'd rather have cleaned toilets than write an essay. I actually think I did that once or twice, come to think of it." He laughed and knocked on Adam's desk. "But it's what you're stuck with until you graduate. I'll make you a deal. Until Ms. Fowler returns, you'll have my help. As much as you need. If you ask for help, you'll get it—and I can guarantee you won't get anything below a B, that's roughly seventy to eighty percent. But if you need my help *and* don't ask for it, you won't get anything higher than a B. I've made this deal with former students and not a single one ever received a lower mark. Some even went on to actually enjoy reading, if you can believe it."

Douggie, who had been a poor student all his life, leaned forward again. The short-haired girl sitting behind him wrinkled her nose at his low-hanging pants that exposed much more than she wanted to see. He said, "Just a B, Mr. Cagey? Why not an A? I mean, all the extra work's got to mean more than a B, doesn't it? Can *we* make that deal too?" He gestured to Ravi, who was already an A student and didn't need the help.

"Hmmm," Theo said, pretending to consider. The boy was dangling from his line like a guppy. All Theo had to do was make the meal more enticing and he could reel them all in with just a single cast. "I'm not adverse to an A, provided you do the work. This applies to all subjects. Come to me for help any time and we'll work to get you that A."

It sounded teacherly enough. Not overly promising. Just the right touch of *you got this*. Nothing Hahn would frown upon. Hell, it could even make him teacher of the year, not that he wanted it. What he *did* want was Adam Brace to spill whatever he knew about the night of Irma Madinger's accident, no matter how insignificant.

"Fuck, yeah," Theo heard as he walked away.

According to his records, Douggie had never gotten an A, not even in kindergarten when they tossed badges around like confetti. His eagerness would bode well for the investigation, provided Theo could naturally squeeze the kids quickly enough. For the rest of the morning periods, Theo leaned on his military experience to keep them in line and by lunch time he felt he hadn't completely lost them, and that was a win.

The bell rang. The kids whammed books shut and abandoned desks with the speed of fleeing buffalo. He needed to talk to Adam but knew that if he were impatient he could jeopardize the investigation and blow his cover. Instead, he settled into Julia Fowler's report and ate a bagged lunch—made by one of UFO's chefs—alone at his desk. He logged into his St. Jude's email account and saw a single message from Irving Hahn, addressed to all staff, welcoming Tyler Cagey from Toronto to their St. Jude's family. It ended with a not-so-subtle nudge that the junior boys' soccer team was looking for an assistant coach. Babysitting, he had to do. Coaching, Theo would not.

"We don't bite, you know," said a pretty redhead leaning into the open doorway. She was carrying a small lunch bag and tumbler that she sipped from as he removed his feet from the top of the desk and sat up.

He grinned. "They all say that, and the next thing you know, you've got chunks out of your planner and spit wads in the shape body parts under your desk." It was a bit forward, but Claire's file stated that she was single, and it never hurt to flirt a little.

"Sounds like you have experience."

"Enough to last a lifetime."

Now she walked into the room. She lowered the tumbler and crossed her arms. "Bet you I can beat that."

"Let's hear it."

"I had a student spike my protein shake with LSD."

"No!" Theo slapped the desk.

Claire nodded. "That's why I don't teach high school anymore."

"All right—?"

"*Claire*," she said. "And the kids here are good kids, but they're only marginally better. I've had fish stuffed in the bottom of my desk and one time it went missing completely. We never found it."

"Maybe I *should* eat in the staff room. Safety in numbers, right?"

She laughed and he found himself enjoying that laugh. Probably because he'd expected her to be as crazy as her father, the dump manager, but she seemed nothing like him. She had both ears, for one, and seemed reasonably intelligent. When Hollis tasked him with babysitting, he'd lugged two boxes of files to his apartment over the Sleepy Sloth and got to work. He crammed as if for a test, memorizing the life of Irving Hahn, Adam Brace, Ravi Das, and Douglas Radway. But he didn't stop there. He studied the files of the other twenty-four kids in his class and the office staff and the fourteen teachers who would be his colleagues until M2 was either captured or too many people were killed and the school was shut down entirely. That's how he discovered that Chief Dan Fogel's buddy, Scotty Waymore, was Claire Bishop's father and that they had been estranged since the old man went off the deep end.

"Are you all right, Tyler? It is Tyler, right?" She waved a hand in front of his face.

Theo blinked. "Sorry. I was just imagining your desk. What kind of fish, did you say?"

"Everyone's a comedian. Whenever my grandfather goes fishing, he brings the guts back for my cat. Remind me to stick some in your drawer before Julia gets back."

"No LSD?" Theo was full-on flirting now, but he couldn't help it. The stress of the last few days had worn on him, and a bit of fun might be just what he needed.

"I'm all out. But now that we know each other so well, let me give you the lowdown on everyone. Mind if I sit?"

He gestured to Tabitha Worley's desk at the front of the center row. Claire sat and unzipped her lunch bag, pulling out a container of salad and a packet of crackers. She smashed the crackers in the packet, opened it and sprinkled the crumbs into the salad. "Don't knock it until you try it," she said when he looked at her strangely. "It's really like croutons, but cheaper and fresher. Want to try?" She offered him her fork.

He politely declined.

"You're missing out," she said, and spied the clock. "Okay, I have fifteen minutes. School is in session, Mr. Cagey. Listen carefully."

Between bites of salad, she told him a lot of what he'd already read in the intelligence reports but also quite a few things that he did not know. He'd learned that two of his students sometimes snuck weed in their pencil cases and that Jason Orr, a thirteen-year-old with raging hormones, couldn't sit near any of the girls because he couldn't concentrate when he was around them. She told him that teacher Fentworth Plumley, an aging Brit from Sussex, couldn't take a joke and was quick to report anything that offended him, and that Ashley Kelby, a twenty-three-year-old student teacher from the University of London, was sleeping with Mack Seaver, the forty-seven-year-old, *married* school counselor. The science teacher, Gwen Hayes, habitually left the school during the third block for a high-needs latte—the kind with twenty-seven subheadings and no resemblance to actual coffee—while her students pretended to study. Edith Yost, a prickly English teacher, had been in trouble with Hahn for gluing dead crickets to the essays of students she believed weren't reading the books she assigned.

"No way," Theo said at that one. "Crickets? Really?"

Claire nodded and a little snort of laughter blew the empty cracker packet to the floor. She picked it up. "It actually seems to work, for some odd reason. But it's not the weirdest thing that's happened around here. We had a teacher marry a student the day after he graduated. They couldn't do anything about it because he was old enough by then, but they fired her anyway. And then there's Larry."

Theo consulted the filing cabinet in his head. Larry Heep was a fifty-one-year-old math teacher. Single. No children. Acrylic left eye. Childhood cancer survivor. Idolized Jim Carrey and was known to hang a personalized, autographed picture of the celebrity in the classroom. Average guy on paper. Nothing remarkable that had caused Theo to remember him.

"There's always a Larry somewhere," he joked. "Tell me about him."

"He's got hands like an octopus and a nose like a bloodhound." She glanced at the open door to see if anyone was in the hall, then lowered her voice. "He's kind of like everyone's stalker. Pretends he's your best friend. Always around. *Accidently*," she air-quoted, "bumps into the female teachers and his hands just happen to be in the wrong places. And he slaps Mack's butt whenever he sees him, but Mack doesn't say anything because he's, you know . . ."

"Sleeping with the student teacher and doesn't want to cause a fuss?"

"Uh-huh."

"Creepy," Theo said, wondering how a man like Hahn could overlook a guy like that.

"There's always an excuse, of course, but don't say I didn't warn you in case you get your butt smacked, too."

He smiled. There were so many ways he could respond, but he held his tongue. No need to be a creep too. Yet she was blushing a little when the bell rang and she packed up her lunch bag. "Thanks for the advice," he said.

Students began rumbling down the hall. Claire went to the door. "You're doing great, by the way. No one has died yet. Just remember that no matter what happens, you get your peace at three every day."

Without thinking, he saluted her the way he would have Hollis. The naval salute of the Canadian Armed Forces. Had Hahn seen it, no doubt he would have been suspicious. But Claire just laughed and disappeared in the hallway. The kids slouched into the room while Theo gathered his composure. He had to be more careful. No matter how much he enjoyed her company, she was a liability. She was Scotty Waymore's daughter and an outsider. An outsider that could doom the Project. He emptied his fondness for her, drained it like a sieve, and had Ravi lead the class to the gymnasium for their next block.

As expected, Adam was as agile as a Martian. Many times, he was tempted to call the boy Mendawall or the pipsqueak Pintree. The Radway kid was even worse. Theo watched Douggie swat his badminton racket, looking so much like a flailing salmon upriver that he thought of the fat turd Adam had drawn. The way the drawing was concealed, Theo had really only seen a snippet. Part of a whole. But now he wondered if it really was what he'd originally thought it was. Maybe it was something Adam had seen that night, or maybe not, but he wouldn't know until he saw the paper.

"Adam, I need to step out for a minute. Can you keep an eye on everyone until I'm back?"

The boy swatted and missed the birdie whipped at him by Ravi. He nodded without so much as a glance in Theo's direction.

Back in the classroom, Theo went to Adam's desk and opened his binder. He flipped through Adam's notes in English, Math, Science, Social Studies, Religion, and finally got to the tab marked *ART*. But the drawing was not there. Then he remembered the drawing had been in a sketchbook and located it by unzipping the binder's interior fabric sleeve. Theo gently turned the pages and saw that Adam had the makings of a gifted artist. The boy might be athletically awkward, but his pencil strokes were sure and steady. He had an obvious penchant for zombies in everyday settings. Zombies walking dogs. Zombies playing hockey. A zombie couple fighting. A few pages of only eyes. A few of decrepit, rotting hands.

He turned a page and the scene that next unfolded was a snapshot of Irma Madinger's accident. Two cars stood on a desolate road. One had a dead female zombie with a deformed head. Another zombie man was peeking in the window. Away from this was the profile of a slightly larger car with a zombie woman on her phone and a zombie boy in the back seat looking *away* from the accident. To the left of the zombie boy in Adam's pencil-shaded ditch was M2.

Theo gritted his teeth. Dalton was right. Adam *had* seen their fugitive.

Forcing himself to remain calm, he turned the page. The murdered construction worker sat on a train car. The face wasn't quite Nick Penner, but it was close. And his eyes were vacant enough for Theo to know no human dwelled inside that body.

On the next page he saw the unmistakable lump of the fat caterpillar-turd wedged behind an open doorway. Only, it wasn't what Theo had thought it was. It was one of M2's long, slithering legs. He knew it because this was the only place where Adam's pencil strokes weren't sure. The certain lines of the door contrasted starkly to the lump. Adam had drawn it in motion, but not steady motion. He had drawn it as though it was vibrating. More, further up the page at the very top of the door crack was the phantom face of Nick Penner materializing as if live on the page.

Theo drew out his phone and sent the images to Hollis.

"Something of Adam's interests you?" Hahn said from the doorway. His arms were crossed and he was looking at Theo yet again with a wise expression that said he knew everything there was to know at St. Jude's, and that if something new were to be found, he would find it.

It gave Theo a start, but he confined the shock to his insides. He casually closed the sketchbook and summoned his inventiveness. "Incredible art for such a young age. I saw him drawing something during the first block, nothing on task, though. I just wanted to see what it was. I once had a student draw his parents shooting heroin, but we had no idea anything like that was happening at his house. A welfare check confirmed it. Just being cautious."

Hahn raised his eyebrows and pursed his lips. "A good story. You know, it's never good to start a relationship with lies. They don't work out. Something you should know about me, Tyler, is that I can spot a liar like an owl does a hare. Does he get the hare because he is stronger? Has bigger claws? No. That's not it. He eats because he *sees*. Even in the dark, even with the hare's camouflage, the owl finds what he's looking for because when he's not seeing, his ears don't let anything pass."

"Forgive me for being concerned—" Theo started.

Hahn cut him off and walked inside the room, his hands in his pockets. He leaned against a desk and sat. "I went to military school when I was younger," Hahn said, sighing through his nose as though he was weighing a great decision. "And something tells me you knew that. You weren't five minutes in my office when you suggested it to Elijah. You didn't even think about it. Just spit it out like that." He removed a hand from his pocket and snapped his fingers. "You might say it was a coincidence, but I don't think so. You see, I may not have been in the military for many years, but a man does not forget his training. Situational awareness is *everything*. Do you know that when you told me about your wife there were four what I call *tells* that told me you were lying? Alone, each could be excused, but add them all together and they're irrefutable *proof*." He raised his index finger. "First, you had to think about the story before you delivered it. I saw it in your eyes. It wasn't sorrow; I've seen enough to know when it's real. Second, there was an intensity that doesn't speak to a death seven years ago. You spoke as though it had happened yesterday, as though you had *contrived* it yesterday." A third finger went up. "And there were several hesitations—almost unnoticeable, I'll give you that—to buy yourself time. Not because you didn't want to share your personal tragedy, but because you were *creating* the tragedy. One does not say *um* or *ah* when recalling such an event. If it has actually happened, a person does not forget." He was at the fourth finger now. "And you never blinked. Not once during the whole story. Could it be that your body was under stress, relaying such personal hardship? Perhaps. But in my experience, people who don't blink under pressure are the ones reinforcing their defences. They don't blink because they're threatened and are trying harder to prove themselves. Why would you have to prove anything but your vocation to me?"

Theo didn't answer.

"I'm distressing you," Hahn said. "I can see it in your jaw. But I need to be clear with you, Tyler. I will not tolerate anything but truth. I bring up my assessment of your story because I believe I've caught you being untruthful again. Maybe you have a good reason for making up the story of your wife, but I can assure you that after only four hours in our school, you do not have an adequate reason for invading a student's privacy, nor do you have a reason for taking pictures of his personal property. Please delete the images right now."

Theo did. Hollis would have the pictures already, so it didn't matter.

"Now, I don't want you to speak. I want you to listen. One more incident of any kind and you will not be teaching here any longer. You will respect everyone in this building, especially our students. And I suggest you get your story straight, whatever it is, so you can believe it yourself when you're telling it."

There was nothing for Theo to do but lower his head and nod like a whipped dog. "Yes, sir."

Hahn glared at him, *through* him, tipped his chin once, and was gone.

21. Tyler Cagey

Theo was in hell. He had reported fifteen minutes early to Principal Irving Hahn's office wearing an itchy tweed jacket and second-hand corduroy pants that were so stiff they seemed to split his balls in half. He was so hot his impenetrable antiperspirant disintegrated. He smelled sour. The chair was uncomfortable. And the crispy-haired secretary—Joan Tobbles, by the nameplate on the reception desk—had been ogling him like his perspiration was coconut body oil and he had asked her to rub it all over him under a tropical beach umbrella. He had smiled politely and when she smiled back, bright pink smears of lipstick were on her teeth and he had to stifle the urge not to point it out.

"You're a new one," she purred when he gave her his name—Tyler Cagey. "Emma and Lauren are our usual supply teachers. Sometimes Morgan. You're going to be with us a while, huh?" Her eyes darted to his left hand where there was no wedding ring.

He avoided looking at her left hand; didn't want her to think he was interested. "Got lucky, I guess."

She took his brief answer for nerves. "First-day jitters?"

Theo nodded. "Is it that obvious?" He flashed his save-a-country smile, the one that got him into beds and out of trouble whenever he wanted. The more she liked him, the easier this would be. "I haven't taught in a while. My sabbatical that lasted much longer than I thought."

"I always thought of taking one myself," Joan said, rising from her chair and coming around the reception desk. "Travel somewhere warm, explore new cultures, maybe meet someone." She leaned against the desk. Her too-large suit consumed her cigarette-slender frame, as though she were a straw bunched inside a parachute. Even through his own sour sweat he could smell tobacco on her and when she opened her ashtray mouth to continue, Theo noted that the lipstick was gone and that her teeth were little brown-yellow capsules in need of a good bleaching. "Where did you go?" she asked.

"Cambodia," Theo said. "My wife and I planned to volunteer in this village."

Disappointment creased her face. "That would have been an amazing experience."

He nodded. "It would have been, but she passed away shortly after we arrived. There was a malfunction with her scuba gear." He cast his eyes downward, remembering his fake wife and her terrible, fake death.

Joan's hand went to her mouth. It was a major improvement. "Oh, oh dear I'm so sorry. That's terrible." She moved as if to reach out and hug him but then two pimply latecomers stumbled into the office. She gave him a sympathetic smile, scowled at the teens, and retreated to her desk to give them purple slips of paper.

He saw it in her eyes that she wanted to talk more, perhaps offer a shoulder of sympathy, but Irving Hahn walked into the office, shoes soaking wet. Behind him was a boy with his head hanging so low that he appeared almost headless. Only when he tripped over Theo's feet did he raise his eyes, and Theo saw that the kid was on the verge of tears.

"Mr. Cagey, I presume?" Irving said, motioning Theo to his office. Theo followed and sat across from Irving, beside the downcast boy. Hahn removed his shoes and tipped the water from his heels into the pot of a giant philodendron in the corner.

"Elijah must've known you were coming, but instead of welcoming you like the rest of us with applause at an assembly or in the student newspaper, he has gone all out with fireworks in the east wing toilets." He leaned over the desk and looked at Theo's shoes. "But I see you missed his welcoming party."

The subject of Hahn's diatribe shrank in his seat.

"Usually an escapade of this magnitude demands a call to the parents, but since you're the guest of honor, I'm wondering what you would suggest, Mr. Cagey."

"Military school," Theo said automatically, having read the intelligence report on Hahn. According to the file, Hahn was soft on his students but liked to scare the troublemakers with military school whenever a more serious misdemeanor necessitated it. Hahn himself had been a student of the Robert Land Academy in Wellandport, the hefty tuition being doled out by his father when Hahn was just twelve years old, after failing to abide by a strict curfew. Intelligence noted that Hahn hated the school and had authored several articles condemning all boarding schools for long-term psychological trauma on their wards.

Elijah yelped. "Please. I'm sorry Mr. Hahn. Don't tell my parents. Please. My dad will kill me."

"Ahh. The proverbial murdering father. The world seems to be full of them," Hahn said, leaning back in his seat.

Theo watched the contemplating principal and the squirming boy. It was taking too long. He needed to be in the classroom near Adam so he could find M2, not sitting here playing what's the punishment.

"How many toilets did you break?" Theo asked Elijah.

"I don't know."

"Three," Hahn said. "Three shattered bowls and one with just a small crack, thanks to the Red Devil that didn't ignite."

"Three," Theo repeated. "That's about four, conservatively three, hundred to replace. Each. Do you have twelve hundred dollars Elijah?"

Elijah said he didn't.

"May I?" Theo asked Hahn, who was watching the exchange with interest. Hahn nodded. Theo turned to Elijah. He steepled his fingertips together on his knees. "A long time ago, a group of students pulled something similar at one of the schools I worked at, but with paint. They thought it would be fun to redecorate the halls, if you know what I mean. They also had murdering fathers and about seven dollars between the four of them. The school was old, not as new as St. Jude's, and needed quite a few repairs. We agreed that if they spent their lunch hours repairing the school until their debt was paid off, we wouldn't send them to the wolves. The thing is, they enjoyed the work so much they offered their services free of charge long after they had to." He raised his eyes to Hahn. "What do you think?"

"I think the question is what Elijah thinks. What do you say? We do have quite a bit of graffiti that needs a good scrubbing. And the baseboards near the shop class need to be stripped of glue before we can reattach them."

"I can do that," Elijah said.

"You can and you will," Hahn agreed. "And you will help reinstall the toilets you broke so you can understand the work that goes into getting them there, and maybe next time you will think twice about destroying them." He asked Elijah if he wanted to discuss the arrangement with his parents, but the boy declined then hurried to class.

"That was a good story," Hahn said when they were alone. He wrung out his socks in the planter and drew a pair of running shoes from a cabinet under the printer. "I thought I was good but you, you are better. My contact at the board usually sends me files on our supply teachers but I have to admit, yours seemed rather thin. You haven't taught in a while, I see."

Though Hahn was occupied with his wet feet, Theo knew he was being sized up. The old man guarded his students with the grace of a swan but the ferocity of a sly crocodile. On the surface Hahn might seem gentle, but underneath his claws were flexed. Theo relayed the fable of his dead wife, willing just the right amount of grief into his face. He wasn't sure if Hahn believed him, but he accepted the man's condolences and followed him to Julia Fowler's noisy class.

They scanned the unattended room through the observation window. Paper planes and wet spit balls zoomed from hands and mouths to heads, walls, and Theo's new desk. Music thrummed from prohibited cell phones. In the back of the classroom the faces of two teens were mashed up against each other, while closer to the front several students were tapping furiously on their devices. Three students were sleeping, if that was even possible, and another was applying lipstick to a puckering blonde.

"Welcome back, Mr. Cagey," Hahn said, and opened the door.

A vacuum of silence swept through the room. It was the same kind of silence that overcame the Under Facility Office whenever Hollis appeared.

"Students," Hahn said simply. He leaned on the edge of the desk and stretched his long legs out. Twenty-seven sets of eyes were suddenly rapt with attention.

"Good morning, Principal Hahn," the students chimed.

"As some of you are aware, Ms. Fowler has swallowed a leprechaun and won a trip around the world." The students whooped with excitement. "Yes. Yes. If we all could be so lucky. Speaking of, we are fortunate to have Mr. Cagey assume the exceptional responsibility of shaping your minds while Ms. Fowler is away." He stretched an arm toward Theo. "Mr. Tyler Cagey, won't you please tell us a little about yourself?"

Theo stood in his stuffy clothes and told them about his imaginary life and his make-believe work experience. Overnight, Cyber Ops had made a point of inserting Tyler Cagey into the largest school system in Ontario—Toronto, to be exact—where there were 584 schools, nearly a quarter of a million students, over 40,000 full and part-time staff, and the inability to recognize change when it invaded their system. No doubt Hahn would investigate Theo's background, but no doubt Cyber Ops was prepared for the peek.

"Be easy on him," Hahn told the students before he departed.

Then Theo was alone with twenty-seven teenagers. He opened Julia's status report and quickly identified the appropriate block (English) and tasks in progress (read up to chapter seven in Gary Paulsen's Hatchet and write a few paragraphs on what their own reactions would be to awakening after a plane crash in the wilderness). He instructed the students to continue their work on the assignment while he familiarized himself with Julia's notes, but mostly he was watching Adam Brace.

The boy, as gangly as a wet calf, was tapping a pencil on his notepad. The kids that Intelligence had identified as his closest friends—Ravi Das and Douglas Radway—flanked Adam and were leaning over his desk, no doubt discussing anything but school.

Theo closed Julia's report and began to tour the rows, starting with Adam's. He came upon the distracted trio so quietly that they jerked and gave sudden yelps of surprise when he spoke. "Anything I can help you with?" he said. He spied Adam's notebook, on which the boy had not written words but drawn something that looked like a fat caterpillar. A turd, Theo thought. The kid's drawing a fucking turd, and I'm the master turd instructor. He wondered what Dalton Byrd had seen in the boy, and for a brief moment Theo Carver figured he might have been fooled. With Theo away from Overlook,

Dalton might perhaps wiggle his way into Hollis' favor. Maybe even get a promotion. But he put on his practiced teacherly smile and said, "I believe art is at the end of the day... What are your names?"

The boys mumbled what Theo already knew.

"And is that part of the assignment?" He pointed to the fat caterpillar Adam was attempting to hide under his arm.

"No sir," Adam said, and Theo did not miss the look he exchanged with the other two.

"Let's put that away and work on the assignment, huh?"

The Das kid swung back to the desk in front of Adam's and the Radway kid slumped back into the seat behind. He didn't want to start the wrong way with them, especially since he needed them to talk, so he said, "I wasn't much of a reader when I was your age and, I tell you, it was torture to do my assignments. I'd rather have cleaned toilets than write an essay. I actually think I did that once or twice, come to think of it." He laughed and knocked on Adam's desk. "But it's what you're stuck with until you graduate. I'll make you a deal. Until Ms. Fowler returns, you'll have my help. As much as you need. If you ask for help, you'll get it—and I can guarantee you won't get anything below a B, that's roughly seventy to eighty percent. But if you need my help and don't ask for it, you won't get anything higher than a B. I've made this deal with former students and not a single one ever received a lower mark. Some even went on to actually enjoy reading, if you can believe it."

Douggie, who had been a poor student all his life, leaned forward again. The short-haired girl sitting behind him wrinkled her nose at his low-hanging pants that exposed much more than she wanted to see. He said, "Just a B, Mr. Cagey? Why not an A? I mean, all the extra work's got to mean more than a B, doesn't it? Can we make that deal too?" He gestured to Ravi, who was already an A student and didn't need the help.

"Hmmm," Theo said, pretending to consider. The boy was dangling from his line like a guppy. All Theo had to do was make the meal more enticing and he could reel them all in with just a single cast. "I'm not adverse to an A, provided you do the work. This applies to all subjects. Come to me for help any time and we'll work to get you that A."

It sounded teacherly enough. Not overly promising. Just the right touch of you got this. Nothing Hahn would frown upon. Hell, it could even make him teacher of the year, not that he wanted it. What he did want was Adam Brace to spill whatever he knew about the night of Irma Madinger's accident, no matter how insignificant.

"Fuck, yeah," Theo heard as he walked away.

According to his records, Douggie had never gotten an A, not even in kindergarten when they tossed badges around like confetti. His eagerness would bode well for the investigation, provided Theo could naturally squeeze the kids quickly enough. For the rest of the morning periods, Theo leaned on his military experience to keep them in line and by lunch time he felt he hadn't completely lost them, and that was a win.

The bell rang. The kids whammed books shut and abandoned desks with the speed of fleeing buffalo. He needed to talk to Adam but knew that if he were impatient he could jeopardize the investigation and blow his cover. Instead, he settled into Julia Fowler's report and ate a bagged lunch—made by one of UFO's chefs—alone at his desk. He logged into his St. Jude's email account and saw a single message from Irving Hahn, addressed to all staff, welcoming Tyler Cagey from Toronto to their St. Jude's family. It ended with a not-so-subtle nudge that the junior boys' soccer team was looking for an assistant coach. Babysitting, he had to do. Coaching, Theo would not.

"We don't bite, you know," said a pretty redhead leaning into the open doorway. She was carrying a small lunch bag and tumbler that she sipped from as he removed his feet from the top of the desk and sat up.

He grinned. "They all say that, and the next thing you know, you've got chunks out of your planner and spit wads in the shape body parts under your desk." It was a bit forward, but Claire's file stated that she was single, and it never hurt to flirt a little.

"Sounds like you have experience."

"Enough to last a lifetime."

Now she walked into the room. She lowered the tumbler and crossed her arms. "Bet you I can beat that."

"Let's hear it."

"I had a student spike my protein shake with LSD."

"No!" Theo slapped the desk.

Claire nodded. "That's why I don't teach high school anymore."

"All right—?"

"Claire," she said. "And the kids here are good kids, but they're only marginally better. I've had fish stuffed in the bottom of my desk and one time it went missing completely. We never found it."

"Maybe I should eat in the staff room. Safety in numbers, right?"

She laughed and he found himself enjoying that laugh. Probably because he'd expected her to be as crazy as her father, the dump manager, but she seemed nothing like him. She had both ears, for one, and seemed reasonably intelligent. When Hollis tasked him with babysitting, he'd lugged two boxes of files to his apartment over the Sleepy Sloth and got to work. He crammed as if for a test, memorizing the life of Irving Hahn, Adam Brace, Ravi Das, and Douglas Radway. But he didn't stop there. He studied the files of the other twenty-four kids in his class and the office staff and the fourteen teachers who would be his colleagues until M2 was either captured or too many people were killed and the school was shut down entirely. That's how he discovered that Chief Dan Fogel's buddy, Scotty Waymore, was Claire Bishop's father and that they had been estranged since the old man went off the deep end.

"Are you all right, Tyler? It is Tyler, right?" She waved a hand in front of his face.

Theo blinked. "Sorry. I was just imagining your desk. What kind of fish, did you say?"

"Everyone's a comedian. Whenever my grandfather goes fishing, he brings the guts back for my cat. Remind me to stick some in your drawer before Julia gets back."

"No LSD?" Theo was full-on flirting now, but he couldn't help it. The stress of the last few days had worn on him, and a bit of fun might be just what he needed.

"I'm all out. But now that we know each other so well, let me give you the lowdown on everyone. Mind if I sit?"

He gestured to Tabitha Worley's desk at the front of the center row. Claire sat and unzipped her lunch bag, pulling out a container of salad and a packet of crackers. She smashed the crackers in the packet, opened it and sprinkled the crumbs into the salad. "Don't knock it until you try it," she said when he looked at her strangely. "It's really like croutons, but cheaper and fresher. Want to try?" She offered him her fork.

He politely declined.

"You're missing out," she said, and spied the clock. "Okay, I have fifteen minutes. School is in session, Mr. Cagey. Listen carefully."

Between bites of salad, she told him a lot of what he'd already read in the intelligence reports but also quite a few things that he did not know. He'd learned that two of his students sometimes snuck weed in their pencil cases and that Jason Orr, a thirteen-year-old with raging hormones, couldn't sit near any of the girls because he couldn't concentrate when he was around them. She told him that teacher Fentworth Plumley, an aging Brit from Sussex, couldn't take a joke and was quick to report anything that offended him, and that Ashley Kelby, a twenty-three-year-old student teacher from the University of London, was sleeping with Mack Seaver, the forty-seven-year-old, married school counselor. The science teacher, Gwen Hayes, habitually left the school during the third block for a high-needs latte—the kind with twenty-seven subheadings and no resemblance to actual coffee—while her students pretended to study. Edith Yost, a prickly English teacher, had been in trouble with Hahn for gluing dead crickets to the essays of students she believed weren't reading the books she assigned.

"No way," Theo said at that one. "Crickets? Really?"

Claire nodded and a little snort of laughter blew the empty cracker packet to the floor. She picked it up. "It actually seems to work, for some odd reason. But it's not the weirdest thing that's happened around here. We had a teacher marry a student the day after he graduated. They couldn't do anything about it because he was old enough by then, but they fired her anyway. And then there's Larry."

Theo consulted the filing cabinet in his head. Larry Heep was a fifty-one-year-old math teacher. Single. No children. Acrylic left eye. Childhood cancer survivor. Idolized Jim Carrey and was known to hang a personalized, autographed picture of the celebrity in the classroom. Average guy on paper. Nothing remarkable that had caused Theo to remember him.

"There's always a Larry somewhere," he joked. "Tell me about him."

"He's got hands like an octopus and a nose like a bloodhound." She glanced at the open door to see if anyone was in the hall, then lowered her voice. "He's kind of like everyone's stalker. Pretends he's your best friend. Always around. Accidently," she air-quoted, "bumps into the female teachers and his hands just happen to be in the wrong places. And he slaps Mack's butt whenever he sees him, but Mack doesn't say anything because he's, you know . . ."

"Sleeping with the student teacher and doesn't want to cause a fuss?"

"Uh-huh."

"Creepy," Theo said, wondering how a man like Hahn could overlook a guy like that.

"There's always an excuse, of course, but don't say I didn't warn you in case you get your butt smacked, too."

He smiled. There were so many ways he could respond, but he held his tongue. No need to be a creep too. Yet she was blushing a little when the bell rang and she packed up her lunch bag. "Thanks for the advice," he said.

Students began rumbling down the hall. Claire went to the door. "You're doing great, by the way. No one has died yet. Just remember that no matter what happens, you get your peace at three every day."

Without thinking, he saluted her the way he would have Hollis. The naval salute of the Canadian Armed Forces. Had Hahn seen it, no doubt he would have been suspicious. But Claire just laughed and disappeared in the hallway. The kids slouched into the room while Theo gathered his composure. He had to be more careful. No matter how much he enjoyed her company, she was a liability. She was Scotty Waymore's daughter and an outsider. An outsider that could doom the Project. He emptied his fondness for her, drained it like a sieve, and had Ravi lead the class to the gymnasium for their next block.

As expected, Adam was as agile as a Martian. Many times, he was tempted to call the boy Mendawall or the pipsqueak Pintree. The Radway kid was even worse. Theo watched Douggie swat his badminton racket, looking so much like a flailing salmon upriver that he thought of the fat turd Adam had drawn. The way the drawing was concealed, Theo had really only seen a snippet. Part of a whole. But now he wondered if it really was what he'd originally thought it was. Maybe it was something Adam had seen that night, or maybe not, but he wouldn't know until he saw the paper.

"Adam, I need to step out for a minute. Can you keep an eye on everyone until I'm back?"

The boy swatted and missed the birdie whipped at him by Ravi. He nodded without so much as a glance in Theo's direction.

Back in the classroom, Theo went to Adam's desk and opened his binder. He flipped through Adam's notes in English, Math, Science, Social Studies, Religion, and finally got to the tab marked

ART. But the drawing was not there. Then he remembered the drawing had been in a sketchbook and located it by unzipping the binder's interior fabric sleeve. Theo gently turned the pages and saw that Adam had the makings of a gifted artist. The boy might be athletically awkward, but his pencil strokes were sure and steady. He had an obvious penchant for zombies in everyday settings. Zombies walking dogs. Zombies playing hockey. A zombie couple fighting. A few pages of only eyes. A few of decrepit, rotting hands.

He turned a page and the scene that next unfolded was a snapshot of Irma Madinger's accident. Two cars stood on a desolate road. One had a dead female zombie with a deformed head. Another zombie man was peeking in the window. Away from this was the profile of a slightly larger car with a zombie woman on her phone and a zombie boy in the back seat looking away from the accident. To the left of the zombie boy in Adam's pencil-shaded ditch was M2.

Theo gritted his teeth. Dalton was right. Adam had seen their fugitive.

Forcing himself to remain calm, he turned the page. The murdered construction worker sat on a train car. The face wasn't quite Nick Penner, but it was close. And his eyes were vacant enough for Theo to know no human dwelled inside that body.

On the next page he saw the unmistakable lump of the fat caterpillar-turd wedged behind an open doorway. Only, it wasn't what Theo had thought it was. It was one of M2's long, slithering legs. He knew it because this was the only place where Adam's pencil strokes weren't sure. The certain lines of the door contrasted starkly to the lump. Adam had drawn it in motion, but not steady motion. He had drawn it as though it was vibrating. More, further up the page at the very top of the door crack was the phantom face of Nick Penner materializing as if live on the page.

Theo drew out his phone and sent the images to Hollis.

"Something of Adam's interests you?" Hahn said from the doorway. His arms were crossed and he was looking at Theo yet again with a wise expression that said he knew everything there was to know at St. Jude's, and that if something new were to be found, he would find it.

It gave Theo a start, but he confined the shock to his insides. He casually closed the sketchbook and summoned his inventiveness. "Incredible art for such a young age. I saw him drawing something during the first block, nothing on task, though. I just wanted to see what it was. I once had a student draw his parents shooting heroin, but we had no idea anything like that was happening at his house. A welfare check confirmed it. Just being cautious."

Hahn raised his eyebrows and pursed his lips. "A good story. You know, it's never good to start a relationship with lies. They don't work out. Something you should know about me, Tyler, is that I can spot a liar like an owl does a hare. Does he get the hare because he is stronger? Has bigger claws? No. That's not it. He eats because he sees. Even in the dark, even with the hare's camouflage, the owl finds what he's looking for because when he's not seeing, his ears don't let anything pass."

"Forgive me for being concerned—" Theo started.

Hahn cut him off and walked inside the room, his hands in his pockets. He leaned against a desk and sat. "I went to military school when I was younger," Hahn said, sighing through his nose as though he was weighing a great decision. "And something tells me you knew that. You weren't five minutes in my office when you suggested it to Elijah. You didn't even think about it. Just spit it out like that." He removed a hand from his pocket and snapped his fingers. "You might say it was a coincidence, but I don't think so. You see, I may not have been in the military for many years, but a man does not forget his training. Situational awareness is everything. Do you know that when you told me about your wife there were four what I call tells that told me you were lying? Alone, each could be excused, but add them all together and they're irrefutable proof." He raised his index finger. "First, you had to think about the story before you delivered it. I saw it in your eyes. It wasn't sorrow; I've seen enough to know when it's real. Second, there was an intensity that doesn't speak to a death seven years ago. You spoke as though it had happened yesterday, as though you had contrived it yesterday." A third finger went up. "And there were several hesitations—almost unnoticeable, I'll give you that—to buy yourself time. Not because you didn't want to share your personal tragedy, but because you were creating the tragedy. One does not say um or ah when recalling such an event. If it has actually happened, a person does not forget." He was at the fourth finger now. "And you never blinked. Not once during the whole story. Could it be that your body was under stress, relaying such personal hardship? Perhaps. But in my experience, people who don't blink under pressure are the ones reinforcing their defences. They don't blink because they're threatened and are trying harder to prove themselves. Why would you have to prove anything but your vocation to me?"

Theo didn't answer.

"I'm distressing you," Hahn said. "I can see it in your jaw. But I need to be clear with you, Tyler. I will not tolerate anything but truth. I bring up my assessment of your story because I believe I've caught you being untruthful again. Maybe you have a good reason for making up the story of your wife, but I can assure you that after only four hours in our school, you do not have an adequate reason for invading a student's privacy, nor do you have a reason for taking pictures of his personal property. Please delete the images right now."

Theo did. Hollis would have the pictures already, so it didn't matter.

"Now, I don't want you to speak. I want you to listen. One more incident of any kind and you will not be teaching here any longer. You will respect everyone in this building, especially our students. And I suggest you get your story straight, whatever it is, so you can believe it yourself when you're telling it."

There was nothing for Theo to do but lower his head and nod like a whipped dog. "Yes, sir."

Hahn glared at him, through him, tipped his chin once, and was gone.

22. THINK MEAT

The sun was just beginning to bloom on the horizon when Scotty came up the steps of his porch, unlocked the door, and put a bucket of live fish on the table. He had fished all night under the Callingwood Bridge and caught several walleye and a small bass. The size didn't matter, only that they were alive when he brought them to the creature.

"Still swimming," he said and sat at his desk where his equipment was humming with noise from Kepler-186f, the creature's home. It was weird to see his own likeness bob into the bucket as if for apples, and weirder to see it come up successful with a flapping fish in his mouth then struggle to bite off its head.

One of the vintage transistors spurted a string of broken words. "Teeth ... not ... not ... work."

Scotty laughed. "We usually don't eat fish heads. Go ahead. It's okay. It doesn't bother me."

His twin's face gathered as if yanked by a drawstring then evaporated. M2 unfurled. His heads brushed the ceiling. His legs thwapped against the floor. Then he was in the bucket again and the fish were consumed in seconds.

"Better," the transistor croaked.

"I still can't believe it," Scotty said, staring at M2, tired from his all-night fishing expedition but too enthralled to rest before work. "All these years. All these years you were under there and talking to me. I thought I was going crazy."

Tears tingled his eyes and he covered his mouth to keep from sobbing like he had when M2 touched him in St. Jude's parking lot and imparted decades of history that dropped him to his knees. The navigational error that brought the Mimics to Earth. Their capture. Their torture. Their longing for home.

"Face . . . *pee*," the transistor said.

"I know. I can't help it." One of Scotty's weathered hands mopped the wetness away. "I mean, what they did to you—"

"Bad," said the transistor.

"Yes, bad. Worse than bad."

What the government had done to those poor, poor creatures, Scotty wouldn't have blamed M2 if M2 had killed him in the parking lot that night and had said as much. But M2 had surprised him. Nick Penner's face had wilted with such melancholy that Scotty had put his arms around the creature and hugged him.

"Oh!" Scotty had exclaimed when M2 then pushed a memory inside his brain.

It was of a cold January night some twenty-eight years ago. Garrett had suffered several weeks of severe weather and a departing storm had wreaked havoc with the waste facility. Two of the trucks had been stuck, and when plows from the city arrived to help them clear the road, ice had jammed the gates and they were unable to enter. And one of the seasonal crews had laid a plastic cover over the pit instead of the ash Scotty had instructed, and it had frozen to the waste below. To top it all off, three employees had been unable to start their cars and had called in to say they couldn't make it to work.

Vera—that cockroach of a woman, who would be there even if the planet imploded—had been the only one on time but was as useful as sand inside a swimsuit.

Scotty had gone to check the leachate tanks when he spotted a small, shuddering porcupine. He had thought it was odd to find the little guy out in the open like that, especially one so *red*, but at the time he figured that it was just the porcupine's reaction to the cold. He picked him up with his thick gloves and put him inside his jacket to keep him warm. Surprisingly—and again, he thought it might have been the chill—the quills did not stiffen against his chest or poke him in any way. He checked the leachate tanks with the porcupine against his shirt, warming it with his own body, then put an old pair of coveralls in a box and set the porcupine inside. Then he warmed some milk and put it in the box, along with half a sandwich that Meredith had made for him. The bread was fresh-baked. The ham was oven-cooked and honey-glazed. The thin slice of tart apple and smear of brie always made Scotty's mouth water and the porcupine took to it quickly. Why M2 had pushed the memory into his head, Scotty hadn't understood, until M2 persisted in showing Scotty what had happened to the porcupine after it disappeared that night.

All these years, Scotty had thought the little guy had run away after he was warmed and fed, or that Vera had kicked it outside when he had gone to help dig one of the trucks out, but that wasn't the case. M2 showed him that six men in white uniforms inconspicuously worked to distract the staff that had shown up, including Vera, and that while Scotty was digging out a truck, two of the men snuck inside the trailer and smuggled the porcupine out. His name is Ebba, M2 had explained without words. And Ebba was the last Plutonian to be caught.

Down below, all aliens were subjected to torture, so they had developed a collective disdain for humans. After the sweetest of the Martians, Pintree, nearly died during one of Lia Geller's experiments, the aliens united. Gossip in Sector East became conversation in Sector West. If a guard sneezed in Sector Center, he was wished a fatal allergy attack in Sector East. Information slipped through the facility as quickly and silently as blinks. Escapes were attempted and exhausted until Ebba shared his experience with the human who held him, warmed him, and fed him. Though they had grown to loathe humans, Ebba suggested that humans *outside* the facility might not be so cruel and that the warming, feeding human might one day help them again.

So began the Voice in Scotty's head. The Voice, in fact, was all Voices. The Martians. The Plutonians. Uranians. Saturnians. Venusians. Mimics. Yoked with the common purpose of finding the one human that might lead them home. Alone, the facility's defences were too much for their gifts, but together . . . together they found Scotty.

"Too . . . much . . . think," said the transistor when Scotty had been vacantly staring at nothing, remembering the first time he'd heard their Voice.

"You would, too, if you heard *you* in my head."

"Head better with me." M2's nine heads smirked, and his nine mouths laughed like organ pipes. His heavy body was too much for the couch and too much for the bed, so he settled on the floor beside the table.

"My head's terrible with you," Scotty said and pointed to his ear. "I tried to cut you out, but you buggers wouldn't go." He went to the coffee maker and began filling the pot.

M2 frowned. "You . . . bad . . . to *you*," squawked the transistor. Then one of those thick legs curled around Scotty's ankle and his toes started tingling. Then his calves. Then his knees.

"What are you doing? Come on now, it's okay. I didn't need that ear anyway." He gently pushed M2 away but M2 wouldn't budge. Scotty's thighs began to itch. His stomach began to rumble. His arms prickled. Nothing unpleasant but definitely something surprising. Then Scotty felt all the tingles and the itch and the rumble and the prickles flock to his phantom ear.

M2 released him. "No cut," said the transistor.

Scotty reached for his ear. Before he even touched it, he knew what he would find. M2 had made him whole again.

"I—" Scotty started. "You—"

"Mouth not work," said the transistor, and those organ pipes laughed again.

"I . . . need coffee," was all Scotty thought to say, and dazedly scooped twice the amount of ground beans into the filter. M2 watched him stumble around until the black-as-tar liquid was in his cup and he was sitting at the table. "Want to try some?" Scotty asked, holding his cup out to the middle head.

"Bad," said the transistor.

Scotty sipped and winced. "You're right, it's bad. But I've got to go to work. Unless you can take my tiredness away, too?"

"Drink the bad," M2 communicated.

"Ah, well, we all can't be perfect, can we?" said Scotty. He gulped the coffee down and poured himself another, needing to be ready when Vera latched onto him. If he didn't have his wits, she would know before he even opened the door. And she would make it her business to know his business. And that would be catastrophic.

M2 sat quiet. His curious heads tilted and twisted like weeds underwater.

"You have to stay here when I'm gone," Scotty reminded him. "Don't open the door. Keep the curtains closed. I'd stay if I could, but we need things to look normal until we figure a way to get you home."

All the transistors crackled. "More," they said. "More. More. *More.*"

"More," Scotty repeated. "More what? The fish? I'll get you fish if it'll help."

Those waving heads seemed to consider, then a compilation of human voices buzzed through Scotty's equipment. They were voices from kitchens, from cars, from playhouses, from bedrooms, from grocery aisles. They came from backyards and bathtubs and phone calls and sleep talkers and bus riders. One word from each, detonating like rockets in planned succession. "More eat think copy red crab get other go."

"Crab?" Scotty said. "You want crab? *Live*?" He scratched his head. "I can't catch those but the grocery's got them." He had three coolers in the crawl space and many more buckets in the shed behind the house, and if that weren't enough, the shop had more.

M2's heads melded into one, then into Scotty's own image. The head shook and the transistors spoke again with words uttered in Florida, in Brazil, in Australia, Israel, Hungary, in the cold waters of the Bering Sea, more clearly now. "Need more think meat . . ." static ". . . to be red crab bad . . . man. To get . . . other . . . out . . . to go . . . home."

The Red Crab, Scotty thought. *Hollis something or other*. He rolled the words in his head, then understood. When M2 had touched him and imparted his history, he had been apprised not only of the torture and the longing for home, but of the creature's gifts. It needed working brains to strengthen its own. Human brains were the most powerful and so the most useful to help him replicate, but multitudes of other brains *could* work. Fish, for example. Mice. Birds. Insects. As long as they were alive, they would do. If M2 had enough of whatever those brains provided, he could mimic the Hollis guy long enough to help his partner escape. Just to be sure, Scotty repeated this supposition. He soaked a cloth with water and rubbed his face as he spoke.

"Let me make sure I'm understanding you," he said, scrubbing his neck. "You need more *think meat*—I'm guessing you mean brains—and if I get you enough, you're going to copy that asshole down there and get your girl out and take her home?"

The Scotty-looking head that wasn't Scotty's nodded.

"Yes," said every transistor now.

It wasn't an impossible job, just a time-consuming one. After all his years at the dump, Scotty had grown used to vermin, but never thought he'd actually have use for them. "No humans," he said firmly.

"No," the transistors agreed. Then, "Small think meat."

"Think meat," Scotty mused aloud, pointing at M2. "That's a good one."

Suddenly, the transistors shut down. M2 glanced at the door, then shrank down to a little cube. A second later, someone knocked.

Scotty snatched the throw blanket from the back of the couch and tossed it on a chair. Then he slid the chair over M2 in case anyone got near enough to see.

Another knock.

Scotty was about answer then remembered that if he knew whoever was on the other side, he would have to explain the regeneration of his ear. He snatched a toque from the coat hook and pulled it on, then he opened the door.

"Sorry it's so early," Dan said. "But I figured I'd catch you before work. Too many eyes and ears in your office." He smiled, and Scotty knew he was talking about Vera. "Looks like you're about to leave. Can you spare a minute?"

There was no putting off the police chief, so Scotty welcomed him in, noting that Dan hadn't parked his cruiser out front so as not to make a scene, and for that he was thankful, whatever the reason for the visit. He offered Dan coffee, but one look at the sludge sloshing around the pot, and Dan declined.

"I don't want to take too much of your time, Scotty. I just have a few questions for you."

"I'm guessing you saw the video," Scotty said of the security footage.

Dan shook his head. "Unfortunately, no. There was nothing on it."

"That can't be right," Scotty said. "Unless I gave you the wrong flash drive, but I swear I took it from my computer and gave it right to you."

Dan was standing, but now he pulled out a chair and sat across from M2. "I don't doubt you and that's not what I'm here for. If you can get me another copy of that video, I'd owe you one, but I have a feeling you won't find it."

"Why's that?"

"You know, maybe I *will* take that coffee. Water it down for me, though, will you? I'd like to have my stomach when I'm done."

Scotty pointed at the bucket. "Went fishing this morning. Needed the caffeine, but I'll make another pot." He got to work, trying to ignore the fact that Dan and M2 were only inches from each other.

"There's this investigation we're working on," Dan said. "It came to us through a sister agency—I'd prefer to leave that part confidential—and I'd tell you it had nothing to do with what happened on that road in front of your landfill, but our sources believe it does. I can't go into detail, but my thoughts are that my department is in the dark about most of it." He paused, considering his words. "And I suspect our partner is intentionally trying to keep it that way. You've heard about the bus stop victims?"

"It's all over the paper," Scotty said. "And you know how people talk."

"I do," Dan nodded. "That's why I'm here. There's no easy way to say this, so I'm just going to tell you as I heard it. We had a report that you were loping around one of those bus stops that were hit that night. The one on Edgerton near St. Jude's?"

A clot of fear rose up Scotty's throat, but he focused on the coffee and getting fresh cups from the cupboard. That night in the parking lot, M2 must have assumed his likeness. Scotty wondered how long

M2 had copied him, and how many people M2 had killed looking like himself.

"I know you've had a rough go the last few years, so don't think I give credit to rumours. People can be terrible. And *bored* people can be worse. This one's between you and me, unless I have a reason to change that."

The coffee began brewing. It was just enough to mask the sound of Scotty's thudding heart. He set a cup in front of Dan and waited beside the machine.

"To tell the truth, I was inclined to dismiss it, but then I remembered you've been volunteering at St. Jude's for a while now. Could be you were in the area for that. Or was it for something else?"

It wasn't an accusation, not really, but neither was it unloaded. Scotty had a half-cocked gun pointed at him. His answer would either release or pull the trigger of suspicion. He lifted his hands in surrender. "I was cleaning the school. Cameras will have me there," he said, sighing. The coffee had finished brewing and he filled Dan's cup.

"I have to do my job," Dan said. He didn't like cornering the man, especially when his instincts told him the city's gossipmongers were just stirring their crap pots. He sipped the decent coffee and stretched out his legs. The heel of his shoe hit something on Scotty's floor but how the man kept his house was none of Dan's business. He pulled his feet back slightly and surprised Scotty with what he said next.

"I saw the school's tapes before I came here. You were cleaning the school during the time of the attacks. Sorry, I must do my job. But you're not the only puzzle that night, and that's why I'm here. We had multiple sightings of Nick Penner all over the city and at almost all of those stops, except for the one near St. Jude's. On its own, the only suspicion that would raise is guilt. The same person showing up at all those murder scenes. You might say it's a slam dunk. But there's two things that bother me. First: he's had it almost as bad as you. He didn't get any of Douggie Radway's *presents*, but a guy who doesn't report a lethal fire might as well have set it himself, in the court of local opinion. I could've chalked those sightings up to a bunch of vigilante justice hunters, but here's the second part of what bothers me. He—"

"He died last week," Scotty interrupted.

Dan raised his cup. "Bingo. We haven't sent out a press release about it, but it's hardly a secret—wildfire gossip and all. So I ask myself, why would we have so many reports of a man known to be dead all over the city? And again of *you*, when I've verified you were in the school?"

"Stress?" Scotty offered helpfully. He kept the house at a comfortable twenty-one degrees, but he was sweating under the toque. If Dan stayed much longer, he'd see the sheen on Scotty's face and suggest he take the hat off. He filled a glass with ice from the freezer, scooped a good portion of Good Host Iced Tea powder on the cubes, and poured tap water to the brim. The crystals hadn't even dissolved when he drained the glass.

"Maybe," Dan said. "And maybe I'm reading too much into all of it. The partner agency I'm working with is convinced one of the killers they've been tracking is responsible. A master imitator. Or *imitators*," he emphasized the word. "Right now, I have to ask myself if someone out there has such a vendetta against you and Nick that they'd go on a murder spree, and the answer is no. Not impossible, of course. Stranger things've happened around here, but I don't believe it. And they're certain that I'm wrong. That we've got a bunch of copycat killers on our hands."

Scotty made a show of looking at his watch.

"I have a favor to ask," Dan said, eyeing not for the first time Scotty's cluttered surveillance station. "We have ears all over the place, but some of those ears like keeping secrets. You're dialed in; maybe even better than we are. Tell me if you hear anything, will you? Anything you think might help me figure this out, anything strange. Can you do that?"

There was only one answer Scotty could give. He nodded, turned off the coffee pot, and pulled his jacket from the coat hook. "Of course."

Dan rose. "I appreciate that."

They went outside. Scotty threw one last look at the house and at M2 hiding like a game piece in plain sight under the kitchen table, and locked the door. Dan was walking to his cruiser and Scotty to his truck when Scotty's phone rang. It was Vera, more agitated than usual.

"Scud!" She hollered so loud he pulled the phone from his ear. "You better get here quick. Frank found a body!"

He ran with Vera squawking on his phone and flagged down Dan's departing cruiser. As he relayed what Vera had just told him, Scotty looked back at the house, wondering if he'd made a mistake.

23. Boy Bad and the Alien Blush

Nothing energizes young boys more than the promise of adventure, especially in Garrett. Larger cities, ripe with danger and surprises around every corner, inure youth to the thrill of exploration. There are no stampedes toward mystery and no young shudders of discovery in Toronto or Vancouver or Montreal. But take a cheap horror flick—*Arachnicobra*—and the hint that the very creature in the movie might be real and living in middle-of-nowhere Garrett, well, you couldn't keep Adam, Ravi, or Douggie away. When St. Jude's tinny bell rang, they thundered out of the school to their homes, begging to go to other homes, where they would not at all be.

Now on their bicycles, the breathless boys gathered under the afternoon sun, pedalling toward Scotty Waymore's cabin.

It had taken Ravi and Douggie only a little convincing to go back to Skitzo Scotty's place. Though they hadn't seen the slithering thing inside Scotty's house morph into Nick Penner, they had witnessed Adam's fright when he bolted from the porch that night, and they had seen the drawings inside his sketchbook. His fear deepened so thoroughly in them that in their minds dead Nick Penner was waiting for them and would strike them like a cobra. The trap thrilled them. And even though Skitzo Scotty no doubt would be watching for Douggie and his shit bags, they were determined to share the spotlight because in places the size of Garrett, discovery meant popularity, if only for a while.

They had gone the far way, heading north to the back of the property, and up through the growing thicket of field. Ahead, the cabin was a dark contrast against the blue sky. There were two rocking chairs on the back porch, a narrow table between them, and firewood piled neatly beneath what looked like a bedroom window. Beside the house stood a small shed, but Scotty's truck was absent.

Douggie had kept up admirably; now he was puffing. "Slow down," he panted.

"Speed up," Ravi called back.

Adam, who had seen a police car at the landfill when they circled behind the property, felt reasonably sure that they had until the car left before Scotty came home. But how long would that be? The car could pull out any minute, and Scotty could come home and catch them. Maybe he would feed them to the monster. Adam wouldn't blame Scotty if he fed *Douggie* to the monster, but Adam hadn't done anything to deserve being eaten. He glanced back at Douggie struggling in the bush and got off his bike.

There was a long hedgerow that marked the end of the backwoods and the beginning of the backyard. Adam laid his bike down behind it just as Ravi and Douggie laid down theirs. As soon as Douggie had done this, he walked a few paces away and picked up a rock about the size of a soda can.

"Put that back," Ravi said. "We're here to look, not break in."

Douggie hitched up his sagging pants. "No way. You saw what Adam drew. What if it attacks us?"

"Drop it, Douggie," Adam said.

"Fuck you," Douggie told them. And because he had pushed past them and was marching toward the house with the rock in his hand, Adam ran after him. Nothing they said would stop him because that was one thing about Douggie, he was as stubborn as a rusty nail. There was no pulling him away when his mind was set.

Douggie was just a few steps from the porch, about to throw the rock, when Adam lunged at his legs. Douggie yowled and both boys went sprawling to the ground. The rock rolled from Douggie's hands, but he elbowed Adam off him and scrambled for it. Ravi scooped it away.

"What the hell, Rav?" Douggie said. He kicked dust at Adam and got to his feet.

The sandstorm burned Adam's eyes. He blinked repeatedly, but Douggie had gotten a few small pebbles under his eyelids and he couldn't get them out. They felt like needles against his eyeballs. "We said *no*," Adam said hoarsely on his hands and knees, unable to see either Ravi or Douggie because his eyes were watering so bad.

Douggie reared back his foot to kick more dust at Adam but Ravi pounced on him. In their scuffle, they picked up the half-blind Adam like a sticky tumbleweed. Fists went flying. Feet went scrambling. Knees cracked against ground, backs, and stomachs. A wild dust-up of earth blackened their clothes, their hair, their faces. The whirlwind of fighting boys banged against the porch.

They might have gone on to do real damage to each other, but Scotty Waymore's door creaked open. Three snakelike limbs whipped out and caught each boy around an ankle and began slowly dragging them up the porch.

"Get off me!" Ravi cried to Douggie, reaching for his confiscated ankle.

"You let go of *me*!" Douggie shouted back, wildly kicking his leg.

Adam, who assumed Douggie had his ankle, struck out at Douggie's arm. But he hadn't remembered Douggie being so muscular.

Or so *long*.

While Ravi and Douggie pushed at each other, Adam narrowed his watering eyes to within a few inches of Douggie's arm. There, one of Arachnicobra's tendonous limbs was clamped around him. Its muscles pulsated like a giant, ancient, man-eating worm's. He opened his mouth to scream at the same time that Douggie and Ravi realized they too had been caught. But before any boy could utter a sound, they were yanked inside. Another limb slammed the door shut.

Hanging upside down by their ankles, the boys were stupefied. Great bleats of terror formed on their tongues but were just as quickly extinguished by yet more limbs that covered their mouths.

Adam could barely see the creature, yet he knew it wasn't the first time he'd seen it. Through his tears, he could make out its shadows and liquid movement. It was the same movement he'd seen on the side of the road the night of the accident. *Please*, he thought. *Please don't kill me.*

Beside him, Douggie squirmed like a fish caught by the tail. He flapped. He whipped. His bladder let go and because the creature had him upside down, a small stream of urine darkened his jeans, then his uncovered belly. He was too terrified to tuck his shirt into his pants and the stream reached his chest before his upended shirt soaked it up.

Instead of struggling like Douggie, Ravi had gone absolutely still. His eyes were the size of moons in his slim head.

Suddenly, a voice came from somewhere in the house. "Rock boy bad."

Their eyes swung past the creature to the bank of what looked like radios on a desk beside the bathroom door. One of the radios cracked and hissed. It spooked muffled gasps from all of them. "Rock boy bad," the radio sputtered.

Adam and Ravi glanced at Douggie, who had gone completely white.

The tendon around Douggie's mouth began to tighten. He thrashed, but his feeble efforts were no match for the beast. Douggie screamed inside his mouth. It was the mewling of a bagged kitten dropped in water.

Ravi and Adam could only watch, helpless. Though Douggie was the most annoying person on the planet, Adam didn't want Douggie to die. Not really. He needed a little lesson now and then, yes, but not a broken head. Something like a really good hangnail or nut-splitting wedgie. Maybe a touch of food-poisoning. Douggie deserved that. He didn't deserve to die. *Please*, Adam thought, harder now in case the creature could read his mind. *Please don't hurt him.*

And then an image came to Adam. It was of Douggie dusting up sand in his eyes. Douggie insulting him in school. Douggie tripping him, laughing at him, being a jerk to him time and time again. Then Douggie shouting terrible things at Scotty and Douggie and throwing bags of dog shit at Scotty's house.

Adam understood. The creature was showing him Douggie's misdeeds. How bad *Rock Boy* was. How it would be better if Rock Boy wasn't around anymore. It didn't want to hurt Adam or Ravi, but it wanted to stop Douggie from being bad, and the only way the creature knew how to stop people from being bad was to kill them.

No, Adam urged the creature. *That's not the way.* He was still upside down, and the rush of blood to his head was making him dizzy. Adam felt that if he wasn't let to his feet soon, he would faint. And maybe while he was unconscious, the creature would eat him. *Please*, he thought again.

The creature seemed to consider Adam's plea, for the limb around Douggie's mouth stopped tightening. "Stop bad Rock Boy," a radio crackled.

One of the creature's heads snaked toward Adam. He thought *thank you, thank you, thank you*, over and over until the words in his own head had no beginning or end but were eternal and not just his, but the creature's too.

The limb around Adam's mouth loosened, and he was able to speak. "He'll stop the bad." Adam coughed, looking at the tiny black eyes next to him then at Douggie. "You'll stop being bad, won't you?"

Douggie nodded emphatically.

Eight dark heads leaned toward Douggie, so close they almost touched his face. He whimpered, squeezing his eyes shut.

"Boy bad," the radio said once more. The heads retreated and Douggie, Ravi, and Adam were delicately lowered to the floor.

Adam, surprised to be alive, got to his feet and stared at the creature. In the confined space of Scotty Waymore's cabin, it seemed gargantuan, yet Adam did not doubt it could get *much* bigger. He counted nine heads, a lumpy round body, and several legs, but these sometimes retreated, sometimes multiplied, so he couldn't get an accurate count. Each head had many eyes, though they did not seem malevolent. They held an almost birdlike curiosity, flitting from boy to boy to understand them, to figure if they were a threat or just environmental noise. He couldn't take his eyes off it, afraid it might capture him again, afraid this was his only chance to see it. He reached out.

Ravi gaped at him. "What are you *doing*?" He backed away while Adam stretched out his hand and Douggie, still shaken, curled into a tighter ball and wept.

Adam's hand went further. Closer. Toward the unearthly creature so slowly he might be there for years before he reached the monster. At least, this is what Ravi thought. But then every second they stayed inside felt like millennia to Ravi. They had to get out. They had to get out *now*. Douggie was closest to him, so without taking his eyes off the beast, Ravi lifted his foot and nudged Douggie's back. It was the slightest movement, really, but one of those nine heads whipped to within a centimetre of Ravi's face and glared at him. It was apparent to them all, then, that the creature despised even the hint of violence, at least to each other.

"S-sorry," Ravi sputtered.

Douggie started to move. He released the death-grip on his knees and began inching toward the door, scooting his rear, then shoulders, then rear against the wooden floor.

Still Adam reached. His fingers, sure and curiously steady, were so close to the creature's hide that Adam could feel thin, wet filaments of coarse hair like old spiderwebs after a good rain. The creature knew this, of course, because one of its heads whipped to face Adam's fingers. Its jaw opened, showing rows of needlelike teeth.

From the floor, Douggie gasped. One of the limbs sprang inside, only for a second, but enough for Douggie to get a mouthful of alien goo. He spat the grey-green slime onto the floor and wiped his mouth with his arm. He turned absolutely white. They had seen movies where aliens invaded people. The people almost always turned into aliens themselves or had embedded hatchlings tear them apart from the inside. Douggie didn't want to become an alien, nor did he want one living inside him. His stomach churned, maybe from fear, maybe because the alien baby was already feasting on him. He wailed, but then all the radios hissed to life.

"Shhh," the radios said. Then, "Sit."

Douggie hushed. Three bottoms instantly dropped to Scotty Waymore's floor.

"Call name. Call boy names," only one radio said now.

Adam had stopped being afraid and was overwhelmed with peace so pervasive, he wondered if the alien was hypnotizing him. He put his hand on his chest. "I'm Adam," he said.

The monster's heads tilted as if to understand. "*Adam*," one of the radios repeated.

Adam lit up. This was progress, he thought. He might still be in danger but the very fact that the creature was at least listening to him and not stringing him up by his ankles was a good sign.

Ravi went next, introducing himself cautiously.

"Ra-vi," a radio clucked.

The alien, too, seemed proud to engage with them, for his heads went to Douggie, waiting for his introduction.

"Boy bad name?" a radio chirruped when Douggie wasn't forthcoming.

Douggie didn't speak, too consumed with wondering if the rumbling in his stomach was a baby intent on killing him.

One of the creature's limbs came out and spanked Douggie's rear as would a mother chiding a young child.

"Say your name," Ravi hissed through clenched teeth.

"D-D-Doug-Doug-eee," said Douggie.

The radio repeated every syllable of the name.

"What's *your* name?" Adam asked.

Those nine wavering heads vocalized silently as though it wasn't sure how to answer or how to answer so they would understand. "Em two," a radio said after a long pause.

To be honest, M2 hated the name, for it was a name given to him by his captors. He had never and would never identify with it, but it was simple enough for the small humans to understand. How could he put into human speak the sound of gravity or the smell of the cosmos, for that was how he had been identified on his own planet, just as M1 had been identified by the feel of lightspeed and the heat of moonglow. Like it or not, M2 had to simplify everything for the humans.

"Em two," he repeated through the vintage transistor.

"M2?" Adam said. "M2's your name?"

On Kepler-186f, confirmation was never needed, for communication was fiercely intentional and so always understood. But during his time on earth, M2 had learned that humans operated in vagueness and nonchalance. They wouldn't understand the clicking of his tongues or the vibrating of his valves. He studied them for only a fraction of a second then his second, fifth, and seventh heads compressed. It was the squeezing of flesh into boy molds, the crafting of art by an experienced sculptor. Then Adam, Ravi, and Douggie looked back at themselves, exact replicas, down to Ravi's moon-wide eyes and Douggie's urine-soaked shirt. The alien boys nodded in unison. "M2 is name," said the transistor.

There is something to be said for looking at your twin. Because it is fashioned of uniqueness only to you, there is an irresistible kinship. For how can one fear *oneself*? Mental fitness aside, similarity invites—no, *demands*—calmness. It slackens the defences and spreads affinity quicker than a baby's coo or a puppy's lick. Somehow M2 knew this and somehow Adam, Ravi, and Douggie knew that he knew this. That M2 was trying to connect with them.

Beneath their mantle of fear, seeds of serenity bloomed. Ravi unclenched his fingers. The knot in Adam's throat slipped down and away. Douggie stopped crying. Adam, who knew they didn't have much time before the police car left the landfill and Scotty came home, recalled the family therapist's advice that delayed communication almost always led to confrontation, and that it was best to speak your mind so as not to let trouble fester.

He said, "Why are you here?" Then, because he felt the rudeness of his question perhaps even before M2, he added, "I mean, sorry, M2. I didn't mean it to come out that way. I just . . . we've never seen an . . ." He was royally mucking it up, but though Ravi and Douggie cringed at his awkwardness, neither of them offered to help. Adam swallowed and tried again. "Where are you from?"

M2 didn't expect these small humans to know much beyond their own planet, so he just pointed with all his limbs, including his imitation boy limbs, toward the ceiling. The effect made the Douggie limb squish up, and for an instant it resembled a great wobbling walrus with Douggie's face. Against his will, Ravi laughed. M2 did it again, now with the Ravi limb, only this time the Ravi limb formed to resemble a toadstool, complete with spotted body and Ravi's thin face. M2's organ-pipe laugh startled them, but then they understood that he was having fun with them. Against all odds, they were in no danger—at least for the moment—talking with an alien in Scotty Waymore's cabin.

From somewhere outside, a sound came. M2 whipped his heads to the windows at the front of the cabin and looked out. In doing so, he'd slid a curtain aside and Adam could see Scotty's truck coming off the highway and onto the long, gravelled road that led to his house.

"He's coming home," Adam gasped, sorry to have the time with M2 suddenly cut short. There was so much he wanted to ask M2, so much he wanted to say. Douggie and Ravi, too, appeared just as disappointed as he was, for they became downcast and sullen.

They had to leave, but then M2 reached out exactly three limbs toward the boys. The ribbed underside of the limbs turned upward and formed three separate hands. Without hesitation, Adam clasped the hand M2 offered him and shortly after Ravi and Douggie did the same. They had all been expecting the alien equivalent of a human handshake, but instead M2 currented his memories to them. His and M1's capture. His telekinetic friendship with the other captured aliens. His longing for home. As Scotty Waymore's truck bobbed over the road, Adam, Ravi, and Douggie learned of M2's torture, and his plan to assume the Red Crab's identity, free M1, and leave Earth forever. All this had taken place in seconds, for Scotty was only meters closer to the house than when the boys took his hands. But it was enough.

"We'll help," Adam said immediately.

"There's an anthill in my backyard. I can scoop them in a bucket. And there are frogs at my grandma's. She's got lots of them." It was Douggie who offered the tiny lives, for out of the three, he had yet to outgrow the creature-catching stage and was quite excited at the mission.

"My uncle works at the hatchery," Ravi said. He had visited the hatchery several times a year when he was younger, eagerly plunking pockets of his mother's quarters into the feed machines just to see the salmon and trout swim right up to his feet. It never ceased to amaze him how many fish could fit in those ponds. Hundreds, maybe thousands of them. They would be perfect for M2.

Besides Scotty Waymore, M2 had never had humans look out for him. But here there were three fledgling men offering their services and asking for nothing in return. His stomach gurgled his species' appreciative expression, but they mistook it for hunger and offered him one of the chocolate bars Douggie carried in his pocket.

"No thank," said a transistor, but they understood what it meant. And they were just about to exit through Scotty's back door when the man himself opened the front door and stepped inside. He had quieted the engine so as not to disturb M2 and parked his truck near the shed, so the boys hadn't heard him.

Scotty's gasp filled the cabin like jet fuel. They felt his unease as his eyes swept over them, lingering on Douggie the longest. He slammed the door and then a string of expletives as long as the Callingwood River torrented from him. He hadn't raised his voice—that was perhaps what frightened them the most—but all the rage he felt toward Douggie came out as if he had, as if he had grabbed Douggie by the neck and shouted right in his ear.

The boys began backing away, but M2, quick as lightning, pressed one of his thick limbs to Scotty's mouth.

"Bad talk," said the vintage transistor, and when Scotty protested, M2 restrained him. The transistors shushed him like slow, incoming waves. First one, then another. "Shhhhhhhh. Shhhhhhh." A cacophony of shushes flooded the house and diluted the jet fuel Scotty had brought in. Scotty's rage-purple cheeks paled back to their natural color, and the veins in his head sank into their familiar trenches. He breathed through his nose, fogging up M2's shiny dark limb.

M2 cautiously removed his limb from Scotty's mouth. Twice Scotty made to speak but couldn't, for his words had rushed out of him and not yet returned.

It was Douggie who broke the silence. "I'm sorry Mr. Waymore," he said, lowering his eyes and speaking not to Scotty's face but to his stomach, twisting the hem of his piss-stained shirt. "I'm sorry for everything. I shouldn't have . . . done what I did. None of it. I'm sorry."

That the city's biggest brat was in his house with M2 made Scotty want to throw them both outside. But he couldn't do that. M2 would be captured and the brat would just blab with that infamous mouth of his. Through clenched teeth, Scotty asked, "What are you doing in my house?"

The boys looked at each other.

"More help," said a transistor.

"Goddammit, you're like a kid," Scotty said to M2, trying to control his temper. "Them? Of all people—and there should've been *none* since I told you *not* to answer the door—*them*? Do you know what kind of trouble you're in? We have no choice but to kill them, you know that don't you?" He glared at Douggie.

Douggie put his hands up. "No, please, sir. Please. I'm sorry. I really am." His knees were shaking and his bladder would have let loose had it not already emptied on his shirt.

Scotty took a step toward him.

This close, Douggie noticed that Scotty's ear had grown back, and he couldn't help but stare at it as Scotty closed in on him.

Scotty scowled. "How does it feel to be fucked with, son?" he said. He took the chair in front of his makeshift surveillance station and sighed into it.

"Y-you're not going to kill us?"

"Would or should?" Scotty said. "No, of course I'm not going to kill you. Damn brats've been watching too much TV. But *you*"—he thrust a finger at Douggie— "have been a class-one asshole. Slinging shit at my house. You've got some mouth, too. I ought to string you up by your feet and let the crows have at you."

"I'm sorry," Douggie said again. "I'll . . . I'll make it up to you."

M2 whipped a broom into Douggie's hand, and even though none of them were happy, everyone, including Scotty, laughed.

"You want to make it up to me, you can start by keeping your mouth shut," Scotty said when the moment passed. "That goes for all of you. Now, since he hasn't skewered you, I can only assume he's told you some things?"

There was the low moan of M2's valves as he bowed his heads.

"I know you didn't mean to do it," Scotty said to M2 of the victims he'd made since his escape. He put a hand on one of the heads. "You've been held against your will and tortured worse than the Leafs." He tried to make light of it, but M2 didn't understand hockey nor could M2 relate to the humor in torture or in death. "Look, as far as you knew, everyone wanted to hurt you. On Earth we call it self-defence."

It did not appear to make M2 feel better. His heads slunk lower and his valves let out the sound of soft, melancholic fog horns muted by wind.

Garlands of M2's memories reeled through the human heads now. He had left nothing out. Not a stab, not a burn, not a tear or a twist, squeeze, break, cleave, or the many extractions he and M1 had suffered. So they could not blame M2 for Irma Madinger or Vishi Chawla or the others. After decades of agony—often to the brink of death—and with no one to show him that not all humans were evil, blame lay with Project Domain and the humans that supported it. M2 had never experienced the tenderness of a human embrace, but now they gathered around him.

"Stink," a transistor said, though M2's alien blush was unmistakable.

They pulled back. Scotty wiped his eyes. "So what the hell do we do now?" he asked them.

24. St. Jude's Zoo

Irving Hahn had always enjoyed junior high. He found that these wonderous years, the budding adults were capable of conversation that often made him marvel. They were self-sufficient and inquisitive and far enough away from advanced puberty to still have their brains. At least, that's what he thought. But now, looking at the hordes of ants crawling out of Douglas Radway's locker, he wondered if some of his students had any brains at all.. The first block hadn't even finished, yet Hahn and his janitorial staff already had their hands full.

Claire, who was returning from delivering a student with a stomachache to the nurse's office, gasped. She stopped beside Hahn and surveyed the community of insects creeping over the bank of lockers. It wasn't the first time Douggie had brought something he shouldn't have into the school. At the beginning of the year when his mother had put the whole family on a diet, Douggie had stored two weeks of lunches inside. The rotting broccoli and souring fish, smelling so bad multiple students uprooted their own lunches in the same hallway, had to be extracted with the schoolyard litter-grabber and put immediately outside. And in the fall, when he was particularly a nuisance, he'd brought two bags of dog shit that were stuffed in his coat pockets. Fortunately, Claire herself had caught that one early, hauled the boy to the office for a lesson on hygiene and civility, and sent him and the dog shit home. Now she watched the army of ants spread onto the ceiling and the vinyl floor beside her feet and squished one with her heel. "Please tell me we can transfer him," she said to Hahn.

Though he had the combination to every locker inside the school, Hahn dared not open the door, not until the day janitor, Grover, arrived with the vinegar spray and the paper towel. Just as he was thinking this, Grover appeared down the hall, pushing the janitorial cart, on whose front sat a big bucket of steaming water. Several spray bottles were vibrating against each other on top of the cart, due in part to the wobbling right wheel.

"That's like blowing a bushfire to the prairies in August," Hahn said of Claire's suggestion. He frowned. "Bishop Parker has its hands full with the spillover from Fauville, otherwise I'd be tempted. Right now I'm inclined to send that boy to the *zoo*."

"Tyler will talk to him," Claire said, and Hahn couldn't help but notice she looked away as she mentioned the new teacher's name, as though she were trying to act casual.

After the incident with Adam Brace's sketchbook, Hahn didn't want the new teacher disciplining a student without his supervision. He had always granted a fair amount of trust to new teachers, but Tyler had obliterated his in an instant when he had taken those photos, and he would have to work twice as hard to get it back.

"No," Hahn said. "He's not yet familiar with the way we do things around here. I'll speak to our prodigal zookeeper."

"Something wrong?" Claire asked.

"Oh, just about a billion ants, as you can see," Hahn said. She eyed him. "And?"

He dug his hands in his pockets. "And the jury's still out on Mr. Cagey. I'm not expecting our substitute to replace our Julia—no one can do that—but . . . it's like trying to put a corner puzzle piece in the center of the picture. Even *time* won't make it fit. That's my feeling, at least." He hadn't told her that he'd caught the new teacher taking pictures of Adam's book as it posed no threat to Adam, and he wanted Claire to make her own judgement. As one of his most trusted teachers, her assessment would be fair and he didn't want to impose any of his own biases on her or any of the other teachers when he really needed subjectivity. It was part of what made St. Jude's so special all these years, and he wasn't going to let Tyler Cagey ruin it.

Claire patted his arm. "You're just jealous she didn't take *you* on her trip, you old softie."

"I do miss her," he admitted.

"Me too," she said. Then, when Hahn started to walk in the direction of Julia Fowler's former classroom, she hurried her stride to keep up with his long legs and nudged him with her elbow. "Give him some time. We haven't had anyone new here in so long, I think it's easy for us to forget what it's like. I think he's just as uneasy as we are, you know?"

"Who's the softie now?" Hahn said, glancing sideways at her.

They parted, Hahn to Tyler Cagey's classroom and Claire to hers across the hall. When Hahn's head appeared in the window, Cagey's otherwise lethargic pupils straightened like arrows. Cagey, who had been writing on the whiteboard with his back to the class, must have noticed a change in the room, for he turned, saw the overly attentive students, and looked at the door.

"My spidey sense was tingling," he said when he gestured for Hahn to come in.

"No need to pretend you're paying attention," Hahn winked at the students. "Carry on. I just need a moment with Mr. Radway."

He wiggled a hooked finger at Douggie and a murmur of trepidation rippled through the room.

Douggie was no stranger to visits from Principal Hahn, but he never failed to adopt a doe-eyed look of innocence.

He should have perfected it by now, Hahn mused to himself, noticing the purple blush of the boy's cheeks. Douggie had just passed him when something in the corner of the room caught his eye. Douggie's backpack, tucked neatly under his chair, seemed to be moving. Hahn had to stare at it to make sure he wasn't wrong, but there it was: a side pocket in the bag *lurched*. The black material suddenly bumped up against the chair leg. And then again. And again. Hahn turned. "You've forgotten your backpack," he said to Douggie.

Douggie, knowing he had been caught, nodded quietly. He grabbed the bag, eyes flitting to Adam and Ravi, then left the room. Theo inventoried the exchange in his mind and went back to pretending to be a teacher.

When they were alone in the hallway, Hahn said, "You do realize that whatever creature you have in your backpack needs to *breathe*?" Douggie didn't respond. Understanding, Hahn said, "Ahh. Well, until you end the little one's life, I should think it's cruel to treat it that way, don't you?"

"It's just a frog." Douggie shrugged.

"Just a frog," Hahn repeated. "Does that mean it can't think? Can't *fear*? If a giant were to put you in the pocket of his backpack, would you be happy about it, Mr. Radway?"

"I guess not."

"And what about the colony of ants in our west corridor? Do you think they wanted to be uprooted and washed away by Mr. Grover? And how about Ms. Stevens' and Mr. Brack's adjoining lockers, are we to assume they were expecting an invasion? A thousand little nibbles on their lunches? Or maybe it's 'bring your pets to school day' and I've lost the memo?"

As he said this, Larry Heep came bustling down the hallway. The math teacher's one good eye swept like a searchlight, back and forth, back and forth, while his glass eye stared forward. Without looking at Hahn, he thrust a finger at Douggie. "*You*. You and your hot fingers. Where is she? Come on. Out with it." One of his cheap shoes tapped furiously against the floor.

Hahn looked from the math teacher to Douggie and raised his eyebrows, but the boy seemed legitimately perplexed. "Not you, then?"

Douggie shook his head.

Heep threw up his hands. His loose watch slid almost to his shoulder before falling back to his wrist where it hung like a necklace. "Come *on*. I caught you in the room this morning. You had no reason to be there. Our class isn't until after lunch."

"And what are you suggesting that Mr. Radway *relocated*?" Hahn asked the flustered teacher.

"Bumper," Heep said. "She was there before *he*"—he pointed at Douggie— "came in."

"The rabbit?" Hahn frowned. Heep's accusation seemed to genuinely surprise the boy, but with the ants and the frog . . . well . . . there *was* a commonality he couldn't deny.

"I left my calculator there. My mom would kill me if I lost another one." Douggie said honestly. He couldn't tell Mr. Heep or Principal Hahn that he actually *had* thought of taking Bumper. M2 needed as many small creatures as they could find, and Bumper was no exception. But when the rabbit snuggled into his hand after he lifted the door on her cage, he just couldn't. It would be like feeding M2 Moakie, his pet gerbil, or Tundra, their golden retriever. He just couldn't do it.

Heep's glass eye wobbled like a lie detector pen, boring into Douggie for the truth, but then settled and was still. "Well, then, if it wasn't you, who was it?"

Douggie said he didn't know. Heep sighed and went stomping back to where he came from.

"You really didn't take the rabbit?" Hahn said when they were alone.

"No, but I petted her."

"How could you not?" Hahn said and led Douggie to his office.

Hahn made it a habit to always keep his door open. In his experience, closed doors bred suspicion, anxiety, and a whole host of negative emotions that rarely helped any situation, especially with children. So his door was seldom shut. In forty years, it had happened once in the case of a runaway student returned to school, twice when one of a student's parents had died, a dozen times during rather nasty custodial disputes, and on the rare occurrences when a student's behaviour required expulsion. This was not one of those times. He gestured for Douggie to take a seat, glancing at the clock on his desk phone. "Second block starts in a few minutes. Shall we make this quick? Now, we both know you're trying to colonize the school with bugs, but the question is *why*?"

He could see an explanation forming in the primitive machinery of the boy's mind. It was like attempting to produce a Rolex with an anvil and hammer. He was about to prod, stick an iron in that clunky machine to pry out the truth when his phone rang. A shriek greeted his ear when Ashley Kelby, one of the student teachers, explained that the pair of tarantulas in the biology lab were missing.

"We have to evacuate the school!" she screeched. There was the muffled sound of the phone hitting her body as she panicked on the other end.

Hahn covered the receiver with his hand. "Know anything about a tarantula?"

"No, sir."

"I'm on my way, Ashley. Just breathe. They're more scared of you than you are of them," he said and hung up on the protesting teacher. He turned his wise old eyes on Douggie, who was fidgeting there like the ants were under his clothes. "Give it to me straight, son. What's going on?"

A lightbulb flashed in Douggie's head. He let his shoulders droop and said, "We were having a contest. I can't tell you who's in on it because I don't know. A bunch of kids, I guess. Someone—I don't know who it was—watched one of those chicken fights on the internet. It was a scorpion and a spider or maybe it was a rooster and a goose, I can't remember. And then everyone got to talking about making one of our own."

"And this animal fight club was supposed to be today?" Hahn asked.

Douggie nodded. "We were going to bring them to the hill out back." Inside, he congratulated himself for thinking of the hill. It was the school's most popular meeting point and also conveniently far from where he, Adam, and Ravi planned to meet before going to Scotty's house.

Hahn couldn't be sure the boy was telling the truth, but if he was, it was more important to let the students know *he* knew so St. Jude's didn't become Noah's Ark before lunch. "Thank you for telling me. I know it's not easy to confess. Makes you feel almost sick, doesn't it?"

"Uh-huh."

"Well, I think for now your punishment is that *feeling*, the queasiness in your stomach. I know it likes to linger and that just might be what you need. Think on it a while, and while you're thinking, I'd like you to help Mr. Grover collect your colony and put it outside. You can make up for your second period during lunch. Does that sound fair?"

"Uh-huh," Douggie grunted and got up to leave.

"And I'd like to make you a deal. You might not have kidnapped the tarantulas in Ms. Kelby's room, but if you help me find them so I can put her mind at ease, we can negotiate some of your lunchtime detention away for good behaviour. No questions asked if they're returned promptly." With that, he dismissed Douggie to help Mr. Grover corral the ants while he hurried to put Ashley Kelby's mind at ease.

When ten minutes passed, Douggie snuck outside. He freed the frog from one side pocket of his bag and inspected the other to make sure the tarantulas were still there. Then he hurried to Ms. Kelby's room, where he overheard Principal Hahn trying to coax the squealing teacher off her desk. He scooped the spiders from the bag and gently cast them into the room, bolting back down the hallway as Ms. Kelby's renewed shrieks filled the school.

Unbeknownst to everyone, Theo catalogued the commotion. Even two rooms away and even with his door closed and even with his back turned, he knew. Thanks to Cyber Ops, pinhead-small Project Domain cameras had been installed all over the school. Live feeds were currented to Overlook's surveillance team but also to Theo's smartwatch. One click of a button and the feed on his watch changed to a different part of the school. So while Hahn was busy digging for answers and letting the student body walk all over him, Theo watched the ants being deposited by Douglas Radway. He also saw Ravi Das stuffing Bumper the rabbit under his sweatshirt, only to have it taken from him by Adam and left in the boy's locker room. And as much as he hated spiders, he had to pretend he didn't know the tarantulas were in Douggie's bag. Turning his back on the class before Hahn had come in, he had imagined them crawling down the collar of his shirt and more than once his fingers went to his neck to check. He would have preferred the rabbit in the bag, but what was the hell of junior high without the torment?

He sipped his cold coffee. They were in the middle of their morning snack break. Students were chatting about nothing that interested Theo. If it were up to him, he would send every single one of them out on a suicide hike, fling his cover aside, and *make* Adam tell him where M2 was. But the funny thing he never understood about kids was that people actually liked them. A bullet in a man or a bullet in a boy made no difference to him, but the latter almost always caused more fuss than was worth the lead. Though with M2 on a killing spree, the lead could be justified. He pretended not to watch Adam and the Das boy. They weren't talking but passing a paper between them. Adam scribbled something, folded the paper, and handed it forward to Ravi. Ravi opened the note, scribbled something of his own, folded it up, and dropped it over his shoulder on Adam's desk without once looking behind him. Whatever they were doing, they were trying to do it secretly.

Theo surveyed his watch. He tapped it twice, scrolled one of the two side buttons, and zoomed in over Adam's desk. Even with their technology, he couldn't see a thing. Adam was hunched so far over the paper, it was all but hidden from the camera, almost like he suspected someone was watching him. The Das boy was just as protective.

Cobra and Tracer had just begun their round-the-clock watch of the three boys, and so far had come up with little information. Sure, it was more difficult to trace a child when excitable community watch groups fingered unfamiliar lingering adults as child predators, but they weren't highly trained spies, for goddsake. They were kids. They should be as easy to pick as berries from a late-summer vine. They should have *fallen* into Project Domain's hands by now. Today Cobra and Tracer would track the boys from school and Theo couldn't wait to see what they discovered. It wouldn't be the animal fight club the fat kid told Hahn about. The camera in the speaker of Hahn's phone had shown Theo that Hahn actually believed Douggie's story, but Theo didn't. Not when the only kids collecting animals were the three who saw Adam's drawing of M2. No. There was no fight club. It had to do with M2.

He wondered briefly if the boys were trying to feed M2 but just as quickly dismissed the idea. First, M2 would kill anyone if they tried to approach him, and second, well, M2 was as tame as a great white shark. He was no puppy in a box. He was bull in a nursery. Only carnage could come from him. Still, there was something there. Maybe M2 was trapped. Theo had never seen the creature stuck before, but it didn't mean it was impossible. If it weren't their break, Theo would have confiscated the note, but if he did that now, everyone would see him single out Adam and Ravi and then he would have to be doubly careful around Hahn. So, against his inclination to haul the boys out and feed them to Cobra and Tracer, whose interrogation techniques made even grown men give up the locations of their own children, Theo waited.

25. Marty's Phone Call

The bell couldn't have rung any slower. Even the urging of three hundred students focused on St. Jude's clocks didn't move those institutional hands faster than the drip of a leaking faucet. Hahn, tired from the day's early events, walked to the front lawn, where the sun was shining, the bikes were still chained and awaiting their riders, and the doors were still closed. He stuck his hands in his pockets, enjoying the last moments of peace before the end-of-the-day stampede.

The city, with a lawn-and-tree-maintenance budget as big as child's allowance, must have gotten an endowment because spring-maintenance was in full bloom. There was the buzz of a chainsaw, the snip-snip of hedge trimmers, and the whir of multiple lawn mowers zipping around the adjacent boulevards and small city-owned park. A road crew was repainting pavement lines and another was fixing a notorious pothole that had jarred suspensions and rattled bones for longer than some students attended St. Jude's. Across the street, a crew was working atop a transformer, while circling its base was another city worker in overalls spraying a thicket of weeds. Never in Hahn's years at St. Jude's had there been so much activity, and he was thinking of making a call to the city to see how his school had won the maintenance lottery when the bell rang.

Doors flung open and a rush of teens poured out. Hahn smiled. Every day these relieved young faces attended St. Jude's was another day of progress. He stood under the shade of an oak tree while the students filed past, into cars and buses, onto bicycles and skateboards. It wasn't long before Claire and Tyler Cagey came out and joined him. Claire, with her tumbler of afternoon tea, was laughing at something the new teacher had said, and there was a faint blush to her face Hahn hadn't seen in several years. It was the unmistakable blush of attraction. Had that color bloomed for anyone else, Hahn would have been happy for Claire. But not only was Tyler Cagey a temporary teacher from Toronto—a three-hour distance that made things a lot more complicated for a single mother—Hahn also didn't trust him. Sure, since the incident with Adam's sketchbook, Cagey was trying to gain his trust back, that much was obvious, but Hahn believed that if one had to *work* for trust, integrity wasn't interwoven into one's DNA. He raised a hand to greet them.

Still laughing, Claire gestured to Theo and said, "Well, he's got Julia's grace, at least. Had to save him back there."

"I slipped down the stairs when they were unleashed. She picked me up before they could trample me," Theo said. He brushed the dust off his knees and watched the students still surging by.

While in the military, Irving Hahn had been taught the importance of assessment. People, places, things. Assess wrongly and it could cost you your life. And even though those years were short and in the distant past, Hahn's assessments were almost never wrong. He'd taken Tyler Cagey for an astute man, a man as sure of his movements as he was his own birthdate. Only the lifers Hahn still knew acted the way Tyler Cagey did, and it made Hahn trust him even less. Cagey didn't just fall down the stairs while Claire was nearby. *He made it so*. Of that, Hahn was certain.

"Ah, the suffering stag. Those steps have seen many of them over the years. I've thought of getting them textured to prevent the slips, but they'd still happen anyway. What with all the girls around." He looked ahead as he said this, not once meeting Cagey's eyes but feeling his resentment and Claire's embarrassment all the same.

Theo laughed as though he didn't want to stab the old man in the eye. "She *is* pretty, but I'm also clumsy. Sometimes I think I was born with toes on my heels and vice versa. Haven't fallen into traffic yet, though, so I'm not completely a lost cause."

"And here comes our little zookeeper," Hahn said, pointing to Douggie. He was with Adam and Ravi, as always, their heads so close Hahn was surprised they didn't knock each other out on the way down the stairs. At the bottom, they made a hard right, avoiding the teachers.

"How do you do it?" Theo asked Hahn, watching them go. "I haven't been in education as long as you have, but I've never seen anyone with your patience. All the other principals I worked under would have sent hellfire down through the classes after the ants and spiders this morning."

It was true that some snarly codgers would have expelled Douggie, but those were the attitudes of yesteryear and better buried there, Hahn thought, along with Cagey's fake flattery. He shrugged. "I like to keep my kids in school," he said simply. Then, spotting Scotty Waymore coming up the hill, said to Claire, "He's quite early today."

Now they were all looking at Scotty, coming slow and with a slight limp. He was still too far for them to fully make out his features, but he appeared to be squinting in the sun.

Hahn pursed his lips. It was a nice day for walking, but Scotty lived almost as far from St. Jude's as you could get. To see him trudging like that, almost as though his bones had jellied, well, it didn't seem right.

Claire must have thought so, too, because a look of concern swept over her face. She seemed to consider going to him but stayed where she was.

For his part, Scotty Waymore was no closer to St. Jude's than Vera was to becoming a decent human being. This was because he was dutifully in his office at the landfill. None of them knew this, of course. M2 had done a fine job of molding his flesh to look like Scotty, right down to the previously deformed ear. It was dangerous for him to be out, but Adam, Ravi, and Douggie had to be warned not to go to Scotty's house like they had planned to after school. Project Domain's eyes were everywhere, and M2 sensed them almost as intimately as he sensed M1. He knew they were up the trees, on the streets, in the fields, searching, watching.

Away from that godforsaken underground dungeon and with all the wildlife in Scotty's backyard, M2's abilities restored like wilted flowers given a cold drink of water. He wasn't what he had been those decades ago before he was captured, but he was more like his old self every day. This was how he knew about the Red Crab's search teams all over the city, and of Adam's own counterfeit teacher. There was no doubt they were watching the boy and his friends. Scotty had planned to tell them to stay away, but then the police chief, Dan Fogel, arrived at the landfill. Recently, there had been a spate of corpses found near the gate. On closer inspection, they were discovered to be mannequins made to look like murder victims—each one with Scotty's name scrawled in pig's blood on their clothing. The cruel pranks were the work of one of the bus stop victims' brothers, who was convinced the man who'd cut off his own ear had gone on a city-wide killing spree.

It was yet another antic by a lost citizen, Dan was telling Scotty at the office when M2 squeezed himself into Scotty's form and slipped outside. To anyone looking, it was just the crazy landfill manager going for a walk, enjoying some air and sunshine on a warm and breezeless day. He had located St. Jude's easily once he adjusted his valves, but the going was slow. Human legs, awkward and stiff, felt like the metal casts the Mad Scientist had once poured on him. Heavy as a black hole. As flexible as the speed of light. It was no feat for him, of course, but it made him realize just how weak humans really were. To make up time, he unfolded his legs in concealed areas and flashed forward faster than a human rocket ship. His fears that someone would talk to him were unfounded, for no one did. The avoidance made M2 sad, for on Kepler-186f, communion was necessary for life. No one avoided another because avoidance meant nothingness. It meant death.

Now, coming toward St. Jude's in his Scotty body, M2 was enveloped with small humans. Joy came off them like vapor. He netted their euphoria in his valves and tried pushing it to M1 to ease her darkness. He wasn't sure if it worked but felt, just maybe, that it did, for there was the tiniest of pushes back. It fortified him and he walked on in his clunky body, looking for Adam.

M2 found him quickly. The three boys he had strung up just days before were rushing down the sidewalk near a small park, oblivious to the activity tracking them. M2 was acutely aware that there were seventeen Project Domain soldiers counterfeiting gardeners, construction workers, dog walkers, utility operators, and joggers. They obviously had their orders from the Red Crab because they were so attuned to the trio that they didn't pay attention to M2, even though he limped like he was missing his bones which, in fact, he was.

A girl on a scooter cut in front of Ravi. It made him look up. Barely a bus-length away was Scotty Waymore wobbling up the hill. Only, Ravi knew it wasn't Scotty. He knew because Scotty was walking like a man with too much alcohol or not enough muscle. And M2's iridescent sheen was in Scotty's eyes, barely noticeable—but once you met an alien, you never forgot.

Ravi's first instinct was to call out, but he remembered that to everyone else Scotty was still Skitzo Scotty. People would notice.

Instead, he nudged Adam and Douggie and whispered, "Marty's here. Don't make it obvious."

The use of the nickname they had come up with at Scotty's house made the other two stiffen and raise their heads. Douggie, who had not yet learned the art of subtlety, shifted his eyes and waved.

M2 stopped. There were no transistors to concoct human communication, so he lifted a finger and rang Adam's phone.

Adam answered it.

Static whirred through the microphone. "Red Crab watch. No come."

Douggie tugged on Adam's arm. "What's he saying?"

Adam looked around. There were a lot more people around St. Jude's than usual, he realized with dawning understanding. "He's saying," he started, then lowered his voice to barely a whisper. "He's saying people are watching us and not to go *you know where*."

"But what about the stuff?" Douggie protested, holding out his squirming bag where he had a mouse, many ants, and several caterpillars.

Ravi elbowed him in the ribs. "Don't, you idiot!"

M2 walked on, afraid of catching the soldiers' attention.

"Dark time," M2 said through Adam's phone. "No light. Come dark."

Adam nodded. Then he whispered, "Go home." He wasn't sure if M2 heard him because the staticky connection had already ended, but he knew M2 wouldn't stay in the area anyway. He turned to see how far M2 was and spotted him hobbling past the school.

Principal Hahn, who had raised a hand to greet Scotty, frowned. "He must be on a mission today. Didn't even see us."

"You know him?" Theo said casually.

"Mr. Waymore is our nighttime janitor. He's been volunteering here for years. We wouldn't have our art program without him." Hahn refrained from adding that he was Claire's father, feeling that it was her information to share, if she wanted to share it.

Claire crossed her arms. "He's my dad. We're not on the best terms."

"He won't even say hi to you?" Theo said, and Hahn gave him a look that suggested he was nearing strike three.

"The last time we spoke I made it clear I wanted space. That's why he walked by without saying anything. He tries to catch me at the school whenever he's here even though he knows I'm not ready to talk to him. That's why he's early today."

If Hahn weren't looking ready to shoot him, Theo would have pressed. He knew Claire's father was crazy. It was the first thing Intelligence noted in their summary of the community. Anything she told him wouldn't be new, but it would give him the chance to make her think he cared. Maybe make her feel like she could confide in him. Maybe tell her something he didn't know about Adam or what kind of man she was interested in. Theo, of course, could be any man she liked, if only for a night.

As the last of the students left the school, Hahn said, "Well, I'm about ready to call it a day. I'll see you tomorrow, Tyler. Claire, may I have a word before you go?"

Theo understood he was being dismissed but he grinned at the old man and departed the school in the old but functioning Camry the procurement department had shoved on him.

Back in the school, Claire retrieved her lunch bag and purse then stopped by Hahn's office. "You don't like him," she said in the doorway.

"No, I do not. But that isn't the reason I wanted to speak to you. I didn't want to mention anything outside because it's not my business to share your business, but the way your father was walking had me wondering about his health. Also, he walked right past the school. Right past it without so much as a hello. He wasn't early. He wasn't coming here *at all*. I don't want to upset you—take from it what you will—but those appear to me the signs of a stroke. The forgetfulness and the limp . . . However you feel about your relationship, I don't believe you want to see him suffer. I asked you in because I think someone needs to check in on him. It doesn't have to be you, but I don't want you to be upset if it's me."

He regarded her with so much tenderness, she couldn't help but be touched. "He *was* acting strange. You really think it's a stroke?"

"Maybe. Maybe not," Hahn said. "But if he had had one and no one thinks to look in on him, he could be in big trouble. It's no imposition for me to pay him a visit. He's done so much for us, it's the least I could do."

Claire was silent. "I should be the one to do it. I'd call my mom but if he needs help, I don't think she'd be in the mental state to drive him to a hospital."

"And *you*?" Hahn asked.

"I'd be okay," she said. "But company might be good. Any hot dates tonight?"

"My dear, after thirty-eight years of marriage, every date with Norma is a hot date, but the heat usually comes from both of us ending up with indigestion in the middle of the night." He chuckled. "Norma is with her walking club tonight. They're hiking the river from the Gazette to that wine bar up near Craig's Valley. And she'd put one of those hiking shoes up where the sun doesn't shine if I didn't insist on coming with you."

"You know I'd be lost without you, right?"

"That's what the women tell me, but only the ones who've lost their glasses. Come on. Let an old man drive you and we can put both of our minds at ease. We might even find him walking somewhere along our way. If we don't, we'll pop in and you can use me as an excuse not to stay too long. I'll drop you back at the school when we're done."

"You'd have made a great counsellor," she said.

"And miss the toilet bombs and ant invasions? *Never*," he said.

As Hahn was locking up the office, Claire took out her phone to let Ty's after-school sitter, Mrs. Puffard, know that she would be late picking him up today.

The retired woman immediately typed back: *No rush. Take as long as you need. I'll keep him until he's graduated if you like.* She followed the message with half a dozen laughing faces, as she often did. That settled, Claire followed Hahn to his car and they left the school for Scotty Waymore's house.

26. Cricket Bolognese

In Canada, April weather is as confusing as puberty. A person can wake to a heatwave and go to bed to a snowstorm. The temperature changes hourly, sometimes quicker than it takes to cook pasta, which Scotty was doing as he spied a canopy of dark clouds through his kitchen window. The weather forecast had been wrong, but somehow the gloom suited Scotty's mood as he threw the salt in and waited for the water to boil.

"What were you thinking? Don't you know they're looking for you? You could've been caught."

He'd been pacing the house ever since he'd found M2 slinking onto the back porch. The sight of himself lurking like a burglar up his own steps first jarred Scotty, then made him angry. He'd only known M2 for a short while, but already his concern for the creature was parental, full of affection, with a good helping of fear. Catching M2 sneaking in was like when he'd caught Claire coming through her bedroom window after a date with Mark Larson. It was a date she'd been forbidden to go on—and the very one that got her pregnant. They hadn't yelled at Claire but let the weight of their disappointment land on her unsheltered shoulders with all the intensity only loving parents could muster. With their continued love and assistance, she had turned out just fine, but M2's situation was different. A slip up wouldn't get M2 pregnant. It would get him captured. Or dead. The consequences were much more severe for M2, perhaps even for Scotty, and for the last hour Scotty had been shaking a wooden spoon, reminding him.

"You want to get back, you have to lay low and do what I tell you. It's not safe." Scotty's famous Bolognese was bubbling in the saucepan, spitting up onto his shirt, but he paid no notice.

M2's faces took on a somber tone. "Red Crab. Kill small shirts," a transistor sputtered.

"Don't you think I know that? We talked about this. One of those kids has been coming here for ages. There's police reports about it. There was a week where he shit-bombed my goddamn front door every day. Everybody knows that kid can't stay away. Them coming here doesn't automatically mean someone's going to follow them. But *you*," he pointed his spoon at M2, "prancing around like a duck with his wings clipped . . . you might as well leave a trail of breadcrumbs to this table."

Outside, thunder began to beat the sky. Scotty turned on the kitchen light. He lowered the temperature of the burner with the sauce and increased the heat on the burner with the pot of water. He breathed the way Dan suggested whenever someone swore at him or wrote *Skitzo Scotty* on his truck. It calmed him a little. M2 must have been doing the same because a breezy whistle came from his valves.

"Look," Scotty said. "I know people have been terrible to you. That's not me. I don't mean to upset you. I'm just worried about you. Do you understand? I don't want you to think I'm one of them. You'll always be safe here, but they'll always be looking for you, so you have to be careful."

One of M2's limbs wrapped around Scotty's waist, another put the lid on the saucepan, and one more put the pasta in the water, which was now boiling.

"All right, all right. Enough with the soft stuff," Scotty said, and patted the arm around his waist.

Rain began tapping the tin roof. Faraway lightning glittered. It was the kind of enchanting spring storm Scotty loved.

Scotty was pouring the pasta into a colander when there was a timid knock on the back door. A moment later, Adam came in, followed by Ravi and the brat. They were sopping wet.

"No come," M2 said through a transistor. "No come. No come." His faces turned a deep purple green, the color and texture of avocado peel. The color of alien worry.

Douggie walked past him and put his backpack on the table. It came down with a heavy *thunk* against the plates Scotty had set out. "Hi Marty. You said not to come until dark," he said to M2. "It's dark."

It was cloudy, sure, but not dark. Not dark enough to obscure three boys carrying big weighty bags. Bags that squirmed, no less. Scotty went to the windows, looking for the search party, and saw nothing but foggy, wet field.

"No one's going to think our parents would allow us out in *this*," Ravi said smartly. Then, when he saw the skepticism on Scotty's face and what appeared to be the same on M2's faces, he confided, "We snuck out. Adam's parents think he's at my house, my parents think he's at my house and Douggie's parents don't care where he is."

"It's true," Douggie said.

"We made sure no one followed us," Adam cut in.

"How can you be sure?" Scotty's hands went to his head as he tugged his hair into wild, unruly tufts. He gestured to M2. "He's got the military looking for him. They don't mess around. They can see the date on the nickel in your pocket from space."

"Tell him, Douggie." Adam nudged him.

Douggie rubbed the back of his neck with his hands. A spray of rain from his fingers fell on the napkins beside M2's plate, warping the dye on the little blue flowers so they looked like weeds. "Uh, every time I . . . uh . . . came here, I went down that row of bushes from the Corner Mart to that church near that ripped sign, you know, the one with the lady in cowboy boots for the rodeo days we used to have?" The route wasn't new to Adam or Ravi, for they had just travelled every mosquito-biting, branch-scratching inch of it, but Scotty's mouth fell open. Douggie stared at the damp spots on the table and continued. "If you turn left there, there's another row of bushes kind of mashed together and if you go in between them, you can get here without anyone seeing you. I used it all the time."

"That's how—" Scotty's anger boiled up hotter than the Bolognese. He gritted his teeth. The muscles in his jaw spasmed. "All this time?"

Douggie nodded. "I'm sorry. I'm so sorry."

"Face bad," said a receiver now.

"Yes, my face is bad," Scotty growled. "It's called anger. And I'm controlling it better than you think."

Just then, the bag Ravi had been carrying toppled over.

"What's in there?" Scotty asked.

"Slugs," Ravi told him. "They come whenever we leave our dog's food outside. There's a bunch of big ones and a few little ones. My sister collects them and puts them in a fish tank. Or, it's like a fish tank, but we don't put water in it." He took the bag, unzipped it, and handed it to M2. "Go ahead. She won't miss them."

Though they knew that any creature they gave to M2 would be killed, none of them wanted to see it. Politely, they averted their eyes to the still-steaming colander of pasta while the bag was upended into M2's mouths. The crunch of shells sounded like someone was walking on gravel in the middle of the kitchen.

"How can you tell it's working?" Adam asked when the quiet made him uncomfortable.

M2 pointed to a picture of Scotty, Meredith, and Claire with sunburns and swimsuits from one of their happy trips to Mexico. Claire had been about ten years old then, and as loveable as ever. She had a small plastic shovel in her hand and a bucket in the other. She had patches of sand on her knees and another on the tip of her nose.

M2 elongated, compressed, changed. Suddenly, Claire was with them. He got all the details right, even the ones the picture didn't show. Every freckle, every dimple, every then-crooked tooth accounted for. When her likeness turned around, there was the small scar on her right shoulder blade from a bad fall off her bike and even the bandages Meredith had applied that very same day, when a honey wasp had stung her calf three times during breakfast.

Scotty's breath escaped him. A tear for his daughter of yesteryear rolled down his cheek and he had to restrain himself from bawling. "Not bad," he said when he was able to compose himself.

"Do me next! Do me!" Douggie yelled, waving his hand.

Ravi pushed him aside. "Me! Me!"

Adam rolled his eyes as though he couldn't believe the audacity of the children beside him.

Scotty bit his thumbnail, thinking. "So, you're better now. Except for her eyes—there's a bit of silver in her whites, but I might be the only person who notices that because I'm her father—I can't tell the difference. Can you talk?"

M2 shook his heads. "No," said a transistor. M2 could talk, technically, but not in a language humans would understand, not in a way that wouldn't blow their simple minds and make what little they had as useless as a ballpoint pen in space.

"Can you ever talk? I mean, even if we get you more—take you to the fish hatchery—can you say something then?"

"Not know," said a transistor.

"Well, then, say you eat all the bugs and a bay full of fish and those slugs you just chomped down on, will you at least walk normal? The way you looked when you were coming up those stairs, I thought your legs were broken. You can't walk like that down there. They'll know."

"Walk better," conveyed M2, and he proceeded around the table in his Claire costume, actually skipping the way Claire did whenever the world was all good. It didn't last long, but long enough for Scotty to almost forget she was only an illusion. M2's color and form returned and then he was just an alien in a kitchen. "Walk better. Stay long time."

"You got all of that from a picture? All that? Jeez, you're better than I thought," Scotty said.

While Scotty was quizzing M2, Adam worked M2's mission over in his mind. M2 was going to impersonate a guy the aliens called the Red Crab. He was the top dog. The leader supreme. A no-nonsense powerhouse with the aura of Joseph Stalin. Adam had read about Stalin in his social studies class. It wasn't of particular interest, but the lesson had come at a time when Douggie was unbearable and, when learning the mass-murdering dictator was barely over five feet tall, he had wondered if squatty little Douggie was on the same path. It was an ignorant thought, because more lessons had taught him just how evil Stalin was, but it etched that piece of history in his young mind nonetheless. Because M2 had shown him when they first met, Adam knew the Red Crab's people reacted similarly to how people reacted to Joseph Stalin. Cowering. Pandering. Cringing. Fawning over his every move, terrified any word of their own would send them away to somewhere much worse. He realized, then, that M2 didn't *need* to talk. He could just walk right in.

He said, "The Hollis guy, the Red Crab, everyone's afraid of him, right? Not just the aliens?"

M2 seemed to think about this, but his answer on the transistor was quick. "All hate Red Crab. Red Crab bad. Bad ones . . . not . . . like Red Crab."

"Then that's it," Adam said. "You don't have to talk. You just have to be as mean as he is."

"Mar-ty not mean," crackled a machine.

It was Ravi who spoke. "You *have* to be. Adam's right. You have to be as mean as he is. Maybe even more. Pretend you're so mad at something that you can't even talk. You got to put veins in his face, make it red, you know."

M2 didn't want to know, but he knew. He knew everything about the Red Crab. Every frown. Every furrow of his brows. The way the lines around his mouth bunched and corded as if bullets were implanted under his skin whenever he shouted. The way his mean eyes grew impossibly large when he was onto something, as though the Mad Scientist had given him special lenses to see through bullshit, to see through people, to see through aliens. He didn't want to, but he did.

"Holy shit," Douggie said, for now in front of them stood Hollis Brubaker. Every creature-killing, person-punishing, self-loving inch of him. His parchment-paper, tanning-bed skin. His coarse hair the color of rotting pumpkin left to the crows. "Is that him? The Red Crab?"

M2's silver eyes, not yet strong enough to fully conceal him, rolled in those paper sockets. He nodded and, nauseated at what he had just done, went back to his better form.

"You sure don't like him, do you?" Scotty said. "Your skin's all grey now. Look at you."

And it was. M2's replicate-sickened skin was as grey as the clouds now roiling across the sky.

Douggie went to the sink where the colander of pasta was and scooped up a heaping bowl, then he added a ladle of Scotty's Bolognese and drew from his pocket a handful of crickets, which he sprinkled on top. He put it on the table in front of M2. "You need your strength. But if you're going to eat that stuff, at least it should taste good." Then, without another word, Douggie made himself a bowl and sat down to eat.

Scotty was about to tell the world's largest brat to get off his chair and out of his house when a small SUV pulled up beside his truck.

He blinked, trying to remember where he'd seen the car before when it dawned on him that it was Irving Hahn's. Worse, that his own daughter Claire was getting out of the front passenger seat.

"Hide, damn it. All of you *hide*. It's Claire, she's here. And your principal, too! They're coming to the door."

At once, M2 compacted to a little cube. Douggie and Adam ran to the bathroom and locked the door. Ravi dove under the couch. Scotty crouched behind the counter, away from the door and the see-through side panels. Seconds later, Claire rang the doorbell.

I'll pretend that I'm napping. She hasn't seen me, so she doesn't know I'm awake, Scotty thought.

The bell rang again. Twice. The tinny chime needled their nerves.

"Dad? Dad are you in there? I need to talk to you. Please don't be mad at me. I just want to talk."

Scotty bit his lip.

A bruising bang hit the aluminum. It must have been Hahn's fist, unless his petite little Claire had *thrown* herself at it.

"Scotty?" Hahn said now. "Scotty, we need to see you. Come to the door if you're in there. I'm going to give you five seconds before we come in whether you like it or not. I'm sorry to have to do this, but you've left us no choice."

There was some murmuring outside and a key slid into the lock. He was so thunderstruck by their arrival, Scotty had forgotten that Claire had a key. He bolted from the counter, steadied himself, then opened the door, keeping his newly regrown ear turned away. "Can't a man nap? Is someone dying?" he groaned as though he'd just woken. His hair, messed from when the boys showed up, fit the part beautifully. Then, pretending he was just getting his wits about him, Scotty said, "Claire? Is your mother okay?" They looked at him with their serious faces. Scotty thought they were relieved, but relieved about what, he had no idea.

Claire threw her arms around him. She hadn't hugged him in so long, he flinched. Actually flinched. Now he was worried there *was* something wrong, that maybe Meredith . . .

"She's fine, Dad," Claire said. "Nothing's wrong. We just wanted to make sure you're okay, that's all."

"Why wouldn't I be okay?"

His daughter looked at Hahn as if she wanted him to answer.

"I'm sorry we interrupted your nap," Hahn said obediently. "If anyone knows how elusive sleep can be when you get to be *seasoned*, it's me. But there is something I wanted to talk to you about that couldn't wait, and I asked Claire to accompany me. If you give us just a few minutes, we can sit at your table and talk to you out of the rain, then we'll be on our way, unless Claire wants to stay, of course."

"Now's not a good time," Scotty told them. But he didn't want to hurt Claire's feelings when he had worked so hard for so long to get her back, so he tugged the shirt he'd wrinkled just seconds before he had opened the door and said, "It was a rough day at the site. I'd like to shower and then I can meet you somewhere. Maybe at Boomer's? You always liked the pie there."

Claire *did* like the pie there, but she didn't want pie right now. What she wanted was to get her father to a doctor and make sure he hadn't had a stroke.

Hahn, who also liked the pie at Boomer's, wanted to get Scotty to a doctor perhaps even more than Claire. This was because when Scotty opened the door, he'd blocked Claire's view to the kitchen table. But Hahn, still healthily over six feet even though his body had begun to stoop as had happened to most of his friends, was tall enough to see over Scotty's shoulder.

He almost wished he hadn't.

It wasn't a large home, in fact by most standards it was almost tiny, and for this reason, Irving Hahn's keen old eyes saw on Scotty Waymore's table a bowl of pasta with something that looked like big bugs crawling over and under the red sauce. More bugs were crawling on the table. Slugs, by the look of it. *Had Scotty been eating the bugs?* Hahn wondered. The evidence was almost overwhelming. And it hardened Hahn's conviction that Scotty *had* had a stroke. He put his hand on the door in case Scotty was tempted to close it and said, "I'd like to come in, Scotty. We won't be but a minute. If you make this easy, we'll be on our way before you know it, but if you don't, well, I'm not a man who takes to invading one's personal space but, in this case, I will do it. Don't make me barge in."

Scotty sighed. He glanced backward. "I wasn't expecting company. It's a bit of a mess."

"We don't mind," Hahn said.

"I live with a ten-year-old," Claire said as if that would make him feel better, but it only made him feel worse. Much worse.

He turned into the house and flapped a resigned hand over his shoulder. "Sit at the table and I'll make some coffee."

Behind him, Claire gasped. Scotty turned and saw that she was gaping at the bugs and that she had just dropped her purse on M2. Hahn was giving her looks as if to reassure her, but she went on gasping and screeching at all the crawly things the boys had collected. "What—" She was about to ask him about the bugs when a cough came from somewhere in the house. Claire's head whipped to the bathroom. "Is someone here?" she asked.

"You're being paranoid," Scotty said dismissively.

"Paranoid? You're calling *me* paranoid?" Claire's frustration vented out like sour gas, pent up after a long fermentation. "Look at your table! The bugs . . . your hobbling walk at the school. I thought you were drunk, but then I thought, no, he doesn't drink like that, it must be something else. A stroke, maybe. And I think we were right. Just look at you. Look at your *place*."

"You think I've had a *stroke*?" Scotty said, almost wishing he had. A stroke would be easier than aiding and abetting an alien and the three kids naively trying to help him. He followed her glance to the table where a sauce-covered cricket was squiggling over a fork. He sought a quick explanation but found none.

Scotty had been so focused on Claire that he hadn't seen Hahn's silent movement toward the bathroom. Hahn knocked.

"I told you no one was here," Scotty protested, angry now at the invasion.

"Tell that to the people whispering near your toilet," Hahn said, frowning. The voices were whispering, sure, but they sounded vaguely familiar. One voice told another to *shhhh* and another groaned like he had been poked in the stomach. Hahn knocked again. "Excuse me? Hello? I know you're in there so you might as well come out."

Scotty threw up his hands. "This is ridiculous. I don't need this. I don't know what you're getting at, but I don't like it. I love you, Claire, but I think you both should leave."

Ravi, who had been still as steel under the couch holding his breath, felt a tickle near his ear. He thought it was probably just a hair or that maybe one of the dust balls under the couch had been disturbed and settled on him. Then he heard the high buzz of insect legs rubbing together on his neck and he couldn't help it. He slapped the cricket off him and scrambled toward the coffee table.

He went a little too far, for looking down at him was Ms. Bishop and, a moment later, Principal Hahn himself.

Seeing Ravi there, caught trying to conceal himself on the floor, Hahn went from surprised to angry, even a little disgusted. The perversion that instantly struck his mind sent a jolt of rage through him and he dug his fingernails into the palm of his hand to keep from striking Scotty. "Stand up, Mister Das," Hahn said kindly and offered the boy his hand.

Ravi took it and stood, looking from Hahn to Claire to Scotty and back to Hahn again.

"Where the seed spreads, the branches follow," Hahn said. "Adam, Douglas, you may come out now."

There was a click and the bathroom door unlocked, then it opened.

"What—" Claire started when Adam and Douggie, heads bowed liked whipped dogs, shuffled out. "Why—" but she couldn't finish. There was no reasonable world where three boys would be hiding in her father's house, including one that he had hated locked inside the bathroom. Was this a . . . a *kidnapping*? Had she and Hahn caught her father . . .? Her stomach soured.

Dawning on Scotty was the realization they thought he was a child predator, one of the sickos they locked away for decades or even killed. It revolted him. His ears turned red. "It's not what you think. It's—"

"Why don't you tell us what it is," Hahn said to the boys. He nodded to the couch. "I think you should sit and tell us why you are in this house. More precisely, I think you should tell us why you felt the need to *hide* in this house."

They sat. Adam first, then the others, squeezing tightly together like wedges in wood. They rubbed their knees and stared at the floor, silent.

"No one?" Hahn said.

Claire went around the couch and took the armchair near the TV. She leaned forward, unsure of what to say but knowing she had to say it. "It's okay, boys. You can tell us. You won't get in trouble, I promise."

No one answered.

"Boys, I want you to think about this. We are here to help you and we can only do that if you talk to us. Tell me, today at the school, I thought I saw Mr. Waymore talk to you. Is there the possibility I saw an exchange of something? Drugs, perhaps?"

Claire hadn't thought of that, but compared to the other, more terrible possibility, she prayed it *was* drugs. That her father had been *dealing* to the students, not . . . not the other thing.

"We don't do drugs," Ravi said. The others shook their heads vehemently.

"First I'm a pervert, then I'm a dealer?" Scotty grinded his teeth. His lips were so tightly pressed they almost disappeared. "You two are rich. Fucking rich, pardon the language, boys. It's nothing like you think, but you wouldn't believe me if I told you because you've never believed me. You took my own goddamn grandson away from me and now you're here accusing me of something unforgivable. Get out of my house. All of you. Get out." He hadn't realized it, but he was on the verge of tears. His throat had gotten thick and his voice poured out of him like syrup. His eyes blinded him like he was under water.

"Oh, I don't think we'll be going," Hahn said. "Not until we get some answers. I'm guessing the bugs are yours? I'm looking at you, Douglas, since I know how fond you are of them."

Douggie nodded.

"And they're here because?"

No answer.

Adam stood then and went to his backpack. There was a great number of caterpillars and a few mice in ventilated containers inside but behind the plastic partition, there was also his sketchbook, which he now took out. He flipped through some pages and got to the one he wanted. He left it open on the table and stepped away.

Claire was confused by the drawing, but Hahn recognized it immediately. It was the image that Tyler Carver had photographed. The one with the alien body and Nick Penner's face. The one Hahn had made Tyler Cagey delete.

Hahn tapped the page. "You're saying this has something to why you're here? Something with"—he pointed at the sketch of Nick Penner's face— "*him*? Answer me in words so I know you haven't lost your tongue."

Adam looked at Scotty, who was leaning on the counter as though the weight of the world had been dropped on him and his legs would buckle without the support.

"Adam," Hahn said gently and stepped aside to block Adam's view of the landfill manager. "Over here, Adam. I want you to tell me. Just you and me. You're completely safe. And as Ms. Bishop said, I promise you won't get in trouble."

In this moment, seeing the old man bear down on the boy like that, Scotty knew there was nothing Adam could say that would appease them. And if the boy told the truth, they would believe he was just as batty as Skitzo Scotty. It was a pain Scotty wished on no one, not even the brat.

"If you want me to explain, I'll need you to move your purse, Claire," Scotty said.

"What?"

"Your purse. It's in the way. I need you to move it so you can understand what we're about to tell you. And before you go hollering out of the house, I want you to know you're completely safe. Safer in here than out there."

For the first time, she looked at him the way the others did. She shed the controlled courtesy and gave Hahn an open look that suggested Scotty wasn't just a little crazy, but outright insane. It was a look that committed him, padded him up, and gave him a little cup of pills three times a day for the rest of his life.

"You know about this?" Hahn asked the boys, who all nodded.

"Marty's safe," Douggie piped up. "He doesn't look like it, but he is."

"Who's Marty?" Claire asked, then she looked down at her purse. "Have you got someone *locked* down there? Under the floor?"

Scotty went to the table, bent down, and picked up Claire's purse. It was one of those big contraptions Scotty had never understood, and it was heavy and laden with books, as evidenced by the open zipper. He put it on the counter. "I'd suggest you both sit down.

Boys, let them take the couch. You're small enough to squeeze on the chair."

Without another word, the boys shifted over to the chair, Adam on one arm, Ravi on the other, and Douggie in the middle. Hahn, understanding that when someone told you to sit, you'd better sit if you didn't want to faint, rounded the couch and sat. Claire followed him.

Hahn looked at the boys and raised an eyebrow.

"Don't freak out," Adam whispered.

27. Vicious Little Bunch

When it seemed Scotty had decided not to share his secret, Hahn said, "We're waiting. We won't *freak out*, as Adam so eloquently put it."

Scotty glanced at the little white cube on the floor where Claire's purse and been. He knew what their reactions would be. They would react not like him—for he had been waiting for the Voice to come—but like the boys had. They would react with outright terror, maybe one of them (likely Claire) would even wet their pants. He tugged at his bottom lip the way he did when he was in deep thought, and an idea came to him.

"I'm going to show you, but before I do I want you to look at me really good and tell me if you notice anything. You haven't yet, but of course you wouldn't. There's no damn way you'd expect it."

"Dad—"

"Just look, Claire. That's all I'm asking. Can you just look, please? *Look* at me."

She did. But it wasn't Claire who noticed the change, it was Hahn.

"Well, I'll be . . ." Hahn said, now leaning toward Scotty with a look on the edge between surprise and appreciation.

"What? What?" Claire asked, almost panting with impatience.

"Your father's got a new ear," Hahn said, pointing. "It's hanging off him like it'd never left."

Her eyes swung to his ear. Her mouth fell open and she covered it with her hands. "How . . . you . . . it's impossible."

"Marty can do anything," Ravi said to the disbelieving adults.

"He can," Scotty agreed. "But he'll also scare the living daylights out of you if you're not prepared. So be prepared."

Claire reached for Hahn's hand. Scotty was too consumed with what he was about to show them to be offended.

Scotty bent down to the little cube and said, "Do your thing, Marty."

M2 had been listening, watching, waiting, but now he released himself up and out. Now higher than the chair seat. Now taller than the kitchen table. Now brushing against the ceiling. Now skimming the front door, the kitchen window, the couch.

Claire whimpered. Her eyes bulged with fear. She drew her feet up off the floor and curled into Hahn, who sat, tight-lipped and silent but watching with the eyes of a man who had seen everything, everything but that.

"Claire, Irving," Scotty said. "This is M2, but we call him Marty. Marty is trying to find his way home and we're going to help him. Say hello, Marty."

At once, a transistor squawked, "He-llo."

Irving Hahn had seen terrible, frightening things. He'd seen children disfigured by war. Babies washed up on riverbanks beside the bloated bodies of their mothers, some with rigor mortis fingers still clutched stiffly around them. Men and women, old, young, able and disabled, shot for no reason. He'd seen gougings and beatings, starvation to the point of death, abandonments, torture, pain. But this terrible thing, rising from the floor like bushfire, snatched his breath and he had to hammer his own chest to get it back.

"My God," he said, over and over.

Claire fainted. When she came to on Hahn's shoulder, her father was above her, fanning her face with a newspaper.

"What happened?" she said weakly, then she remembered the monster and scrambled up. She thrust a finger at M2, who was quietly waiting for the commotion to settle. "What is that? Get it away! Oh! Get it away!" She squeezed her eyes shut.

"Marty won't hurt you," Adam said, and, to prove it to her, stood from the chair and walked over to M2. "See, Ms. Bishop?"

Reluctantly, she opened her eyes. She cried out, "Don't do that! Get away, Adam! Don't touch him."

Adam ignored her. He touched M2. M2 draped a limb over Adam's shoulder, then Adam became Claire herself. He grew red hair, breasts, and those freckles she had despised and Scotty had loved ever since she could remember. Ravi and Douggie burst out laughing. Unable to help himself, Hahn joined in, first gasping at surprise, then chuckling at Adam's metamorphosis.

Claire turned on him. "What are you laughing about? You all think this is some kind of joke?"

"It's no joke, I can assure you," Hahn said, wiping his eyes. "But in the few seconds you were out, Marty here shared something with me."

"*Marty*? What the hell are you talking about? Have you lost your *mind*?"

"If anything, I've *gained* my mind. What would you call that, Marty? What you just showed me? *History*, I suppose? Everything we've put you through? Is there a word for that?" For once, the old man was stumped.

"Me," said a transistor, meaning *I showed you me*. M2 released Adam and now stretched out to Claire. She recoiled as though a great wall of lava were coming at her.

"He's not going to hurt you, honey," Scotty said.

"He's nice," said Ravi.

"Your father's right, Claire," Hahn said gently. "Those voices he's heard, they're more real than this room. Marty isn't going to hurt you. But if you let him, he'll explain all you need to know." He rose and went to M2 as Adam had. Then Irving Hahn threw his arms around the monster in front of Claire's own eyes, and hugged him. He leaned his head against one of those dark, waving heads and said, "I'm sorry for you, Marty, but it's nice to meet you. It's so damned nice to meet you."

"Nice. Meet," said a transistor, and the alien blush the color of oranges bloomed on his faces.

Again, one of M2's limbs stretched to Claire. She looked at the monster and Hahn, her father, the boys, and it dawned on her that she was the only one afraid. She reached out her hand, pulled it back, stretched it forward again. Then she closed her eyes and bit her lip. M2 closed the gap. Instantly he imparted everything he'd shown her father, the boys, Hahn, and when he was done, he let his arm slip to the floor.

A dam burst of tears flooded Claire's eyes. She was no longer afraid but felt a sadness so pervasive, it irreparably hurt her heart. She didn't go to M2 as Hahn had but now to her father, throwing herself at him as though she were that scrape-kneed girl of six years old and needed her daddy.

"I'm so sorry," she blubbered into him. "I didn't believe you. I'm sorry for not believing you. Oh, Dad. I'm so sorry. All this time you were right and I was . . . I was so wrong. I'll never forgive myself. I'm so sorry. Oh, Dad." Even with the others in the room, she held nothing back.

Her dripping nose leaked onto his shirt, but Scotty just held her tighter, rubbing her back to soothe her. "It's okay, Claire Bear. It's okay. We're good now."

Scotty felt the pressure around his stomach ease, and he let her go. She turned to M2, wiping her face with the palms of her hands. She sniffed. "I'm sorry, Marty. You didn't deserve that."

M2 drew her in for a hug and she let him. All those limbs, all those faces, all that slick skin, yet Claire felt more at peace than she had in years. There was something about M2, something that calmed her, and she settled in deeper.

"Good," M2 said through a transistor.

When their shock resided to an acceptable curiosity, Scotty and Hahn cleared the table while Claire made tea. With the humans occupied, M2 quietly emptied the contents of the backpacks, trying not to disturb—or disgust—his new friends. Claire found cookies and gave them to Douggie to plate. Ravi and Adam worked together to make iced tea, with just a tad too much sugar, as they liked. When they were done, they sat at the table, all except M2, who was too heavy for the chairs and sat on the floor.

Hahn accepted a cup of peppermint tea from Claire, unable to take his eyes off M2. "I can't believe you were under our feet all this time. How many others did you say there were?"

"There's forty-seven of them. Martians. Some from Saturn, Pluto," Scotty started, but Douggie rushed to finish for him.

"They're from everywhere," he exclaimed, holding up his fingers to count the planets as he named them. "Pluto, Mars, Uranus, Saturn, Venus, and the Kepler one where he's from."

"So is the plan to get all of them out? I mean, we have to try, don't we?" Claire said as she sat, warming her hands on her cup. "We can't just leave them there."

"In a perfect world, we would," Hahn said. "But I fear that if we overfill our basket, it's apt to spill and we'll get nothing at all. Marty needs his partner, there's no doubt about that, and even if he plays the part of that Hollis fellow and manages to get her out, I doubt those guards will look away from a mass escape." Claire had started to protest but he held up a palm to mollify her. "I'm not saying it's right, Claire. But I don't think those people down there care about what's right. And they'd just as likely kill them all than let even one escape, so we have to be careful. My hope is that we help him get her out of there, and when they're free and off this doomed planet of ours, they can somehow help their former cellmates find a way out or at least convince those bloody people to leave those aliens alone."

None of them liked Hahn's reasoning and they said so. The kids looked downright gloomy.

Scotty sighed. "He's right. I don't like it any more than you, but we can't reason with those people. We can't just break into a government facility and expect them to care about our feelings. They'll shoot us. But if we can help at least one of them, I say we do it." He frowned at the eagerness on the boys' faces. "And when I say *we*, I mean us adults. I know you want to help, and you've done that, but now you have to leave the rest of it to us. It's not right to ask you to help us, it's probably not even *legal* for you to be here. Even if it is, I know more than anyone how people talk. I don't want to put you in danger, and I don't want you to be treated like me. It's almost better for you if you pretend none of this happened."

Their protests deafened Hahn's ears. He covered them with his hands until their complaining died down. "Viscous little bunch, aren't they?" he said. Claire and Scotty nodded, agreeing. "That gives me an idea. I do agree with Scotty that it's too dangerous for you to help either here or down there, but not at the *school*. Ms. Bishop knows I've never liked your new teacher. That Tyler Cagey. What's his real name again, Marty?"

"Th-eo," a transistor sputtered. "Bad."

"That's right. I remember now. Theo Carver. Clever, but not too clever for you three. Marty, I suggest you make for your girl during the day. They most likely believe you're active at night, hiding in the shadows, don't want to be seen sort of thing, but I don't think anyone will expect you to walk in during the *day*." Hahn spun to Adam, Douggie, and Ravi. "When Marty's down there,

I want you to give that soldier hell in school. Bomb the toilets. Bring on the insects. Unleash the bees. Spill some superglue on his chair. All the things you're good at, Douglas. Keep him busy." Hahn winked at Douggie, who was positively gaping at him. "And, Adam, I think you should draw more of those pictures, but with a different background. Something far away but still in the city. Something recognizable like city hall or the Garrett Gazette. Limbs all over it. And accidently lose your book or drop a paper. We need that bully to call his resources away from here, to anywhere else. Just for a little while."

"Sounds like you've done this before," Claire raised an eyebrow at Hahn.

"I've rounded up soldiers, yes, but the rounding up of children takes far greater skill and, thankfully, I have a lot of experience in that department," he said.

Scotty had been watching Marty as Hahn's plan unfolded. The alien had given no indication as to his thoughts on the plan, he just sat there undulating like weeds under slow-moving water. "What do you think, Marty? Can we do it? Will it work?"

M2 seemed to think about it, then told them through a speaker, "More. Think meat. Work. Red Crab. Long time."

"Think meat?" Claire's face twisted in confusion. "What's he talking about?"

"Brains, of course," Hahn said with a chuckle. "Good one, Marty."

"I thought so, too," Scotty said. Then he pointed at Ravi. "You said your uncle works at the fish hatchery. Damn good idea, kid. I think it's our best option to stuff this pig over there."

M2 gave Scotty a gentle, brotherly slap to the back of his head. "*You*. Pig," squeaked a transistor. Then those limbs reached into the cupboards and pulled out Scotty's sizeable collection of junk food, dangling potato chips and chocolate bars and pork rinds in front of his face. The boys pounced on the food and were quiet. Claire and Hahn laughed.

Scotty elbowed M2. "All right. All right. We're even. Anyway, I was getting to the fish. From what I remember, they keep most of them inside, in that blue building, in holding tanks. Some will be no more than eggs, you know, but I'll bet there'll be thousands that aren't. It'll be impossible for us to get them for you, Marty, but if we tell you where they are, do you think you could get them?" He was aware that any step outside his home was unsafe for M2. And a journey of that distance would be dangerous, one that could capture or kill him, as they all knew.

"I live out that way," Hahn said. "What if I drove you? If you could go as Claire and Claire stays here, I don't think anyone will suspect a thing when they see us. Just coworkers heading home after a long day.

"That's a great idea," Scotty said.

M2's heads nodded. "Maybe. Stay. Claire." It was only three words, but they knew what he meant. He wasn't sure if he was strong enough to stay Claire, or an adequate version of Claire, for the entire ride. Though as long as no one stopped them, it could work.

"Try," he told them.

28. Do You Paint?

Dan hated stakeouts. In his younger days, lured by the glamour of Hollywood police action, he had eagerly anticipated his first stakeout assignment. But after Tom Widlow appointed him to a fraudulent credit card investigation, Dan found himself stuck in an overheated car for three weeks, staring at covered windows and a door that rarely opened. Worse, his partner at the time, Arthur Teddy, a thirty-year veteran of the force with leaky bowels, napped for most of it. The experience taught him not only to avoid stakeouts but that too much takeout can give even guys in their twenties terrible heartburn. He stared out the window and sighed.

If the task were on the books, he'd have thrown it on Brander or Collins, who liked sleeping on the job as much as any of them, but this one was his own. It was a curiosity detail, off the record because surveilling the RCMP could cause trouble. They liked being investigated as much as the Catholics. But, just like the Catholics, it had to be done. There were too many lies and not enough truth, and with a killer on the loose Dan couldn't afford to turn circles any longer.

After he had threatened to go to Hollis and the RCMP's rented space in the Adequate Accounting building and demand answers, Hollis had come to him. Despite being a member of a supposed partner agency, Hollis had obviously not wanted to meet him. He had kept looking at his watch and giving short answers with all the clarity of brick. When Dan mentioned that Gina Totwsither had stopped returning his calls, Hollis had said she was sick, which was odd because a point person was critical to any investigation with an active serial killer known to be in the area. Gina neither told him she was sick nor returned his messages, and Dan hadn't been apprised of a temporary replacement. None of it added up. It bothered him so much that he visited the RCMP website for law enforcement partners. He found Hollis' info quickly, then identified Gina Totwsither's. But something still didn't ring right to him.

Over the years, he'd developed good, even deep relationships with people in partner offices. Many had been to his wedding and several had commiserated with him through his divorce. But he still couldn't tell just anyone about his frustration with the RCMP or his suspicion of Hollis or Gina. It had to be someone discrete, someone willing to drill past the bullshit veneer and get at the truth, knowing that doing so could cost him or her their job, but willing to do it anyway. It had to be Digger Sky.

He had scrolled through his phone and dialed her number in Ottawa. When she answered, he'd said, deadpan, "Excuse me, miss, I was hoping you could help me get my fish back. It's buried with my neighbour, you see . . ."

Nadine "Digger" Sky grunted a little chuff of laugher. "Exhume the wrong body one time and you never live it down."

The memory of that fiasco decades ago when both had been fresh to law enforcement made them smile. Two neighbours had been fighting over a trophy catch from a fishing trip when one of the men died and had the fish buried with him. Not to be outsmarted, the surviving neighbour went to court and sought an exhumation of his adversary's casket to get the stuffed fish back. He won, and Nadine Sky worked with the Garrett funeral home to exhume the casket and get the fish to the rightful owner. But somehow, during what she since termed *the great paperwork debacle of 1997*, another man with an identical first and last name (John Clark) was exhumed instead of the John Clark with the largemouth bass on his lap.

She'd overcome the career blunder by becoming one of the finest officers in Garrett, an accomplishment that got her noticed—and also a senior role with the RCMP in Ottawa. "To what do I owe the honor?" she said. "Is this a professional call or has that reporter girlfriend of yours sent you packing and you need me to pick up the pieces?"

"Ouch," Dan said. "Neither. She's still burning my breakfast, but at least she's making it."

"Misogynist," Nadine said, laughing again.

Pleasantries settled, Dan told her about the Zombie Killer investigation and Hollis Brubaker and Gina Totswither.

Nadine excused herself while she closed the door to her office. When she came back on the phone, she said, "Sounds like they're dickin' you around. I know we can be assholes, Dan, but we're generally not dirty when it comes to serial killers. We want to get those guys as much as anyone. Why would we stop cooperating in the middle of an investigation like that? The answer is we *don't* unless something is sour. And I know you're not the rotten fruit there, as much as you smell. Let me do some digging on those two and get back to you."

She had called back later that afternoon with the news that although Hollis Brubaker and Gina Totswither *were* listed as employees, their names were affiliated with absolutely no case files or committees, they had no employee number assigned to them, and were basically ghosts as far as their files with Human Resources were concerned. "This isn't just sour, Dan," she had said. "It's foul."

"Are we talking a bad egg or a whole dozen?"

"Anything out of the carton—the people I know—are fine, but I think anyone in proximity to these two has to be checked twice. This speaks deep, Dan. I'd be careful if I were you."

Now, sipping from a thermos of coffee, Dan regarded the building with suspicion. Who were Hollis Brubaker and Gina Totswither? He wondered if the Zombie Killer was even real or if, as had happened on occasion, the good old Canadian government was fucking with its own people. Could the bus stop murders be another government blunder? Or were they just so incompetent that they allowed a foreign entity access to their internal systems? It wasn't impossible. God knew it had happened to other countries across the planet. But to have a trespasser in your own backyard . . . well, time to close the blinds and lock the safe.

He was yawning and rubbing the glaze off his eyes when a small car pulled up behind him and parked. Dan felt this was odd because the street down Waste Way was practically deserted but for the few cars in Adequate Accounting's parking lot and the lone truck parked in front of the Sleepy Sloth. Of all the places to stop, why behind him, so far away from the two buildings, which were really the only places to go? From the rearview mirror, he saw the woman get out of the car, carrying a briefcase. She didn't look at him, but still Dan had the feeling of being watched. When she passed the car without so much as a glance in his direction, he noted she was wearing a shapeless suit and large, clunky shoes, but had a soft pink scarf and carried a matching pink jacket slung over her arm. She displayed all the makings of government trying not to be government. Like a skunk with a dyed stripe.

After a moment's consideration, he got out of the car and followed her, leaving a reasonable distance between them. She padded to Adequate Accounting's entrance and went inside. A minute later he too mounted Adequate Accounting's front steps and tried the door.

It was locked.

He knocked. When no one came to answer, he took out his phone and called Hollis. It rang five times. Six. Then it went to voice mail.

"I'm standing outside your building, Hollis, and I know you know I'm standing here because there are four—make it *five*—cameras pointed at me. I saw Gina Totswither—if that's even her name—go in here about four hours ago. And one of your people just parked behind me. She should've done a better job of hiding the dash camera. Do me a favour and cut the bullshit. Either we talk or I'm afraid we're going to have to go our separate ways. I'm extending you courtesy because I *suspect* you're law enforcement, but . . ."

There was a click of the door being unlocked. Dan looked at one of the cameras and went inside.

There was nothing remarkable about the office. It was your typical stale and colorless professional building, as exciting as old paint; except that from behind the reception desk and a dozen different low-level cubicles, everyone was staring at him. They tried to make it look like they weren't, but Dan was a noticer. Generally, people don't type while looking away from their computers or file papers with their eyes in other places. He waved and the office zombies blinked like startled deer.

The woman he'd followed into the building came from a door behind the reception desk. "Follow me, Mr. Fogel," she said, and turned without another word.

She led him down a narrow hallway much too long and sloping to be part of the office. The walls seemed to close in on him in this strange place, but the comfort of his gun, heavy at his hip, powered him through to the room on other side.

It was a command center. There was a wall of surveillance monitors, an oval table with a conference set up in a center console, and rows of computers. The people at them did not turn their backs but worked on as if he wasn't there.

The woman with the pink scarf stopped and turned. She glanced to her right, where there was a set of large steel doors opening. Then she nodded curtly at Dan and went back the way they had come.

He stood there, being ignored by the people but no doubt being scrutinized by the cameras, and waited. There was the rattle of an engine, the opening and shutting of a car door, then the steel doors opened wider and Hollis Brubaker was strutting toward him, looking like the many criminals Dan had caught. His bottom lip was thrust forward in a pressed and menacing grin and his eyes speared Dan with all the vengeance of actual weapons. And when he finally entered the room with a soldier in fatigues and the doors swept closed behind them, Hollis did not offer Dan his hand.

"I'm not much for wasting time, so I'll just remind you that the oath you swore when you were a rookie includes circumstances of national security, which has federal jurisdiction. One word of what I'm about to show you and I'll rain a shitstorm so heavy on you, you'll need a goddamn wetsuit. Are we clear?" He stood stiffly in front of Dan with his arms clasped behind his back, now with an eyebrow raised.

Without hesitation Dan said, "About time."

Hollis tipped his chin to the soldier ever so slightly, but it was enough. The man flashed a key card and tapped it to a small silver wall plate. Then he pressed his thumb to an adjacent reader and the doors hissed open. "Follow me," Hollis said.

The man, whose embroidered nametag read *Rollins*, led the way. He took them down a steel-lined passageway maybe fifty or sixty feet then used his thumb and key card to open another set of doors. Behind these laid a winding dirt road at the bottom of which was an enormous subterrane.

When things were good with Brandy, they had taken a trip to Poland to visit some distant relatives and toured a salt mine that reminded Dan of this big empty space underground. There had been a restaurant and banquet facilities and even a chapel, and it had seemed huge to them. But this behemoth of a vacuum beneath his city was somehow greater and more terrifying than billions of tons of rock-hard salt dangling over his and Brandy's heads.

When he sucked in his breath, Rollins—just a kid, by the look of it—peered at him as if to say, *you haven't seen anything yet*.

They brought him to a G Wagon. Rollins took the driver's seat. Hollis sat beside him in the front and Dan sat in the back. As Rollins started the vehicle, Dan noted many more men and some women, all in fatigues, sorting pallets of equipment, talking and clustered over electronic screens, and patrolling points of entry and exit, including several grate-covered ventilation shafts and a massive transportation shaft leading deeper underground. The mammoth military operation had to have been there for decades, and it made Dan wonder just how much he didn't know about his own city.

As they started moving, Dan said, "JTF?" Meaning Joint Task Force, Canada's most elite military unit.

"They wish," Hollis said without looking back. "Project Domain is too sensitive even for those guys, and you're going to see it. Keep your head on and your pants buckled, Chief, because you've got a front seat to one hell of a show."

Rollins, who did look back, smiled at their shared secret—and it was a little eerie to Dan because the young soldier's lips were so scabbed they seemed almost bitten off. When he smiled, one of those scabs cracked open and a pinprick of blood gleamed bright red in the middle of all that crusty brown. The symptoms of post-traumatic stress disorder, written all over the soldier's face and the jitter in his hands, put Dan on edge.

They went down an impossible distance. The further they went, the more apprehensive Rollins seemed to get, but under Hollis' stern glare, he kept driving. When they stopped at a gargantuan steel door a short time later, it appeared Rollins wanted to take the G Wagon and leave, but he waited behind the wheel without saying a word.

PROJECT DOMAIN

The soldiers guarding the door saluted Hollis; the door whirred open and Dan was led inside.

A thin woman in glasses wearing a white lab coat was waiting for them. Like Hollis, she didn't reach to shake Dan's hand. Instead, she said to him, "You understand your oath?"

"He knows," Hollis said, but it wasn't the oath Dan was concerned about. The oath was as sacred to him as his own allegiance to God. In normal life, above ground where giant militaristic caverns didn't exist, breaking his oath would get him fired, fined, or possibly even jail time. But Dan suspected that if he revealed any of what he seen or heard *down here* . . . he might not survive the penalty.

"Good," the woman said and spun on her heels.

"Your name, ma'am?" Dan asked, hurrying behind her.

She turned her head to Hollis, who gave her the nod. "Lia Geller, Director of Bioprocess Technology."

"Bioprocess . . ." Dan trailed off, thinking, following behind. "*Biology*. You're talking living cells, right? Living things? Animals?"

"See for yourself," she said, and led him through an airlock and then a sterilization chamber, both with *Sector Center* painted in yellow letters above their thresholds.

On the other side of the sterilization chamber was a long hall with what could only be jail cells. A row of iron bars on the left, a monitoring room and doors in the middle, and a row of glass-fronted cells on the right. The sound of an old how-to-paint show—Bob Ross, Dan thought—came from a TV in the iron-fronted cell.

"It's a new one, everyone! Oh, we haven't had anyone new in so long! Nice to meet you," said a small voice from behind the bars.

Dan looked down. Standing before him was a knee-high silver-skinned creature, shaped almost but not quite like a human, with the longest eyelashes he'd ever seen. He sucked in his breath.

"Oh, don't be afraid. We don't believe in violence. I promise we don't bite, sir." Then her eyelashes elongated even more and weaved into the shape of an arrow pointed at Hollis. "But *he* might."

"Stab the Red Crab," another silver creature muttered weakly.

"Cut the power," Hollis ordered.

"Noooo," cried the creature with the eyelashes, and she continued this way until Lia Geller glowered at her, then she went quiet.

Dan knelt beside the bars. "*Aliens*. I'll be goddamned."

"*Martians*, to be exact," Geller said. "Twenty-eight of them. As you can see by their enclosure, they pose no threat to humans, though they can be a bit whiny at times. They've developed a somewhat dependent relationship with the painter, Bob Ross. If we don't play his videos, they become testy and uncooperative. Like children without their pacifiers."

"Well, I'll be . . ." Dan said again. "May I?" he asked Hollis and Geller, mimicking a handshake.

Hollis flapped an approval. "Go ahead. Like Pintree said, they don't bite."

Dan felt that he probably *should* have been afraid. He should have been terrified, but what he felt instead was an overwhelming curiosity. As a boy, he had loved the UFO stories his camp leader told around the fire. Most of his friends had been scared, shaking in their sleeping bags all night, but not Dan. At eleven years old, he had tugged his sleeping bag outside the cabin and slept under the stars, hoping to see a comet or—even better—a flying saucer. Had the little alien Pintree appeared the way the camp leader described, dark and murderous, Dan might have thrown himself back to the subterrane and Adequate Accounting's dreary office faster than a sneeze, but she was as sweet as syrup.

He stretched his arm into the cell. "Nice to meet you," he said. And then he felt the cold clasp of her Martian hand. Her skin was colder than ice and firmer than stone, but her smile was warm and pleasant.

"Do you paint?" Pintree asked him.

"I *could*," Dan said. "But not well. Not like *him*, that's for sure."

PROJECT DOMAIN

Pintree looked disappointed. Just then another with Martian with a long silver-blue beard sidled up beside her. Dan thought it was a boy, though he had no way to be sure. The little guy put his face to the bars and whispered so low only Dan could hear. "*Help us.*"

"Mendawall, you spreading trouble again?" Hollis said, trying to appear genial, but Dan detected a hostility in his voice that warned the alien to keep his mouth shut.

"No trouble," Mendawall said and quickly backed away from the bars.

Dan stood. He had been in law enforcement so long that few things surprised him. But this . . . this *wonder* below the city seemed to have tied his tongue. For a long time, he couldn't talk. He just stood there, looking at all those small silver bodies worshipping the painter on TV like their own earthly deity, already wishing he could visit again.

"It gets you the first time, but you get used to it. The rest aren't as nice as these ones," Geller said.

"There's more?"

"Of course," she said. "Though Martians make up more than half of our guests. We have five Venusians, three Plutonians, and six Uranians in Sector West; three Saturnians right over there"—she pointed— "and our Kepler Mimicas—your Zombie Killer—are, or *were*, in Sector East."

Dan wanted to know more about the Zombie Killers, the Kepler-somethings, but when Lia Geller pointed at the wall of glass on their right, three fluid sponges rolled their bodies forward. They were dark yellow, the color of honeycomb or autumn leaves. Unlike the almost humanoid Martians, the three sponges—resembling stringy mold now that he thought of it—were difficult to relate to. And though the impenetrable prison-glass suggested they were more dangerous than the Martians, Dan didn't back away.

The sponge-mold in the middle rose its fluid body high to face Dan. Ropes of floating flesh dripped off its sides like candle wax.

"Say hello, Templeton," Hollis ordered.

There was a tingling in Dan's head, then the headache that had been forming since he'd followed that woman into Adequate Accounting was gone. Dan's fingers went to the nape of his neck.

"Good boy," Geller said.

"How—when—?"

"Like I said, you get used to it. But I suppose we haven't had anyone *new* here in so long, we forget what it's like." She paused and sighed slightly. "This was the easy part. I brought you here first because these ones are the easiest. They've never made anyone tuck tail and run. Not that you could, but you know what I mean."

Dan raised an eyebrow.

"Once you see the others, I think you'll understand. We're just like every other prison, really, so I don't think it'll be too much for you."

And before Dan could thank the alien Templeton for relieving his headache, they whisked him out of Sector Center.

In another corridor as he followed them to Sector West, Dan asked, "Back there . . . that was incredible, but I couldn't tell which sponge-thing was which. How can you tell them apart?"

Lia shrugged. "They all have their own personalities, except for the Uranians, which share *one*. And Templeton is a little crusty around his edges. It's hard to spot, but once you see it, you know it's him."

They went through another airlock chamber and another sterilization zone. While they were being decontaminated yet again, Dan said, "Those Keplar things —"

"*Kepler* Mimicas," Lia corrected.

"Sure," Dan said. He lifted his arms, raised his feet, put everything down again. "You said they're the Zombie Killers? You're saying there's more than one? And they've escaped? They're the ones that got Irma and all those people?" The realization that all this time they'd been searching for aliens while Dan and his team had been scouring the city for a person that didn't exist drew red hot anger through his veins. But he also knew they were willing to lock him up (or worse) if he didn't *fall in*, as the military demanded. So he gritted his teeth to keep himself from exploding on them.

A buzzer sounded and they were cleared to leave, then the great double doors to Sector West hissed open. When they went inside, Hollis stopped abruptly. He put his hands in his pockets and brought his shoulder blades together so that his chest puffed out. "You're angry about the misrepresentation."

"In my line of work they're called *lies*," Dan said. "This circus you're showing me, it's a great little show, but I've got fourteen families who won't give a lick about any of it. Whatever goddamn thing you've got down here killed good people. Deaths—at least thirteen of them—that could have been prevented if you'd have told me the truth from the beginning. And I don't believe your oath is so far off mine that you don't put the safety of citizens first. Above *everything* else."

"Are we done?" Hollis said. He was not looking at Dan but past him, over his shoulder.

Dan spun around.

Facing him were six creatures pressed up against the glass. They were the blue of cresting waves, light and glittering, with ruffles of shaggy tissue from bottom to top. They reminded Dan of the scrubbing columns in automated car washes.

"Truth is the way," said they in their English-like language. "You are not happy. We can make you happy." Their vertical eyelids blinked expectantly.

"These are our Uranians," Lia said. "One of our most unique species. We call them Hyph-A—collectively—because they are similar to some species of fungi that communicate via electrical impulse. You see six creatures, and to us there are six unique creatures, but to them they exist as one. There's no point in differentiating any of them, conversationally speaking." She gestured to Dan, whose jaw had fallen open. "Hyph-A, would you like to greet our new guest? This is Dan."

"*Dannnnnnn*," they said as one.

"You were saying?" Hollis said to Dan. "Something about nobody giving a lick about this?"

With great effort, Dan pulled himself away from the glass. "Show me the Keplar thing."

"Kepler," Lia corrected again.

"*Now*," Dan said.

Hollis wiggled a finger at the surveillance room. A door to their left opened. "Let me be clear. You have as much authority here as the grit on my shoe. I've allowed you here as a courtesy, nothing more. Your opinion of how we operate is of zero relevance because I don't care what you think, and the people that sign my goddamn paycheck don't care what you think or they would've told you. Ever think of that? So you're welcome to go back to your little station up there, but if you want answers, you're going to keep your mouth shut and follow me." He had inclined his veiny neck toward Dan to make his point, but now he pulled it back.

"People are dying," Dan said.

"And many more will die if we don't take you through this slowly. Want to dip your toes in lava, Chief? What good would that be? Had we skipped over Pintree and Mendawall and Templeton, would you be ready to see Hyph-A now? I don't think so. You look like a kid who snuck a horror film and now regrets it. Like you're going to piss your pants. This isn't an ordinary SWAT situation, Chief. They won't just blow you to pieces. They'll *eat* them, too."

It took a long while for Dan to respond. He just looked from Hollis to Lia to Hyph-A, to Hollis. Then he said, "The day I'm immune to the peculiar is the day I retire, that's my word. I'll go at your pace because I have no other choice but as you string me along your sideshow, I want you to know that the people who sign your check don't tell you everything. Ever heard about Anabelle Cheever?"

Hollis raised an eyebrow. "The electrified girl?

PROJECT DOMAIN

"That's the one," Dan said.

Just over a year ago, a tour bus had crashed into the Callingwood River, killing all forty passengers except one, a nineteen-year-old woman. The case had been tragic, drawing emergency response personnel from across the province, but it had also been the most mysterious case of Dan's career. Shortly after being rescued and arriving at the hospital, Annabelle became electrified, actually *electrified*. Dan worked with the hospital, a team of engineers, and the IESP—Ontario's Independent Electricity System Operator—to draw the current from the girl's body. The ordeal drew not only local and provincial attention, but that of the Feds. Given the operation directly beneath the city's landfill, of course Hollis would have been aware of Annabelle Cheever. But the circle aware of *why* the girl had been electrified was much, much smaller. Dan was one of them.

"She's no secret," Hollis said. "Everyone knew about that. Hell, my own grandmother was stitching a pillow with the girl's face on it."

"And what about Sylvia Baker?" Dan asked.

Hollis pursed his lips and lifted his shoulders. "Another electrification?"

"You don't know, do you?"

"Wouldn't tell you if I did."

But it was obvious Dan had stumped him. For a man who purported to know everything, Hollis was missing the biggest piece of the puzzle. This was good. Dan wasn't a fan of all-powerful, all-knowing, buck-stops-here types. The force was full of them. Arrogant officers were in every city, in every department. Even the best teams seemed to have that one chest-beater, puffing him or herself up like a blowfish, and while Dan was patient with all of them, it was also necessary to poke a little hole in their surface and let some of that pomp out.

"Whoever signs your check is definitely looking at mine," Dan said. "So let's be done with the bullshit and show me what I need to see."

Lia had been silently watching their exchange but now clicked her tongue at them. "Since you two are done fighting over who's got the biggest gun, let's get on with it, shall we?" She spun away and started walking again. She showed Dan the Plutonians, which looked like dark red porcupines and the Venusians, which looked like bug-infested sea coral. They were interesting all right, but all Dan could think about was what the Zombie Killer looked like.

"You're actually doing better than I expected," Lia said to Dan when they exited Sector West and took the long corridor to Sector East. "It could be that everyone's behaving today, but it's obvious there's little that surprises you."

Hollis harumphed but said nothing.

"I wasn't expecting an extraterrestrial operation beneath our landfill."

"And yet you haven't fainted or dashed back to the office."

He shrugged. "Wouldn't help."

They came to a junction guarded by at least a dozen soldiers, most carrying rifles but two with machine guns. A soldier sat beside a tall, rolling cabinet, opening a sterilized pouch.

Upon Hollis' last visit to M1, he'd instituted frequent saliva tests—another layer of precaution to be sure everyone present was human.

"Open your mouth, sir," said a soldier brandishing a long cotton swab.

Dan opened his mouth. The soldier, a short man with a long nose and receding chin, rubbed the cotton swab on the inside of Dan's cheeks then the swab was dipped into a liquid solution at the bottom of a thin vial. He snapped off the end of the swab stick, capped the vial, and swished the remaining swab and solution around.

PROJECT DOMAIN

"We'll have our results in ten minutes," Lia said after her own mouth had been swabbed and their vials had been inserted into a compact centrifuge.

"Results for what?" Dan asked.

"To make sure you're human," Hollis answered. He was standing beside the soldier, observing the procedure.

The soldier seemed to consider opening a third pouch, glanced at Hollis, and then returned the package to the cabinet drawer.

Seeing the expression on his face, Lia said, "It will make more sense once we show you their file. The crux of it is that the Kepler Mimicas have the ability to replicate other living things; namely you or me or any of us, down to the shadow of our fingerprints. Back when we first captured them, they could even match retinal identities, but we found that if we limited their diet to non-encephalic nutrition, we could control this. Sorry, I tend to employ scientific terminology that not everyone understands. M1 and M2 are encephalic-reliant creatures. They depend on living brain tissue for most of their processes. Specifically the temporoparietal lobes—the neocortex—though the wider cerebral cortex in mammals do work, as do insect ganglia, just to a lesser extent. It's what allows creatures to copy. The part of the brain a child uses to mimic a parent teaching them to bring the spoon to their mouths or brush their hair. Copycat processors. In the wild, predators use it to catch prey, or avoid being eaten themselves. It's an adaptation genius, and it's what's been working against us since M2 escaped."

The centrifuge let out a long beep. The solider removed their vials, extracted portions of the solution with sterilized pipettes, and dripped the solution on strips. The strips were then inserted into a machine beside the centrifuge. The soldier studied the monitor. "All clear," he said, and they were finally permitted to pass.

They crossed yet another airlock threshold and sterilization chamber. Unlike in the chambers for Sector Center and Sector West, here Hollis, Lia, and Dan changed into biomedical suits. "It's absolutely imperative no outside material is brought in," she explained. "The Mimics will use anything they can to escape, as happened with M2."

Dan said, "If they're that dangerous, why have them in the first place? Seems to me like having a serial killer man a parade."

"Bioprocess technology is imperative to—"

"Keep classified," Hollis interrupted.

Lia had been about to say more, but now she tipped her head to Hollis. "To keep classified," she agreed.

Dan didn't pry. Instead, he followed them into Sector East. There was only one cell in that area, but the security detail was noticeably more involved. Whereas in Sector Center and Sector West a handful of soldiers patrolled the cells and adjoining antechambers, here dozens did, if not more. The surveillance room was filled with men and women, and the space from the antechamber to the far wall of the room was lined with more soldiers carrying machine guns.

"Heavy hitters," Dan said, and looked for the Mimic in the glass-encased cell. He didn't see it. Then Dan understood. "You took it somewhere? That's what they're for? Some kind of transfer?" Dan had overseen many prison transfers, a mostly benign procedure, but sometimes—as in the case of dangerous offenders or prisoners considered a flight risk—Dan didn't just delegate the procedure, he accompanied them from their simple cells in Garrett to the macabre cells in Millhaven or the South Detention Centre in Toronto. He knew that it was dangerous to consider any prison transfer routine, and that the soldiers in Sector East obviously thought the same.

"We rarely transfer *guests*," Lia said. "And M1 is here; she just wants you to think that she's not."

Hollis stepped forward. He went to just inches from the glass and stopped. The soldiers that had been near the glass stayed near but fell behind. Then he pointed to a little white cube on the floor no bigger than a die. "You can blame that little bitch for your bus stop murders and the Madinger woman. She has a partner. They work in unison like fire and wind. One sparks, the other spreads. The trick is to put the fire out before the other catches wind, but they've got a damn good head start on us."

Dan's eyes swept to the floor. The little cube was there, looking . . . well . . . like a little cube. He thought for a moment that maybe Hollis and Lia were putting him on, but in no sane world would so many soldiers be dispatched to an unimportant figure, so he went to the glass and crouched. "I don't get it," he said.

Lia spoke loudly. "M1, please show yourself to our guest."

The soldiers readied their guns. Many of them stepped back even further.

Hollis, as stolid as ever, did not move. Neither did Dan.

"*M1*," Lia warned, and then the little cube rose, distended, inflated, elongated. Nine beastly heads glowered down at them. There were so many eyes, Dan couldn't count, and what looked like gills ran down the length of its neck, angry red and blistering, as though they'd been recently burned.

"My God," Dan gasped, gaping up at M1.

"This," Hollis waved a hand at the thing on the other side of the glass, "is M1. A Kepler Mimica. Up until now, she and her partner, M2, enjoyed a peaceful existence at our facility, but—"

All those nine beastly heads struck out, lashing at the glass in front of Hollis' face, then toward Lia Geller. Though M1 did not do the same to Dan, he fell over from his crouching position and stared at the beast above him.

"This is her most natural form," Lia explained calmly. "Vicious. Completely violent. So focused on brain matter, she's willing to eat her own arms off if it means escaping and getting at us."

"Is that how the other . . . ?" Dan asked.

Hollis grunted. "Incompetence is how it happened."

"We've contained them for decades without a problem," Lia said quickly. "Remember what I said about their diet? The only way we've had even a smidgeon of control is the strict regulation of their diet. We don't allow social gatherings here, for obvious reasons, but an employee recently retired and our staff decided to throw a potluck when senior employees went home for the night. As luck would have it, almost everyone got sick, including the chef who was responsible for dispensing M2's meal. We can't confirm it, but we believe something entered the nutrition capsule, a fly or something even smaller, before it was sent to the enclosure. The only way he could have escaped is by assuming the body of another living creature, something small enough to get past our protections. Now he's out and already feasted on those victims, God only knows what his capabilities are."

"Can we capture it?"

"We *can* once we find it," Hollis said. "We have operational teams scouting all over the city. So far our best lead is a boy, a thirteen-year-old kid, Adam Brace, whose family car came upon Irma Madinger's accident. The investigator who interviewed the family suspected the boy saw something, so we put a man in his school. St. Jude's. He discovered some pictures the kid drew, and they look exactly like that." He gestured again to M1, who was ineffectually gnashing at the glass. "We've been watching the kid, but there hasn't been much activity to lead us to M2. Our best guess is that the kid saw him that night but that M2 didn't see him, otherwise he wouldn't be alive to draw those pictures." As an afterthought he added, "And your dump manager, Scotty Waymore, he had a tape of the accident. Didn't show much, but we destroyed it before you could see it."

Dan nodded as if it all made sense. He wasn't mad at Hollis or his team. He himself had been in many a tricky situation where he couldn't be truthful but understood that sometimes it had to be done. "I know Scotty. I'll talk to him again and see if he knows anything. Delicately, of course."

"Fine," Hollis agreed. "And we'll need everyone you can spare to look out for anyone they think are suspicious." He held up a hand.

"Yes, I know you do that anyway, but let them think there is a serial killing *team* in the city. It'll make them even more vigilant."

Dan couldn't argue with that. "And in the meantime?"

"In the meantime, we're going to put some heat on that kid. There's no doubt he saw something, and we need to know what it is. We can't be too careful with these beasts, but mark my words, we will get him if it's the last thing we do. And then maybe we'll put an *end* to this part of the program."

M1's nine dark heads followed their movement toward the door. Law enforcement had a sixth sense bred into them, something beyond intuition. Dan felt it now. The hair on his arms stiffened and there was a tingling at the base of his neck and along his shoulders. It was the feeling of having your back turned to an armed gunman, knowing he was about to shoot. He glanced at M1 but she didn't lash out at him as she did Hollis. The behaviour spoke of consciousness and of selective contempt. And as they took him back to Adequate Accounting, Dan thought about those angry red gills on the beast and wondered how *peaceful* the alien's time in Project Domain really was.

29. Get Mar-ee-a

The sky was still dark and full of stars when Hahn and M2 arrived back at the house. Scotty and Claire, awake through the night, jittered nervously, drinking coffee and revisiting the things he had insisted were true but she hadn't believed. He brushed off her apologies yet relished the reunion.

She was holding his hand when the car pulled up. Their heads whipped to the window, hoping it was Hahn and M2 but terrified it wasn't.

"Maybe you should go in the bedroom," Scotty said. "Just in case."

Claire nodded and slipped from the table to the small bedroom and closed the door most of the way. When Hahn had left with M2 for the hatchery a few hours before, M2 had been the spitting image of Claire. They'd agreed that M2 would return as Claire as well, as long as he was strong enough to maintain the façade for the duration of the trip.

Scotty squinted into the darkness. The bright lights of the vehicle shut off, then Hahn and M2 got out of the car. "It's them," he said.

"Come on out. They're back. Thank God they're back." He opened the door for them, saw his daughter's likeness, and sucked in his breath. To Hahn he said, "You take my daughter out and bring her back pregnant. Shame on you, old man."

Hahn laughed and smacked M2's bulging belly. "Not bad for ten thousand fish, eh? We're lucky we caught the batch before they were released. He had a formidable buffet, wouldn't you say, Marty?"

M2 burped his answer.

"And apparently they need time to digest," Hahn continued. "He can make us see the world but gets stuck on fishbones like the rest of us. So much for a higher being." He grinned sideways at M2 and got a nudge that almost knocked him over. To Scotty, it was as if Claire had the power of fifty men inside her. He quickly waved them up the stairs.

They hurried inside. When Claire saw M2, she burst out laughing. "I look like I'm having triplets."

"Triple that and you're close," Hahn said. "He's come down some during the ride. Had to damn near push him into the car."

"Weak-ling," said a transistor.

"Hey, you try pushing a whale through a keyhole and see how *you* do."

"Anyone see you?" Scotty asked once they were seated and M2 returned to his natural form, which was now a dark and bloated mess.

"I don't believe so. There looked to be some surveillance vehicles near the landfill, but we managed to avoid them with that back route you suggested. It's possible someone saw us driving, but it really would have been fleeting, like any other car, really, and we hit only two red lights, but it was so late the streets were more or less deserted. And *he* took care of the cameras at the hatchery, so they'll be no evidence it was us. Except, of course, who steals ten thousand fish without a trail?"

"You're saying they'll know?" Claire asked. She had taken out a cup for Hahn and was filling it with coffee.

Hahn shrugged. "Hatcheries aren't immune to thieves, but they're also not as smooth as this guy." He jerked a thumb at M2. "They can leave quite the trail."

"Which is even more reason they'll know Marty did it," Scotty said. "But it doesn't matter now. What matters is we get you down there and help get Maria out." The name was jarring, but they had agreed that using the Mimics' institutional names could be dangerous. If any of the snoops around them heard, they would all be swallowed up by swat teams or even gunfire before the next word.

Claire came around the table with a glass of water for M2. He laid one of his arms over the glass and drew the water in, condensing it upward into his skin. In the short time she'd known M2, she'd come to worry for him almost as she did for her own son Ty. The alien was kind, caring for her father and the rest of them as though they were family, and hadn't a mean bone (or any bones, for that matter) in him. "Do you think you're ready for it, Marty?" she asked.

There was a pause while they all looked at him, but M2 was as steady as a steel pipe. He spoke in his usual way, but without a crackle, hiss, or sputter through the transistor. The sound was as clear as a megaphone in a library. "Ready. Get. Mar-ee-a."

"Good," Hahn said, but Scotty didn't feel good about it. He didn't feel good about any of it. M2 had been part of the cacophony in his head for so long, Scotty wasn't sure he could live without him. Even if the other aliens continued the interior conversation, it just wouldn't be the same, like a song without a melody or a laugh without mirth.

M2's heads swooped around Claire to Scotty. "Ba-bee."

"You're the baby," Scotty sniffed and pushed M2 away.

Hahn said, "Well, even though you bump around like a blind old dog and you smell like a walrus, I'm with Scotty on this one. We're going to miss you."

"Me too," Claire said.

M2 blushed his tangerine blush. "Me. Too."

Scotty wiped his cheeks. "All right, so let's go over this again. You two are going to school like usual. The boys are going to raise hell, and when you grill them about it, Claire, you're going to conveniently see a drawing that will lead our fraudulent teacher and his bullies to the river behind the Gazette. Irving, today you happen to have a midday craving for those pizza rolls at that gas station bakery out near Canary Junction, where you've parked the Land Rover you borrowed from an old college friend. I'll happen to be at the same gas station. While I'm filling up, Marty, who will look like Hollis, will slide into the Rover. Then you'll drive to that accounting building and try to bluff your way in." He looked at their solemn faces. "Have I missed anything?"

"My uniform," Hahn said.

"Yes, you have to wear one. Even if it's not the right one. As long as they think that Hollis guy is coming in, I don't think they'll stop you."

Claire had been following the plan, reasoning it out in her own head, and now she said, "But what about Hollis? We don't know he's going to run to the other side of the city with the others. In fact, he probably won't. From what Marty's shared about him, he'll think that kind of work's beneath him. He's almost certainly going to stay back and wait for Marty to be caught and dragged in, so he can confront him there. If you run into him while you're there or he sees you on a camera, or if someone else sees Marty on camera where he shouldn't be, you could be in big trouble."

Scotty sighed. "You're right."

"Yes," Hahn said. "But it's the only plan we've got. We might be a ragtag bunch of amateurs, but that doesn't mean we're ignorant. Far from it. Not only do we have the advantage of all that terrible knowledge Marty shared with us, but there hasn't been a single indication they know he's here, nor that we're helping him. And they couldn't possibly think we're *helping* him because they think he'd kill us before we did."

"No," M2 said.

They stared at him, gaping, because the sound hadn't come from a transistor or a radio or even the TV speakers he sometimes used, but from one of his own mouths. It was an undeniably human sound, maybe a little like Scotty, a little like Hahn, a little like Hollis, appearing so smoothly that Scotty looked around to make sure no one else was there.

He pointed at M2. "Did you just *talk*?"

"Well, Marty, you just about struck me dumb," Hahn said, putting his hands on his hips.

"I talk," M2 said, now sounding more like Hollis than the others. He drew in his heads, his limbs, compacting his expansive, after-meal body into only one head, a torso, two arms, and two legs. His skin lightened to an almost translucent color, then gathered auburns and reds and oranges and pale, pale yellows. The healthy alien sheen gave way to a droughty, sun-damaged human dermis and a frown-furrowed face. "I no kill you."

"*A plus*, Marty," Hahn said appraisingly. "Though you do sound a little German. You'll need to tweak that."

"Is this what your . . . what the *think meat* did?" Claire asked. "Is that why you can talk now?"

"Yes," said M2, now without an accent. "Think meat work. Small words."

Scotty put a hand over his gaping mouth. "You're him. You're really him, aren't you? I know you told me you could, Marty, but I wasn't sure, you know?"

M2 nodded, and when he stepped away from the cover of the table, Hollis Brubaker's nearly invisible penis came into view.

They howled with laughter, Claire most of all. She wiped the tears from her eyes. "No matter what happens today, Marty, you got him.

I wish he could see that. Oh, you know humans so well. Sorry, I know it's crude, but it's funny."

Suddenly feeling quite comfortable with himself, Scotty went to the dresser in his bedroom. He took out a pair of black trousers, a belt, his best shirt and suit jacket, and the tie he had worn to his wedding to Meredith over twenty years ago. He brought them out to M2. "I guess we should've thought about this earlier. Maybe we could've got you something better from Irving's closet. I know it's not the best, but—"

"It's fine!" M2 bellowed and pounded his fist on the table. Hahn, Scotty, and Claire shrank back, stunned.

"Good God, Marty," Hahn said. "That was frightening. If that man is really like that, God save his soul. I think you're ready. Don't change a thing. Put on the clothes, but I think you're ready."

The tenets of decency overcame them, and they averted their eyes while M2 put on Scotty's clothes.

"Let me get that for you," Claire said and stood to fix M2's tie. It reminded Scotty of all the times Meredith had helped him in the same way when they were married.

By now the sun had risen and the room was bright. M2's tie was adjusted, his pants and shirt were smoothed, and his jacket was buttoned. Scotty retrieved his only pair of dress shoes and put them at M2's feet, then held the tongues up so M2 could slip them on.

They appraised him. M2 worked Hollis' face, tested his scowl, his glower, maneuvered gritting teeth and narrowed eyes and forking eyebrows and air-tight lips. He flexed his Hollis jaw and clenched his Hollis fists.

Hahn looked at his watch. "Claire and I have to be at the school in an hour, but if we show up like this, they might think we belong down there; not that any of you ever belonged down there, Marty. I'll drop you home so you can shower, Claire. I suggest you change as quickly as you can while I wait since your car is still at the school. With your permission, I'll take some of your books and make a show of bringing them to my car. If anyone asks why we carpooled today, we'll just tell them we've been asked to collaborate on a potential curriculum change and need the research. Language arts are always being jabbed by *supposed* moral authorities so it wouldn't be unusual. And then we'll stop by my house since it's on the way to school. I'll be ready faster than Marty gobbled up those fish."

Claire reached for her purse but then threw herself at M2, squeezing him tightly. "I guess it's goodbye, Marty. Don't forget us, okay? We're not all bad. After all they did to you, I wouldn't blame you if you never come back, but if you do, we'll be here for you, okay?"

It was unsettling for Scotty and Hahn to see the tyrant hugging Claire, but M2 softened his tough outer hide, conditioning it like leather. For the first time, Hollis smiled. Crescent moons pushed up under his eyes. His eyebrows rose in happy arches. His thin upper lip all but disappeared, and the likeness of Hollis Brubaker was all teeth. "Won't forget," M2 said, and they knew that he meant it.

"I'll see you later, old boy," Hahn said to M2. "But I suppose once I'm in uniform and we're in the car, we won't have much time, and we'd pretty much blow our cover if I hugged you, so give me a squeeze, will you? God knows I'm not the hugging sort, but sometimes a handshake isn't enough." He took Claire's place in M2's arms and crushed him around the shoulders. "You take care up there, okay? We're better than what we've done to you. I know it doesn't look like it, and some people will never live up to it even if they live as long as you, but most of us are all right. Maybe not perfect, but all right. I'm sorry, Marty. I really am. It's been good knowing you." There were tears in his eyes when he pulled away

"All you better," M2 said, wiping the seepage from his valves, which in his current form were Hollis' tear ducts. It wasn't tears, for his species didn't cry like humans did, but a jellied outpouring of emotion too great to be contained.

Hahn shook Scotty's hand. Claire hugged him. Then they were off.

30. Quiet Business

Claire had loved daycare when she was a toddler. She'd wake up, throw off her covers and bound down the stairs in her underwear, begging to be taken to Tiny Timbers to play with her friends and make her crafts.

But it hadn't started out like that.

Those first few weeks had been terrible for all of them. Separation anxiety clamped down on mother and daughter as though the umbilical relationship had never been severed and doing so then might kill them. When Claire held her breath, tantruming to be returned to her departing mother, Meredith had confessed her own panic and that she found it hard to breathe. She had felt terrible, like a bad mother, because wasn't that what bad mothers did? Leave their weeping children in the arms of strangers and then stuff their ears with reassurances so as not to hear them? Scotty, who had never been part of the mother-daughter daycare drop off because of his conflicting schedule at the landfill, had wondered what all the fuss was about. They had scrutinized potential day cares as carefully as agents at the Prime Minister's residence, maybe even more. Scotty himself had toured Tiny Timbers to ease Meredith's mind and ensure Claire would be as safe away as she was with them. But even with those precautions, Meredith had felt the rending of her own soul each morning for weeks.

Now he knew what it felt like.

After Hahn and Claire were gone and Scotty had showered, he left M2 for the landfill, feeling a terror that drummed on his heart and played fire with his nerves. The difference was that he knew Claire had been safe. Claire hadn't had a brigade scouring the city for her. She hadn't been in danger of being captured and dragged underground. She wasn't going to be tortured or shot. It hadn't crossed his mind. Not once. But all these worries and more he had for M2. The alien was facing real dangers. Lethal dangers. And as he drove away in his truck, he fought the urge to look back, afraid of what he might see.

A few minutes later, he stopped his truck beside Vera's car, too consumed by his worry for M2 and the day ahead to mind the severely angled parking job that had taken out the *Visitor Parking* sign. He adjusted the toque over his ears, sure she was going to grill him about it because the day was already warm, on the verge of shorts weather. He pocketed his keys and began his short walk toward the office when the sound of tires on gravel made him look at the entrance, which had just now opened to the public.

It was a police car.

He muttered an expletive under his breath. A visit from Dan Fogel was the last thing he needed, but sure as the sun, Dan pulled into the parking lot and waved through his open window.

The door to the trailer banged open. Vera came out, pinching a lit cigarette. She blew a mouthful of smoke in his direction. "They arresting you, Scud? I knew you were up to no good."

Stressed as he was, Scotty wished M2 had swung by the trailer for a visit with Vera instead of Irma Madinger, figuring a little lobotomy would've done her good.

"Just here for a visit, ma'am," Dan answered for Scotty. He turned off the ignition and exited his cruiser.

Vera snorted, gesturing at Dan with her cigarette. "You check him out good. And tell him to take off that damn hat. He looks like a cancer patient, for goddsake."

Dan raised an eyebrow at Scotty.

Scotty rolled his eyes as if to say, *can you believe this woman*? He knew the toque was out of place for such a warm day but if he took it off, they would see his ear. "It's not cancer, Vera. I'm . . ." He paused as though he were embarrassed and put a hand to the back of his head. "I've got a transplant. I have to wear this for a while so infection doesn't set in."

Vera's yellow eyes widened. "You got *plugs*, Scud?"

"Just in the front," Scotty said, wondering how he was ever going to remove the toque.

"Good for you," Dan said without a trace of sarcasm. It was why they had always gotten along. "In a few years, when Jessica makes more of my own hair fall out, we'll need to talk about it, but for now I want to pick your brain about something, if you've got time." He glanced at Vera. "Privately."

Stung at being left out, Vera took another drag on her cigarette. "Hair won't fix all your shit, Scud. Still be a sack of it." She wheezed, fixed them with her eyes, and banged back into the office.

"You really got plugs, man?" Dan asked when they were on the red clay loop that surrounded the facility.

"Something like that," Scotty said, and changed the subject. "You find out who's been leaving those dummies here?"

"We have an idea, but not anything solid enough to share. That's not why I'm here, though it *is* related to those transit killings."

"How so?"

They slowed in front of the fenced-off conservation area, far enough for Vera to hear or see and remote enough for Dan to be sure Hollis hadn't planted any bugs in the area. He didn't want Hollis to overhear his discussion with Scotty because although he'd been apprised of Project Domain, Dan still didn't trust him. If anything, he trusted him even *less* after the alien tour because it was one thing to hunt for a killer but another to hunt for a killer held captive for decades beneath an innocent city. Dan knew with certainty that if he weren't law enforcement, Hollis would've had him killed by now. The government was good at covering things up. Dan would be coyote feed, and no one would know because that's how it worked.

A pair of geese landed in the marsh. Dan studied them while he spoke. "I've always been honest with you, and I've never shared what you told me, you know, about the voices and your problems with Meredith?"

"Uh-huh," Scotty said a little uncertainly.

"Well, I was hoping you could return the favor. I've got some tricky business I'm dealing with. *Quiet* business, you understand." He looked at Scotty, waiting for the green light of secrecy.

"Of course."

Dan leaned forward against the short fence. "That night Irma died, do you remember anything funny about it? Anything that made you take a second look? You said she came to your door, acting strange."

Scotty nodded. He'd heard the best way to lie was to tell the truth, so he balanced on that narrow edge carefully. "Not the strangest thing I've ever seen, but close to it. I didn't know she'd been in an accident."

Air wooshed up Dan's nose. "That's the thing. Now, don't think I'm strange for asking it, Scotty, but are you *sure* it was Irma? Absolutely sure?"

"I mean, it was dark, but it looked like her," Scotty said.

"Hmmm," Dan said. He picked a stone off the grass and threw it the marsh. It landed far from the geese, but they squawked their disapproval.

"Do you know how hard it is to admit to hearing voices in your head?" Scotty asked. "Damn near killed me when I told you. It's not easy for a man to admit to something like that, but it was God's honest truth. I know you could've locked me away, but I'm damn thankful you didn't. I owe you one. If that's what you need to hear, consider it said. Least I could do. I'm the last person who's going to talk. They already think I'm crazy."

Dan considered this for a moment, then he said, "I have it on good authority that we have a killer in our city. My sources tell me it doesn't just kill but does things to the victims' heads. People are talking about it, so I'm sure you know what I mean."

"Uh-huh."

"Well, the thing is . . . I guess what I'm trying to say in my clumsy way, is that . . . it seems the killer likes to role play. Dress up as the victims. It's rather morbid, but the minds of killers are work for psychologists, not for people like us. We suspect this killer dressed up as Irma. Did a real good job of it too, almost like they were the same person. And when it was done with Irma, it went on to other people. We need to catch it before it kills anyone else, and I think that if there's any chance you saw something that could help us locate it, well, you might be saving a lot of lives."

"You said *it*," Scotty said, watching more geese settle on the marsh.

There was a pause, then Dan said, "I did."

Scotty wasn't sure if Dan had come because he knew M2 was at his house or because he knew something inhuman was out there and Scotty was the only person crazy enough to hear him out. He stayed silent.

"Anything you're not telling me? No judgement, no matter what it is. Promise."

Again, Scotty stayed silent. He thought of M2, alone in his house, and how nervous he must be, how nervous all of them were and of the bad things that could happen if their plan went wrong. Color began to flush his cheeks and he bit the inside of his lip, thinking.

"I can be here all day," Dan said. "I just want to talk to you. Off the record, for your sake, but for mine too. I'm not leaving until you talk to me. Something tells me you've got something to say and I want to hear it. I swear on my mother's grave it won't get past this fence, no matter what it is."

Scotty wanted to run, to go away, send Dan back to his policework and tell him not to come back. Not today. Definitely not today. "I can't."

Dan raised his eyebrows and stepped away from the fence. "Can't or won't?"

There was a tingling in Scotty's ear then, the one that hadn't been and then was. The one that M2 had put back. He felt M2 was telling him it was all right to tell Dan. At least, that's what it felt like. What he sensed. Did M2 have that power? He wasn't sure, but he wasn't sure of anything anymore. Not even of his own sanity. The tingling grew stronger. Maybe M2 was telling him *not* to tell Dan, but if that were so, he felt M2 would just adopt someone's exterior and call out from the bushes or squawk a message through the phone in his pocket. He reached in and grabbed it now, but it didn't ring or make any sound at all. He thought briefly of calling Hahn, who would know what to do, but knew that people were listening and that any conversation he had with Hahn would have to be made in private, which was a luxury Scotty didn't have.

"You still with me?" Dan said, tilting his head.

Scotty didn't answer. Instead, he turned to face Dan fully. Then he took off his toque.

Dan inventoried Scotty's head. "Well fuck me to heaven," he said. It was a phrase his father had used when he was a boy, and it had stuck with him, unravelling its coarseness only when Dan was exceptionally surprised or stumped. "Sorry, Scotty. Didn't mean it to come out like that, but you mind telling me how you managed that?"

"I think it's better if I show you," Scotty said, and led Dan to his house.

31. Here's Looking at You, Larry

St. Jude's was typically a happy school. The noise that sprang most often from its glossy corridors was that of shuffling feet and of good-natured, yet hormonal, chatter. But this morning the shriek that rang out, louder than the end-of-day bell, brought instruction to a halt and students to the classroom doors to see what the matter was.

It had come from Larry Heep, the math teacher. He had arrived at his classroom, about to teach the Pythagorean theorem to the grade 8B students, when something had fluttered at his feet. Curious, the teacher looked down to see the shredded remains of his beloved autographed Jim Carrey poster, one he'd had for over thirty years, since the comedian and actor appeared in the TV series *In Living Color*. One Jim had signed, *To Larry, Better have one eye than be cockeyed. Here's looking at you. Signed, Illegible*. It had been funny to Larry because he'd waited in line nearly two hours to get the autograph, and when his turn came to have the headshot signed,

Larry froze and couldn't speak. When he did, he didn't tell the comedian his name—not immediately, anyway—but only that he was a childhood cancer survivor and lost an eye. It just came out of him. Splat on the autograph table. He had always been the awkward sort and people let him know it, but that day the comedian was not only patient but made Larry feel comfortable, more at ease with himself than he'd ever felt in his whole life. So the picture hadn't just been a sentimental icon to Larry, but proof that Larry wasn't socially incompetent and that people weren't all that bad.

But that proof had been snatched from the picture frame and torn to pieces. On one of the larger pieces, Jim Carrey's smiling teeth beamed up at him as if to say, *here's looking at you, Larry*.

"Who did it?" Larry roared. He had been carrying a fresh cup of coffee, and in his furor he threw up his arms and splashed it all over. Now the picture was not just shredded but it—and Larry—were wet. "You fucking brats! You beasts! Who did this? Tell me!" He thrust his finger at the closest student, then the next, and the next.

The students shrank in their seats, but none of them could get small enough to escape Larry's wrath.

The commotion surged through the school and then Hahn was speeding into the classroom, gaping at Larry, at the floor, at Larry, at the shuddering students. He frowned. "All right, let's settle down now. We'll get to the bottom—"

"Right now! I want to know who did this right goddamn now!" Heep cried.

Theo's and Claire's heads appeared in the doorway, then that of several other teachers. Fentworth Plumley. Ashley Kelby. Mack Seaver. Edith Yost. Gwen Hayes. They, too, surveyed the tattered remains of Heep's beloved poster. Plumley, who had only had a chilly relationship with Larry Heep, shrugged and returned to his classroom. The school counsellor, Mack Seaver, squeezed past the others to offer his immediate assistance. Edith Yost scowled at the students, which was her normal look and so didn't increase their terror.

"Ashley," Hahn said calmly. "Please take Larry to my office and give him some chamomile tea. I'll talk to him after I talk to the students." She nodded and tiptoed into the room.

"But—" Larry hissed.

"*Go*," Hahn said more sternly, knowing that once Larry Heep was in the hallway with Ashley, her prettiness would subdue him and he would be able to have a reasonable conversation. Unfortunate, but true.

Heep grunted at the students, kicked the ribbons that were his beloved poster, and left. Hahn instructed the students to review their last lesson and ushered the crowd of teachers back into the hallway. From open doors, hundreds of students stampeded back to their desks.

"Now," Hahn said, but didn't get the chance to finish because at that moment, water from the girls' bathroom flooded into the hallway.

Gwen Hayes jumped away from the water near her feet. "What the hell is happening today?"

The scowl on Edith Yost's face hardened like stone.

Theo had been standing beside Claire. She touched his arm and whispered conspiratorially, "Bet you it's Douglas Radway. He's flooded the bathrooms before. Stuffed the drains with socks and underwear. Let's just say they weren't all his and they weren't all *clean*."

Theo raised his eyebrows. *Of course*, he thought. Any class Hollis stuck him with would be full of delinquents. He hoped Julia Fowler was enjoying her government-paid vacation while he festered with the rest of the teaching staff. "I'll speak to him," he said.

"He won't listen," said Claire, stepping further back while Mack rushed into the girls' washroom to shut off the taps. "Irving tries, but Douggie's a special case. He's so far past three strikes, he could sink an entire baseball *season*."

Just then, the day janitor, Grover, came rushing down the hall with his cart. He stopped the cart just outside the bathroom, glanced at the gathering of flustered teachers, and went inside to survey the damage.

Hahn moved to the cart, took out a *Wet Floor* sign, and set it in the middle of the slowing spill. There were stanchions in the gymnasium storage room, and he directed Theo and Claire to retrieve them and set up a safety boundary around the spill until it could be cleaned up. Outwardly, Hahn appeared slightly unsettled, as he was expected to be, given the chaos in the school. But inwardly he knew their plan had started and that the boys had done a fine job of distracting Theo. He also knew that the Jim Carrey poster Larry Heep kept raving about was only a copy and that the authentic poster—and an apologetic note from a mysterious prankster—would be found later in the back seat of the car Larry consistently forgot to lock.

Ironically, he was prouder of the boys than he had ever been.

Over in the gymnasium, meanwhile, Claire and Theo were packing a trolley with stanchions when they heard whispering.

"Do you hear that?" Theo asked.

Claire said she didn't.

He pushed the trolley out of the storage room, and when the sound came again Theo fell very still, putting a finger to his lips. Claire stopped walking and listened. There was a stage in the gymnasium and coming from under the wooden bottom were the muffled sounds of feet shuffling and of someone whispering.

Theo went to the apron of doors at the front of the stage, clasped a handle and pulled.

Adam, Ravi, and Douggie's not-so-subtle whispers gave way to grunts of alarm as they were caught.

"Out with you," Theo commanded. "Come on, out."

The boys crawled out obediently. They stood with dusted knees, hands behind their backs, eyes downcast.

"Adam, would you mind telling me what you're doing under the stage?" Claire said. Her tone was rigid. She crossed her arms and waited to see what they had come up with.

"What've you got there?" Theo said, pointing to the bucket Douggie was holding.

Douggie didn't answer.

"I want to see your hands," Theo ordered. "*Now.*"

Ravi, who was standing between Adam and Douggie, nudged him. Douggie brought the bucket forward.

"You too," Theo said.

Adam and Ravi stretched out their own hands.

Theo and Claire looked at the screwdrivers, then peered into Douggie's bucket and saw several dozen screws, maybe even more.

He tried to be calm, to be the patient and reasonable teacher he was expected to be, but at that moment control was beyond him. His anger detonated on them like mustard gas, and they shrank away and closed their eyes as if his shouting and fist shaking were actually stinging them.

"What in God's name do you think you're doing?" Theo roared. His face, so red and bulging with veins, not only scared the boys but Claire too. She put a hand on his arm but he shook it off. "You trying to kill someone? Do you know what you could've done? If people were *on* there? Christ, I've had it with you. No more. No more chances. You're expelled. All of you. And I'm calling the police. Let them deal with you."

He paced away from them, hands on hips, biting back the urge to yank all three of the delinquents out of school and drag them to M1 and let *her* deal with them.

With Theo's back still turned, Claire winked at the boys to tell them it was okay, that they wouldn't be expelled and that they were, in fact, doing a very good job. Then she said, gently now, "I'd like an explanation, Adam."

Adam hesitated but said, "We . . . we were building a trap."

"And why would you build a trap?"

No answer.

"Is someone bullying you? Is that why—" Claire started but Theo let out a sarcastic push of air. She gave him a look as if to say, *you're not helping*. He glared at the ceiling but stayed silent. She continued. "What's going on, Adam?"

"You won't believe me," Adam said.

"Try me," Claire said. "Why don't you give me those and tell me what's going on."

They gave her their screwdrivers and the bucket.

Adam stared at his feet. His arms were rigid at his sides, but he worked his fingers against his thumbs so hard that the occasional rubbing squeak came out. "I think something's after me," he said after a time. "I don't know if it's a person, but I don't think it's a person. I just know that sometimes I see it in the bushes and sometimes I think it follows me home."

Theo swung around, not angry now, but interested and very alert. "What do you mean?"

"When the grocery lady had that accident, we were driving on the same road and when my dad went out to see if she was okay, I saw it on the side of the road. In the ditch. It was like a spider, a giant one, or something, or maybe a snake. I don't know. It was dark and hard to tell but . . ." He thought of adding that M2 had morphed into Irma Madinger and run off like a cat but felt it might make him even more of a target. A strange animal could be explained or rationalized. An animal that transformed into a human could not. Not without giving up Project Domain's secrets. It would mean that Adam would have to go. It would mean that Adam would have to die. "Whatever it is, it's been following me."

"And you think it's coming *here*?" Theo asked, white-faced now. "To the *school*? You're planning to trap it under the stage with a bunch of loose screws?" The idea was mind-splitting. Trapping a Kepler Mimica under a rickety stage was as likely as halting the charge of an elephant with a matchstick. Or a mother grizzly bear allowing her cubs to be cuddled. It just wouldn't happen.

"Maybe," Adam said. "But I usually don't see it during the day. Only when I leave school by myself or my parents take me to our . . ." He paused, trying to seem embarrassed by the sessions with the family therapist, even though shame was the furthest thing from his mind. "We go to a therapist. I see it there almost every time. But it hides so no one else sees it."

"Where is this, Adam?" Theo asked.

"It's near that church that burned down, but on the other side of the river behind that newspaper building. Kind of between them."

"Holy Redeemer?" Claire asked. "You think it's behind there? Or the Gazette?"

Adam's small shoulders went up. "Both places, I guess. It moves around a lot. Here," he said, and pulled from his pocket a drawing he'd sketched that morning. It was another picture of M2, but more detailed than the previous pictures. There were nine heads and a body that seemed to squirm off the page. For good measure, Adam had drawn the beast with fangs and dozens of terrible, ravenous eyes.

Claire's face squished in pretend confusion. "Looks like an upside-down octopus," she said. She reached out and touched his shoulder. "Are you sure, Adam? You don't think that maybe it's some deer or something? They do like to travel together. Maybe it's just a few of them close together? Or some elk have got their horns tangled? I know we don't see them often around here, but maybe that's it?"

"I believe you," Theo said before Adam could answer. The veins in his temples had stopped throbbing and now he spoke to them not with anger, but with urgency. "I'm sorry for yelling at you. I didn't realize you felt threatened and didn't feel comfortable enough to come talk to us about it. We can put the screws back later, for now I want you to go back to the classroom and stay there while we have someone investigate. Nothing is more important than your safety, okay?"

Adam nodded, and when Theo looked them in the eyes, Ravi and Douggie did too.

"Go on now, boys. We'll take care of this." He shooed them away.

When they left, Claire said, "I know they can be a handful, but I feel sorry for them. Poor kids."

"Yeah," Theo said absently. "Hey. I know a guy here. Police. You want to bring the stanchions over while I call him? I'm sure he'll check it out for us."

"Good idea," Claire said, and thought, *Tell that bastard crab to send everyone there.* Then she left Mr. Tyler Cagey to make his call.

32. Professional Redirection

It was going on thirty hours without sleep for Scotty, but he'd never been more awake in his life. Back in his kitchen after telling Vera that Dan wanted a more formal interview with him at home, he triple-checked the curtains to make sure Hahn wasn't speeding toward the house. Now he returned to the table where Dan was gawking at M2.

"I still can't believe it," he said. "They had me so convinced you were a . . . you know, Marty." He made a predatory face and curled his fingers into claws. "I mean, I haven't seen anything like you before—*good Lord,* your girl wasn't happy with them. And it's the strangest thing that I didn't feel she thought the same way about me. I remember actually thinking it. Now I know."

"Red Crab bad," M2 said, sounding like the man on a cat food commercial that had been on TV before Dan walked in. "Mad sci . . . mad Geller more bad."

"She was fine with me," Dan admitted. "But I saw the way the others looked at her. They were afraid."

"All afraid," M2 agreed.

Scotty poured coffee and put a tray of M2's favorite cookies on the table. Soon after, they were gone.

Dan absently stirred milk into his mug. He was quiet, trying to make sense of the last few days, few weeks, wondering what other secrets he didn't know. "I owe you an apology, Scotty," he said. "I didn't believe you. All those times you talked about that voice, I thought it was stress over Meredith. I know it doesn't make it right, but I just thought you needed some time, and maybe when you weren't so stressed things would get better for you. It's hard to believe something like that is real, even if it's sitting at your kitchen table eating cookies."

"Good," M2 said, and patted his belly.

"Don't apologize," Scotty said. "No one believed me. I wouldn't have believed it myself if they weren't in my own head. Tried to get them out and they just stuck around like shit paper on a shoe." He winked at M2.

One of M2's arms reached into the bathroom then whipped a roll of toilet paper at Scotty's head. He ducked and missed it. Dan laughed, but an hour ago he hadn't been laughing. An hour ago, when Scotty brought him up the porch steps and opened the door, Dan had instinctively reached for his gun. But Scotty had slapped it down. Before Dan could react, the door was closed behind him and M2 had pushed his knowledge into him. To Dan, it was as if all the secrets of the universe were being pulsed like blood into his brain. In that instant, he discovered the rest of Project Domain's blood-curdling secrets, and that even with the grand alien tour, Hollis and Lia had lied to him. None of the aliens were a threat. And they were being tortured like criminals in the name of biomedical advancement. Now the trouble was that if Dan acted any way but with a total and absolute obsession of catching M2, Hollis and the unnamed, faceless, heartless people above him might have him not only *professionally redirected*—as Hollis had threatened on his way out—but *killed*.

"It's a lot to take in," Scotty said when Dan became quiet.

"Yes," Dan said. "But I'm glad for it and glad to help any way I can. You've told me your plan, now I'm just thinking about mine. I can't be seen abetting an enemy; no offense, Marty. That's just how it is. I want to help you, but I just have to figure the best way to do it. When—*if*—they go rushing over to that church, we need to do everything we can to keep them there. Or at least keep away as many of them as we can, for as long as we can. I can't block off the road because, first, I'd have to do it in both directions. East of that godawful accounting getup and west of it too. Can't be done without a bunch of arrows pointing at me. Second, I'm supposed to have all my people looking for *you*." He stopped as an idea came into his head.

"What?" Scotty said.

"Well, if something serious came up, I couldn't realistically ignore it, could I? I still have a job to do."

"What do you mean?"

Dan told him. It was a brilliant idea, and not unusual given the situation at the landfill as of late. "That takes care of one direction. Let's say *south*. You think you could figure something to get the north covered? Not too close, of course. Don't want to make it look like we're in on it together."

Scotty pulled at the whiskers on his chin. "Remember Frank's first day on the job? We had to call the police because he pressed the wrong button on the truck. Ended up with thirty thousand pounds of trash in front of the mall. Traffic stalled in all directions. Ah. Maybe you don't remember. It was Tom Widlow back then."

"Of course I remember," Dan groaned. "We were in the middle of a heatwave. It smelled to high heaven. Tom had us patrolling the area the whole day. I don't think the stink left me until the fall."

"Still stink," M2 said, and his valves whistled with alien laughter.

It should have made Dan laugh. Instead, it tugged his heart. "I'm sorry, Marty. You're too good . . . I don't know how they could do what they did to you. It doesn't mean much, but I'm sorry for everything you've gone through. I give you my word I'll do what I can to get you and Maria out of here."

M2 nudged Dan's shoulder just as Scotty's phone vibrated. He picked it up. "Message delivered," he read. It meant that Theo had found out about M2's non-existent hiding place and that, ready or not, the plan had begun. "She said Irving's already left the school."

Dan stood. "We better get going. I'll go first, and I suggest you two go out the back. As much as I'd like to see you again, Marty, I hope I don't. I hope you leave and never come back. It's been a real pleasure and I wish you worlds of goodness up there." He stuck out his hand. M2 coiled around Dan's arm, vibrated, and released him. Then Dan tipped his chin at Scotty and left.

M2 began sliding toward the back door, but Scotty had stayed at the table. When M2 looked back, he saw Scotty's head in his hand, and his shoulders were quivering.

The alien heads tilted this way and that, pondering the weeping human. "Go now," M2 said gently.

Scotty pushed away from the table. When he looked up, his face was wet and his eyes were red. He raised a hand. "I know we got to go but I need a second, okay? I'm . . . I'm not used to this."

Alien limbs stretched across the living room. They coiled around Scotty's ankles. Knees. Thighs. Middle. Then he was lifted and carried to the door and wrapped in a tight, warm hug. "Love Scott-tee," M2 said, for it was the closest emotion on Kepler-186f to what Scotty would understand.

A snort of emotion puffed from Scotty to M2. A valve puffed back. "I love you, too, buddy," Scotty said, wiping his eyes. "Can't believe I'm saying that but it's true. God, I don't want you to go. I know you have to, but I'm going to miss you." His lips quivered. "If anything happens, you know, if something goes wrong—"

"Not go wrong," M2 said.

"Yeah, but if it does, don't worry about me, okay? Get Maria and get out. Whatever happens, don't look back." He wrapped his hands around M2, then let go. M2 carefully lowered Scotty to the floor. Then M2 drew in his limbs, compacted his body, and became the man in the cat food commercial.

Scotty gave him the thumbs up. "Let's go get some gas."

33. Ready Prisoner

Canary Junction, so named for the flock of Canadian geese—not canaries—that swarm the adjacent fingers of Southern Ontario's Buttonbush Preserve, was as slow as the snapping turtle M2 now watched plodding into the dusty parking lot. The Gas-O station, an isolated and unincorporated holdout, fought the city competition not with cheap gas but with an instore bakery that put grandmothers everywhere to shame. To Scotty's great relief, the morning rush had come and gone, and only two midday snackers were in the store when he stopped at a pump.

He turned off the truck and looked at his alien friend. "He'll be here any minute, I'm going to pay inside, and when I get back in the car you should be gone. Stay as you are until you're with him, understand?"

M2 nodded his cat-food-actor head. "See me in sky."

"I will," Scotty said, trying not to tear up. Then added, "I'll look for the ugly one."

"Thank you," M2 said seriously as Scotty took the keys from the ignition.

"No, Marty. Thank *you*. I mean it. I'm not going to hug you now because this is supposed to an ordinary car on an ordinary day, but you've changed my life and I owe the world to you. Now go and give'r hell." He opened the door and went outside, mouthing *bye* with no trace of the heartache or worry that weighed on him. It took everything he had not to look back as he rounded the front of the truck and went inside.

M2 had seen boredom on people. The guards that had watched over him, old and new, had yawned and played entertaining games inside their heads and sometimes even snoozed. He tried to look bored now. Just a guy with his head against the window, admiring the old Land Rover parked behind a weather-beaten *Best Buns in Garrett* sign with half-interest.

A car was dusting up the road toward him. No doubt it would be the principal, rushing to take him back underground. The plan filled him with anxiety. He wanted—*needed*—to see M1, but if he were caught . . . if he were caught it would be worse for both of them. Spending decades in detention and getting tortured was bad enough, but at least they had each other. If they didn't . . . if they held them apart, it would be worse than floating alone in the great desert of space for all eternity.

His valves tightened.

He watched the principal park beside the store, far enough to be out of the way if the station became busy, but close enough to appear ordinary. Ever cool, he exited his vehicle and whistled his way into the bakery for a half-dozen pizza rolls. One that he would eat on the way out, still steaming, and five that would be cold as stone by the time the rescue mission was done.

M2 yawned and stretched. Now he was just a guy looking for the bathroom. He left Scotty's truck and walked casually to the west side of the building where the public restrooms and the unlocked Rover were. He was almost at the entrance to the men's restroom when he looked around, saw no one, and changed direction to the

PROJECT DOMAIN

Rover, then casually slipped onto the front passenger seat. Shortly afterward, the driver's side door opened and Hahn got inside.

"Ever had a pizza roll?" Hahn asked.

"Like pizza," M2 said, and the bag was emptied.

"All right, then. We just have to wait until we see the cars go by. There should be lots of them. Claire said Theo has already left the school, so hopefully he'll be with that godforsaken terror squad. Once we see them, we need to go. It won't be long." He had been wearing an olive-green cardigan but now unfastened the buttons and removed it. Underneath was a gleaming white dress shirt and long black tie that matched his pants. A suit jacket, pressed and absolutely wrinkle-free, hung from the back of his seat. He put it on. The man looking back at him in the rearview mirror was a high official, one of the elite, a decision maker. It was as if the military academy and short postings in Vietnam and Zimbabwe had prepared him only for this moment. Irving Hahn was ready.

The shrill antique peal of an old rotary phone rang through the car. Hahn looked at this cellphone. It was Claire.

"There's a bunch of cars heading north," she said urgently, meaning away from the river where Adam had said the monster was hiding.

"And south?" Hahn said calmly.

"Both," she said. "There's more than I thought. Dozens of them."

Hahn frowned, wondering if he'd arrived too late, if the search party had already been dispatched. He had left the school after sending Claire and Theo to the gymnasium, and he was sure he'd made good time. But had he beaten the outgoing calvary? He thought so, but he couldn't be sure. "They're being careful. They're sending people to Adam's house and to the river. It's to be expected."

"How's he holding up?"

"As good as a prisoner sneaking back *in* could be, I suppose," Hahn said. "He's fine. Stronger than anyone—"

A wave of cars sped past the Gas-O with such fervor a cloud of dust enveloped the parking lot. There were many of them. Cars. Trucks. Vans. All unofficial yet somehow more ominous than black clouds on a hot day. "Hold on. They're passing us now. I've got to let you go."

"Good luck," Claire said, but Hahn had already ended the call.

"That's our cue, Marty. You ready?"

In the borrowed Rover, under a thick cloud of dust, M2's television-handsome face weathered and bunched and furrowed. The healthy glow gave way to a sun-spotted, sickly orange exterior as crispy as dry leaves. M2 shed the actor's golf shirt and khakis and donned a suit of severe brown, the color of dried blood, and a tie so tight on his gobbly neck that loose folds of skin bulged overtop. "Ready," M2 said sharply in Hollis' voice.

Hahn waited until he was sure the last car of soldiers had passed, then he gave it another minute for good measure and put the Land Rover into reverse. As they left the parking lot, Scotty returned to his truck and filled it with gas, trying hard not to wave, trying harder not to cry, hoping they would be all right.

34. General Allen Daniels

They took the direct route to Waste Way. Only a short kilometer north, a right toward the landfill, and they were on the road. Hahn had driven within the speed limit, trying to calm himself, and found that although he was treading into evil water, he felt no real fear.

The aliens weren't going to attack him. It would be the real criminals, the *people*, who might, and Irving Hahn had dealt with their kind before. His experience in the military and with decades of children and their families taught him that most behaviours could be predicted. There was never a real surprise because change in people was slow, like the continental drift. Knowing your surroundings didn't just stop at the tree in the road or the downed power line but started at the water that trickled through the dam for years before it broke through and took out the city. It was the same with people. The people in Project Domain, hidden for so long, would do everything they could to not only catch M2 but also retain their anonymity. It meant that if Hahn were caught, he might be locked up with the aliens, but more likely they would put a bullet in his brain before he'd even get the chance.

He sighed and straightened in his seat. There was a police car ahead and a cold tine of fear spread through him, but as he got closer, he saw that it was Dan Fogel.

Both men pretended not to see the other, for after Scotty explained to Hahn and Claire they had Dan's help, all agreed it would be best to acknowledge him as little as possible. As the Rover passed the cruiser, Hahn noted tracks in the adjacent field and understood that Dan hadn't taken a road to where he was now but *made* one. Once the Rover was further ahead, Dan took his cruiser from the field onto the road, then went to the trunk.

"We're getting closer," Hahn said, glancing sideways at M2.

M2's skin ruffled as though thousands of balls were circulating underneath.

Hahn frowned. "You okay, Marty?"

"Okay," M2 said, though without muster.

"Marty, I'm going to ask you once because we don't have enough time for more. I know you went through hell down there, and I know you want to get her out, but if you tell me it's too much, then I'll turn around right now. God knows I wouldn't blame you." He gripped the steering wheel, preparing to turn.

The balls under M2's skin receded and he became nasty Hollis Brubaker again. But he didn't feel as confident as the mask he now wore. Returning to the place where he had been stripped of his dignity and of the qualities that made him better than his captors was almost worse than getting injected with acid in the Mad Scientist's lab. But if he didn't go, he would be stuck on Earth—maybe with Scotty, maybe as an alien vagabond—while M1 suffered, *truly* suffered, for both of them.

"I go get Maria," he said, more confidently.

"Well, all right then," Hahn said, and sped up.

They arrived at Adequate Accounting two minutes later. Hahn pulled the Rover into a parking lot across the street and cut the engine. "Marty, I'm going to leave the car and point some things out to you. You need to look interested, like we're searching for something. It's the only believable way we can walk in the front door. They almost certainly have a different entrance for their goons somewhere, but we can't look like we don't know what we're doing. There will be cameras everywhere and we'll have to pray to God the real guy doesn't appear on any of them at the same time as you. Don't follow me too close. I'll go to the door first, got me?"

"I do," the deep and terrifying voice of Hollis Brubaker said.

They exited the car.

Hahn, serious and stern, adjusted the buttons on his jacket, then as M2 rounded the back of the car, Hahn pointed away from the building to the chain link fence that surrounded the parking lot. He had noted the need for razor wire on the top and said this now to M2. M2's frown deepened, and he grunted. If he hadn't knew they were being watched, Hahn would have given M2 a hearty thumbs up for his performance.

They strode over the parking lot, across the street, and up the steps to the haunted accounting building. Hahn maintained a good five-foot distance from M2 because he wanted to appear as though he knew what he was doing. His hope was they would see him walking with the big man, Horrible Hollis, the Red Crab, and think that he was from one of the ambiguous and powerful echelons above them and let them in.

There was a momentary pause as cameras scanned Hahn's face. He had made sure to use the exact second the cameras whirled on him to bend down and tie his shoe. But then M2, scowling, raised his pelican neck and bored into one of the cameras. The door unlocked and they went inside.

As Hahn had hoped, only a handful of people were in the office. Although maybe fifteen or twenty cubicles and a big reception desk filled the space, only a third of the cubicles were occupied. No one seemed to be armed, though Hahn knew that guns or tasers wouldn't be far away. They stood in their suits, looking so much like the office staff at the school board that Hahn had to remind himself that any one of them would have orders to detain or even kill them, should their plan be revealed.

"Sir!" said one of the women, and saluted him. The others followed suit.

"General Allen Daniels," Hahn said intensely. It was the name, though not the rank, of his American counterpart in the Zimbabwe mission, and he and Hahn had remained close. "Take me down," he said without preamble.

The woman who had first saluted M2 looked to him now for his approval. M2 nodded curtly. She spun on her heels.

They followed her down a long, sloping corridor; at the bottom lay a command center, bustling with people. A trio of men in fatigues were deliberating over one of the big computer screens, but when they saw M2, they abruptly stood and saluted. As in the office, everyone fell in. They clicked their heels and raised their inward-facing palms to their heads. Hahn and M2 returned the gesture. Then M2, completely surprising Hahn, walked over to the screen where the trio had sat and said, "Development?" His voice was strong and steady, with no hint of the gentle alien underneath.

"Cobra, Tracer, and Grizzly are on scene behind the church, sir. Missile, Shadow, and Bloodhound are scouting the kid's house," said one of the soldiers.

"Good," M2 said in deep monotone.

A set of steel doors in the room was big enough for a vehicle, and there was no doubt as to their purpose. Hahn strode to them, waiting. M2, pursing his lips in pretend concentration at the monitors and screens, tipped his chin at the soldiers and stood beside Hahn. Neither man pressed security cards to the scanner, but their collective glare settled as discomfortingly on the soldiers as glass on eyeballs until the woman who had brought them there withdrew her own card and pressed it to a small metal plate. She pressed her thumb to an adjacent reader and the doors groaned open.

She said to M2, "I'll call Rollins to bring you down."

They walked through another hallway, longer and lined with steel. When they got to the end, the enclosure opened to a vast underground cavern. A vehicle sped up a winding road toward them. At the wheel was a soldier, so pale and lanky it was as if he'd been *born* underground. He stopped the car—a G3, Hahn noted—and hurried out of the vehicle.

"Master Corporal Rollins, sir!" The gangly soldier saluted and opened the door for M2 and then Hahn.

They got inside.

Rollins pulled the G3 around the earthen platform and back down the way he'd come. Multiple soldiers, far enough from the G3 to have to pay the senior officers homage, worked on various activities absorbedly. Rollins, Hahn, and M2 entered a tunnel befitting a cruise ship.

For a time, Rollins was quiet, but then he said, "I didn't see you come up earlier. Did Berger take you up?"

Hahn dug his fingers into the palm of his hand to tame his apprehension. Rollins' comment meant that Hollis most likely *hadn't* come up and that he was *in* the facility right now. And if they ran into Hollis, the whole plan would be over.

"*Quiet*," M2 ordered angrily, and appeared to brood on something.

Rollins jittered at the rebuke, then went on driving them down, down, biting his scabbed lips.

They came to several more soldiers guarding a colossal steel door. Hahn and M2 got out of the G3, frowned at Rollins, who could barely contain his quivering, and slipped inside the door now whirring open for them.

They were in.

35. Nothing to Worry About

Hahn expected to be greeted with a platoon on the other side of the door, but there was only a single soldier. The woman, tall and with her hair gathered tightly at the nape of her neck, paid her respects but otherwise continued mulling about her post.

They passed an airlock chamber and came to a junction guarded by several soldiers. One of them pulled a sterilized pouch from a drawer in a tall cabinet. Hahn saw a long cotton swab through the translucent vial. The hairs on the back of his arms rose in terror. *They want to take our DNA*, he thought apprehensively. But his fear was short lived because M2, ever the actor, growled, "Let us through."

The soldier obliged and put down the pouch. M2 nodded superiorly and then they were past the junction and the guards. The breath Hahn had been holding came out of him. M2 looked at him sideways and winked. It was the subtlest movement, maybe not even discernable by Project Domain's sensitive cameras, but Hahn caught it and relaxed. They proceeded to a sterilization chamber. Hahn took a biomedical suit from the wall and put it on. M2 did the same.

They were so close now, M2 could sense M1 as if she were right beside him. He felt her frustration, her fear, her anger, and a deep, despairing loneliness. *I'm here*, he conveyed through their internal language. He took his time dressing, wanting to give her enough time to respond, if she were even able to.

She immediately clutched him with her mind, hanging on to him as an ocean drifter to a piece of wood. The sound of gravity and the smell of the cosmos came to him as she cried his name inside his head.

They didn't have much time. He urgently pushed his message to her. *Man with me is good. More people good. Do not hurt him. He helps us. Red Crab there?*

No, came her nervous reply. *But Mad Scientist here*.

"What?" Hahn whispered when he saw the look on Hollis' fake face.

"Mad woman," M2 whispered back, and Hahn understood. Lia Geller, the woman the aliens deemed the Mad Scientist, was with M1. It would make the rescue much more complicated, but if they turned back now, their departure would make the soldiers curious. And curious soldiers were dangerous soldiers.

"We must continue," Hahn murmured under his breath.

"Yes," said M2, adjusting his Hollis armour, tightening his scowl, ironing his jaw. He pressed a button and the door opened to the Sector East's solitary, cheerless cell.

M1 was in her cube, unable to avoid Lia Geller's advance because the divisor was down. M2 instantly felt it trying to drain him, syphoning his abilities out of him. Had he not eaten a lake full of fish the night before, his façade would have disintegrated. Still, he had to concentrate on repelling the divisor so his face didn't shift.

Five soldiers stood outside the cell and saluted M2 and Hahn's arrival. Another soldier at a bank of monitors briefly stood, saluted, and sat back down.

"Good news, I hope?" Lia Geller said, her eyes locked on M1. She was approaching the cube with what looked to be a scalpel.

"Nothing yet," M2 said steadily, wanting to rip the scientist's head off.

The lights flickered.

Now it was Hahn who frowned. "Is that normal?" he grunted to one of the soldiers standing near the cell.

"It happens occasionally," the soldier said. "Nothing to worry about."

The power flickered again. Then the man sitting at the bank of monitors began typing furiously and smacking a monitor with the heel of his hand. "What the hell?" the man muttered to himself.

Lia Geller lowered her scalpel. "Cupps, check to see what the Venusians are up to. The Plutonians too."

Foster Cupps went to the phone, put it to his ear, tapped the hook switch several times and replaced the receiver. "No dial tone," he said.

"Damn it," Geller sighed. "Go to Sector West and check on them. Tell Y2 if he doesn't cut it out, he'll need a parka for a week. No heat. Understand?"

Cupps nodded and was gone.

"Acres!" Geller shouted next.

"Yes, ma'am," Jeffrey Acres responded quickly.

"Go to Centre and ask them what the hell is going on."

"Yes, ma'am," Acres said, and sped away.

There were now four soldiers, including the one at the monitor, and Lia Geller. *Better odds,* Hahn thought, *but still terrible.*

"You need to fire your systems manager," Hahn said brusquely to M2. "We've never had this issue at ALIEN."

The three standing soldiers couldn't contain their gasps. They'd never had a visitor from the Artic League in Extraterrestrial Naturalization before. At one point or another, every employee had been threatened to be shipped up north. It was the cold place. The nowhere land. It was the place where nobody wanted to go because they never came back. Suddenly, no one wanted to look at Hahn, afraid he'd been sent there to collect them. They averted their eyes.

Hahn took the opportunity to survey the room, looking for an escape route, but a quick scan yielded nothing but the cell and the soldiers. If they managed to get M1 out—and that was a big *if*—they would have to go back the way they'd come.

Do your thing, he thought, hoping M2 could read his mind. *Whatever it is, do it now before we're caught.* He wasn't sure if M2 heard him, but when the lights flickered again, he remembered all the times M2 used a transistor to speak and knew that M2 was working Project Domain's sophisticated equipment like an organist. Yielding this. Countering that. Stretching and manipulating currents to his will.

The lights went off. In the two seconds of darkness, M2 charged into the cell. He focused his newly strengthened talents and brushed the Mad Scientist. But her coming scream was caught in her throat as she shrank down, down, down into the shape of a tiny white cube which M2 pushed to where M1 was waiting.

It took all of one second.

In the next, he wrapped himself around M1's diminutive and weakened body and gave her his strength. She grew larger, grew two arms and two legs, grew a single spectacled head, and dressed herself with a long white lab coat and biomedical suit. But M2 had to pull her to where the Mad Scientist had been crouching because she was still too weak to repel the grip of the divisor.

The lights went back on.

Their movements had been so quick and quiet that not even Hahn knew what had happened.

M2 raised a pointing finger. "You two," he grumbled to soldiers Joe Osborne and Tobias King, whose last names were printed on their fatigues. "Osborne. King. Report to Overlook. *Now.*" The words exhausted him, but he glowered expectantly at the soldiers as if they should know what he wanted them to do, until they nodded and finally rushed away.

Now there were two soldiers. One slapping at the monitors, one standing, pistol holstered at his hip near the cell. He frowned. "Ms. Geller?" he said. There was a touch of concern in his voice because since the light had flickered off, Lia Geller hadn't moved.

Hahn glanced at M2, and there was that almost imperceptible wink again. Then, as if the development was the last thing he needed, M2 said, "Come with me."

He tensed his body for the pull of the divisor and went into the cell. Inside, so close to the divisor, it felt as though he were being ripped apart. His cells were jerked and snapped and stretched, but he held on. He grabbed M1's humanlike wrist and suffused her until she took a step, then another, then another.

"Shut it down," M2 ordered once they were outside the cell, but he had become weakened and his voice cracked.

"Sir?" said the soldier with the pistol, now looking at M2, now at M1. He wasn't at the point of alarm, not quite yet, but they could see it rising in him like smoke in dry grass.

"Demagnetizing sickness," Hahn said. "What's your field ratio setting?"

"I don't understand, sir."

Until now, Hollis had been the most terrifying person the soldier had ever seen. But Hahn, a practiced disciplinarian, outmatched Hollis' manner with a look so terrifying, the soldier bowed his head. "How many times had you failed basic training, soldier?"

"Two," the shaking soldier admitted.

"We have a program at ALIEN for incompetents like you. Shut the divisor and close the cell while I get these two to the infirmary."

"Yes, sir," the soldier said.

Then Hahn, M1, and M2 left.

36. Do it, Marty

In the sterilization chamber, M2 had to hold M1 up to keep her from falling. She glared warily at Hahn when he took her biomedical suit and put it inside a decontamination chamber that hissed when he opened it.

"He good," M2 said to M1 so Hahn would understand.

"Nice to meet you," Hahn whispered. "I'm sorry, but you're going to have to walk once we get out of here, otherwise they'll insist you go to the infirmary. Let Marty do the talking."

Lia Geller's artificial head nodded weakly.

Outside the chamber, the same soldier who had brandished a buccal swab stood from his post. He pointed to M1, whom he thought was the scientist.

"No time," M2 growled. And it was true. M1 had walked from the chamber of her own will, but he could feel her strength already ebbing away.

M1 put up a hand as if to say, *This time I'll pass*. But the soldier, so familiar with Lia Geller and her insistence on entry and exit tests for herself, frowned.

"Is there a problem?" he asked. A group of soldiers was standing nearby. One of them looked toward the man with the swab.

Neither M2 nor Hahn had an answer, and M1 wasn't strong enough to speak.

"Well?" the soldier asked again.

Now two soldiers were looking their way.

Hahn, about to conjure up another lie, opened his mouth to speak but the soldier with the swab winced and put it down. The two soldiers looking at them also winced as a docile and compliant look fell on their faces.

"Proceed," the soldier said robotically.

They continued down the corridor. When they were out of earshot, Hahn whispered, "What was that?"

"Help," M2 said, for as the unified voices of the aliens had reached Scotty Waymore, so had their gifts reached M1 and M2 and Irving Hahn. Over in Sector Center, the Martians had stopped watching Bob Ross and were taunting the Saturnians, throwing shoes and pillows and great balls of fallen hair at the Saturnians' cell. The Saturnians pretended to give the Martians headaches and the Martians pretended to have them, all to keep the guards occupied so they wouldn't rush away. In Sector West, the Plutonians had launched gobs of red viscous tissue at their cell walls until they were almost fully concealed. It was all they could do, really, besides contribute to the headaches, but it occupied the guards who had to ensure the cell walls were clean so the aliens could be observed. This while the Uranians vibrated great buzzing noises from their bodies, sounding so much like swarms of bees that several guards whirled around slapping at their necks, which the Venusians flicked with their minds. Meanwhile, down in Sector South, the employees imprisoned at the beginning of the fiasco suddenly found their cells unlocked. Then the mothers and fathers and loyalists converged on their stupefied counterparts responsible for guarding them.

Hahn, M1, and M2 were near the steel door from which they had entered when M1 stumbled.

Hahn caught her arm and lifted her. "We're almost there," he said. She went forward. When he let her go, she fell to her knees.

M2 put his fingers on the back of her neck, willing his strength to her, but the effort of playing Hollis Brubaker and keeping the Mad Scientist a cube and was too great. He could only help M1 if he released the scientist.

He began to withdraw. The scientist slipped from her casing. Her full body spilled onto the cell floor and into the view of the confused soldiers who were still in Sector East. Believing that M1 had transformed, they immediately tasered her with 50,000 volts. And again when she lifted her pinky to explain.

Having heard M1 stumble, the solitary soldier who had been guarding the steel door came down the corridor. "Are you okay, Ms. Geller?" she said.

"Demagnetizing sickness," Hahn said instantly, now helping M2 hold M1 up.

She reached for one of the phones that were interspersed along the corridor. "I'll call the infirmary."

"Unnecessary," Hahn said. "What she needs is distance from that blasted divisor. Something's wrong with the current. Call maintenance and have them inspect it."

The soldier's brows knit together. She looked from Hahn to M2 to M1, whose skin was now pulsing with the strain of trying to keep her body inside. "*Maintenance*, sir?"

"You heard me," Hahn snapped, charging toward the door with M1 leaning heavily on him.

The soldier unbuttoned the holster at her hip and squeezed the handle of her gun.

"Fall back, soldier," M2 commanded, but the soldier did not fall back because the divisor had taxed M1to the point that the whites of his eyes had turned silver.

"Put your hands up," the soldier said shakily and withdrew her gun. A headache struck her. "Stop that!" she cried. "Stop t . . . s . . . ohhhhh!" She clutched her head with her free hand.

And fired with the other.

A surprised groan escaped Hahn's lips as the bullet lanced his shoulder. Blood poured down his chest. More fell from the hole in his back.

M2 tore through his costume and lashed the weapon away. His nine heads advanced on the soldier and she let out a spine-tearing shriek. Then she wet herself.

"Don't!" Hahn wheezed, clutching his shoulder. "Don't do it, Marty! Don't be what they tried to make you."

But his efforts were in vain, because as M2 backed away, M1 threw herself at the soldier's feet, knocking the woman unconscious.

"Not dead," M2 said to Hahn.

Thank God, Hahn thought. He brought his left arm to his right shoulder and pressed. The pain was exquisite. White hot embers of agony seared through him, but he lurched forward, gasping and grunting until he was in front of the vault door. In the seconds before the alarm wailed, Hahn used the soldier's key card and—with M2's help—her finger to deactivate the lock. He dropped her card, saturated with his own blood, and knew he could go no further. Hahn slumped against the wall. "Go," he said as the suction around the door broke and it began to open.

M1, now fully in her alien form, wrapped a limb around Hahn's waist and pulled, but she was so weak it felt to Hahn like the tug of an infant.

The high call of the siren rose and fell, rose and fell. A barrage of rushing footsteps sounded from the center corridor. The west. The east.

"Go," Hahn said and brushed M1 away.

The footsteps were almost on them. There were shouts and orders and the clicking of safeties being unlocked from many guns.

The siren wailed.

Hahn, nearly panting now, waved the aliens on. "*Now.* You've got to go now. You'll never get another chance."

"No," M2 said, and took Hahn and M1 under his arms. He charged through the door and slammed it shut. He worked the electronic locking mechanism with his mind, and when he turned his Hollis head around, there was Master Corporal Rollins, open-mouthed and shock-white, shuddering in the G3.

The G3 began to reverse, but M2 snatched at it with one of his limbs and pulled it back. Rollins screamed.

Shadows of soldiers approaching from the subterrane on foot and in vehicles descended the tunnel. M2 ripped open the G3's rear passenger door and threw Hahn and M1 in the back seat, then he got in beside the cowering Rollins.

"Drive," he commanded in Hollis' voice.

"D-don't e-e-eat me," Rollins pleaded. In his fright, he had bit his lips so hard they were openly bleeding. "P-please." He put his hands up.

"Goddamit, you heard him, *drive!*" Hahn bellowed from the back seat with a burst of energy. "He *will* eat you if you don't drive right now."

Rollins reversed and spun the vehicle around just in time to see several G3s with soldiers hanging out the windows and their guns raised. "Oh shit," he groaned. The deliberation over which was the lesser evil played over his face, then he gritted his teeth and slammed the gas pedal.

Two vehicles usually only passed each other at specified locations where the tunnel widened to accommodate turns or to provide contingency space for rescue operations. Rollins, as quivering and gangly as he was, knew every inch of the place. The G3s bulleted toward each other, but he edged the steering wheel to the left, where the tunnel wall curved at a slightly more moderate angle.

A soldier in front of the approaching G3 sighted Rollins and was about to fire a warning shot when M2 stuck his head out of the open door. If they knew that M2 was not actually Hollis Brubaker, the soldiers in the other vehicle gave no indication, for they lowered their weapons and gawked as Rollins banked the tunnel wall and passed them within inches.

Rollins sped on, knowing that he was the only driver capable of turning within that narrow space. The speed sent daggers of pain through Hahn's shoulder. He was losing a lot of blood, and when Rollins wasn't eyeing M2, he was watching Hahn in the rearview mirror, bleeding over the backseat. M1, in her weak state, was trying to stop the bleeding by plugging the holes in the front and the back of Hahn's shoulder. It was curious to Rollins, who had been taught that the Mimics were lethal creatures, and that they would sooner bite off your head than let you breathe. He wondered if the bleeding old man was perhaps a third Mimic and the other two were working to heal him, but from what he'd heard of Lia Geller's experiments, Mimic blood was not red but an iridescent silver. He figured the blood could be a trick, too, and didn't say anything for fear that any one of them would attack.

They came to where the subterrane opened, but only two soldiers were there; the others were either in the G3s down the tunnel or had gone to find the fictional hiding place of Adam's drawing. Both soldiers had their weapons drawn, listening to the radios clipped to their breast pockets.

Hahn squeezed Rollin's shoulder before they stopped, at which the soldier let out a bleat of surprise. "As far as you know, Hollis is right beside you. You have your orders but make no mistake he will take the three of you out before you can blink if you tell them otherwise. Their lives are in your hands, soldier."

It didn't escape Rollins that M2 might kill him the moment he left the vehicle, nor the fact that there were other people to think about, not just himself or Loredo or Plosch, whose steady aims had become unsure once they spotted M2 glowering at them. M2 could kill hundreds, if not thousands of people if he were free.

Hahn seemed to read his mind because he said, "I would've been dead a long time ago if he was what you thought he was. You people made him that way, but that's not his nature." To M2, he said, "What do we do about Maria?"

But there was no time for M2 to help M1, for at that moment, Loredo and Plosch were inching toward the G3. If they went any further, they would see M1, who was spread low over the floor.

"Out of your vehicle, sir!" Gus Loredo barked.

"Man down!" M2 returned with equal gusto.

Hahn lowered his window and pointed to the tunnel. "He got me at the entrance. There's more hurt down there. We need help!"

Loredo glanced toward the tunnel but kept his gun sighted on the G3.

"Fall back, soldier," Hahn ordered.

"I can't do that, sir," Loredo said, now looking at Rollins, who was staring ahead with a pressure-white grip on the wheel. "Rollins, you okay?"

There was the sound of the other G3 nearing the subterrane. They had only seconds before being surrounded.

"Do it, Marty," Hahn whispered. And before Rollins, Loredo, or Plosch could react, all three were stripped of their guns and hung over a support beam in the ceiling like laundry on a line.

M2 gathered his strength and yanked M1 and Hahn from the back seat and went to the door. He pressed the security key he'd lifted from Loredo, but he still needed Loredo's fingerprint. In another moment he had snatched the squiggling and shouting soldier and mashed his hand against the reader. When the sensor beeped and flashed green, M2 delivered Loredo back to the support beam four stories high.

By some miracle, and a lot of Irving Hahn's blood, they had made it inside Adequate Accounting and into the command center.

Where a dozen guns were pointed at them.

37. I'm Yours, Maria

"Put them down," ordered Dalton Byrd, who had rushed to Adequate Accounting from the Sleepy Sloth on Theo's command when an agent overheard one of the brats wondering if M1 had escaped yet.

It had been Douggie, of course. In his excitement at fooling the Canadian military, he had forgotten to use the nicknames they had given M1 and M2. The boys were back in class, but the bugs Theo had placed at their desks picked up the whisper as clearly as glass, and it took only seconds for the monitoring agent to convey the development. Twenty vehicles were now on route to the Under Facility Office and would arrive at any minute.

"I said put them down," Byrd ordered again. He was flanked by soldiers, none of whom were fooled by M2's veneer.

M1 slipped from M2's hold. She writhed on the floor like a pile of mating snakes. The soldiers stepped back, tensing the grips on their guns.

Hahn, weak from the blood loss, backed away and slumped down, leaving a bright red smear of blood on the wall.

From behind the line of soldiers came the clank of metal on metal, then a hiss, then the iron voice of Hollis Brubaker. He had been in his office when the alarm sounded, and the reports had come in like gunfire. The lights in Sector East had gone out. Lia Geller was sick. Someone named General Allen Daniels from ALIEN had carried her out. Soldiers were getting brain-splitting headaches. The aliens were acting up. A gun discharged near the entrance. Rollins was driving erratically with Hollis in the passenger seat. But Hollis hadn't been with Rollins. He had been in his office with the growing awareness that something was cataclysmically wrong. The reports continued, but he hadn't heard about Rollins, Plosch, and Loredo strung up on the rafter because he had already bolted to his secret lift, used only once before.

Now, standing across from the Mimics and some pretend general Hollis didn't know, he glared at the glowering version of himself and didn't care if all three of them died. They already had decades of research and the only way to guarantee the Mimics didn't escape again was to not have them in the first place.

"Kill them," he ordered.

The soldiers readied their guns.

Hahn's eyelids were heavy. He was conscious that he was dying and there was no hope for him whether they shot him or not. As a man who'd lived for the benefit of others, he felt no fear, only a deep disappointment he hadn't been able to do more. A thought occurred to him in his final moments, a grotesque but beautiful thought. His wife, Norma, would expect it of him and—after grieving as she would—immensely love him for it.

He clenched a shaking fist and put up his thumb, not to M2 . . . but to *M1*. "I'm yours, Maria," he panted. Then his thumb turned into a middle finger directed at the soldiers and he squeezed his eyes shut.

It takes a bullet only a few centimeters to accelerate to the speed of sound; a marvel by any human standard. But more astounding is that Mimics are neither limited by gravity nor by their bodies, for their adaptive capabilities are incomparable. In the nano seconds it took the first bullet to exit its chamber, M2 looked at M1 and then at Hahn. Neither were in good shape. If they made it out, M1 would survive, but Hahn—having suffered a small nick to his radial artery—would not. Although he regrew Scotty's ear, M2 could neither repair Hahn's catastrophic injury nor raise him from the dead. But in the man's dying moments, Hahn proved braver than the soldiers and the Mimics combined because he had given the ultimate permission.

Hahn's last thought was, *Use it for good and get the hell out of here.*

Then M1 was on him, knocking him out so he wouldn't feel pain or see the ugliness of her attack. She took what she needed—no more—and advanced on the soldiers with new strength.

Bullets flared from chambers. But no one got to squeeze their trigger a second time because the soldiers were battered unconscious by M1 and M2.

All but one.

And for the first time in his adult life, Hollis Brubaker wasn't scowling. He wasn't scowling because . . . because you need a head for that.

38. Parting Gift

Thirty minutes after Scotty had released thirty thousand pounds of garbage a kilometer north of the landfill and Dan Fogel had cordoned off a fictional crime scene with one of the bloodied dummies a kilometer south, Meredith arrived at the house. She had rushed over at his call but was forced to walk nearly two kilometers through the northeast field to avoid the backlog Scotty warned would be there.

Panting up the steps, she spied him on the porch, as jittery as when Claire was born. She knelt beside him. "You're acting like someone's died," she said. "What happened?" When he told her that maybe someone *had* died, she gripped his leg. "Tell me already!"

He was sitting with his hands between his knees, looking at his feet. His new ear had been hidden but now he deliberately turned his head, knowing she would study him as she always did.

She didn't gasp as he suspected she would but drew her head back to really look at him. Then she said, "Whatever it is, tell me and I'll believe you."

But Scotty didn't have to tell her because among the quiet of the field, the grass rustled up to greet him. Then M1 and M2 were standing there.

Meredith's jaw fell open.

Scotty took her hand and led her down the porch steps. The two aliens, shifting their bodies so that several heads and legs were here and there, then none, then many, approached the house. "Nice to meet you, Maria," Scotty said, and stuck out his hand.

M1's heads twisted as if considering the gesture, then she tapped his head with one of her limbs. Then she did the same to Meredith, who was still too stunned to do anything but whimper.

Scotty pointed above. "Well, I guess the sky is about to get uglier, isn't it?" he said to M2.

Meredith elbowed him.

"I don't mean *her*, I mean him. Never mind. It's a guy thing."

M2 whacked Scotty in the stomach. "Guy thing," he said, and his valves quivered with laugher.

Sirens were drawing near, and a buzz of commotion drifted from the highway. "I'm glad you made it," Scotty said, "but you better get going. You can do it?" Again, he pointed to the sky. He hadn't worried about how M1 and M2 were going to get home because he hadn't been confident the plan would succeed, but now he wondered.

"Can do," M2 said simply.

"All right, then. Oh, before you go: You think you could —?" Scotty tipped his chin to Meredith.

She turned white and put up her hands. "Think you could *what*? What did you ask him to do? No. No. I don't want—"

But it was too late. M2 already had a limb around Meredith's wrist and pushed his knowledge into her. It was a parting gift to his best friend on Earth.

Then M1 and M2 were gone.

39. ALIEN's New Guests

The subsequent months were bittersweet. Irving Hahn's death hung heavy over the community, with many surprised mourners wondering how a man so fit could have a heart attack. The few who knew the truth of his death—namely Adam, Douggie, Ravi, Claire, and Scotty—grieved as though their own parents had died. It was Claire who suggested a memorial at the school, giving them something into which to channel the deep waters of their sorrow.

To appease public anxiety, Dan had the enormous and complicated responsibility of recasting the events as a convergence of occurrences that could be rationally explained: there had been a serial killing *team* in the city, which had since been contained with lethal force.

Meanwhile, the UFO's new commander—an astute woman named Gail Barra from ALIEN—ordered a comprehensive investigation into the escape of the Mimics and the myriad failures of Hollis Brubaker's team. Several members, including Theo Carver and Deborah Mills, were sent to ALIEN's elite training facility for a refresher on expected conduct, while—after an unusual consultation with the alien residents—Lia Geller was imprisoned in one of ALIEN's cold and miserable cells. Barra was part of a contemporary leadership that prized secrecy but equally understood and respected moral sensitivities. She immediately shut Lia Geller's lab and replaced the macabre sub-section with a library and entertainment room the aliens could visit for their good behaviour, and vowed to work with the aliens on improving their spaces. She did not, however, extend her good graces to setting them free.

And on clear, warm evenings, when the sun was down and the sky was full of stars, Scotty looked upward, hoping to see his friend.

Sometimes he thought he did.

<u>Other Novels By S.L. LUCK</u>

Redeemer
Interference
Lords of Oblivion

Authors need reviews! If you enjoyed this novel, please consider giving an online review at your favorite store.

Many thanks!

Check out my short stories and blog at www.authorsluck.com

Connect with me at:
www.authorsluck.com
Twitter: @Author_SLuck
Instagram: @authorsluck